SCIMITAR

HR

A Henry Robbins Book

E. P. DUTTON

NEW YORK

SCIMITAR

a novel by

Rick DeMarinis

Library of Congress Cataloging in Publication Data

De Marinis, Rick.
Scimitar.

"A Henry Robbins book."
I. Title.
PZ4.D3742Sc   [PS3554.E4554]   813'.5'4   76-41228

ISBN: 0-525-19805-9

Published simultaneously in Canada by Clarke, Irwin & Company Limited, Toronto and Vancouver
Designed by The Etheredges

10 9 8 7 6 5 4 3 2 1

First Edition

PART 1

It flashed at me from blocks away, a neon message in cryptic blue against the muddy sky:

THE LOVELY FIST

a beacon for the brand new martial arts emporium in the shopping center next to Arabian Heights, the condominium where I live. Under the flashing sign, in steady red neon script, more information was given. *Eclectic street fighting techniques, Scandinavian massage, Sauna, Power counseling.* I wedged the Olds into a parking slot under the sign. Rain pelted the black asphalt, puddling, the puddles nervous with neon. I pulled my collar up, got out, ran, wings of water rising from my heels. A large, bald man on a skateboard swerved by me, grinning, silver swastikas dangling from his ears. "Don't get wet," he said.

I gave him the finger, but left my hand strategically in my pocket. He sensed the gesture anyway, made a lazy turn, circled me, leered. I didn't accept the challenge. He was wearing cutoff sweat pants, a sleeveless tee shirt, open-toed sneakers. At least thirty years old. A happy, permanent child with the body and disposition of a defensive end. *This is the future,* I told myself. Senator Leander, on the six o'clock radio news, had said, "I am deeply troubled by certain invidious tendencies in the nation today." His use of limousines had been questioned by a militant consumer group.

I entered The Lovely Fist. Basho Lovely, owner and chief instructor, was standing rigidly in the center of a matted area like a contained explosion. A big, muscular man who radiated danger. Face like the moon, tree-stump neck, hair the color of iodine. I let the door bang shut behind me. "Pork chops or rib-eye steaks?" I said.

No one looked up. Basho's hands began to cut long slow slices of air. *The Art of Weaponless Street Fighting.* I'd seen the brochure on Louella's vanity. *They want your money, they want your body, they want your life. Don't give it to them. Blunt their attack in three easy lessons, mount your own in three easy more.* Louella had been thinking about rape. "I am deathly afraid," she told me.

Basho's sterno-mastoids bulged. Pink surge of explosive power. I cleared my throat. But nothing could interrupt the process now. It was called *getting into the moment, and outside of time.* I'd seen the lesson plan. Louella had told me that concentration is everything. Self-consciousness leads to drubbings. The rape victim is hopelessly self-conscious. *The ego must yield to the inner savage.* A motto, one of many. The mottos, taken together, make up The Method. An eclectic method. Karate, judo, boxing, wrestling, and street techniques. This, and Power Counseling. *Think of yourself as a knife, dangerous to touch, or perhaps a loaded gun.*

Bang. Lovely went off. Blur of white followed by a green jungle roar. Bird shriek from Louella. I sneezed. Louella was on her back, Basho's clean naked foot on her chest. His moon face was stone. Contrary to the brochure, Louella tried out a submissive little smile. Her eyes bright and friendly with a cloying admiration for the master's uncompromising discipline. The little smile did not drag him out of the moment or lure him back inside time.

4 • •

Unself-conscious stone. The Method. The Path. Look closely and learn.

"Pork chops or rib-eye steaks," I said. I was talking to myself. I took off my coat and flapped rain from it. Basho, with the practiced contempt of an elite assassin, began to pick his nose. Dignified probing. *They want your body, they want your life. Sometimes they want your dignity. Do not yield.* Louella didn't move. I blew air into my hands, warming them, accidentally lipping a fartfrap. Snappy little trumpet of sound. I cleared my throat, covering the slip. It didn't matter. She was wired to the mat with what looked like fear. The little smile was gone. Basho, looking down at her like a king snake at a field mouse, nodded very slightly: *now we're getting somewhere.* Her touching vulnerability did not reach him. But it reached me. So tiny and frail in her loose-fitting terrycloth combat jacket. Girlish. Rag-doll housewife with absurd physical ambitions. (*Stick to tennis, honey,* I had said. And she'd replied, rather splendidly, *You can't stop a rapist with a picture-perfect backhand.*)

Basho knuckled his toes and pressed. Louella winced. I said, "Hey, take it easy, champ," but my voice didn't carry to the mat.

Then Louella was on her feet—quick roll to the left, back somersault to a standing position, hands carving those automatic, lethal arcs. Her skill and speed took me by surprise. I sat down on a folding chair nicely placed in shadow. A damp stranger. An outsider. I felt a chill, sneezed again. Then Basho, looking left and right for imagined accomplices, uncoiled at her, bellowing, and took her to the mat again.

I cupped my hands over my mouth: "Lou-ella? Pork chops, rib-eye steaks, or what?"

No eyelash dipped or eyeball swiveled.

"Screw it," I said. I didn't feel good. It had been a bad day. It promised to get worse. I went to the large plate glass window that overlooked the parking lot and watched their images knife back and forth above a field of wet cars. I took out my little Rollei 110. My hobby. Something for the hands to hold besides cigarettes. I took a picture of the window. Art shot. *Ghosts Condemned to Spar in Neon Glaze.*

Basho missed with a generously slow roundhouse kick to the throat and was doubled over by a short punch to the balls followed by a lateral, ankle-high kick that sent him ass-over-tea-cup to the mat. A finely honed act. The window hummed dangerously with the impact of his two hundred and thirty pounds. I turned away from the rainy images and pulled the folding chair up to the edge of the mat, camera ready. Louella was on her back again, trying not to wince. Basho held his knee over her heaving rib cage. A teenaged boy who had been gathering towels in a rolling hamper took my picture with an imaginary Kodak of his own and winked obscenely. I glared at him, as the circle of combat started again.

I toured the studio. There was a poster scotch-taped to the door. *How to Hobble the Rapist.* A primitive ink drawing of a woman in an evening dress hobbling a surly tough with a zippy heel to the crotch. The masked sociopath, holding a Colt .45 but unable to squeeze off a round, went slack-jaw with astonishment. "Aaaargh," he said. Next to the poster, an announcement. "Dahlia Delaney will lead next Tuesday's power counseling session. Ms. Delaney holds a black belt in Karate Sho and is author of the best-selling *Facing Down the Deviate!"*

I turned back to the duel. A visual shock: Basho vertical in the air, upside down, apparently motionless, law of gravity suspended. A trick of retina and brain, for in the next instant he was rolling to the mat and bounding again to his feet, shouting, "Number one, Lou! Dynamite!"

Only a trick of retina and brain, but the damage had been done. I suffer from vertigo. An easily triggered disorientation. The Army gave it to me. I woke up vertiginous one morning in a field hospital. Earlier, I had taken a hard crack on the head running away from annihilation. It didn't go away with the years. It became a chronic thing. A visitation. There was no predicting it. Seeing Basho vertical, head down, arms and legs out like spokes, frozen that way, brought on a small attack. The floor rose under my feet, tilted up and to the left, began to plane, like a surfboard. To fight it back, I closed my eyes tightly and concentrated on the seventh grade.

I was a poet then. A secret star. I wrote whole shoe boxes full of rhymes. Some of them I remember. Animal jingles, mainly. A few warbling lover's complaints, that I, mortified incendiary, burned above the toilet minutes after composition. But it's the jingles I remember and on occasion still compose. I walked across the tilting floor receiting *Pigs*, for comfort and stability.

> *pigs in wigs*
> *look so fine*
> *but underneath*
> *they're still swine*

Back and forth several times, chanting, until I found level ground again. The rhymes, the concentration they give, help me. I don't know why. A mystery.

Louella had a leg scissors on Basho's neck. She was attempting a complicated wrist lock, her pale arms twiglike against the hairy stumps of her mentor. Basho's big moon face, red with impending harvest, was cinched tight in her thighs. He was grinning like a teased dragon.

I walked out. All I wanted was an answer. Pork chops or rib-eye steaks? It was my night to cook, Louella's Ladies' Defense Association night. Three new arrivals wearing their terrycloth uniforms came out of the locker room. They stopped as I walked past, eyed me with unsmiling serenity, ready for sudden moves.

I smiled: *I am a decent man.* It didn't register. Still, I don't grudge them this hysteria. It probably has some value. Unlike the Santa Peggy bomb shelter of 1962. (*The art of self-defense disciplines the mind, Jay,* she said. *Your perspective on everyday things changes subtly.* I said, *Why change your perspective when you're comfortable?* She does not like to be reminded of our middle-class allegiances. She looked at me, pity and scorn flashing in her eyes like warning beacons. *If you don't understand that,* she said, *think about rape, and in the context of rape, think about your daughters, and not only your daughters, think about your son. The maladjustment index is climbing.* She talks like that, six units and a senior thesis short of a B.A. in social psychology.)

In 1962 Red missiles in Havana fingered the nation's radarless underbelly. We got the heebie-jeebies from Key West to Seattle. The end was on its way. I shared in the general trembling. Any minute, a prodigious thermonuclear reaming would arrive. We laid in cases of tinned meat, soup, dried beans, boxes of powdered eggs, great wheels of cheese, vitamin supplements. But Kennedy was quick and firm. He guaranteed his survival in the national mythology. That heroic shock of rusty Irish hair on TV, the warm but alarming blue eyes, the steely, unwavering Boston twang. *Cuber,* he said, and we dug giant holes in our yards. Millions were made in prestressed concrete. In Santa Peggy, the low-budget tract we lived in at the time, they excavated in the children's park to the tune of one hundred and fifty thousand dollars. A shelter spacious enough to keep a hundred families for weeks. Stocked it with food, magazines, medicine— and .30 caliber carbines for the anticipated ant-versus-grasshopper war that was sure, in our paranoid imaginations, to come. Madness, in retrospect, that national wildfire of digging in. And I take responsibility for my share in it.

Many bleak calendars later the emphasis shifted to the human missile, the lonely heat-seeker, and the context of rape. Whispering panic, akin to the scare of 1962, traveled among our women, but now, no heroic young president with an unwavering twang was available to put their fears to rest. All they had were wistful politicians, Senator Leander and his crowd, who had canceled whatever potential they might have had between the anode of special interest and the cathode of public obligation. They became focal points of nullity.

8 • •

Thus, The Lovely Fist, which I do not grudge. What I grudge is the context of rape and the Basho Lovelies it creates.

It was not a good day to watch a two-hundred-and-thirty-pound martial arts expert do a toe dance on your wife. When I got home I was ready for a lift. A four-ounce shot of Wild Turkey. Then I fixed the kids, Debbie, Nell, and Chris, their "Safari" dinners. Halibut squares, vegetable cubes, amorphous spuds. Thirty minutes in the oven at 350 degrees, peel back the foil and serve. This is the future. They took their piping trays into the living room and plopped down in blank obeisance before the regal RCA, not noticing who it was that handed out the loaves and fishes.

That's not a complaint. They are fine kids. Bright, friendly, compliant. They'll make their way. The girls, at ten and twelve, already show signs of remarkable citizenship. They are neat and efficient and speak with gravity. Chris, the boy, is eight, and a possible question mark. Not to me. To Louella. She takes him to a local university for "gender counseling." She's read the books, knows the signals. (*Watch his hands, Jay. He splays the fingers, he limps the wrist, he extends the fifth digit. Watch how he holds his elbow, and see the way he pats the back of his head with the palm.*) Chris is under scrutiny. He is a little, unathletic fellow with thick glasses and a hunger for Mozart that borders on the pathological. He is pale and ineffective next to his tall, round-limbed sisters. Louella found a doll under his pillow, one of Nell's castoffs. At age four, he preferred *Snow White* to *Jack the Giant-Killer*. In the gender counseling lab, they spy on him electronically. (Report: *When he urinates, he fondles his scrotum.*) They offer him a choice of dolls and guns. Usually, it's dolls, little Charlie McCarthy marionettes with puckish expressions and movable limbs. Guns are guns. Who wouldn't choose the dolls? Poor Chris, you're in for it. They are going to make a recognizable man out of you.

We fight over this, and other things. Not fiercely. Louella

• • 9

reads paragraphs to me. I name androgynous men of genius. Chris is catching on. He picks up an M-16 now and then to please the technicians. He will survive.

My own survival is another thing. Today was an indicator. I had been cheated. Robbed. Told in a single gesture of my declining worth. I am a technical writer for Dynablast, the aerospace company. I repair the mutant English of engineers and scientists until their schemes have the ring of plausibility if not good sense. I'm good at it. Specialists who can only speak in the esoteric jargon of their trades court my good offices. ("Arjay, can you get this report to sound, you know, 'colloidal'?"—You have to know the man before you understand his adjectives.) My degrees are in electronic engineering and English, with minors in art history and organic chemistry. Early in my adult life I discovered Lord Snow and decided to become a man of the future, a bridge over the troubled waters between the two cultures of science and humanity. Arjay Ponce, conciliator. I had a mission. But no clear idea how to carry it out. Teach? Write? Politics? Time solved it for me. I got married, needed a job. A man with a job is a secure man. So is a man tied up in ropes. Idealism is a by-product of freedom. Only the young are free. Bitter words. I sweeten the aftertaste often with macho bourbon.

But today the bitterness was compounded with a deliberate piece of malice: I had been cheated. Of my promotion to management, something I had been expecting. Instead, it had been given to Tobey Bacon. Eighteen months less seniority than me, goosey, a bad speller, and yet they moved him up to mahogany row, the purple badge of management gleaming on his precious lapel.

I've never been able to roll with a punch. I stand flatfooted and stare bovinely into the slings of fate. Unable to adjust swiftly. Easy come, easy go. A motto not in my repertoire. I sulk. I drink. Even so, I tried to give the office girls the opposite impression. I joshed and grinned and lightfooted it around the office like a good sport. But their knowing eyes avoided my act all day, as if I had just been

10 • •

diagnosed for the big C. The doctor jovial and unafraid. Only the lucky ones on the business end of the shaft are good sports. (A friend once thought he had contracted jaundice in Mexico. The jovial and unafraid doctor said, No, your liver is probably sitting on a big nasty cancer.)

Flexibility. A more flexible man might say: Hey, nineteen years with Dynablast isn't exactly a lifetime. Opportunity *exists*. Get out there and root, ass to the wind. Hang tough. A man is free, young or old. That's the *definition*. Free to do whatever he wants to make a living. He draws a line in the primitive dirt we all stand on and allows no traffic to cross. He reaches the borderlines of self-respect and says: *No, I don't need this*. Right?

On Mars, maybe. On Earth the years of shifting fault lines play footsie with those borderlines. Adjustments are made. With your help or without it. And you're caught by surprise by what you've become. Oh, the fear and trembling comes like gray hair and flab. One day a superior asks you in the kindest terms to lay one on his rosy buns and, God help you, you find yourself puckering. Through the pride-eroding years you've evolved involuntary lip muscles of the spirit. You look at your dying face in the mirror and ask it several stirring questions. The answer is a smirk: *You, of all people, ought to know better*. You make yourself pucker theatrically, gag, then spray raspberries of contempt at the treasonous glass because the world is a stage and the pucker is true. You sign up, in middle age, for gender counseling at a local university. You sit in the electronically watched room with the little boys who have their parents fretting. But it's too late. You play with the safe and pretty dolls because the guns in the real world are always loaded. You live in a context of humiliation, and though you transform it on occasion with a snifter of Wild Turkey, you remain a crafty survivor. Chris, it's the best I can offer you.

Other jobs? At my age there are no other jobs. Unless you go to extremes—shit shoveling, straight commissions, or this: On TV last night there was a commercial for a deep-sea diving school. Hard-hat diving. Only heroes need apply. *Did you know,* said the announcer, *that hard-hat divers make up to three thousand a month for only thirty minutes of work a day?* But that half hour is in 220 feet of shark-infested silt and likely as not, it's in the rusted hull of a sunken tanker, and the noodle working the compressor that keeps your air coming down the tubes does not have a mother's interest in your survival but is fresh from a pep pill and mescal weekend in Baja and has forgotten, temporarily, how to count to ten. No, I'm not Errol Flynn. Remember his flashing smile as the giant squid came sliding out of a dark hold, tangling his tentacles in the air hose and safety line? Remember Errol's quick knife and the squid's rubbery flesh? No respect in that man for terror.

Terror. The polar opposite of boredom. We knew, as kids, the hidden message. The future was going to be unbearably boring. The terrified are not bored. If you survived you became—*Errol Flynn!* If you didn't, you went out in glory, like an Evel Knievel attempting a final canyon. Twist that throttle, leap the stacked sedans of boredom! Not me. Evel may be waiting for me behind the sky with a cool six-pack and a bowl of chips, but between us there is the killer whale of calamity, and, as long as I have the choice, I know I will avoid that confrontation. Cowardly? Yes. Of course.

What I'm saying is, I did not quit my job.

The kids fed and out of the way, I poured myself another half fishbowl of Wild Turkey, fired up an L. T. Brown, and stepped out onto our tiny patio. The rain had stopped. The late autumn sun was red as a freshly removed tumor, spreading its noxious crimson sloppily between the spires and obelisks. A mean-spirited poetry, I admit. Arabian Heights should inspire a craftier mood. Why didn't the sales brochure promise a happy Arabic fatalism, too? An easy acceptance of the-way-things-are? Kismet. "Three bedrooms, two-and-a-half baths, swimming pool, laundry facilities, gymnasiums, steam rooms, tennis courts, and, last but not least—*kismet!*"

It's kismet that makes them—the Arabs, I mean—the world's most perfect billionaires. So guilt-free that the money is almost incidental. A form of manna. An amusing incarnation of the djin. Feeling Arabic for the moment, I laughed at myself, this American stranger and clown, so controlled by his petty emotions. I saw myself as the subject of a racial joke, great bulb-nosed caliphs laughing sandily into their hookah smoke. The joke long and complex, part of it dealing with Basho Lovely knuckling his toes into Louella's sternum, part of it dealing with my losing out to a twit like Tobey Bacon. Laughter all the way from the Red Sea crackled across the tarnished sky, as the cold sun dimmed and the drizzle started up again with miasmic fury.

2

I smelled her before I saw her. Orange blossoms.

"You're getting wet," she said. Her appearance was sudden, unexpected, a sorcerer's trick. Poof.

She held a transparent umbrella over her head, leaning against the chest-high grapestake fence that separates our patios. Lisa Dennison. The sunbather. Take this as a confession: I knew her body well. A bronze decal pasted to the windows of my reverie. The Arabian Heights brochure promised private patios. Private, but not secluded. And from your second-story bedroom balcony the patios of your two adjacent neighbors are open books. And I confess, I knew the Dennisons' patio by heart, every paragraph.

Sunday was her day. Sunday morning, still in bed, Louella burrowing away from light and sound, I'd tune the clock radio to the twenty-four–hour weather station. A small act of infidelity. I hoped for hot and sunny. Hot and sunny meant the thong. The thong bikini, and plenty of oil. I'd load my big Nikon, attach the long lens, ease myself like a commando onto the balcony and lift her image, over and over, shutter clicking like a castanet. I have a thick sheaf of eight-by-ten glossies hidden away, some of stunning quality. On rainy days I warm my hands on them. Mild perversion? No.

A respect for form. A high-minded sensitivity to the glorious incandescence of flesh. With any luck, the temperature on a Sunday would climb into the eighties. On these occasions she'd loosen a string, revealing the avenues to Mecca.

"I like the rain," I said, thinking of brilliant Sundays.

She was wearing a fluorescent tangerine sweater that hugged her breath-stopping hills and valleys like second skin. Slacks to match.

"Three days of clouds and my tan turns yellow, like mustard."

"Ah, but I hate clouds," I said, quick as judo. "Love rain, *hate* clouds."

She smiled, amused. I fought back a gut rumble. In her eyes there were challenges to face. I looked away. Gave her my best profile. A spherical cloud fell like a bomb toward a hillside. My L.T. Brown went out.

"Isn't this *dumb?*" she said.

I looked at her again. "Dumb?"

"I mean, we've been neighbors for, what, it must be two months now, and we've never actually met."

She was large. Larger than I thought. Or I was shrinking. She loomed, a warm patch of flame in the gray ambience, an effect of color, of contrast. I felt light. Small and light. Almost airborne. There was a suction in the air. I felt my feet skidding against it.

"Ponce," I said. "Arjay Ponce."

"Call me Lisa." She smiled and extended her hand. I took it in mine. It was hot, long, and narrow, and it had teeth. The teeth pressed the fat of my palm. The ground refused to give me traction. I was sliding, downhill, toward a fragrant furnace, and simultaneously rising.

A dream I once had spoke to me of my vertigo. I was in a skyscraper, the one hundredth floor. The room was empty, except for an old man. He pointed to the window. I shook my head, began to look for the door out. No door. Clouds outside were changing colors and shapes, suggesting time-lapse photography. The old man caught my sleeve and tugged me toward the window. I looked at his face. I saw that he was bitter. I saw too that he was more afraid of the window than I was. I also saw that the old man was myself. I went to the window and looked out at the terrible distance to the traffic below. I looked back, but the room was empty. I climbed on the ledge, more afraid of the empty room than of the drop. I stood there in the wind, teetering. In my feet I felt the delicate momentum of the building. Delicate because it belonged to the greater momentum of the planet. I felt the planet's momentum, too, caught in a storm of vectors, momentum added to momentum, the solar system, the galaxy, the great wheel of galaxies, and it was all delicate, precarious, and the sense of this uneasy balance came to me through my feet.

"Sippy," she said.

"What?"

A cold rivulet followed the crease of my spine until it reached my waist, where it warmed.

"You're kind of distracted, aren't you?" she said, pointing to my glass.

"Oh. I guess I am." I handed her my drink. She took a long sip.

"Ding-a-ling," she said. "Cru-*ell.*"

"Wild Turkey." I touched my hairless upper lip, wondering how I'd look in Zapata moustaches. Probably like a Tijuana barber.

Her neck muscles tightened and her breath hissed between her teeth.

"*Muy fuerte,*" I said, transfixed.

"I feel *raped,*" she said. There were tears in her Mediterranean gray eyes.

"One-oh-one proof," I said.

She touched her wrist against her forehead. I knew that gesture well. I had it in black-and-white. Often, in the heat of Sunday, she would lean up from her chaise and sip lemonade and after sipping she'd touch her forehead with her wrist. The gesture meant *I'm hot, but am I too hot?*

16 • •

"Ponce," she said, studying me now. Her eyes moved over the faintly Iberian contours of my face. It was my turn to feel warm. "Is that Spanish?"

"More or less. I mean, yes. 'Ponce' is Spanish, but my father was born in Saskatchewan and my mother is a Swede from North Dakota."

"Another lump from the melting pot."

I made my jawline assert its geometry cleanly. "Not a very flattering way to put it, but true enough, I guess."

"I'm sorry. I was thinking of myself. I think of myself as a lump, a hodgepodge alloy, from the melting pot." She smiled, creating new imbalances in the air. *Some lump*, I thought, keeping my eyes decently high, by brute force. "I'm English, French, and Hungarian," she said. "Also Italian, Irish, *Samoan* for God's sakes, perhaps Moroccan, and one-sixteenth Cherokee princess—*de rigueur*." She laughed, bouncing girlishly on her toes, and my eyes broke free. Her breasts, unchecked by brassiere, leapt like fun-crazed puppies, the well-defined nipples turreting the smooth acrylic of her sweater, and, oh, an abstract thirst raged in me like a desert wind among the hollow mesquite canyons.

I took a drink and said, "How do you know all that?"

"Genealogy. A hobby. It's fascinating. I know, for instance, a great-great grandfather of mine was a slave trader out of Liverpool. Enormously wealthy, but the wealth got lost someplace long before my grandfather's time."

A sudden tightness in my chest made me mumble something into my drink.

"What?"

"Nothing. I mean, I was thinking about something that happened today."

"Nothing awful, I hope."

"I don't think you want to hear about it. Boring, really."

It had stopped drizzling. I made a Bogart grimace, squinted through imaginary barroom smoke, suggested with my furrowed brow that my life was the polar opposite of boring. My words were a smokescreen, too. I wasn't thinking

about Tobey Bacon, Dynablast, or Basho Lovely. I was thinking of her, how her arms, in another lifetime, might call me
to her bed, those perfect, Coppertoned arms.

"Oh look! A rainbow!" She pointed at the sky behind
me, but I didn't take my eyes from her. Her eyes were wide
with what could have been guileless enthusiasm, and in the
smoky nightclub of my mind, I buried my face between her
breasts.

There's a robot in the laundry room. Someone's idea of
fun. It makes change and it talks to you. Funny, meaningless
phrases with each dollar you shove into its mouth. "It's
lonely in here, lady. Give us a little smooch." It's seven feet
tall and looks like Fred MacMurray. Change rolls out of its
belly. "You got cold hands, lady!" it complains. "Are we
alone?" It rolls its eyes. It sings "Some Enchanted Evening."
It wants to gossip. "Did you hear about Mrs. Roper?" There
is no Mrs. Roper in the building. The robot is not in touch.
But it's got the right idea. The laundry room is where the real
gossip gets started.

The laundry room consensus: Lisa Dennison is dangerous. A troublemaker. "Oh dear God," Louella told me,
scoffing. "That woman is the epitome of self-indulgence. She
has all the social responsibility of a cougar." The list grows
daily: She smokes pot by the pool. She vacuums her apartment in the raw. She has boyfriends, even though she's married, and her husband doesn't even care. Once, when I was
feeding Fred MacMurray dollars (my night to do the laundry), I heard some interesting fragments: ". . . wrapped in
condoms . . . drugs . . . husband comes and goes . . .
dealer . . . secret organization . . . dirty movies . . . " And
another time, the single word that makes the hackles rise,
"nymphomaniac," followed by an eyewitness account of a
midnight orgy that spilled out to the pool, and afterward
. . . but Fred MacMurray interrupted with a booming song,
"I'm fit as a fiddle and ready for love."

The heat and tempo of the gossip increased. Louella:

"She is definitely a bitch-wolf. She feeds on men. It's a reflex, the nymphomania, out of control. Actually, I feel very sorry for her."

All this by way of warning the menfolk. But what man would take such fine character recommendations as warnings? The men of Arabian Heights did not feel sorry for Lisa Dennison. The truth was, the menfolk felt sorry for *themselves*. Those tireless readers of *Playboy*. In fact, half of them, their torpid imaginations inflamed by these descriptions of Lisa's personality defects, were ready for anything that might stray across their paths. Visions of those unsettling attributes stalked the dull, eventless corridors of their lives. They wanted very dearly to believe the voices in the pages of *Playboy* were real: *My boyfriend goes down on me, but gets impatient. Please advise. I travel with three women in a Winnebago. I find it hard to steer when getting head from Darla. Ted is in electronics. Last night he attached an electrode to my clit. Wow. But should I fear cancer?* And if they *were* real, then they belonged to real people, people right here, in their world, on this planet, in this city. The only thing to do was to keep alert. Readiness is all.

Warnings. Is there something devilish in the wives who issue such red hot bulletins as warnings? Or are they just blind to the dormant randiness of their broken-spirited clock punchers? Of course, as I said, the context is harmonious. I wanted to keep it that way. I didn't want to rock the domestic ark, much less capsize it. Too much at stake, and the water is deep. And I guess those wifely advertisements for such richly fleshed succubi take the clock puncher's basic and reliable fear of deep water into account. But it doesn't allow for the Dutch courage of the *stoned* clock puncher who has had a bad day.

So when she declined the Wild Turkey I didn't beat an apologetic retreat back to the safety of the kids and RCA. Errol, Evel, or any hard-hat diver would not do such a thing. I searched for words that would quickly and irretrievably escalate the situation. Something from the depths of a squid-killing fearlessness. I cleared dead smoke from my throat and broke the mushrooming silence.

"What say to a little Benedictine, inside, after I get the kids put to bed?" There. It was done. No backtracking. I coughed harshly, covering a sudden tremolo and the persistent feeling of weightlessness.

She looked at me, looked at me, and smiled. Her teeth were large and glossy with health. Mouth big, and true to gossip, hungry. She ran her tongue quickly over full Sophia Loren lips. Her nose was aquiline, predatory. My heart flapped against my ribs, like a caged hawk.

"My place, nine-thirty," she said, adding from below her throat in a dark, soul-squeezing whisper, "My husband, Gil, won't be home." She turned and walked slowly away. Her walk was (right again, oh matrons) an open invitation to follow.

The clouds parted for the occasion. The spheres and obelisks gleamed in magnificent erection, as the dying sun erupted in one last orgasm of light.

It was an unmistakable symbolism. Even the detritus-packed air of Los Angeles had become an aphrodisiac, irresistibly Persian with her subversive perfume.

A reader of omens would have taken to the hills.

She was gone. But the darkening air still was tuned to her presence. She was magnetic. I stood there rocking on my heels like a lodestone, wondering in what direction my failed life was trying to point. I had actually made a date! An assignation! Oh, the sobering prospect! Of course, I couldn't keep it. I was no Errol Flynn. I was not even a Fred MacMurray. Besides, Louella would be home by ten. What did I expect of myself? One drink, a hasty apology, and run? Foolish man-mouse approaching the roulette wheel of life with nickels and dimes!

I went inside and refilled my tumbler. I sat in the gloom of the kitchen, the crackle of canned laughter filling the air

20 • •

like static. No. I could not go. Impossible. I'm forty-four, forty-five in the spring. Lisa Dennison, no more than twenty-three. Mistake, mistake. Wrong league. A mismatch, apples and oranges. Louella and I often laugh at middle-aged celebrities *falling in love* with women young enough to be their daughters, even marrying them, as if their celebrity status and their money didn't have anything to do with their success. People in that category can have anything they want, and when you can have anything you want you can't stay satisfied confined to one thing for very long, whether it's a Mercedes 450 SL or a wife, and you name this itch *love*. I'm not in that category. Never will be. Never. And yet, unrestrained images rose to the surface of my thoughts. Images of those long sunny legs, glistening with oil, shimmering with purpose. "At ten o'clock I turn into a husband," I would have to say, nickels and dimes ajangle in my soul. Where would we be then? At the bar? On her couch? Would it be possible to get up and walk out without shame? Without her thinking, *Oh, this lame turkey, this chickenshit old fool.*

I got up and knocked over a chair with my shin. Pain brought a new image to the surface: Basho Lovely holding Louella by the front of her jacket, forcing her slowly backward, leering. I kicked the chair out of my way and went to the freezer. I took out a nice rib-eye steak and put it on the table to thaw. I found Louella's grocery pad and tore out a sheet. "Honey," I wrote, "I hope this isn't too large for you," adding, "I'll be home soon. Don't wait up." And then, the afterthought: "Card game."

I didn't like the tone. Clever lying is not one of my strong points. I tore up the note and threw it down the garbage disposal. Then I wrote it again, same words, and pinned it to the steak.

I drank methodically, two ounces of Turkey in twenty-three–minute intervals. By nine-thirty the fifth was half gone. I went into the living room and ordered the children to bed. Seeing my condition, they filed out of the room obediently, the little citizens. I caught Chris by the arm as he went past.

"Chrissie," I said, "way you feel to the whorl, they mightn't say it, but watch out for them even so, okay?"

Chrissie nodded slowly, with polite caution, one of the few people I know who takes me seriously.

"World, I mean. Didn't I say world?"

The patient lad nodded again and went to bed.

I went back into the kitchen and wrapped myself in the thickening mood. Fueled it with another taste. "Take it easy," I told the glass. "There's an evening ahead." And the rebuttal: "Give me to drink mandragora, that I might sleep out this great gap of time!" For that is what I really wanted. Unconsciousness. A solution my warring halves could live with. Errol Flynn and Fred MacMurray, cavalier and hubby, can snore out the night together. No honor lost, no domestic harmony risked.

But it didn't work that way. Turkey didn't understand the strategy. My thoughts had a military precision and coldness. My trooper was flushed with hot courage. The trumpets were sounding.

A final ploy: I conjured up my lost promotion, a genuine damper. Here's what it meant: no tenure. Forget the raise. The raise is reason enough, but that's not the big item. The big item is tenure. Do you know what that means in a company whose dealings are one hundred percent with the Department of Defense?

A hypothetical for-instance: Suppose Dynablast is bidding on a contract for, say, the testing and development of the rocket boost system for a carrier-based target device. Call it the RBS/CBT. Well, right away they fill the newspapers of large cities, coast to coast, with ads such as:

WANTED IMMEDIATELY!

DESIGNERS!
ENGINEERS!
SYSTEMS ANALYSTS!

MACHINISTS!

22 • •

DRAFTSMEN!

KEY PUNCH OPS!

And so on. For months the place is buzzing with eager faces looking for something to do—the result of deliberate over-hiring. They overhire because they want to look prepared, ready to go. They want to look like world beaters, not afraid to take chances, gamble big. They think this impresses the military. It does. But then, catastrophe! Corporate thrombosis! The contract is given to a competitor, United JetVac, say, because Senator Z owes one to somebody there, and the president owes one to Senator Z. The big boys worry about these allegiances, but they have to pretend they don't exist. Besides, such allegiances are complex and often subject to modification. Betrayal is an operational parameter, just as lies are inoperative statements. Nothing to get upset over.

Until the layoffs begin. Mercy is not an operational parameter. It's not just the new hirelings that get the ax. More bodies have to be shucked than were hired because of the reckless and uncompensated overspending. Even old gray heads roll. One year short of a pension? Sorry about that, old boy. Guilt is not an operational parameter, either. This is business. We try to run a tight ship here. We are not the Sisters of Charity.

Conspiracies form. The empire builders get together and try to salvage their power by forming minicartels within various departments. Belt-tightening becomes a euphemism for noose-tightening. It is ugly, it is sad, And, given the system, it is necessary.

I've been laid off four times in my nineteen years. I know how it feels to sit across the table from the personnel man who gives you the company's final kiss-off. All the counterfeit compassion in the world oozing from his pores. He's scared to death himself, knowing well that personnel is butterfat. No one in personnel ever slammed a rivet into missile skin.

Yet, I've stuck with Dynablast. I rode out those long periods of no work and managed, through my savings and one or two decent investments, to keep my head above water. The family was fed and clothed, the mortgage payments were met on time. In short, I survived. Why do I stick it out with a company that's tied to the whims of the Department of Defense, the DOD in turn tied to the whims of power politics? As much as it hurts to admit it, especially now, the reason is simple. I like my job. Damned if I don't. I like the working conditions, I like the liberal policies of the company, and I like the people I work with. I could even tolerate Tobey Bacon, to a point, until this little knife-twist of fate.

Conjuring the little knife-twists of fate called a halt to nothing. It only raised the need for solace. The solace of sunny legs. But by the time I knocked on Lisa Dennison's back door (I climbed the grapestake fence to avoid the too-visible front door approach), it occurred to me that I might have read her signals wrong. Maybe I'd seen and heard only what I'd wanted to. Maybe a neighborly chat over tea and cookies was all she had in mind. All that gossip was only *gossip*, after all.

But wait—she had said, "My husband, Gil, won't be home." What was that supposed to be? An evening of Scrabble and Twinkies? No, no, she had written a blank check with those words and pressed it into my palm.

Turkey roared in my blood. My hands tingled with blood pressure. *The husband, the husband,* I told myself, *won't be home.* It flashed in my brain like neon. I'd never met her husband, and wouldn't meet him again. I knocked with a confident knuckle, sounded a merry tattoo. *The husband won't be home. The husband won't be home.* A song, a refrain, a ticket to ride, a gift certificate to a Sears and Roebuck of the libido. I knocked again and again, joyful iambs chugging in my heart. *The husband won't, the husband won't, be home, be home, be home.*

24 • •

No answer. I peeked into the curtained window next to the door. Dark. No lights. I began to lose the rhythm. The iambs became trochees, the trochees, pyrrhics. I sighed. But. I also felt. A glimmer of relief. Miserable relief. *You nervous skulker,* said the thin nasal voice of Errol Flynn coming over the speaking tube from forty fathoms below. Still I felt relieved. I had, after all, not betrayed myself. I had acted. I had climbed the grapestake fence of my timidity and knocked boldly on the gates of paradise. Was it my fault if the angels forgot I was coming? I looked over at the lighted windows of home. Clean, domestic, butter yellow light brimming in the windows, Fred MacMurray seated at the table, reading the *Wall Street Journal.* A plaintive harmonica caroling the happy scene. The harmonious context. I shrugged and started back.

Then the door opened. "What is it?" she said.

Her hair was pulled back severely into an American Gothic bun. She was wearing a plain brown dress buttoned ominously to the neck. Her eyes were not Mediterranean but arctic, and her voice was wedged with ice. The three opening witticisms I'd been practicing turned into small lumps of sour clay on my tongue. My Wild Turkey stone crumbled and the fragments crawled miserably away. I felt tired.

"I get it," I said.

"*What?*"

"You forgot." But how could she have?

"Oh, shit. You're right. I *did* forget."

But how could she have? Unless what was chateaubriand to me was a handful of crackerjack to her.

"Little drinky?" I said, making little drinking motions with my right hand.

What a fool. I suddenly wanted nothing more than to be home, in my big recliner, Debbie, Nell, and Chris upstairs in bed, "Hawaii Five-O" on the tube. Life was exotic enough for me.

"Well, now that you're here, you might as well come in."

She took my arm and led me inside. It was dark, but the

floor plans in Arabian Heights are all the same. I knew the room. Kitchen. She led the way past the breakfast nook, the dining room, short hallway, den, and into the sunken living room.

"Saving electricity?" I asked, a fading cavalier, not really thinking about technique any longer, knowing I'd be home in ten minutes, kicking at the defenseless furniture, but thanking my lucky stars that fools like me sometimes are allowed to get off the hook, bloodlessly.

"What? Saving electricity?" She looked puzzled. "Oh, you mean the lights. No, it's just that I've got this terrific headache. Migraine. Light aggravates it."

A single laugh barked out of my chest, but I cut it off and sputtered into my cold hands, pretending to warm them. But I kept on laughing on the inside. The old venerable bedtime wifecode! The last-minute headache. But after climbing fences and crossing moats filled with the squids of catastrophe? What do you say now, Mr. Flynn? Mr. Flynn drew a rapier, touched her throat with its point, then cut the strings of her bodice, teeth agleam, and watched her dress tumble around her ankles.

"You find headaches kind of funny?"

"I'm sorry. No, of course not. I understand. I'll just, you know, go home."

Then it was her turn to laugh. Good-natured, though. Not more than one or two syllables of meanness in it. A rich laugh from behind the weighty tits, modulated sensually in the splendid throat. She turned on the lights. They were on a rheostat and she turned them down low.

The room was black. Black carpet, black walls, sharply punctuated by chromium furniture with white leather cushions. There were little ebony figures on the coffee table, toothpick thin and in assorted attitudes of nervous embrace. The expressions on the faces of the figurines were blank, without personality, blind. Hanging from the center of the ceiling on two silver wires was a carved elephant tusk. At first glance the tusk seemed merely eroded, a casualty of time. But the carvings were intricate, tiny, meticulously detailed. And what they showed was the confused interlocking of the everyday world. The tusk was long and its curvature reminded me of the hull of a ship. A single ship carrying the whole human drama through endless night.

Lisa went to the stereo and put on a record. "I've taken a rainbow," she said. "They seem to work best. It should be gone in a few minutes."

"A rainbow?"

"A pill."

"For the pain?"

"Say, you're *quick*. Yes, Mr. Ponce, for the *pain*."

The music came on then. A single drum, joined, after a few solitary thumps, by another. The two drums moved toward each other, timid at first, two strangers testing each other's sense of reality, determining if there was a friendly frame of reference they could share, then, finding one, they merged into a single rhythm that broke over the agreed-upon world like a sunrise. At this point they were joined by a speedy sax blowing planets out of its bell. I got caught up in it. I tried to believe that my apartment was just next door, but that seemed a growingly absurd notion. There are warps in space that do not meet the eye. I lived light-years away. This was someplace else. Another world, watched over by another sun.

She touched my arm. "You really want this?" The smile was still there. But now it held a warning, too. *This?* I looked around the room, knew that my face was hanging, stupid with booze.

"This?" I finally said.

Her eyes hardened, their sharp light accusing me of naïveté at best. I went to the bar, searched it for the bourbon. Poured myself a bomb. Stupid is as stupid does.

She followed me and sat on a stool. "My flick, I mean," she said. "You really want to come into my movie?"

I drank. All this mod talk. Ho ho. I watched the drunk in the mirror raise an eyebrow. Mellow rooney. Old tool from the school of cool. I drummed a bebop rhythm on the grained formica. The sax was trying to tear holes in my brain. It was succeeding.

"I'm a bad actor, lady," I said, a fair imitation of Lee Marvin in good grim humor.

"Hardly, Mr. Ponce," she said, keeping the advantage.

I was in the school yard suddenly. Years mean nothing. She was at least seven centuries older than me. The school yard of Horace Mann Junior High, 1943. I was winding up a yo-yo, trying to find a rhyme for *turtle*.

"If you come into my flick, which is far down the street from *your* flick, you might not find your way back."

I acted as if I knew exactly what she was talking about. I nodded soberly, drank. "Girdle," I said, thirty-four years late.

The sax had carved out a cul-de-sac in the stone of time and space, making room for a stately trumpet. They mated, and the harmonics they bred rattled the glass against my teeth.

"Hey, listen," I said. "I'm ready for anything, kid." But she had seen me glance at my watch—nine-thirty-nine—and the drunk in the mirror behind the bar began to think poorly of himself.

"Maybe you *had* better go home, Mr. Ponce. Really."

I wanted to. I admit it. But there would be unbearable humiliation in that. *Grow up, fool,* I told myself. *Get your ass out.* "No," I said, aloud. Then, "How about calling off your dogs, Mrs. Dennison?"

"Lisa. Maybe I won't be able to." She said this softly, almost to herself.

"You don't look all that dangerous to me," I said, realizing suddenly that everything I was saying was the perfect opposite of what I meant. My intestines began to chuckle at me. Little liquid pipings.

"You're a man who believes in the surfaces of things," she said.

"What's not to believe?"

Coy sparring, just like the two drums at the beginning of this record. An attempt to discover the rules of the game we would soon be playing for real. Psychic feel. I put more weight on my elbows to buck the four-cornered rhythms of the quadraphonic machine.

"Spoken, Mr. Ponce—"

"Jay, dammit. Jay."

"Spoken, Jay, like a true believer. The gullible Americano. A model consumer." She laughed at me, not in an unfriendly way, but it stung just the same. "You have the correct perspective on things. Just the man they want."

A college girl. Stuffed with bogus smartass ideas. I didn't ask who "they" were supposed to be. That was the Great Assumption. General Motors, ITT, General Foods, Steel, Copper, Aluminum, Oil. Aerospace. Corporate Farms. I'd heard it before. Sophomoric claptrap. Fribbles. I started to ask something, something with an edge to it, but she left the room, giving me a look over her shoulder as she went out that answered my question, whatever it was.

I looked at the drunk in the mirror. Shitfaced to the knees. Hair blowing wild. I looked at my watch. Only nine-forty. I held it to my ear. The little insect was still thrashing. The Disneyesque black magic here held time in its giddy jaw. I traveled around the room, checking out the art objects.

There was a photograph taped to the wall. An eight-by-ten glossy. A shot of a human head. By itself. Severed. The eyes glistened under heavy lids. Lips parched and slightly parted, as if the head were sighing. Nose like a white bone jutting out of the face. It was inscribed. "This is S.B. 8/1." The head was mounted on a metal frame, a cart of some kind. The background was blurry, but it looked like the front panel of a large computer.

I recognized the head. I'd seen it before. The face, I mean. But I couldn't put a name to it. A man of real importance, no transient star. A man not given to little jokes, either. Still, this photo had to be a gag of some kind. (*I've lost my head over you.*) The name, the name. It wouldn't come. I went to the couch to think about it. I needed to lie down. Too much booze, old tool. I dozed.

I am photographing her. She's wearing the thong. We are on her patio. A hot, dry Sunday fragrant with body steam. "Your movie," she is saying, "strikes me, how shall I put it—as *dull*. Dull city. Predictable. Moribund. Played in the same theater before the same bored audience with the same bored cast of characters for years and years. And you don't even notice that the celluloid is wearing thin, that the best scenes, the most believable ones, are pinholed, washed out, the sound track tinny, false, hashed with static. That static is from the void, Mr. Ponce, the very thing the play is supposed to cancel out." As she tells me this, I snap frame after frame, catching each change of posture, each challenging expression, but concentrating mainly on the powerfully sheening breasts, the boldly impertinent mons. "I'm not an actor," I tell her. "I'm just a photographer."

Lisa was kneeling next to me, tickling my nose with her fingernail. "Such heavy dreaming," she said. I sat up, too quickly. My head kept floating, floated across the room, bumped against the wall, rolled down to the floor, came to rest in the thick black pile of the carpet, where it throbbed with pain and the panic of dislocation. Lisa took my face in her hands and massaged my temples with cool and delicious fingers. And my head rejoined my body.

"Here, take this," she said. She had two small white pills in her hand. Gave me a small paper cup filled with water.

"What for they are?"

She laughed. "For your syntax."

I took the pills, worried about them for three seconds, swallowed.

"Perk you up a bit. You're getting rubbery."

I touched her hands, discovered them. Her face, a bright oval, flawless as a Hollywood dream, a carving in alabaster, the most beautiful face I'd ever been this close to. I pulled her toward me. She didn't hold back. But when her lips were one inch from mine she braced.

"Hold the phone," she said. Her eyes had a calculating gleam. Further progress now was going to be conditional. She backed away, slipping her hands out of mine.

"Hey, what gives?" I said, stupidly.

"I'll be back in a flash," she said. "Try to stay awake, okay?"

I tried to stop her, but she was quicker than me by seconds. I rolled, a trout in molasses, to a sitting position. I had lost track of many things, my glass included. Then I saw it, back on the bar, signaling to me mutely. I got up and walked a skinny Z across the room, a tune in my head. A rattling harpsichord. A manic clavier.

"Jay."

I turned, the clavier died. *Ding.* A ruler out of memory, edged with brass, cracked down across my knuckles. She had returned, wearing a nun's habit, black shoes and all, face framed in black, her forehead hidden behind a starched white band.

"Well don't just stand there, dickhead," she said. "Make us a drinky poo."

It took a minute, but then I understood the routine. The starched white band across the forehead did not signify a sterile purity of thought. This was her movie. *The Foul Nun.* 8 millimeter. Sister Libido. Typical scene: *Sister Dementia is interrupted at vespers by the oafish plumber.*

She posed for a moment and I applauded. But a remnant chill of childhood was trying to surface. I had gone to parochial schools for the first six grades. I remembered the sour nuns and their shameless lust for the brass-edged ruler, the final instrument of the inquisition. The child is the father of the man. The man is a fake, an elaborate disguise, layers of effective pose, so effective he believes it himself. But a well-honed image from the distant past cleaves it easily. I applauded, smiled, but knew I couldn't talk.

"Scotch and water, you old dog-fucker," she said.

I made a noise. I hoped it sounded like a laugh. "Hey, sister, *sister*," I said, woozy. I poured something into a glass, added water. I handed it to her.

"Kiss me, numb nuts," she said.

I put down my glass and pulled her close. Oafishly. Her lips were clean and parsimonious. Her wide-open eyes were churchy, cool, convent-remote. There was the smell of palm fronds and censers about her, the musty air of cloisters, tattered catechisms. But my workman's hands were full of the truth: flesh, solid and warm, nondenominational, and, sweet Jesus, yielding.

I kissed her. Dry cool lips closed tight and prim, but then her tongue unnunned itself and slid under mine, strong, fierce, searching, flexing with secular greed. I shortened the distance between us and our teeth clicked. Then she pushed off and went to the couch. I followed, retracing my Z. She sat down heavily and crossed her legs. She lit a hand-rolled cigarette. Dope. A seam separated slightly in the front of her habit and a patch of bronze skin blazed archly in the gap. Her perfect navel roamed in the shifting hiatus. She held the cigarette toward me but not for long, knowing I'd refuse. She sucked on it deeply. *Sister Sexualis, at the succulent age, encounters Father Goat, the papal scourge.* "Would you help me with my surplice, sister?" Midnight in the vestry.

"Isn't this a groove?" she said, appreciating her own invention.

I knew I was going to lunge. Something massive was taking charge. A maniac in the muscles. A Hun in the cerebral hemispheres. A voice, the voice of responsibility, argued for calm. *Stay cool, count to one hundred, think of a jingle. Think of what you can lose.* But it was a telephone voice, long distance, nervous, vertiginous, waiting to be cut off for lack of funds.

"Groof?" I said, snorting the word. A Hun.

"I mean, isn't it more exciting to you than a kimono or

even a black lace nightgown—a Frederick's of Hollywood special, complete with straps?" She leaned toward me, lips parted and curled slyly at the edges, an I-know-what-is-happening-to-you smile. "With that Spanish name of yours, you must have some Catholicism in your background, right? Isn't your head getting all stormy with wierdo-creep ideas?" She touched my knee, gave a little squeeze. All erectile tissue stepped forward, crackling.

Give me a break, said the long-distance caller. But the Hun was remembering, now, all the old gray-faced nuns he had known and feared as a child, and a vengeful Teutonic uncoiling commenced in an embarrassing place. I grabbed her.

But the nun was quick. She broke my hold and dodged out of reach and I missed her when I tried again, landing across her knees, my face in her hip. She was up then like a dancer and I rolled inexpertly to the floor, got to my hands and knees, rolled again, stayed put. Directly above my face was the carved elephant's tusk, a great phallic curve, mocking me. I made binoculars out of my thumbs and forefingers and swept them across the room. Into my wobbly field of vision came the photograph of the severed head. The face, its living-dead quality, gave me a chill. An image from memory: white sheets, clear plastic tubing, the compact Frankenstein machinery of modern medical technology. But nothing more. It was like a fractionally remembered nightmare, the will dividing itself unevenly because morbid curiosity is not a motive entertained by reasonable men. I swept past the photo with my zero-power glasses and concentrated them on the tusk above me.

A thousand images. The world. Out of the confusion, one scene stood out. A man coarsely mounting a woman from behind. The man had a loving interest in what he was doing. The woman was eating a handful of rice.

3

Above the chrome cannister that grudgingly gives up one single sheet of membrane-thin paper at a time, I wrote:

Basho Lovely
picks his nose
while nudging tits
with his toes

I was in the stall farthest from the door, the favorite stall of malingerers and graffiti artists. The "D Area" men's room, Dynablast. I had a bristling hangover. A brute. Bright whistling shadows winged through my head. Pulsing ovals the size and weight of Easter eggs slid across my iridescent retina. *Symptoms of high blood pressure,* I thought, glum and shaking. My legs were numb from the kneecaps down from sitting on the john through coffee break. I crossed out the jingle. It added nothing to the wall of excretory wisdom. No entertainment value. Obscure. Too private. Too ambivalently malicious—it had humiliating backlash potential. An element of masochism, of self-wounding spite. The art, here, is to transform private rancor into public scorn, with wit. What my jingle failed to do was multiply the targets. Dump on *all* the Basho Lovelies of the world on behalf of ninety-eight–pound weaklings everywhere, in one succinct flash. In terms of those esthetic requirements, my jingle didn't get on the chart. Fizzled and died, a stillborn effort. I thought hard for the right combination, but it was too much for me.

> Get me
> to a
> nunnery

I wrote, cryptically, crossing it off, too.

A pair of impeccable yellow Wallabees approached my stall. They stopped in front of it.

"Is that you in there, Arjay?"

The voice was boyish and avuncular at the same time, as well as painfully nasal. Not a welcome sound, it sent rasping needles through my brain, grazing the bundles of dying cells.

"Mah-Jongg! Are you all right? What is that frightful sound you're making?"

Tobey Bacon. Probably spying on me. I wasn't aware of it, but it was true: I was groaning.

"I'm dying."

"You simply mustn't joke about such things, chummo."

"If I'm joking, then the joke's on me."

"That noise—"

"Karg. What noise?"

"Mah-Jongg! Oh, my dear *man*."

"I'll be okay, Tobey. Karg. Just leave me alone for a while."

Someone who did not understand the rules of this stall had drawn a beautifully detailed penis. The penis was airborne, heading for the moon. The moon was smiling. Its craters were oddly labial. "This is demented," I wrote. "A for form, F for content. Study, meditate, try again when you have attained wisdom."

"Listen, Arjay, let me get you something from the dispensary."

"Get me a gun." I coughed, covering the karg. My stomach was inching upward, afloat in poison stew.

Two flies walked into my stall. Big slow winter flies, savoring the perfume of death. Their movement was random, but they managed to bump heads anyway. Both buzzed angrily but neither was able to fly. A fierce rumbling began inside me and I erupted foully, an inverted volcano.

"Mah-*Jongg!* Aren't you going to flush that?"

"No. It's alive."

One of the flies climbed up my shoe.

"Arjay, the vileness!"

The fool had given the penis windows. Passengers were waving good-bye. The 6:15 to Salt Lake. Somewhere behind my wounded brain, a mind was trying to understand what it was looking at.

"We're in a lot of trouble, Tobey," I said, philosophic in my misery.

The Wallabees changed configuration. Less aggressively helpful. More thoughtful. The insteps were furrowed.

"Listen, chummo. I want—I mean, I *really* want—to talk to you about this, you know, promotion thing."

The fly on my shoe had been washing his front legs, but was frozen now, senilely, in prayer to the Fly God who, he believed, lived on my knee.

"Ugly little monster," I said.

"Jay? Jay-o?"

"Go damage yourself, Bacon."

"Please. I'm saying *please.*"

"Up your box, sideways, Tobey."

"But, really, it's not what you think at *all,* whatever on earth *that* may be. You are angry, aren't you, because you think you've been treated unfairly?"

The fly moved from my shoe to my pantleg. It lumbered up the vertical polyester, drunk with age.

"Well? That's it, isn't it?"

"Go jump on a doorknob, Tobey."

"Oh, you're such a headhunter today!"

"You love it."

The fly reached the plateau of my knee where he rested, a grubby pilgrim. I flattened the winded bug easily, picked him up by a wing and dropped him into the grim lake. His reward. The other fly was still on the floor, asleep.

The Wallabees edged confidentially closer. "Listen, Arjay, if you're feeling *très mal*, I can get some pills for you from the dispensary."

One of the passengers in the flying dork seemed dubious about the whole idea of this form of travel. The others wore simpleton grins, but this one was clearly downcast. His expression seemed to say, "How did I let myself get talked into going to the moon in this big cucumber?" This depressed fellow was clearly a portrait of the artist himself, disturbed, no doubt, by his unwholesome obsession.

"How about it, chummo?"

"Okay. Okay."

"But I still want that chat, Arjay. I'm very serious."

"Okay. Okay."

"Well, at least you're acting civilly now."

"Go sit on your face."

"*Quel gauche!*"

The Wallabees pivoted smartly then, and Tobey left the men's room, stimulated by the abuse.

I wrote:

> *Lobo suffers*
> *but*
> *Lobo lives*

in my best grammar-school hand. Then crossed it out, too.

Tobey was waiting for me when I returned from my ordeal. He was sitting in my chair, feet propped up on my littered desk. Coyness bloomed in his face, a garden of self-satisfaction. When he saw me, he jumped to his feet. He took a handful of pills out of his pocket. There was something implied in the preoccupied way he handed me the painkillers.

"Listen," he said, looking furtively around the area. Two hundred identical desks occupied by two hundred identical-in-most-ways bodies. D Area. The hum of idle conversation. The miniature gunshots of typewriters. My pain-sensitized eyes were picking up the sixty-cycle flicker of the overhead fluorescents. "Let me show you my new office, Jay."

I felt too humbled in mind and body to indicate where he could put his new office. Besides, he thrived on insult. I followed him. Down an endless aisle of typists, of navy gray desks, of navy gray faces, clamped knees of unit secretaries, standing coffee-drinkers, bursts of banal jibing, endless tedium of duplicate lives, the air itself torpid, failing to enrich the blood, crossed with bilious shadows, this place where no sun ever spread its warmth. Ah, the transformations made by spite. The job I liked so much had become an insult to dignity. All because of the little man ahead of me, tripping along with insufferable aplomb, now that he was management.

We came to a wall of doors. Each door was made of real wood. Each had a nameplate. This was mahogany row. We stopped in front of a door with Tobey's label on it. "Tobias Q. Bacon."

I grinned nastily. "Tobias Q.?"

He gave me a sidelong glance and a bittersweet wince. We went inside.

The rug was blue, the walls paneled in real walnut, and the giant desk was solid mahogany. I sank into a cool, real leather chair. The lighting, thank Edison, was not fluorescent. On the wall opposite me there was a piece of electronic sculpture.

"Ever see one of these?" he asked me, pointing to the tangle of wire, capacitors, coils, bulbs, and transformers. He walked over to it, and as he approached, the sculpture began to react. The lights flashed on and off in increasing tempo. "It senses me," he said. "The closer you get, the more body vibrations it picks up." He stopped a yard away and then moved toward it again an inch at a time. The thing went berserk. If there is an electronic equivalent of panic, then this machine was experiencing it. When Tobey was half a foot away, its chaotic switchings and unswitchings became audible. It began to grunt and sizzle. A three-inch spark danced between two electrodes. "My God, Arjay, you'd think it was going to wet its pants!"

"Clever," I said.

He came over to me. "Ciggy, chummo?"

"I'm trying to quit."

"Oh my poor viceless man!"

I gave him a look that suggested a new vice might be in order. Murder.

"I know exactly how you feel, Jayvino. I mean, my promotion coming ahead of yours, and you having a year seniority on me and all."

"Year my ass. Eighteen months."

"Whatever. And your work record, so spotless."

I didn't want to listen to it, this simpy bleating. All it amounted to was a spineless gloat. I raised my hand to my eyes and rubbed at the pain between them.

"Water," I said.

Tobey jumped up at the oversight, went noiselessly out of the room and returned with two paper cups. He hovered over me, motherducklike, while I swallowed the pills with the water from the first cup. I dropped the Alka Seltzers into the second cup. I leaned back into the chair, letting my head rest against the gently sighing cushion. I watched the calmly flashing lights from the electronic sculpture for a few seconds, then closed my eyes. Tobey disappeared.

That's all there is to it. Close your eyes, snap, you turn off the world. Something the electronic sculpture was unable to do. It was condemned to vigilance. Not me. Survival can be thought of as a problem in selectivity. Here's how to improve your life: Cancel your newspaper, sell your TV, buy earplugs, encourage tunnel vision and myopia, don't read books written after 1840, develop a corpse's interest in current events, and when the Citizens for Responsible Action come to take you away to the internment camp for the un-committed, tell them, *Too late, too late, ha ha, the joke's on you,* and grin like an imperturbable winner. Try to under-stand that you spotted the opposition too many points the moment your mama squeezed you into the light.

But there's a flaw in this system. With my eyes closed against the present, the recent past began to take shape and parade against the cinerama curvature of my skull. Lisa Den-nison's face. First a coin, a Lincoln-head penny. Then, subtly, the coin grew large and the head, no longer Honest Abe, turned to me. And licked its lips.

El Eye Ess Ay. Who are you? The thought, the mystery of those letters, plodded through the marshes of my mind like weary guerrillas as I lay there under the intricate tusk. There were other scenes in the ivory. Somehow, I felt a clue to her personality was present among them. Across a bridge from the fucking couple, an old man was beating a dog with a stick. The dog was rolling over submissively, abused beyond simple humiliation. On the other side of a miniature range of mountains there was a busy marketplace. A rickshaw carry-ing an elegant lady was parked before a silk merchant. The man was displaying an armload of fabric. But the woman wasn't looking at the merchant or his wares. She was looking down the street at an obscenely fat monk. The monk was standing flatfooted next to a palace. He was smiling bea-tifically, pointing a finger toward heaven, and pissing on a rock.

I got up. She had left the room. The apartment seemed deserted. Quiet. A terrible dryness in my throat needed at-tention. I went back to the bar, refilled. I could have gone home at that point, it was only ten-thirty—no real problem in explaining thirty minutes—but retreat now was the last thing on my mind. I was an underwater hero, ready to go against the parrot-billed squid with my trusty blade. "Lower the cage," I mumbled, accent impeccable, "to fifty fathoms." Lisa was the ocean. A sea of possibility. An unknown quantity beyond any high-ground algebra. A sea of quick tides governed by invisible moons. "Reason has moons," I recited to the head of the living dead man whom I knew in the serious way you know your worst recurring dreams, "but moons not hers lie mirrored on her sea, confounding her astronomers, but, o, delighting me!" A befuddling notion to the responsible, to those keepers of the world's glittering mechanical gardens. (But don't look too deeply into night-black subsoil!) Yes, I was stone to all the forces of balance, enjoying a galloping case of the raptures of the deep.

I called her name. "Where has the tide swept you, sister?"

I called her again. "Ahoy! Man overboard! Name the game! Spit in the ocean, jacks or better, hide-and-seek, finish-what-you-start, I'm ready, ready, lady. I'm a good sport!"

Nothing. *Nada*. I jogged heavily up the spiral staircase that led to the bedrooms. The upstairs was dark. I caromed into the hallway, groping, finding my way by a braille of fixtures, switches, doorways. One door backed away from my fingers on soundless hinges. My heart began to sprint at the sound of rapid breathing in the welcoming dark.

"Who's there?" A frightened girlish voice. It took me by surprise. A tropical storm rose in my blood. The sweats came on, pins under the skin. Hidden manias longed for liberation.

I said, "That you?"

A "yes" so small it was almost lost in the dark. A tiny voice from the bottom of a canyon. Jaw quivering with despair.

"Hey," I said, booming, spreading reassurance through the valley of fear, a friendly, competent ranger. "It's me. Arjay. Your neighbor."

I could hear terror in her short, choppy breaths.

"Go home now, Mr. Ponce. Please. Forget what I did."

But the room was awash with perfume, newly sprayed,

tingling, sharp, a welcoming committee of attars. "I understand," I said.

And I did. More of same. Game within the game. Movie within the movie. A brief outline: *Little girl of twelve, returning from a guileless romp in the park, the night closing unexpectedly around her, and now, a strange man, stalking. The Virgin and the Creep.*

There was something in all this that appealed to the buried child. Playacting. How delightful. What a treat. How bland life is without the chance to wear alien masks. Think of the benefits. Banker playing Pimp for a Day. Housewife commanding a battalion of executives. The retired clerk leading the civic symphony. The hobo adored. The wino applauded. National Role-Swap Day. April first. I proclaim it.

CREEP: Now, now, my child.
CHILD: Oh, *please* go.
CREEP: Don't whine, child, it offends me.
CHILD: Oh, dear sweet Jesus help me!
CREEP: I sense a fine upbringing, youngster.
CHILD: (Strangling sounds, paralyzed with fear.)
CREEP: Think of me as unclekins.
CHILD: (Screams)
CREEP: Ah, there, there. Do not fear old unclekins, lass!

My knee touched the bed. I swallowed my drink and put the glass on the floor, under the bed where it would not be later stepped on by the forgetful shoeless foot. Lisa was still wearing the habit. I touched her. She quaked away from me. Convincing, convincing. Then she turned the lights on.

"You're quite the actress, aren't you?" I said, squinting.

Thinking the game was over, I sat on the edge of the bed and removed my shoes. I turned to say something, caught a roundhouse right on the left ear, and a big chime went off in my head. She grabbed my hair and pulled me off balance. As I fell over, I felt her knee work at my crotch.

"Hey, Mrs. Dennison! Take it easy!"

Then her knee hit home plate. Starburst. Not a direct shot but close enough. Squibs of black light dotted the room. My stomach lost its last swallow of bourbon, which had to be reswallowed. Not without a little wincing.

"Crazy goddamned bitch!" I yelled into the pillow she was trying to smother me with.

"You're going to have to fight for it, Lobo!" she said.

Lobo? I grabbed her legs and rolled her over on her stomach. But she was agile and strong. Another of Basho Lovely's trainees? She kept rolling away from me and then a foot out of nowhere caught me on the chest and another on the shoulder.

"Oh Lobo, *punish* me!" she said, as her heels banged into my clavicle like little pistons. "Punish me Lobo! I've been a bad girl!"

I ripped off one of her shoes, then the other. The heels were metal. Who the hell was supposed to be punishing who? Then I grabbed her by the habit and pulled. The entire garb came off in one piece. A breakaway habit! No end to her grab bag of little tricks. I began to laugh. I kept laughing and grabbing until there wasn't anything left to grab or laugh at.

"No!" she said, but this time in a different spirit. "Don't *finesse*. Ramrod the son of a bitch!"

Then she began to whoop. Great lungfuls of whoop. Too crazy and loud for smart gamesmanship. As her fine patio brown calves sawed my kidneys.

Tobey was staring at me with a curious, tender expression on his pallid face. The pills began to wrap my pain in gauze.

"Feeling better, chum?"

I nodded. But I wasn't thinking of myself, my pain. I was thinking of Louella. Thinking this: *I love her, I do love her. How can I make her believe it now?* Too much damage had been done for roses and candy. Nothing short of some form of self-mutilation would do. I thought of Lisa. *Lobo,* she said,

● ● 43

and the strange word whipped the animal in my blood awake. El Lobo! A streetfighter's name.

I felt like a schoolboy. I thought of myself, again, in Zapata moustaches. The look in my eye no longer the easily turned back glance of the middle-class desk jockey. Steel. Rock bottom calm of the man with nothing to lose except his dignity. Warrior pride singing in my heart. Thinking of Lisa and myself in this way made my stomach tense. Teenage tense.

Did Louella ever inspire such feelings? Easy to answer that one. No. But was that love? Isn't that part of the definition? Aren't you supposed to get butterflies, at least during courtship, with the memory of her spell-casting loveliness? I've never gotten butterflies thinking about Louella. Not that she wasn't lovely in her own way. I knew she was beautiful, knew it as objective fact, but never felt the beauty, never experienced it as an assault on my entire being, like a wonderful disease. From the start our relationship seemed to be governed by the spirit of pragmatism, good sense, and careful planning for the future. I was thirty-one when we were married. Louella was twenty-five. A little beyond teenage acne-jitter years.

But we left something out. Something locked away in the back rooms of personality. Something that hated the spirit of pragmatism, good sense, and careful planning. The animal. The spirit of appetite. The sovereignty of desire. *Lobo*.

Can you have it both ways? Probably not. The two spirits are negative images of each other. Matter and antimatter. Bring them together and the result is wreckage. Lobo does not lie down with Lassie.

Which way, then, do you want it? Easy again. Though the thought of Lisa started a tic in my soul, I was not about to buy a chopped Harley Davidson, black leathers, put her on the back fender and dissolve into asphalt landscapes of comic book existentialism. What I had with Louella outweighed that prospect. Call it domestic stability. A context of compati-

44 • •

ble routines. I needed that. I didn't want to lose it for an erotic pipe dream that could easily exhaust itself overnight.

Domestic love, it gets my vote. Thanksgiving turkeys. Christmas tree mornings. Sunday newspapers. TV evenings. Drives to the mountains after the first snowfall. Finding that, after the budget was figured out, enough money was left for a brand-new waffle iron or toaster. The makings of a soul-dissolving ennui? For some, maybe. But not for me.

And yet, I'd put the gun to that friendly image and had blown its brains out. Bang.

Tobey was seated at his desk, leaning forward intently, as if reading my thoughts. He was nibbling inoffensively on a scarred yellow pencil. In the subdued atmosphere of his office, I felt my hostility slipping. Even the neurotic sculpture on the wall was barely awake, flashing a dull bulb every fourth or fifth second. I checked the slide toward indifference by reminding myself that he would keep this plush cubicle and I would be out on the streets when the next big layoffs came.

He put his pencil down and cleared his throat. "Arjay, may I let you in on some inside information?"

I should have walked out. It was a crack. Inside information for Christ's sake! Insider to outsider! But there was a wistful pleading in his eyes that stopped me. He hadn't meant it as a slap in the face. He bit his lip realizing the special impact his words now had. His eyes glistened, misty with regret. I sighed and relaxed deeper into the soft chair, feeling, suddenly, sleepy.

Then he was on his feet and leaning out eagerly over his desk. The veins in his forehead were large and blue. His skin almost transparent. Mournful skull shadows showing through.

"Okay, Tobe," I said, yawning. "Shoot."

He waited a full ten seconds. Then, "Arjay, we've landed the biggie. Sugar City!" He darted out from his desk and went to the electronic sculpture, taking it by surprise, and threw his arms around it. It went berserk.

Sugar City was the in-company code name for Scimitar. Project Scimitar was going to be the biggest plum since the Artemis ICBM contract was let a dozen years ago. Artemis was a super program that provided a hundred companies, as well as the prime contractor, United JetVac, with years of rich activity. And in addition to the initial contracts, there were long-range extension programs for systems modification and maintenance. Then there were proposals for a whole new generation of Artemis-MIRV which SAC subsequently bought, and several more years of prosperity were thrown to UJV and its subordinate subcontractors. UJV was also bidding on Scimitar, but as some cynic said, "They're out of the running because it's our turn to get a big one." A cynic in this business is a man who has worked in it for at least a month. It takes about that long to understand the chemistry.

Scimitar, without a doubt, was going to be the grand-daddy of the big gravy contracts. Whoever grabbed off this one was going to be king of the industry. At least for the next decade. I felt a deep glow, a hearthside warmth. Code word Sugar City was not coined indifferently. The untenured would be safe for a long time to come.

Although Scimitar meant all of this, it remained almost totally shrouded in mystery. No one knew what it was. And the company wasn't saying. There was a lot of talk about a new missile. A new concept in ballistics. A revolutionary new launch facility. New guidance, new propulsion, maybe, even, satellite-based warheads. But reasonable as all this speculation sounded, it didn't take into account Helsinki, or, more recently, Vladivostok. Besides, the present arsenal of ICBMs didn't need to be replaced. *They* were the ultimate weapon. Complicating the speculation further was the odd way DOD officials were acting publicly toward questions directed at the program. They seemed to have developed a schizophrenic twitch on the subject. On the one hand they seemed to be pushing it. While never giving an unambiguous hint as to its purpose, they clearly wanted to get the program rolling before the congressional watchdogs got into the picture with their endless committee hearings. Support in Congress, even among the old hawks, was thin on this one, even though the Secretary of Defense called it "the single most important defense project of the latter twentieth century." On the other hand, there were public statements by top DOD officials that suggested a general bureaucratic malaise, a reluctance of spirit, an uncharacteristic fatalism in regard to this new project. "We've got to have this one," they seemed to be saying, "but, O God, do we really want it?" If this stance was not upsetting to the man in the street, it did cause a few ripples of concern in the industry itself. When bureaucrats worry, those elephant-skinned functionaries, then it's time for the average citizen to dig in deep and say his prayers.

For the past few weeks I'd noticed groups of haggard Army, Navy, and Air Force brass in and around D Area, where I work. D Area is where advanced proposals are drawn up and management teams established to implement the various phases of a given project. All the liaison work between the military and our engineering departments takes place here. D Area is also responsible for the administration of contracts to our many subcontractors, the small and not-so-small satellite companies who are the manufacturing specialists in the defense industry complex. They are responsible for supplying the prime contractor with the highly specialized parts and equipment, the "hardware" which, when assembled, becomes the "end item," a completed unit. In fact, the prime contractor contributes very little hardware to a given project. Its main function is to oversee the whole operation, provide interface liaison between the subcontractors, and to assemble the various systems into the completed "end item." Finally, the prime contractor must check everything out to ensure the project will function as specified by contract. Dynablast is such a company.

Though everyone I knew was excited by the prospect of a new gravy contract, there was an unsettling chill of apprehension generated, in part, by those jittery statements by the DOD officials, and by the fact that no one had an inkling about Scimitar itself. A new instant-retaliation weapon seemed to be the consensus, promoted by a technological breakthrough of startling proportions, serious enough to nullify treaties and formal agreements. I mean, what else? Eleven-digit figures aren't thrown around for anything less. It was a zapper, all right, trumping the Red aces.

Tobey pirouetted away from the snapping wall sculpture and sat on his desk. "How does that grab you, Jayfonzo?"

I showed him where it grabbed me. "Beautiful, Tobe," I said. "Just beautiful."

"Beautiful isn't the half of it, *mon chèr*."

He hadn't told me all. He was holding back something, radiant with secret knowledge. He hopped off the desk and feinted at the wall sculpture. The sculpture had dropped its guard. The new threat was too much for it. It farted unhappily and burnt a transformer. The burning insulation stank.

"Well *what?*" I said, annoyed again, but suddenly attacked by hope.

"Not *what*. *Whom*."

"Whom? Whom what?"

"You! *You*, chummo!" He jumped up and down twice, like a child on Christmas morning. It was hard to believe he was really a part of management. The air was filling with blue smoke. "You, Jaybrinski, are going to be a purple badge, too! Document chief, if you can believe that. All Scimitar paper, the technical stuff, is going to be your baby! An empire, Arjay!"

He came toward me with the twinkling speed of a delicate forest animal and embraced my shoulders. I began to duck the kiss, but he pulled something out of his pocket instead and in the same movement removed my ID badge. With toy soldier military ceremony, he pinned the big purple disk on my lapel, the badge of management.

48 • •

"Mr. Towne's idea," he said. "I mean, to spring it on you this way. You know what a great kidder he is."

I knew now. But it was an outstanding turnabout, and I was ready to forgive everyone, from Nixon to Xerxes. "I don't know what to say, Tobey."

He went to his desk and raised a cut glass decanter from a lower drawer. My stomach was ready. The morning's hangover belonged to someone else, some nondescript boozer with failure on his mind. He poured out two glasses of something candy amber. It didn't matter. Gasoline would have been acceptable. We raised the glasses in the blue air of his office.

"To Scimitar," he said, his eyes brimming. "And to you, my friend."

"To Scimitar," I said, "whatever the hell it is."

I returned to my desk. There was a memo from Byron Towne waiting for me:

> Ponce: Report to conference room 33-A 0900 hours sharp tomorrow for informal briefing and introduction to Scimitar Project Chief, Spear. Your loyalty, diligence, and general performance have not gone without our keen awareness and appreciation.
>
> My heartfelt congratulations,
>
> By.

By! No one I knew ever called him that. Towne is the boss of D Area, and part of the oligarchic inner circle that runs the company. Intraoffice memos were always signed B. Towne, or B.T., or with his full name, but never this nickname, By. This, more than the purple badge itself, brought home the reality of my elevated rank.

Several typists were staring at me and at the purple circle on my lapel. Alice James, an aggressively cheerful girl from London, gave me a strong handshake. There was scattered applause. I bowed, offered a beneficent wave of the hand. I felt moved to say something, read the shine in their faces as a mute hunger for wisdom, guidance from the higher echelons. Something about loyalty, patience, endurance, and the essential decency of the system was called for. I wanted to give a word of encouragement to those who now found themselves several cuts below me in rank. I felt smug, definitely smug, liked the feeling, wanted more of same.

"They also serve who stand and wait," I said, but loud enough for only Miss James to hear.

"How true, Mr. Ponce," she said, a West End music in her voice.

"Lincoln had a phrase for all of life's more poignant moments, wouldn't you say so, Miss James?"

"Indeed I would. But that one's from Milton. He's one of ours, Mr. Ponce."

Her eyes were merry and good-natured, her sharp Anglo-Saxon nose pugnaciously close. I accepted the challenge. "How about a bit of lunch, Miss James?"

She gave the suggestion mock-serious thought, finger in cheek, then said, "I'd love to."

It was not quite noon, but this was one of the rewards of the purple badge: Lunch Hour Lapover. A fringe benefit, one of many, of my new status.

I took Miss James to a neighborhood restaurant and bar. It was of a Spanish motif, called La Mujer Caliente, a fine enticement, but the music inside was from a very cool—so cool the music was beatless—jazz quartet. Flute, harp, drum, vibes. Each note was held as long as technically possible, great sailing arrows of sound, before being nipped off by a languid rap of the cymbal. A music that avoided the notion of time.

I had never taken an office girl to lunch before. Not once in nineteen years. My position didn't allow it. I don't mean I couldn't have if I'd wanted to—there had been opportunities, and reasons for vetoing caution—but it just wasn't done. A graybadge taking out a typist for lunch would have had sleazy overtones: another unhappy slob on the make, home life a grim mess, the desperate little ego trying to punch itself up. But a purplebadge lunching an office girl is just another instance of the cavalier generosity of management. Of course, everyone knew better, but knowing better doesn't necessarily mean the hypocrisy wasn't proper. In this business, as everywhere else, form is everything.

We had two martinis apiece, Alice making witty remarks about the Americanization of her appetites—eyes up over the rim of the glass, darkly blue, on the word ''appetites''—and then a pair of seven-dollar steaks.

"This is hardly lunch, Mr. Ponce," she said, squaring her shoulders as if for an ordeal.

"Consider it the victory feed, Miss James."

"Then let us feed like amorous birds of prey."

"Like which?"

"Andrew Marvell. He's one of ours, too."

"Of course. 'To My Coy Mistress.' I remember." I let my eyes take managerial liberties. An ivory V from throat to midbreast occupied me. Boldness goes with rank. The lovely pears curving jovially under the blouse. Trim waist, trim spirit. I liked her very much.

"His. 'To *His* Coy Mistress.' Wrong pronoun, wrong persona."

"What's an educated girl like you typing engineering reports for?" I asked.

"What's an educated girl like me *supposed* to be doing?"

Her merrie-olde-England eyes had me by the throat. What indeed, what indeed. I smiled, jawline firm, the winner's smile. A purple squib of light darted up at me from my lapel. The perfume of success surrounded me.

"Beats me," I said, winking.

"Have we touched on the subsoil that belies appearance?"

"Who said that, Miss James?" I said.

"Me. I just did."

"How about that? Do you say things like that very often, Miss James?" I felt like a big horny cat. I decided to buy a Cadillac as a personal reward. Perhaps a Jag too. In honor of

Miss James. The Cad in honor of Lisa. Lisa. The word spending itself in the soul's woozy interiors like a sigh.

"Only after two double Beefeaters, Mr. Ponce," she said. Her smiling eyes did not release me.

"Oxygen starvation," I said.

"What?"

"You know," I said, leaning toward her. "I really feel stupid. Here we've been working together practically side by side for who knows how long and I feel as if I've never really noticed the real Alice James until now."

She raised an eyebrow. "Backwards, Mr. Ponce."

"Backwards?"

"I'm the one who noticed you. The *real* Mr. Ponce."

I leaned away from her, fished in my pocket for an L.T. Brown. The waiter, a tall skinny kid with shoulder-length hair, approached the table. He looked at me, eyebrows arched expectantly. I resented his expression, glared at him. He dropped the check on the table and left. I blew a ring of smoke at his back.

"You always seemed so worried and harassed," she said. "You'd come to work distracted. There was an air about you that warned people away. Did you realize that? No, of course you didn't. But today all of that seems to have vanished. I can't believe a mere promotion is responsible for such a stunning change."

"I didn't realize I was such a clod," I said.

She reached across the table and touched my hand. "Oh, not that. You were never a clod. Just remote, you know? Unreachable."

"And now I'm reachable?"

She laughed. "Well, *friendlier.*" She looked at me directly, her eyes an open door, I believed, to her thoughts. And such thoughts they were. Ah, the magnetism of rank. "I hope I'm not embarrassing you with all this instant character analysis, Mr. Ponce."

"I'm not embarrassed, Miss James," I said, lying slightly. "I'm flattered. Very flattered."

"Beware the flatterer."

"Flattery from you, Miss James, doesn't make me wary."

"I'm glad."

"So am I."

There was one of those important pauses between people that marks the turning point in their relationship. I glanced at my watch. Let us not turn this corner too swiftly. I felt a bit drunk. My body was a fine apparatus geared for great, raging excess. But there was a traffic cop in my head. Ease off, ease off. Remember the priorities. I tried to make a mental list of them.

"Mr. Ponce?" she said.

"Yes?" *Home. Family. Job.* Maybe it was too late for two-thirds of that list.

"Will you call me sometime? I mean, at home, my apartment?"

I smiled. A great sailing corsair of an Errol-Flynn-in-his-prime smile, but my chest was sinking under a lead weight. My fine apparatus felt a little sick again.

"Gather ye rosebuds, and all that," I mumbled.

"I like you very much," she said.

When I got home I found a note pinned to a defrosted chicken: "Put your dirty thing in this, hotshot." It was signed L. I had to think for a minute. L. *Louella?* But the phrase was so uncharacteristically simple. Another glance around the apartment, though, settled the improbabilities. It was empty. Furniture, pictures, knickknacks, kids. Empty. Clean. The works. I made for the liquor. Louella, a non-drinker, had left the bar intact. I uncapped a fresh quart of Wild Turkey and lightened it an ounce.

There was more, in a more characteristic tone: "You're not a man. You have no respect for me or for the children. You thrive on diseased images inspired by your flagging masculinity. Degenerate self-indulgence makes you feel functional, evidently. Basho was quite right."

I unpinned the note and put the chicken into the microwave oven. I set the electronic brain for "chicken—defrosted." I went to the den. My desk was gone. So were my books. Even my old college texts. One slip-up in thirteen years and you become buzzard food. Bones picked clean. Well, not quite clean. My cameras and equipment were still in the closet. So were my eight-by-tens of Lisa. Scattered on the floor, some of them ripped, others bent and creased by the claws of outrage. I'd taped them to the bottom of my desk. No doubt a mover had discovered the manila envelope.

It was a shock, but not a surprise. Like deliberately touching a high-voltage wire. She hadn't said she was leaving, but it was implicit in the scene. I came home, two or three in the morning, expecting to find her in bed. But no, she was waiting, grim as Madame Defarge, sitting erect, scrubbed of makeup, symbol of domestic sanctity. She did not speak. Just took one long look at my wet and naked body, the little heel-bruises on my chest, gave me a faintly famous smile—Mona Lisa, or better yet, Parmigianino's long-necked madonna looking down at the writhing four-foot dwarf in her lap with the pity and disdain of a queen—and it worked, I felt small and stupid, a trapped delinquent without defenses.

Oh God, yes, wet *and* naked. After rollicking about her rooms we decided, devil-may-care, on a midnight swim, sans garb. The pool is lighted, but we had no sense of caution to inhibit our spree. We played underwater games. *Spear-fisherman and Mermaid. Spawning Grounds Hi-Jinx. Flipper Flips Out. Jaws.* We were both extravagantly impressed by the stamina of my aging trooper. "Well, I swan!" she said, time and again, playing Scarlet O'Hara to my Rhett Butler. Rutt, she called me. "You're in a rut, Rutt!" "I aim to please, ma'am." In a slower mood, under the jovial gaze of Fred MacMurray, whom we'd accidentally jarred into action, she said, "I thought men over forty were inclined to fade in the backstretch and die coming home." So did I. So did Fred. He was singing "Full Moon and Empty Arms" in a boozy baritone, a rasping nasal lament. We climbed into a huge dryer meant for carpets. We made the big, perfectly balanced cylinder rock on its soundless bearings. No one was counting, but it was probably our sixth. And neither one of us was going to look the gift horse in the mouth, especially this one who began to feel his oats more and more as the evening galloped on.

Call it the at-long-last release of my "pent-up aching

rivers." Over the years, Louella and I had wound down to a mechanical, nondisruptive, weekly routine. We told ourselves it was normal and proper. We even talked about rededicating our energies to "more important areas" of our lives. We called it our "Saturday Night Special." Christ. (*Hurry dear. Don't touch it there! You really have a dangerous surplus of unutilized pregenital tendencies! I'm going to speak to Dr. Vapori about this. Get back up here! You know how I feel about the polymorphous perverse! Oh glick!*) Once a week is plenty, she said, *for integrated adults. It is infantile to put yourself constantly before the greater need of society.* Something to that effect. Very responsible, very adult. Exemplary. *You can't fuck society,* I once said, a lame little non sequitur after a Friday night turn-down. *Tell that to the rapist,* she snorted cleverly, rolling over into sweet durable sleep. And I'd lie there with the clamoring beast, hungry, red-eyed, chained by the logic of responsibility and the negatively wagging finger of reason.

The lie was terrible, but I tried it anyway. Something about a few of the fellows throwing me into the pool, naked, hiding my clothes in the bushes somewhere, all because I won heavily. "Where's your winnings?" she said, crisp as scissors. Her eyes pinned me to the wall. I was a destructive moth. She saw through my disguise. The flesh, hair, and bone of a man didn't fool her a bit. I rallied: "Look, where I go is my concern, Louella!" I tried to recall the brute realities of the frontier. Sterling Hayden explaining animal need to a spinster. "Once in a while a man has got to follow his impulses without being made to feel as if he's exposing his family to some kind of vicious degradation." She did not answer. Oh, the forbidding strength of the wronged. She rose slowly, a tower of heatless morality, cinched her robe tight, and slammed me out of her bedroom forever.

Still, I loved her. It hit me, standing there, alone and shivering. I thought about that sudden and gratuitous impulse. *Do you? Do you really?* But it was real, it was decidedly real. Yes, I loved. Loved something, and felt, now,

56 • •

the chill of vacuum. Something had gone out of me. A vital organ of the soul.

It was my life I loved. My routines, my arrivals and departures, my place at the table, and those indelible moments when the sense of well-being overwhelmed me. Family life, the nucleus. The safety. The bulwark of worthy possessions. Gone, all gone.

The microwave oven buzzed for me. I took out the sizzling chicken, slid it onto a coat hanger which I had straightened into a skewer, and carried it, with my bottle of Turkey, into the living room. "Basho was quite right," she said. I thought about his probable evaluation of me. Hated him for it. I ate the chicken without tasting it.

I drank until I cried. Real tears. Real sobs. The throat pinched with salt. "A maudlin drunk," I told myself, chuckling without pity through the self-pitying tears. "A crier," I scoffed, merciless.

Then it was dark. I got up to turn on a light. I approached the invisible wall, arms outstretched. The room around me was, I knew, preparing to rise. I tried to block out the idea. Try not to think of an elephant: Swarms of elephants graze in the sunny veldts of your brain. I stopped resisting it. The room soared. Soared and rotated, as it gained altitude. The axis of rotation was just behind my heels. Behind me it rose, in front of me it sank. I tilted forward, almost fell into starless space. *It's all in the head, all in the head,* I reassured myself. *What isn't,* came the pat reply. The rotation speeded up. My home, emptied of its life, had become a dangerous centrifuge. I was pressed against the wall by an enormous hand. I begged for mercy. I tried to sink to my knees, but the hand wouldn't let me. Chicken began to crawl up my throat. My heart was on fire. I couldn't feel my feet or legs. The room's axle was belted to a flywheel. The flywheel belonged to an underworld engine. Clear in the dark air were the dull hammerings and the groans of the miserables who fed the eternal furnace. Then a new force. A lateral yaw added itself to the rotation, a gnarled confusion of vectors, and I began to cartwheel through space, a space station made of blood and bone and beating heart.

I searched for a rhyme. Tried to say something, but chicken got in the way, soft metallic lumps of it, a vengeful acid searing my throat. We floated, liberated chicken and me, through the cistern of galaxies. I raised my infinitely massive but suddenly weightless hand and struck a light switch. The engine slowed. The invisible hand let me go.

I stood, face to the wall, snivelling and puking.

I did not want to be alone. In the air around me, the wheels of vertigo were poised. I cleaned myself up, then went out to the patio and climbed the grapestake fence. I knocked on her door. No messing around this time, just a cup of coffee and a few words about the ups and downs of life. Somewhere in the neighborhood, a lonely beagle grieved for itself. I knocked again.

She opened the door. "Hi, Lobo," she said, her smile thin.

"Can I come in?"

She looked behind her quickly and I realized then she wasn't alone. "Sorry," I said. "I didn't know you had company."

"No. Come in. It's no one."

We sat in the kitchen, at the breakfast bar. The place was dark again, except for the little light above the range. She was wearing a sleeveless sweater and slacks, and her long hair was hanging free.

"Headache again?" I asked.

"What?"

"The lights."

Something was wrong. She was not looking at me. She kept her head turned slightly to her left.

"You don't look too chipper yourself," she said, pouring out two cups of coffee."

"I'd be surprised if I did."

"Bad day?"

58 • •

Her smile didn't work. A partial flash of teeth, a half-smile, a weak show of spirits under duress.

"What's wrong?" I asked.

I got up and turned on the overhead lights. She turned her face away from me again, but not before I saw the damage. Left eye closed, the skin around it blue-green and puffy.

"My God, what happened to you?" I asked, but I was afraid I already knew. The husband came home.

"Oh. You mean this?" She touched the eye gingerly. "I walked into a cupboard door. It was dark, and I didn't see it."

I swallowed some coffee. "I'll bet," I said, under my breath.

She sat next to me. I took her hand. "He socked you, didn't he?"

She took her hand away, pushed loose hair from her forehead. "Forget it, Jay. Take my word for it, it was an accident."

Sure. And snakes piss uphill.

I got up and went into the living room, turned the rheostat up high. It was a mess. A bomb had gone off in it. The ivory carving had been broken in half. The two halves hung down like victims of a lynching. A lamp shade had been crushed, the lamp bent out of shape. The little ebony figures were scattered all over the carpet. A chair was overturned. Papers, magazines, records, scattered everywhere. A dumped ashtray. I carried my cup to the bar and sat down.

"Looks like you bumped your head in here, too."

She was biting her lip, trying to hold back. But her eyes were glistening. Then I noticed her other bruises. On her arms. An odd butterfly mark, a perfect blue butterfly, or the shadow of a butterfly, on her left shoulder, repeated several times on her upper arm.

I reached for her. "You poor kid," I said, but she waved me off.

"Look," she said, "you ought to know something. What we did, you know, last night—" Upstairs a door slammed.

There was an urgency in her face that complicated things instantly. I looked up at the landing. No one appeared.

"You'd better go," she said, whispering now. "I'll talk to you later, okay?"

But I wasn't listening to her. My neck hair was stiff. Mouth dry. The husband was up there. Gil Dennison. Probably soaking his sore knuckles in epsom salts. I looked at Lisa and nodded toward the stairs. She lowered her eyes. Her mouth was weak at the edges. Scared. I took her by the wrist. "Come on," I said. "Let's get out of here. You don't need this."

She jerked away from me, terrified. *"No,"* she hissed. "We'll talk *later*. You don't understand."

I looked at her for a long second, then left the bar and went to the foot of the stairs. "How's it going, slugger?" I called, my heart alarmed suddenly at the suggestion of heroics.

He didn't answer the challenge. I started up the stairs. Lisa came up behind me and pulled my arm. "Don't," she said, "be stupid." She wasn't crying now. I looked at her. For a second I suspected another skit. A wiggy *ménage à trois*. Complete with bruises. Blood. I tested the pressure against my arm. It was honest. She didn't want me to go up there. I went back to the bar, searched it for something medicinal, something for the stomach, found the aquavit, poured a shot.

"You have a problem, lady," I said.

She shrugged. "Who doesn't?"

I saw the photograph then of the severed head. It was on the floor, torn into quarters. I picked up the pieces and put them together, like a puzzle for three year olds, on the bar. And then it came to me, the full memory of the bad dream. It was Skylor Blue, the billionaire, and the memory was of a story carried in *Life* or *Look* years ago. He'd been terribly sick, on the verge of death, and it was big news because, like a ten-thousand tentacled octopus, he was at the nerve center of a vast and various corporation. A large full-color photograph of Blue in the hospital connected by transparent tubes and wires to life-sustaining machines, surrounded by doctors and well-wishers, as well as a few eager vultures, is the bad dream I remembered. *Pull your plugs, Mr. Blue,* I recall having said to the glossy misrepresentation of a life. *Pull your plugs.* Medical technology had climbed on his back, and like a lamprey, wasn't about to let go. For reasons such as this, it is possible to pity the rich. The bloody mechanics aren't interested in the wheezing machinery of the poor.

"Skylor Blue also has a problem," I said.

She tapped a cigarette out of the package, dropping two of them on the floor. "What do you mean?"

"That's him, isn't it?"

She blew smoke between us. "Don't be crazy. It's a joke. Pop art, I guess you'd call it."

"Looks real enough to me. Do you know him?"

"Of course not."

"I didn't think a man like him would be very interested in playing practical jokes."

But how would I know? Skylor Blue, the almost mythical industrialist, owner of Dynablast's chief competitor, United JetVac, as well as a superconglomerate that included oil companies, copper mines, fruit plantations in Central America, shipping companies, airlines, God knows what else, a man of means, one of the world's proprietors.

"Lisa," I said, "what's going on here? Why—"

Behind us someone cleared his throat. We both turned around, between heartbeats. A man wearing only slacks stood on the landing. He was big. A weight lifter. Arms like railroad ties. Washboard stomach. Armor-plate chest. A blond man with a dark tan. His wide-open eyes were the color and indifference of daylight. The husband. The husband.

"You'd better go now," Lisa whispered.

"Come with me," I said.

"No." Then, leaning toward me, she whispered, "Come by tomorrow night. I'll be in a position to tell you more."

"But you haven't told me anything, yet."

The ape on the landing cleared his throat again and began to descend the steps, slowly, his movements suggesting an awesomeness that had better be recognized.

I didn't want to appear rushed. I finished my drink in three sips, slid off the stool, yawned quickly, patted my stomach. He was on the bottom step now, and grinning.

I grinned back, hoped it was a grin, but it probably looked more like a flinch. *The Cuckolder Caught*. Old codes die hard. Gossip is easy. But it ignores the reality of pain. A loose wife sours life. Behind the big man's grin there lurked a sourness on life I did not want to tap. My earlier inclination toward heroics had vanished. I blamed the aquavit for diluting the Turkey, and headed for the door.

I went home, found my bottle, brought it with me into the shower. I sat under the nozzle until the water turned cool.

Louella had left my clothes in a pile against the bedroom closet. I put on fresh slacks and a depressingly festive shirt. Red and yellow hombre stripes. I buzzed the blue stubble off my chin and splashed on a strong lime after-shave. Then, because I was unhappy and drunk and willing to experiment, like an incautious surgeon, on the body of my paraplegic spirit, I looked up her number.

"I didn't think you'd actually call," she said.

"What made you think that?" I asked.

"It was in your face, Mr. Ponce. A definite 'no thank you.' "

"Well then, so much for your powers of tepelathy, Miss James old bean."

"Telepathy. What made you change your mind?"

"The English bulldog is known for its tenacity, right?"

"What?"

"Disaster, Miss James. Always alters the decision-making process."

"I don't think I'm following. What disaster?"

"Nothing newsworthy. The big news floats above a submerged continent of little miseries. Big news is just a pleasant distraction. Entertainment. Let's call up Walter Cronkite and give him the lowdown."

"Are you drinking, Mr. Ponce?"

"Am, was, and will be. Anyway, I called. That's the upshot of all this, as I see it."

"I'm glad you did, Mr. Ponce."

"And I'm glad you're glad I did, Miss James."

There was an undeclared moment. She claimed it. "Well, *are* you going to ask me out, or not?"

I had a fleeting impression that her aggressive manner was not in good taste. Let us at least cover our crude designs with ornate hypocrisies. What am I, after all? Meat in the roaster? Let it go, let it go. Who are you to judge. I said, "Why not," and noticed a sober resignation in my voice.

She laughed. It was a hard laugh. I warmed up to it. Life is hard. Either harden against it or become bread pudding. "Why not indeed?" she said, softer now, but a long way from pudding.

"Just one thing, Miss James. I am slightly *borracho,* you know? A little dizzy. Will you pick me up, here, at my place? You have a car, don't you?"

"Give me directions. But are you sure you want me to come? I mean, to your *home?*"

"Like Speedy Gonzales. Like an ambulance, Miss James."

"That's me ringing your bell, Mr. Ponce."

Actually, it took her nearly an hour to get here. "Got lost," she said, looking around the hollow apartment with slowly widening eyes. "This neighborhood has its share of tricky streets."

"Tricky streets, tricky people. It's a pattern, Miss James."

"Well, anyway, I'm here."

And so she was. Aglow in satin. Sunset pink, a color to arouse pretty nostalgias. Long skirt, coolie jacket, and a tank top that plunged suicidally, half exposing her boldly unencumbered breasts.

"You like?" she said archly, following my tactless stare.

I nodded. "You had your dinner yet, Miss James?"

"Hours ago. It's after nine, you know."

I knew nothing, a piece of smooth driftwood on a strange beach, waiting for another tide. "Oh," I said.

"But if you haven't eaten, I wouldn't mind going along."

"Have you ever been to one of our drive-in restaurants?"

"Mr. Ponce, I've been here for six years. I'm practically native in my tastes."

The lilt in her voice gave everything she said a subtle importance. It kept you alert. I liked that.

Her little car was quick and low to the road. She nudged it smartly through the gears. The little engine hummed. The top was down and the chilly air felt good, the cockpit was awash with it, as we jolted along on the hard, sports-car springs.

I became full of a nostalgic but antecedentless admiration, watching her drive. I took out my little camera and took her picture, the flash igniting her face.

"Don't do that," she said, downshifting. "You'll blind me."

A bumper sticker on the car ahead of us said, *Jesus Isn't Tired Of You Yet.* Another sticker in the rear window said, *Honk If You Understand.*

We followed the car into Jack's Big Bite. The drive-in was packed with high school kids and the rock music from their car radios was loud and competitive.

I ordered two cheeseburgers, a root beer, onion rings. The car next to us, the one with the stickers, was still idling. It sounded like a tractor.

"We didn't honk because we didn't understand," I explained to the driver, a heavy man in a sweatshirt and earphones. He looked at me, puzzled, took off the headset.

"I'm listening to the Kings. This heap makes so much noise you got to use the phones."

"What's the score?" I asked.

"One up. One up."

"He's listening to the *king?*" Alice asked.

"It's the battery," said the man. "I got to leave this clunker on or I won't be able to get it started again. Listen, if I get the job at K-Mart, I'll get me one of those little Jap bombs. *Varroom, varroom.*"

"Good luck," I said.

He put his earphones back on and gave me a little wink.

My food came. I tore the foil away and got busy.

"I love to watch men eat," said Alice. Her steady blue eyes missed nothing. I grinned, squirrel-cheeked. "They're— I don't know—*primitive,* I guess. Set the jawbone into action and the mind goes back thirty thousand years."

The lilt was becoming a delight. It told of unrevealed enthusiasms. She was an exciting girl. Jack, a neon robot standing on the drive-in, encouraged the traveler to stop in and get those jaws working. I emulated Jack's eye-popping jaw action and took the burger down in three enormous bites. Alice clapped her hands and laughed. "Greed," she said, "is healthy. Quite normal."

No doubt. But I couldn't swallow. Too big, Jack. I grabbed the root beer and washed it down.

"Mr. Ponce?"

"Let's get off that, all right? You're Alice. I'm Jay. Try to remember."

"Jay."

I hit the second burger. Shark into tuna. The man in the clunker lifted an earphone. "They scored," he said.

"Why was there no furniture in your apartment tonight?" said Alice, her mood shifting toward pensive.

"Wife left. Took everything not nailed down. Furniture. Kids. Bank books. Left the booze, my clothes, cameras, and the microwave oven. Always claimed she hated it. Talked about waves in the air jammed with cancer. Always covered her breasts with aluminum foil when she was near it. But she couldn't resist the convenience."

"I'm so sorry." And she appeared to be. Domestic tragedy is one of the universals. Everyone understands it, has a stake in it. But then she smiled. "Hasn't affected your appetite much, has it?" I looked at her. Tucked cozily into her bucket seat, immodest little ski-jump breasts bathed in red neon from Jack's moving jaws, her watchful eyes deepening with promise. Affect my appetite? Nothing affects the miserable shark that lives in this deplorable house of flesh.

We sat in her Westwood apartment drinking Irish tea laced with Jameson's and listening to 78 rpm records of the early and mid-fifties, rhythm and blues mainly, a music the nostalgia craze had so far left pretty much alone. A man called Big J McNeeley poured the ragged texture of his mighty black soul into a split-reed B-flat tenor sax in a wall-clawing piece titled "Texas Turkey." Alice, in her stockings, danced to it, dividing the speed-of-light rhythm into eighths and still shimmying.

I felt relaxed and at home, shoes off and feet propped up. Alice's apartment was small and convenient, neat and efficient. A lot like Alice herself. I thought of my barren rooms, took the Jameson by the neck and drank. I didn't want to think about my own barrenness. I wanted to fill it.

Alice led a sensible, well-ordered life. I forgave her aggressiveness, her quick assault on the new purplebadge. Then bit my tongue. Who was I to forgive her? Forgive her for being honest? For saying what's on her mind?

She was dancing in the middle of the living room, letting the music play her bones. I studied her, and her apartment. There was a small, framed photograph of a gray-haired couple, her parents probably, on a clutter-free desk. Next to this there was a small wicker basket containing letters. The furniture was straight-edged, functional Scandinavian. The whole interior was woody, fragrant, clean. A refuge for the battered, world-weary Viking.

"Texas Turkey" was replaced by an Ivory Joe Hunter ballad. Music to grapple by. She came over and took my hand. I didn't budge.

"Can't do it," I said. She pouted for a second and then began to dance with herself again. "I'm dead. Knocked out.

Can't get started, kid. If I get the job at K-Mart I'll get one of those slick Jap bombs. Varroom."

She smiled a little but kept her eyes closed. She was hugging herself, swaying nicely, lips still in a slight pout. But the pout now was a kiss for the music, not a judgment. I got up.

I took her in my arms. We leaned in two or three directions, our bodies colliding, a half beat out of sequence with each other. I scuffed her foot, she pushed me back, I began to slide downhill, she held my wrist, I sensed the invisible vectors of my old war, she became alarmed.

"This isn't dancing," she said.

"I'm such lousy company tonight," I said.

"Listen, would you like a rubdown? It can be very restorative."

"Shouldn't drink so much. Should get in shape. Feel sixty sometimes, way I'm going, you have to wonder."

"Let me open the Murphy."

"You'd really do that? For me?"

"I really would."

Ah, the radiant smiling girl here before me. Among the mean and angry traps of this hard hard world there lie bright islands of marvelous beings.

"You just pop out of those clothes and let me go to work. I've very good at it. No one at work knows this, but I used to do it professionally. At the Riverside Rub Club. Under the name of Cherry Sweet. 'Let Cherry Make You Merry,' said the billboard."

"You surprise me, Alice."

She smoothed out the Murphy and waited for me. I stripped down to my shorts. She looked at me, arms folded, waiting. Eyebrows arched, amused.

"Shy?" she said.

"What do you mean?"

"Shy. I mean, shy."

I dropped my shorts, lowered myself with forced nonchalance to the bed.

"Of course I'm shy," I said into the pillows.

Her hands worked the length of my back like firm little machines. Muscles in my shoulders, back, and lower back let themselves go under their mistressing stroke. Then the arms and hands, legs and feet. Then, lift up now, that's a good chap, and over to the chest—whoops, look at this, hello, we seem to have an uprising on our hands, patience, patience you little rotter—the thud-thud of the heels of her hands jostling the flab, and I regretted having let my chest muscles go flaccid and titty, the regret absorbed quickly in pleasure, thud-thud-thud sending shock waves of titillation toward the brain and spinal cord, as she removed the body from the mind's jealous noose, thud-thud-thud sending impulses of light through my blood, my brain luminous with it, and I floated, vertigo without panic, amorphous blossoms outside time and space surrounding me, incandescent pollen tickling the marrow, freedom, real freedom, freedom without will, without desire, the universe seen in this internal light as a living orgasmic cell, whole, unfissured, distributing itself in ecstatic lines of force, the atoms dancing in an eternal circus of delight, thud-thud-thud, molecules in the skin mating, ageless molecules in the aging skin. I sighed with gratitude and glee, my shyness gone.

"How's that, Jay?"

"Jrrrmm?"

"I said, how does it feel?"

"Gaaaaa . . ."

We sat in her kitchen drinking coffee. It was bitter, but the bitterness came from me. Humiliation soured the morning. A red lake from the smog-fused sun flooded the apartment. The red was mine, too. It was my shame. The day would be red, the week, maybe all time to come.

"Don't go on about it, Jay."

"Easy enough for you to say," I said, trying to make a feeble joke, but the grin wouldn't stay put. I took out a

68 • •

twenty dollar bill and put it on the table between us. She didn't look at it.

"It isn't as if everything depended on it, you know."

"Easy enough for you to say," I said again, without the grin. I put a ten on top of the twenty.

"Really, Jay," she said, not looking at the bills at all. "It's just nonsense, this carrying on. The single major flaw in American men is their dogged refusal to grow up. Honestly, it means *nothing*. I don't keep a list of the top ten, you know. I'm not going to distribute handbills notifying the world of your—difficulties."

She was being so reasonable I wanted to break her arms. I hid my evil thoughts in my coffee mug.

Dead in the water. Doornail dead. I slipped out another ten and dropped it on the pile with stiff, nihilistic fingers. She was looking out the window. Her clever masseusing didn't resurrect the dead trooper. In fact, her skillful attempts at resuscitation only made things worse. Her having to work over it like a dying coal. But it was numb as a plum, indifferent to the varieties of sweet friction she had to offer.

The pent-up aching rivers had gone dry. Dry bed disaster. After Lisa they needed recovery time. I hoped, at least, that was it. But I wasn't about to use that as an explanation. I remembered Lisa's white pills. The culprits? I had finally said, after ten mortifying minutes of useless emergency treatment, "I guess I'm not a kid anymore, Alice," acutely aware, too, of her disappointment. It was—generous to me—disappointment in herself, in her failure to excite. But as far as I was concerned, the fault was all mine. I slept in her bed, tame as a monk, and dreamed of a tideless chemical sea choked with dead fish.

"Let's talk about something else," she said, taking the English muffins out of the toaster and applying the butter with a subject-changing flourish.

"How about the weather?" I suggested, schoolboy-bitter.

She looked at me, a scold in her face. "How about the Sheik?" she said.

I guess my face went blank.

"You *have* seen him, haven't you?"

Her kitchen window overlooked the front entrance of an import shop. A fat man in a white suit was feeling the arms of a bamboo chair.

"Big man in a burnoose," she said. "Wears dark glasses, even indoors. Chin whiskers. They call him Sham, I think."

The fat man sat in the chair. The chair sagged to the left. The shop had just opened. The owner was putting pieces of wicker and bamboo furniture out on the sidewalk. The fat man stood up and looked at the frail import. He said something to the storekeeper.

"What are you talking about?" I said.

"The Sheik. Sham. He's been conferring with Mr. Towne and some military men for the past few days. You haven't noticed?"

I spooned marmalade onto my muffin. I didn't know what she was talking about, didn't want to know, my thoughts still mobilized around last night's catastrophe. *On top of everything else,* I told myself, *I've lost my manhood.* I knew I was striking a melodramatic pose, hated it, knew that these things should be taken in stride, but failed nonetheless to rise above my petty self and snuff out the memory of that sullen traitor, half-up only once, a brief nodding awareness, then only to wilt shabbily like a sensitivity plant.

"He's one of the oil Sheiks," Alice said. "They say Arab oil money is heavily involved in the new project."

I shoved the image of the absurd fern out of my mind. "Scimitar?" I said.

"*Yes.* Scimitar. Supposedly, these Arabs have bought into Dynablast. The project is a cooperative effort. Our technology, their money. Partly their money, anyway. I think it's very complicated and very political."

The fat man sat in another chair. This one didn't sag. He

took off his hat and wiped his forehead on his sleeve. I said, "That explains the name, doesn't it? Scimitar. Usually we use the Greek pantheon."

"Mr. Towne picked the name himself. Symbolic, I suppose, of the arrangement."

She heated two more muffins, poured more coffee. I thought of Louella, the kids, the kitchen smells of home, my other loss. I sighed. Alice looked at me, looked quickly away.

"What do you suppose it means?" she asked.

"The Arabs buying in? Probably nothing much. They're buying into everything else American, so why not aerospace, too? That new drive-in chain, Ali Baba's Beef on a Bun, is supposed to be owned by an Iranian. Technically not Arab, I guess, but Moslem, *and* oil rich."

"But *aerospace*. What about security things, top secrets and all that?"

"Who knows? I guess they've made some kind of deal with the DOD. Maybe Scimitar isn't a weapon system after all. Maybe it's an oil-carrying zeppelin."

"But it seems so odd, seeing this Bedouin type hanging around Dynablast."

"International politics makes strange bedfellows," I said, instantly regretting the figure of speech. I made a face, as if there were coal oil in the marmalade.

The fat man was stuck in the bamboo chair. He tried to stand but the chair hugged his hips like a woody mouth. He minced back and forth in front of the store and slapped at the chair with his hat, a turtle unhappy with its shell.

Alice got up and clattered around the kitchen for a while, refusing to let silence have an opening. I watched her. She had nice, positive movements, her body reflecting an enviable frame of mind. She stood at the sink, her weight on her left foot, apples flexing in her calves, as she rinsed the cups. I put the marmalade jar on the money so it wouldn't get up and crawl away.

I went into the living room and put on a Ray Charles record. "Drown in My Own Tears." The old Ray, before he

• • 71

opted for popularity with middle America. It was a suitably maudlin piece, choked with the ragged chords of defeat. End of the road music.

She came in. She looked at me with all her healing powers turned on. She hugged me around the middle and pressed her face against my neck. So warm, so soft, so free of reluctance, but I pushed her away, remembering the icy hollows of failure, tasting the acid of a brand-new species of fear, common, I suppose, to middle-aged men.

"Work," I said. "We have to go to work."

And the bloody light of Los Angeles blessed nothing.

She sighed. "Work," she said, the stale word triggering a weariness in the face, automatic resignation in the spirit. But, quickly, she brightened. "We can take sick leave today, and make a day of it!"

I shook my head no.

"I can call in sick, and then fifteen or twenty minutes later, you do the same. No one will make the connection."

I headed for the door.

"We can lie in bed and eat candy bars and watch TV movies. Or we could go to the zoo."

I opened the door.

"Well?"

I was suddenly struck by the enormous improbability of practically everything. I imagined that the apartment building here in Westwood, the import shop across the street, the city itself, were surrounded by a halo of crackling energy, an aureole ribbon that held the gift together. For a moment I saw her own halo, a bright band shimmering fragilely, the gift it held, her unspeakable uniqueness and improbability, and a sharp jolting nostalgia expanded my lungs with the sure knowledge that everything that happens happens only once and then is gone forever. I sighed raggedly, nearly sobbed.

"I gather that is a final no."

The impulse to stay was strong but it was vetoed by my new importance. I was not geared to take promotion lightly. "Today is the big day," I said, almost apologetically. "You know, the Scimitar briefing. The Project Chief is going to be there."

"I'd forgotten."

Carpentry. I could take up carpentry. I could hire myself out to families wanting to convert their garages into game rooms. We could live here, in her apartment. I would simplify my life. Meat and potatoes. Hammer and saw. Muscles hard and lean, mind clear and free, skin brown and sequined with the salt crystals of honest sweat.

I said, "Let's go. We're going to be late as it is."

Dynablast is situated in what is known as an industrial park, a complex of buildings as far removed from the old smoke-belching factory image as you can get. The buildings here, in fact, are designed to fit in with the dominant architectural styles of the immediate neighborhood. Dynablast seems less like a factory than a large version of the neighboring suburbs, with the exception of the DC building (Development Center) where end items are assembled and tested. DC is a little too large to disguise, but even at that it is decorated pleasantly and is far from being an eyesore.

The motif is California Modern, a blend of Spanish, Mexican, Moorish, and Futuristic styles, with an occasional touch of old New England. It makes the workers (who live in such settlements as Villa Conquistadores, Cambridge Palms, Rancho Del Futuro, Old Nova Scotia Palisades, and Arabian Heights) feel at home. The building where I work, Proposals and Liaison, was built along the lines of a hacienda, even to the extent of cactus gardens, tiled fountains, and patios where the workers might enjoy an outdoor lunch. In place of the archaic steam whistle announcing lunch breaks and shift changes, Flamenco guitars signal the workers over a high fidelity paging system. It is a windowless hacienda, big as a stadium, and shaped somewhat like a headless turtle, but, all things considered, not a bad place to work. I've heard of worse.

Conference room 33-A, more of a theater than a conference room, is the largest one in Proposals and Liaison. A small crowd of nervous men in blue suits traded small talk with near-hysterical energy. Their laughter clattered off the bare walls like spent bullets. The purple disks of management were prominent, high up on the lapels, each man displaying his rank with desperate pride. The metallic perfume of deodorized sweat was everywhere.

A girl from the typing pool, doubling now as hostess, handed me a steaming styrofoam cup. Another, carrying a tray of enormous doughnuts, offered jellied treats to the managers. She had an angelic face that sat on a doughy jowl handsome as a bladder. I declined, but she lingered a moment, nostrils flaring in the manner of Raquel Welch. I joined my colleagues.

"The big day," I said to a man with prematurely white hair. He had a speedy smile-tic that uncovered unnaturally brilliant dentures in startling, hallucinatory flashes. He looked at me and the smile-tic became a frown-tic, the corners of his mouth flicking downward, his brow a semaphore of moving furrows.

"Where is your *badge?*" he said. He spoke out the side of his mouth, looking away.

I glanced at my chest. I was still in hombre stripes, no jacket, badgeless. "Left it home," I said. "Forgot it. Real bitch of a hassle at home this morning. Wife on her ass with the flu, kids croupy and feverish." I used the jocular, no-sweat tone of my new club. Management. The unruffled insider. I chuckled, grandly at ease with myself, badge or not, but he had lost interest in my little performance, knowing it all too well himself, and looked over my head at the door.

"They're late," he said, checking his Bulova.

I looked at mine. "I've got five to."

He checked his electronic digits again. "You're slow. It's two minutes past the hour."

"Okay. You tell them they're late," I said.

He looked at me hard, the ravaged look of a centerless man, tic on the rampage, and walked away.

I stood back from the group, unable to penetrate it. The hombre stripes a temporary talisman against entry. Now and then someone would take the trouble to peer at me for a long second, flickers of disapproval kindled in his brow, then duck back into the jittery blue mass. I watched, an insider on the outside, the continuous checking and rechecking of cuffs, tie clasps, collars, badges, lapels. The meticulous lint-picking, the tugging of earlobes, the fingering of moustaches, the absentminded nose-picking. The doughnut girl dug my ribs with the edge of her tray. "No thanks," I said, and she turned, showing her profile, weighty breasts strapped up high, fun-loving torpedoes, nipples like thumbs. I pictured fat babies dazed with lovemilk. I winked.

Then they came in. Byron Towne leading the way, followed by a man I hadn't seen before, and, lo and behold, Alice's Sheik. The Sheik was a big man, not as tall as Towne, but wider, resplendent in a flowing burnoose. He was smoking a long cigarette in an ebony holder. Eyes concealed behind smoky glasses. They were laughing. The booming, unrestrained laughter of the highly placed. Inner circle merriment. The men in blue instantly picked up the mood. They started chuckling, a few coughing noncommittally, the cautious let's-wait-and-see cough of the shrewd flunky. The three men went to the front of the room, where a raised dais had been erected for the occasion. There were three cushioned chairs on the dais, a podium, and a microphone. The Sheik and the new man sat down. Towne remained standing. He raised his arms for quiet, even though no one had taken a breath for thirty seconds.

"You all know what you're here for," Towne said into the mike, his voice flooding the room. He leveled a frank gaze at the rank-and-file managers. It moved from face to face. It excited a new wave of nervous coughing. The overhead fluorescents danced on Towne's shining scalp. A long gut rumble whinnied furiously from the center of the crowd. Towne savored the pause, let it hang for optimum effect.

Then he freed the mike from the stand and jumped down from the dais. "First things first," he said. "You—" He pointed five times. "—five men come with me." The singled-out men followed him to one side of the room.

He came back then to the main group and singled out five more. He had each group of five stand in a line. The lines faced each other.

"This is for the Sheik," he said. "Damon and I—I'll introduce Damon a little later—Damon and I have been trying to explain American football to Sham here, but it's nearly impossible to do it in abstractions. So, with a few of you volunteers, we're going to give him a little demo."

The Sheik smiled and nodded to us. He held his cigarette holder underhanded, sipping the smoke carefully.

"Now," said Towne. "I need three more. Racehorse types, this time." He looked us over, quick eyes of a wholesaler. "You," he said. "And you, and you." His eyes culled through the milling men efficiently, resting finally on me. "You, Ponce. You are number three, my safety."

He stationed us behind the second line of men, three points of a triangle, two linebackers and a safety, the abbreviated teams evidently sufficient for the demonstration.

"Okay. Dame? Will you assist?"

The new man, Damon, stepped down from the dais with athletic grace. He was a well-built man with delicately handsome features. Next to Towne, who was a very big man—six-five and close to two-fifty—he seemed small. But it was easy to see that he was hard and sinewy, the sculptured perfection of his face tending to obscure this, and that he possessed an enormous reservoir of self-confidence that spilled over into downright arrogance. The new man, who had to be the Scimitar Project Chief, was clearly a winner.

"Now," said Towne. "When I say 'hike,' the center will pass the ball—this briefcase here—to Dame, and he'll follow my lead block over the number five hole, the guard and center clearing out the area. Get it?" He turned to the Sheik. "This is a rough and tough game, Sham. But it's not without its subtleties." The Sheik nodded, sipped smoke. "Watch," said Towne, "how Dame uses me as a shield, timing his own penetration to mine. It's stylized warfare, Sham." Then, turning to us, he said, "All right, you linemen! Get into a three-point stance and keep your asses down!"

The Sheik smiled pleasantly. He clapped his hands together once. "I am your estudent, Byron," he said.

The ten linemen squatted, five against five, wheezing, wondering what was expected of them. The white-haired man with the tic was one of the guards expected to do the blocking for the runner. He was stricken with worry. Towne had created a procedural problem. A problem in politics. How seriously were we to take this demonstration? Would halfheartedness be met with disapproval? In this business, aggressiveness, or at least its trappings, is admired. Seriousness is respected. Singlemindedness is rewarded. Unswerving dedication is met with a warm show of gratitude from the highest offices. Everyone here knew that Towne took football seriously, that he was a former Little All-American. But did he expect, now, that these flaccid, middle-aged, Maalox-sipping purplebadges should go all out, do their best, exert themselves, become *physical?* You could almost hear the gears of decision stripping themselves. Then, before the gastric acids had a chance to start new pinholes in our stomach linings, Towne said, "Hike!"

The briefcase was passed back to the new man, who quickly lined up directly behind the eclipsing Towne. "Keep your eyes on Damon, Sham!" boomed Towne. "Watch his deceptive hip and leg movements!"

Towne bulled past the slow-moving white-haired man, and, with one thump of his forearm, dropped the first worried tackler on his butt. The man hit the floor hard, and change—nickels, dimes, quarters—shot out of his pockets. The runner danced and swiveled like a dervish, blinding the defenders with his quickness. He knifed to the left, cut back toward the middle, spun full circle out of the feeble arms of a linebacker, lost yardage deliberately to build up speed in an attempt to get to the sidelines, jitterbugged handily into the open, lowered his head, and turned upfield. We stood and watched him, amazed.

I hung back, sipping coffee from the styrofoam cup, hoping to go unnoticed. But suddenly I realized that the demonstration had been reduced to an open-field situation between me and the runner. A duel. The others were on their feet, watching with soaring pleasure.

The runner, running low and very fast, aimed for me. No sign of deceptive hip and leg movements now. He was smiling with anticipatory glee, a thin humorless baring of the teeth, his back almost parallel to the floor, building momentum. Towne yelled, "He cuts through tacklers like a blade, Sham!"

I knew that if he hit me at that speed and angle I'd wind up in the dispensary, sternum separated, ribs bruised, or worse. He was an efficient machine, a runner against obstacles, a compact unit designed for scoring, and I had no intention of using my body as a roadblock. So, at the last moment I stepped aside. He was holding the briefcase easily in his left arm and as he brushed past me I stuck out my hand —showing Towne that I at least tried to impede the runner —and the handle of the briefcase grabbed my fingers. The "ball" snapped out of his arms. I knew enough to realize that I had recovered a midair fumble and that the ball was still alive. Taking care not to spill coffee, I cakewalked into the enemy end zone. Where I spiked the briefcase.

The Sheik said, "Haw, haw. Seex points, eh?" and applauded.

The runner, Damon, walked slowly back across the conference room. The girl with the tray of doughnuts tried to interest him in a cinnamon bar but he ignored her. He was mad. I saw his jaw muscles lumping under the whitened skin. He wouldn't look at me.

"Still got that old fumble-itis, right Dame?" said Towne. Then to the Sheik he said, "Damon and I played football in college together. I think he set a conference record for fumbling the ball on kickoff returns that still stands. Correct me if I'm wrong, Dame. We used to call him 'Old Polio Hand.' "

There was some laughter at this, but it was careful laughter because by now everyone had figured out for himself that the new man was Scimitar Project Chief, the boss they'd have to be dealing with day to day. But Damon was a good sport after all. He gave Towne a generous hug. Towne hugged him back. The Sheik chuckled. The managers chortled among themselves. Good sportsmanship gladdens the heart. Someone nudged my ribs, a friendly elbow. It was the white-haired man. I nudged him back. We were a team, after all. A jolly group destined for good times. Towne was now hugging his old teammate with both arms. A bear hug that reddened the smaller man's face. Towne lifted Damon from the floor. The veins in Damon's face were standing out. "Zis boom bah," said Towne, dropping Damon to the floor, "bust their jaw!" An old cheer. We all picked it up. The doughnut girl did a cheerleader step, fanning her skirt.

> *Zis boom bah*
> *Bust their jaw!*

The Sheik was laughing immensely. He removed his dark glasses and wiped the tears from his eyes. His eyes were small and weak looking. Tired, world-weary eyes. He was an old man, much older than he had seemed.

Towne and Damon joined the Sheik on the dais. Towne went to the podium, rapped his knuckles against it. "As you have probably guessed," he said, using the mike, "this little scatback here is Damon Spear—Dame to his friends. A few of you might know that Damon Spear has been involved in our solid propellant program up north where he—and I do not think this is an exaggeration of the facts—accomplished a bloody miracle."

Spear, standing rigidly at Towne's side, accepted the praise soberly.

"And I think," Towne continued, "that we can expect the same kind of leadership from him in the Scimitar program." He put his hand on the back of Spear's neck and squeezed it possessively. "This little Mickey Rooney s.o.b. is one in a million."

Spear grinned at this reference to his height. He wasn't short, but next to Towne he was dwarfed. He grinned, though, the same baring of teeth I'd seen during his broken-field run. A blower came on somewhere and cold air poured into the room. I shivered, sipped my cool coffee. There was an uncomfortable silence. It went on, unmolested, for nearly a minute. I looked around for the doughnut girl. That soft, nourishing presence. That link to warmth. But she had left the room. Then Towne said, "I want each and every one of you to get to know Damon personally. To know him is to respect him. To respect him is to respect the importance of your assignment. We're going to have a smooth management team on this project, gentlemen. Tight interface. No foul-ups. Above all, *no cost overruns.* And the key to all of this is communication. Keep your channels open, gentlemen."

"*Wallah!*" said the Sheik, clapping his hands appreciatively.

Towne led Spear around to each of us for personal introductions and a handshake. When it was my turn, Spear gave me a bone-crushing grip and a stony stare that went to the back of my head. It was a probing look, cold, clinical, searching, I felt, for chinks in my character. What I had seen as delicate in his features now seemed sharply chiseled, strong as steel. He held my hand for embarrassing seconds, much longer than he had anyone else's. His grip tightened slowly, his brown eyes opaque, bird-glossy, hypnotic. I didn't try to compete with his grip. Or with his stare. I grinned and looked away, first at Towne, then at the Sheik.

The Sheik leaned forward in his chair, holding his cigarette high between thumb and forefinger, like a dart. He appeared to be waiting for the outcome of the contest. I raised my eyebrows at him, smiled affably. *No contest, Sheik.* But Spear persisted. He wanted me to commit myself, and I finally decided that this uncompetitive hand of mine was an admission of weakness and a wanton style of life. You can understand why this occurred to me. So I tightened my grip, but, as luck would have it, just as Spear was withdrawing his hand. I only managed to clamp the tips of his fingers together, so hard that I heard the fingernails click. In that wayward instant, I saw my new boss wince.

"Wallah!" boomed the Sheik.

After Spear had made all the rounds, Towne said, "And, for those of you who don't know, this august gentleman from the Middle East is Sheik Muhammad al Shammari, a new and very important stockholder in the company. I get that pronounced right, Sheik?" The Sheik tilted his head slightly and made a little kismet gesture with his hand. "Anyway, it's 'Sham' to his pals, and I sure hope I qualify on that score." He looked at the Sheik and the Sheik, who now looked a thousand years old, smiled thinly.

The meeting lasted about forty-five minutes more. The responsibilities of each manager were given, but the details were abstract, dealing with each man's function in the broadest and most general terms, never with the specifics. By the time we adjourned we still didn't have an inkling as to just what Scimitar was, although Towne did refer to it once as a *lollapalooza.* No one had the gumption to step forward and ask the question. I was given the ground rules for "need-to-know" access to the microfilmed document library that would be under my control, but the contents of those future documents, the very thing required to make need-to-know priorities, was excluded from the discussion. I sensed, among my colleagues, a timid conspiracy to remain unenlightened. A conspiracy based on an implicit trust in the stra-

82 • •

tegic decisions of the top executives. Byron Towne, Damon Spear, possibly the Sheik, had decided that our need-to-know priority was below some prearranged threshold. At least for the present. It smelled of politics.

As we left the conference room I said to the white-haired man, "Well, that clears everything up, doesn't it?"

He didn't smile. He looked at me, saw my grin, looked away. Tics of bewilderment flared across his face with the speed and delicacy of heat lightning. He said, "Zeus was something like this. They held back on us for a long time. I remember setting up test sites months before we had the key details."

"We knew it was a solid propellant IRBM a year before we got the contract," I said. "I read about it in *Time.*"

"But we didn't get the *details.*"

"That's because we got the contract before the design was finished. Those were the days, weren't they?"

"Maybe Scimitar isn't finalized yet. Maybe—"

I laughed at him. He knew as well as I that contracts weren't written that way anymore. The DOD had long since lost the keys to Fort Knox. Prime contractors now had to work under the harsh requirements of producing a working prototype before the production contracts were signed. Life is hard.

I went to my new office. It was next to Tobey's. I loved it. My state of unenlightenment didn't worry me. The politics of the new program would eventually work itself out. It had nothing to do with me. I sat in my leather swivel chair and put my feet on solid mahogany. The real thing under the deserving heel. It felt wonderful. Arrival. Finally. Top floor. Here I was. Enveloped in cushy privacy. There are compensations. Lose some, win some. Let us not dwell on loss just now. The carpet, thick blue pile, was a buffer between old losses and new gains. So were the walnut walls. So was the absence of typewriter noise from the outer work area. So was the low, sexual throb of the air conditioner. Not to mention the half-ton desk. Or the soft, eye-caressing lights.

I felt gleeful and childish. No, my problems hadn't disappeared. There was definitely a struggle ahead to normalize my life. But now I had *position* on my troubles. From this office, from this rich dark interior, *solutions would come.*

I reached into the front of my slacks and took hold of the quisling. "Turncoat," I said, without rancor.

But the old trooper sprang to attention, renewed by that top-of-the-world feeling professional advancement brings.

"A word with you, Ponce?"

I snapped out of my drowse, yanked my wayfaring hand out of my slacks, jumped to my feet. Damon Spear leaned into the room. He hadn't knocked.

"You bet, sir," I said. "Come right in." I tried a club-member smile, but my trembling tenor undermined it.

Spear stood in the doorway another moment, leveling his strong, character-assessing gaze at me, then stepped in, closing the door softly behind him. He pulled a chair up to my desk.

"I believe in speaking my mind," he said.

I chuckled. He showed me his teeth. "Oh, absolutely," I said.

"Mind if I smoke?"

"Not a bit." I handed him my L.T. Browns.

He took one out of the pack and examined it closely. "What the hell are these?" he said.

"Cigarettes," I said.

He put the cigarette back and handed the pack to me. He lit a cigar, filled the space between us with smoke. "You didn't exactly make a big hit with me today, Ponce."

"It was luck," I said, shrugging. "Dumb luck."

"I know it was luck. But that doesn't really alter what happened out there, does it?"

I shrugged again. "Well, it sure wasn't my idea to play football."

He blew a ring at the ceiling, chuckled soundlessly.

"Say," he said. "You ever see one of these?" He showed me his wrist.

"The watch?"

"It's a Pulsar. The best." He showed me how a flick of the wrist made the numbers appear. "You can take this little bugger to hell and back and it won't quit on you."

"That's quite a timepiece," I said.

His eyes narrowed. "Isn't it though?"

It dawned on me suddenly that we weren't talking about his fancy wristwatch at all. He was giving me that look again, milking the awkward pause for all it was worth. He seemed on the verge of saying something deeply significant, but I realized it was only a technique, a way of putting his subordinates off balance. He was a man who demanded the advantage.

"Those cigarettes of yours, Ponce," he said.

I touched the pack in my shirt pocket. "These?"

"Only vaginas smoke those."

Technique, I reminded myself. But he had me leaning.

"I like them," I said. *Fuck you, Project Chief.*

"I don't doubt it, Ponce. It never occurred to me that you *dis*liked them."

He grinned again, having scored. *Compensations,* I reminded myself. *There are compensations.* I pulled a hangnail loose. A pellet of blood formed in the tear. I started to say something, but the slippery riposte got away from me, and I cleared my throat instead.

"He's going to rub it in, you know."

"Pardon?"

He laid a perfect cylinder of white ash on my desk. "Towne," he said. "Towne is going to rub it in until it squeaks, Ponce."

"Oh. You mean the football game."

"That cheap shot of yours is going to cost me. Maybe you noticed how much it tickled him."

"Hell's bells, Mr. Spear, it was only a game."

● ● 85

"Oh, that's very good. Only a game. Wonderful. Damned keen of you to see it that way. Marvelous insight."

The cylinder of ash began to crumble under the steady breeze from the air conditioner. *What the hell, what the hell.* I lit an L.T. Brown and tossed the match on the desk. *Tenure,* I reminded myself. *Prestige. Money.* I formed an image in my mind of the Cadillac I would buy. *Maroon.*

"Only a game," he said. "Only a game. Next you'll tell me that humiliation is relative? You believe that, Ponce?"

I didn't know what I believed. I believed in peace, comfort, and reward for service. Not exactly ideals to set the upcoming generation on fire.

"You're a native Californian, aren't you Ponce?"

"Yes sir," I said. "Born in Venice, when Venice was Venice."

"And you probably went to one of those state colleges where some vagina taught some sort of nonacademic oriental mysticism and you walked away believing that everything is relative. I can hear the pussy now: 'Defeat is a state of mind.' 'The ego thrusts itself upon others in the mistaken belief it is sovereign.' Blah blah blah."

"I studied engineering and literature," I said.

"Were you ever in a combat zone, Ponce?" He was giving me his hardest look.

"Yes," I said. "Korea. Early part of the war."

He leaned back a foot. "Oh," he said. "I didn't know."

"How about yourself, Mr. Spear?" He'd dumped the advantage in my lap. I picked it up.

"Beside the point, actually."

"You were going to suggest that a man with a gun aimed at his nose probably wouldn't be ready to agree that his life is relative."

He shrugged, examined the tip of his cigar.

"Well, you're right, Mr. Spear. Mortal danger has a way of turning your pet philosophy into so much shit. There's only one philosophy you have in those conditions. Survival."

"I'm glad you see it my way," he said, deftly taking back the advantage.

"But wait a minute," I said. "We weren't talking about real danger. We were talking about a football game. A fake football game at that."

He stood up, leaned over the desk at me. "Ponce," he said. "There are no games."

It was a conversation stopper. Invent the premises, and all arguments are yours. *There are no games.* Q.E.D. It was a winner's premise, the only one needed.

"I believe in speaking my mind," he said, restarting the interview.

I nodded, reminding myself that my life was on the verge of a stunning improvement. Just play his game. Or his nongame.

"I'd like to get something out front," he said. "I hate to begin a relationship on a misunderstanding."

"Of course, of course," I said quickly.

"It's you and me, Ponce. We're not going to get along very well. You sense it, don't you?"

I took a deep breath and looked at my hands. "Well—"

"Don't be embarrassed. Speak your mind. You'd like to speak your mind, wouldn't you? Although you probably haven't had much practice at it."

The room began to turn. Five r.p.m. I took another breath. *This is just his style,* I reminded myself. *Hang on. A little initiation. Tomorrow he'll buy you a beer.*

"Enough said, Ponce. I'm getting the message, loud and clear." He stood up and toured the room. "Say, you ought to get some wall hangings in here. Get yourself settled in. Personalize the place." He walked along the wall, running his fingers over the paneling.

His quick change of pace didn't stop the attack. The room tipped as it turned, the axis of rotation in the middle of my desk.

"Titman," he said, introspectively.

"Sir?"

He came back to my desk, sat on the edge, avoiding the crumbled ashes. "The runt of the litter. He's the pup who always gets hind titty because he's too weak or retarded to compete. 'Only a game,' he tells himself, while his sturdier brothers and sisters hog the up-front nipples where all the milk is."

I rubbed an old hairline fracture at the back of my head.

"Am I going too fast for you, Ponce?"

I rocked my head back and forth. But everything *was* going too fast for me. The room was skimming through space. I felt little shoves of gravity from nearby asteroids.

"Either the titman is going to curl up one night and die, or he's going to make it. Now if he makes it, here's where your trouble starts."

If I kept my eyes closed, I could see the texture of space. It doesn't come in big easy quadrants. It's more like a magnified tongue. Rough, vulgar, tricky, holding little surprises for the unwary traveler.

"See, Ponce, the titman is never going to forget how it was sucking those dry dugs. His frame of mind, his perspective, his whole attitude toward the world, is fixed before he's weaned. And nothing under God's blue eyes is about to change him."

I looked at him through my fingers. He was leaning toward me, his face less than a foot away. His cigar was in the center of his mouth. A heavy white ash fell away from it, hanging for a moment on a little hinge of leaf. It was like a door opening and the deep red core of the cigar seemed like a tunnel that went into Spear's mouth, into his head, his brain, opening finally on a wide red lake of flame. I closed my fingers.

"Oh shit *yes*, he'll be a good house dog. A pet for the kids. A lap warmer for granny. But let me tell you this, Ponce. He won't be worth a thimble full of piss in the field!"

We were riding now on the end of a seven-hundred-foot boom. It was a thin boom, pencil thick, untrustworthy,

88 • •

capable of buckling catastrophically at any point along its length.

"You *read* me, Ponce?"

I lowered my hands and looked at him. He looked like Richard Widmark. Prettier. Meaner. He was playing with his left earlobe. He had nice ears. Little pink shells. His act was good. It had taken him far. I remembered something Louella said to me the day she signed up for Ladies Defense. "Jay, everybody we know is hiding a terrible secret. The world isn't safe anymore, for anyone. Society is dead, not God."

"Titmen, Ponce," said Spear, resuming the lecture. "Vaginas, Ponce. You get my drift?"

I nodded.

"And now, if that wasn't enough, we've got the Arabs shoving their dirty feet into the door."

"Beg pardon?"

"Titmen, vaginas, and Arabs. Everywhere I turn." His voice had become abstract, distant. He was listening to a different drummer. "They're coming out of the woodwork. The true competitor, old-school hard-nose rock'em-sock'em get-it-while-it's-hot competition is going the way of the whooping crane. And now the bloody camel jockeys are taking over everything in sight."

"The Sheik?"

"They're fucking us over, Ponce. It's an invasion. Their second try at it. Remember 711."

"711?"

"A.D. The camel jockeys took Spain that year. Twenty years later they were in France, where they got their heads whipped by Charles Martel and the Franks."

Charles Martel and the Franks. That great rhythm and blues group.

"But this time they're doing it with money. Oil money. Buying up California, Ponce. Big tracts of undeveloped land. Heavy industry. Electronics. Farms. Recreational areas. The Sheik and his cartel wanted to take over Dynablast, lock, stock, and barrel, but the government, a sorry bunch of titmen and vaginas if I've ever seen one, stopped them at forty-nine percent. What do you think of that, Ponce?"

"What do I think of what?"

"Aren't you listening to me? Jesus, we're going to have one beautiful relationship. I mean the *Sheik*. How do you think you're going to like working for him?"

I shrugged. It didn't matter to me. Work is work. The man I'd be seeing every day was Spear, not the Sheik. And at this point, the Sheik seemed like a prince by comparison.

Spear grinned, nasty merriment crinkling the corners of his flat eyes. "You live in one of those camel jockey condominiums, don't you?"

"It's called Arabian Heights, but—"

"Barf."

"—I don't think it's owned by an Arab company."

"I don't think it's owned by an Arab company," he mimicked, mincing the words in cutely puckered lips.

"It was built by Corelli Construction," I said defensively. Corelli was one of the biggest housing developers in Southern California.

"Sal Corelli, Ponce, died ten years ago. That outfit has been bought and sold six times since then. The latest owners are camel jockeys. You'd better wake up, Ponce, before you find your wife trucked off in a caravan headed for a slimy harem." He leaned close again and gave me a dirty little smile. "Those desert goons are supposed to have prongs the size of tent stakes." He winked and made a clicking noise in the back of his throat. He leaned a little closer. "Listen," he said, his voice hoarsely confidential. "Don't let the trappings fool you. The world hasn't changed a centimeter in fifty thousand years. It's still fuck or be fucked. You see it all around you. It's your choice, Ponce. Line up with the vaginas, or line up with the cocks. I tell you this man to man, rank aside."

"Isn't that a rather simplistic metaphor?" I suggested.

Spear stood up and shook his head, grimacing with disbelief. Disbelief in the condition of the world he was trying to compete in, disbelief in the hordes of titmen and vaginas he had to work with, disbelief in the depths and reaches of my ignorance.

"We are going to have one beautiful relationship, Ponce," he said, shaking his head, unable to believe his own bad luck.

He left. I sat in the deep hollow of my executive's chair. The glow of my promotion somewhat diminished. I tried to think of Scimitar and all the beautiful billions it would funnel into Dynablast for years and years to come, how it would, like a cornucopia, shower my life with the symbols of advancement and worth: Cadillac or Continental, closets full of new clothes, a condominium in, say, Malibu; another in Mammoth where, come January, I would take up skiing and the cold pursuit of gleaming Nordic blondes with a realistic eye for men of substance and an arctic will to add themselves to that treasure-store. And then, a good performance as Document Chief would surely lead to an even higher station, and that in turn would ensure another brisk shaking out of the horn of plenty, and—Gambling on the Riviera! Photographic safaris! Sexual explorations in darkest Tokyo! It was all a matter of opposites, you see. Balance is all. For every negative feature of life (and I was sure that Spear qualified as one of these), there is a balancing positive. Out of misfortune comes great gain, says the poet. Balance is all.

D Area knocked off work early that afternoon and adjourned to La Mujer Caliente for an informal celebration of the Scimitar contract. Alice walked with me in spite of the flurry of gossip we'd started when we came in together that morning. It was a fine day. The smog had been blown into the eastern valleys by a strong sea breeze.

"Feeling better?" she asked.

"Still reading minds?"

I took her hand, gave it a squeeze. "That was the titman book, Miss James old bean. I've banished it on the advice of a follower of Charles Martel."

"The *what?* Did you say 'tit man'?"

"I'm going to compete for the up-front nipples from here on out. That's where the milk of success is, you know."

"You're crazy."

"Only because society is dead."

"Bonkers."

"Tonight?"

She gave me a friendly sidelong glance and a fractional smile. "Feel up to it?"

"Never felt better."

"We'll see."

Everybody got drunk in less than an hour. No special trick for this gang of office party veterans. The jazz quartet was gone. In its place on the bandstand a convulsive rock group called The Burbank Brain Trust exercised itself on amplified equipment. Everyone's mouth was going at a fantastic rate, but I couldn't pick out a syllable above the electronic din.

Byron Towne stood in the middle of a gathering of secretaries and engineers, his big arms engulfing the group. I could see his mouth opening and closing, his white teeth in flashing contrast to his tanned face. The others in the group looked up to him and made grimaces of hilarity timed to his delivery, but I couldn't hear their laughter. The music, pure gales of undifferentiated sound, made it impossible. I felt deaf in the decibel storm. Even the man seated next to me at the bar was out of range. He was a despondent drunk putting on a mellow act, feigning good cheer. But the lines and spheres of contentment were obvious strangers to his face. It was a bad act, pinholed, washed out, hashed with static from the void. A bad act, but not an uncommon one. I recognized the gestures. He slapped me on the back and chuckled noiselessly into his martini. But just as the glass reached his lips, the cheer dissolved and the primary mask emerged, hungry for its gin.

I turned back to the merrymakers gathered around

Towne. They were still at their guffawing. I could tell that Towne was really rolling along in top form. His audience understood his timing now and he was playing it for all it was worth. Then, for no clear reason, I thought one of his jokes had to do with me. I thought I saw his eyes flick surreptitiously in my direction, then quickly away, followed by several sneakily swiveling heads. The group tottered then on the brink of collapse. Knees buckled in uncontrolled merriment. Faces crimped with the pain of too much hilarity. I felt the back of my neck redden, then dismissed the whole thing as crazy. Okay, Towne loved a good joke, especially when it was on someone else. But what did I have to be suspicious about? I *had* been given the purple badge and a private office, hadn't I? We'd landed Sugar City, hadn't we? I turned back to the bar and my drink. A gorgeously garnished frosted marvel. The drunk next to me was talking. Reasoning with the air. His eyes moved from glass to glass. Then he pointed. Then I understood. He was concerned about Alice's drink. The ice was melting. I read his lips: *That is no way to treat innocent gin!* Alice's drink hadn't been touched. She'd left for the powder room a few minutes ago and hadn't returned. In the meantime, her drink, her second, had arrived and the ice was melting. The drunk tapped my shoulder with an indignant finger. *Wasteful,* said his numb lips.

I picked up her drink and left the bar. The only lighting came from strobe lamps on stage, behind the guitar-walloping group. The strobes gave the packed clubroom a sputtering-rainbow reality. Visual assault, the eyes attacked by a new incarnation of the same demon that attacked the ears. I had to close my eyes for a few seconds at a time to keep my precarious sense of order intact. Sound moved in the floor, hummed manically in my shoes. Then I was in the center of a crowd of strobe-splintered dancers. Shoulders and hips nudged me, ghostly fingers stroked my neck, an incandescent woman put her hands in my pockets. I didn't stop. I pushed my way through the stormy dance.

No Alice.

I asked a lady who was on her way into the john to inquire within. I waited five minutes for her negative report. I weaved in brain-dicing light back to the bar. She hadn't returned. The despondent drunk was now face down on his arms, weeping. I went to the booths, checked out each one by squinting into the spectral faces of the occupants. I got a few soundless laughs. But no Alice.

La Mujer Caliente is divided into three parts: a dining room; a clubroom, where the bandstand and dance floor are; and a small, soundproof bar for serious, no-nonsense drinking. I decided to look in the barroom, in case she had managed to get herself sidetracked.

It was quiet, and to my strobe-fogged eyes, very dark. A few unwholesome types sat slumped at the bar. The bartender was whistling "Jada."

Alice. Lovely London Alice. Who drinks Irish Whiskey. In her Irish tea. *Dónde está,* my little cockney señorita? Where are you, Cherry Sweet?

There. Not at the bar, but in an alcove apart. And with her, the muscular arm of top management, draped with easy ownership around her gentle, grotesquely available shoulders. Damon Spear. No wonder Towne had everyone splitting at the seams. Aced out by Old Polio Hand.

Poor Alice, caught up in the arms of survival politics, was doing her best. This, according to the unwritten rules of personnel utilization, was his rightful territory. He had the imperative. He knew it. She knew it. I knew it.

Spear nodded hello, a threatening gesture. I took a long sip from Alice's drink. I caught her eye. *Do you want me to get you out of this?* my eyes asked. She made the cheery grin-and-bear-it smile. I took another sip of room-temperature gin. Spear, watching me, let his arm slip farther down her shoulder. His hand came to rest inches above her right breast. There was a frozen moment. I lowered my drink slowly. Property was being claimed here, right before my eyes. My throat tightened. Time rubberized and the seconds became elastic quantities. We were, the three of us, in an express elevator, accelerating upward. Then, in a single, slow, deliberate act of contempt, his hand cupped her game little tit.

"Whoa there, Chief," I said. "Just a goddamned minute."

Alice's eyes widened. I thought of capsized boats. A sea of capsized boats. The end of my career. My life. A whirlpool developing, sucking boats, lives, and the debris of high hopes.

"You'd better check your hole card, Ponce," said Spear, almost tenderly. But he was a man who lived at the absolute zero of emotion. It was a simple, heatless instruction.

This is what could have happened:

"Outside, Polio Hand," I could have said.

"Suits me," he probably would have replied.

We could have gone out to the parking lot, squared off. He most likely would have thrown the first punch. I might have taken it well, got up, jabbed lightly with my left and clipped him with a surprisingly solid right. He might have gone down. On the other hand, he might have stayed on his feet and knocked out my front teeth.

I could have handed him my purple badge, if I had it with me. I could have tossed my drink in his face. I could have pulled Alice out of the bar and headed south for Oaxaca to take up a life of humble craftsmanship. Pottery. We would rent a hut and merge with the natives. We would regard *turistas* from the north with the indifferent gaze of the rude artisan. We would live humbly and we would be at peace with ourselves and our world.

These things may have even happened in a universe parallel to our own. But this is what happened here: I took a deep breath, hid my face in one great swill of tepid gin, and pretended not to see his iron fingers spider her unhappy little breast.

And this is what happened next: I walked past them and into the men's room.

Where I drained my titman's spleen.

I had avoided her eyes but not before I saw something in them turning off. Of course, she didn't expect me to sacrifice my career in a tantrum of chivalry. She too, after all, was a survivor. Still, the alternative to chivalry was not the stuff dreams are made of. The gray-skinned coward who inspires only lethargy in the soul is not embraced by the dreams of the entowered maiden.

I skulked out of the bar and called a cab from an outdoor booth. It took five minutes to arrive, half a lifetime. The driver took one look at my face and said nothing, all the way to Arabian Heights. I paid him and added a five. Hush money, I guess. Still, he said nothing, his eyes as impartial as coins. The oracles and judges of this world.

I felt a meanness in my mouth I could not spit out. What are the rewards of this life that they leave an unspittable grief.

Oh yes, there are compensations. To every plus there is a minus. The world is a bad marriage of opposites, and the healing divorce is not possible.

This is what should have happened: I should have shown him my hole card. Freedom. Evel Knievel roaring up the ramp of no return. Errol, sinking into the silty depths among the coiling monsters.

But no. The misty squid and I keep to our separate schedules. If we meet, it will be by accident. And if she finds herself aground in his lagoon, the ocean will taste like tears. Alice. Oh Alice. I am sorry.

There was a strange car parked out front. A red convertible. I went into the apartment. It was still shockingly empty. I found my Turkey and we had a quick reunion. I marveled irrelevantly at my capacity for the stuff. My recent prodigious drinking had not exacted a price. I was eating my Turkey and having it too. One-oh-one proof in these quantities should have curdled the liver. I patted my side, congratulating it, that stout peasant among the internal organs, tougher than the others, the noble brain a feeble inbred by comparison.

96 ● ●

I took the tour, one last time, through the mausoleum that had once been home. The dead echoes of children at play rattled the air. I had a drink in every room. A kind of ceremony. The place was beginning to take on its original smell of carpet and plaster. What the hell. This is your future, my friend. I went into Chrissie's room. Empty as a box, clean as an M-16, traces of no one, no hint of the small scars he was beginning to collect. I went into Debbie and Nell's room. The shock of that double absence, gone the bunk beds, gone the color storm of record albums and posters, gone the charming menagerie of stuffed animals. And on the wall, in blunt crayon:

DADDY IS HOPELESSLY IMMATURE

I left the room, the simple and just verdict cutting my heart out.

I decided to lock the place up and get a room in a noisier part of town, close to P & L if possible. But leaving here meant deciding to leave. And that involved more than just walking away. There were ghosts here. Ghosts of good times. Innocent ghosts. Flesh can pick up and leave, but the ghosts stay on. Until the walls come down and the ground is bulldozed flat. I had betrayed, but I had not deserted. Now, I too would have to desert, walk away from it, and the household ghosts would stare out the windows until they finally died, alone.

One last pull from the Turkey and good-bye. I went downstairs to the garage. The Oldsmobile was a decent old friend saying, Let's go, old buddy. It's all over around here. Let's put on some miles, friend.

Right. A machine after my heart. Begin the cure with miles. But as I approached the car, its interior lights came on. There was a commotion, a panicky blur of white in the back seat. Legs. Arms. A woman's head, hair flying. An ass.

The big white ass of Basho Lovely.

He was out of the car like a cat. He was naked except for a heavy leather wristband that held a watch. A diver's watch. And naked in the back seat, covering her tits as though i'd never laid eyes or lips to them, was Louella. They'd been at it in my car. There was humiliation here, it hung in the cool air of the garage, but it was tied in big giddy rubber bands. I sagged against the wall. Kismet. Arabian Heights had finally given me kismet. Defeat sandwiched in defeat. A steady diet of it. My life. Too much to handle without a shot of kismet. Basho's trooper was still up, its passion not much fazed by my intrusion. "It's not polite to point," I said. A giggle began to move around under my ribs. I bugled at them, an amused moose. I suddenly wanted a passport into that parallel universe where it was possible to spray Damon Spear with seltzer, shouting, "Unfinger that defenseless tit, you fiend."

Basho took up an attack stance. Hands up like ax blades. His trooper, finally distracted, began to retreat. The giggle broke through.

"What's wrong with you?" he said.

I looked myself over. Wrong? Was I bleeding already? I touched my forehead. Cool. No fever.

Louella had left the back seat and was crouching behind the open back door of the Olds. Her face was averted to one side. *Shame? My God almighty! Shame?*

"We came for the car, Jay," she piped from her barrier, still not looking at me.

"And got sidetracked in the process, right?"

"Stow it, old-timer," said Lovely. I noticed that he had moved toward me several feet, imperceptibly. Part of the killing art.

"Stow it yourself, sailor. That car is mine. I bought it. I feed it. I like it, it likes me. It's mine."

"Just hand over the keys, mother."

His hands began to cut small arcs in the air. He was within striking distance now, but the nice cuts he made in the narrow space between us had a hypnotic beauty.

98 • •

"The keys, Ponce. Am I rapping over your head? You're not thinking of going up against me, are you, friend?"

"You've never had a friend in your life, killer."

"Jay, for God's sakes, give him the keys! He *teaches* self-defense. Don't be a hero *now.*"

Something about that "now" I did not like. A mixture of terror and sarcasm that soured in my ear.

"What do you mean, 'don't be a hero *now'?*" I said, ignoring the more immediate threat.

"Come on, lardass, give me the keys and we'll go."

"Dammit Louella, what was that supposed to mean? That *now* business?"

"She's referring to your balls, my friend. She means guts was never exactly your long suit. She doesn't want you to give yourself a cardiac. Isn't that what you meant, Lolly?"

"*Lolly?* What's this Lolly crap? You let this cretin call you that? Lolly?"

"You talk like a man with a paper asshole, friend. She likes me to call her something you never did. Makes her feel like a different woman. Cleaner. Especially after all your dumb clowning around."

"Jay, *please,* for my sake, give him the keys and we'll go."

"For *your* sake? What the hell do I care about your sake? Is this what you call the changed perspective? Christ, it's my sake I'm thinking about right now."

I felt the fullness of outrage, a marvelous feeling for the usually divided sense of self.

Louella looked at me. No hint of recognition. Perhaps it had always been that way. We do fool ourselves, don't we. We agree on certain blind spots. Through the years they increase. They become the grid we use to filter each other through. I was seeing her, too, for the first time. Mutual recognition of mutual strangeness. Lolly. All these years she had been Lolly. Her awesome secret. But who had I been?

Basho began his growl, moving into the timeless moment. I kept my eyes on Louella. She turned away first.

Listen: I wasn't scared. It amazed me.

To Basho I said: "You want the keys, you come and get them." It was a perfectly calm statement. Not a note of hysteria or false courage. It took something out of his act. He hesitated a second.

Then he said, "My friend, you're breaking your bones with your mouth."

I smiled. He'd been reduced to bravado. I'd ruffled him. I knew it. Bumped him out of the moment. His perfect concentration was rippled. Morality, after all, was on my side.

"Please, Jay!" said Louella. "Don't be a fool!" She stood up, her nice round boobs all pointy with their shivering nipples. "Karate is—"

"A social disease," I said.

I still had my Wild Turkey with me, held by the neck and partially hidden behind my leg. In the dim garage I was sure he hadn't noticed it.

There was still enough room to turn tail. I let him know with my eyes and shit-eating smile that that's exactly what I intended to do. The play of manliness was over. You win, stud. We losers know our place.

I turned to walk away. The way it's done in the classic Westerns. As I turned, I drew the half-full bottle from my hip and rifled it at the massive skull of the naked master. It caught him between the eyes, making a modest *blenk,* a sound to remember. Basho held his flawless crouch for a full second, then went down hard. Like a sack of rice.

The world is loaded with traps. One step out of line and iron teeth bite your leg, wire nooses snare your neck, the sharpened sticks of a Malayan gate run you through. Or if you avoid the obvious ones and make it home free, a crazy mob opens you up like a Christmas package and strings your bewildered guts into a decorated tree, singing carols to the gods of commerce. What I mean is, insider or outsider, you get nailed.

Louella, my meek, faithful, socially responsible wife of

100 • •

thirteen years, had jumped at the first chance to get on her back now that I'd given her the excuse. I don't mean to say she wasn't justified. It was her taste that appalled. And to use the back seat of my car, the one thing I could still call mine, smacked of downright nastiness. As if to make me, by proxy, an accomplice in my own cuckolding. The whole thing lacked style. Useless crudity. But then, I am not one to talk.

I backed the Olds out of the garage and into the diminished light of afternoon. I drove the red convertible into the garage. Louella and I loaded the groaning master into the back seat. I held the door for her as she got behind the wheel. She'd pulled on her clothes blindly. Her skirt was twisted. Blouse buttoned wrong.

Basho, still nude, tried to sit up in the back seat as the car pulled away in graceless, head-snapping jerks. I waved bye-bye. To Lolly and her man.

And to life, as it had once been known.

PART 2

6

My last bottle of Turkey lay smashed on the garage floor. I went back to the liquor cabinet, hoping for a reasonable substitute. There wasn't one. A half-empty bottle of vermouth, a swallow of sherry, a decanter of something yellow. I picked up the vermouth. I toasted the day. Something final had happened and a toast was called for. But I spit the toast, pure ether, into the kitchen sink.

I went to the bathroom and brushed my teeth with my finger. In her rush to exchange her life, Louella took all the toothbrushes. No toothpaste either. I used a thin sliver of Zest. It tasted better than the vermouth.

I washed my face. Looked at it a moment too long in the bright mirror. Louella once said I looked like Glenn Ford. I searched, moved by an urgency I couldn't explain, for that likeness. There was no discernible Glenn in the mirror. No self-effaced but winsome confidence in those desperate eyes. The longer I looked the less I recognized. No likeness in memory to that pallid mask. The fictions of name, place, occupation, past life, hopes for the future, pet peeves, particular fears, attitudes, all ran through my mind, but they skimmed a surface that hid an unpredictable world of arcane purposes. There were new erosions everywhere, and I didn't understand their meaning. I looked fifty-five. Felt one hundred and ten.

Your mirror reflects every telling detail if you approach it with an unbiased eye. Bias in my eye was gone. No reason for it now. The family man with so many claims on his ass needs to convince himself each morning that what he is doing with his life makes good sense. His mirror, willing accomplice, shows him the face of a sensible man, a man who makes admirable adjustments to life's little misarrangements, a man of commendable judgment, a man approaching, in his middle age, a serviceable *wisdom*. He actually tests the sagacity of his smile in the fork-tongued glass. But this new absence of bias did not give me new grounds for understanding. The man in the mirror scared me.

I needed to get out. The household ghosts had become malevolent. The dark air seethed with spite. I gathered up my clothes and cameras, carried them to the street.

I drove to the shopping center, idled past Basho's studio—no red convertible—kept rolling, the bright window displays of the many shops suggesting a world of pleasant rewards for stable behavior. I stopped in front of a bar called Our House.

Our House was only a room, a small one at that. It held a twelve-foot bar and a half-dozen midget booths. The bartender, a glamorous woman out of 1946, was looking at her fingernails and shaking her head with disgust. Madame DuBarry special complete with rats.

"Nails," she said, rolling her eyes.

"Double shot of Wild Turkey," I said.

She poured it from a nearly full bottle, took my money. There was no one else in the bar. It looked as if there never had been anyone else in the bar. The clean smell of new vinyl. The unscratched formica. The absence of cigarette stink.

"You like to get started early, don't you?" she said.

I shrugged. There was a sign above the cash register.

106 • •

FOR SALE
1969 HENWORTH
LIKE NEW!

"What's a Henworth?" I asked.

"Two dollars plucked," she said mechanically, looking at her nails again.

"I always fall for those things," I said. I let a little wave of Wild Turkey roll over my tongue. The confined, vinyl-sweet air was niggling and humorless. I finished the drink, slid off my stool, and thanked her.

"I'd sell my caboose if I could grow inch-long nails," she crooned, holding her ten fingers out for inspection.

I entered the central indoor mall, remembering the Saturday afternoons Louella and I would window shop under the soft electrical sky among the tropical polyethylene shrubbery, the girls skipping ahead, Chrissie loitering at toy displays. An image to carry into old age. A painful reminder. Memory, my enemy, my cross.

A massage parlor beckoned. The Warm Body. The sign in the door said that "Tango" was *Set To Go!* "Let Tango Untangle Your Snarls." A tempting inducement. Her photograph next to the sign: a stormy-eyed redhead sneering with MGM lust, zealous breasts thundering toward the passerby like silicon warheads.

Back in the parking lot a dog tied to the bumper of a pearl white Mercedes whimpered at me. It was a monster, an unfortunate blend of gargantuan ancestry. Great Dane, St. Bernard, perhaps some Irish wolfhound. A great, hairy thing with soulful eyes and a small voice that mourned for itself demurely. I stopped to pat its head.

It accepted my caress dolefully. It had a nose like a bear, nostrils big as nickels. Enormous ears that half flopped, half flexed, as if the great beast was caught between perpetual vigilance and perpetual repose. It had the soft, seductive eyes of a camel. I went back to Our House and bought a Polish sausage. I offered it to the grotesque dog, who sucked it down like a noodle, swallowing without chewing, its huge nostrils dilated with ecstasy, its heavily lidded eyes wet with gratitude.

The storm returned. A fine drizzle at first, then gradually asserting itself until full-fledged drops began to pelt the asphalt. I trotted back to the Olds and sat in the front seat listening to the rain drum the roof, wondering whether or not to start the engine. For starting the engine had serious implications. Starting the engine was a positive and important act that implied several things. It implied a destination. It implied a will to arrive there. It implied a future. (I have seen the future and have found it wanting.) Three fastballs letter high and the bat stayed on my shoulder.

I was thinking of Lisa, of course, and her promised explanation. Sitting there in the dark, rainy parking lot, I wasn't too sure that I really wanted to know what had happened to her. My own troubles seemed adequate. Still, it was a place to go.

But there was a distinct reluctance in the going. It was simple enough: Drive out of the parking lot, cross a boulevard, enter the wide white gates of Arabian Heights, drive the artfully twisted streets to my own, and park. But I entered the wrong lane on leaving the parking lot and was forced to turn left on the boulevard, forced to join a traffic stream that took me west at fifty miles an hour with No U Turn signs snapping at me for an endless succession of intersections. "Why did you do that?" I asked, but the Olds shouldered through traffic with sullen impatience. I crowded it into the left lane and made an illegal U that wrung smoke out of the big flabby radials.

The reluctance switched from simple driving mistakes to something tangible in my mood. A queasy foreboding. I sat in the car in front of Lisa's apartment for five minutes trying to isolate the meaning of my unreasonable inclination to get on a freeway to anywhere and floorboard the big Ninety-eight until the tank went dry.

108 • •

Once again I avoided her front door. I went back into my apartment, mental blinders in place, out the back door to the patio, and over the grapestake fence. The rain was coming down hard now. Her apartment was dark, but the back door was open. Open. Wide open. I knocked anyway, stepped in out of the downpour.

"Lisa?"

There was an unnatural quiet to the place. Double-quiet. Not the relaxed quiet of empty rooms. A flexed quiet. Surprise-party quiet. The enforced quiet of the held breath. I backed out into the rain, knocked again.

"Anybody home?"

I remembered the ape on the landing, Lisa's bruises, was tempted to leave, but something like fascination made me go back inside. I turned on the kitchen light.

I smelled food. Then, seeing it on the plate—a nice steak, baked potato, crisp salad—the reason for my uneasiness surfaced: Warm food and empty apartments don't go together. I'd smelled the food before I'd smelled the food.

So. She was here. "Lisa?"

Again the deliberate hush. Games?

I went into the living room, snapped on the lights. It was still a mess. The twin halves of the tusk-world hung down in the stillness. I examined it. The break was clean. It severed the joined couple, the man's cleaved penis buried forever in the ivory haunches that now dangled light-years out of reach. The woman who had stolen his penis did not appreciate her singular success, continuing to give her attention to the meager handful of rice, and the man did not seem morose. The photograph of Skylor Blue was still on the bar. The pieces were askew now, and his eyes glittered mucously in different directions. The two halves of his torn mouth made a sharp V, signifying manic delight. I went back into the kitchen.

Games. After all, she knew I was coming over this evening. A date of sorts.

Why else this food? Why else the open door? Oh yes, the

little trickster had seen me drive up, watched me sitting out there, waited until I got out of the car, then took the food out of the oven and put it on the breakfast bar. And now she was hiding from me. Upstairs. Costumed as a Bantu princess. Or a meter maid.

But I had no stomach for games. "Come on down, Lisa," I yelled. "Let's just talk, okay?"

She persisted. I sat down at the breakfast bar. Waited. Tapped the knife against the plate. Hummed. Whistled. Picked up the fork, tinged it against the knife. Food fumes rose, reminding me that I hadn't eaten yet. I cut into the meat.

It dawned on me. *Goldilocks.* A variation on the theme. I was supposed to be the intruder, the lost waif. Upstairs there was an opened bed ready to be violated by the errant way-farer. Lisa in the closet wearing a bear suit, growling with lust. I admit the prospect produced twinges of greed.

I ate my fill.

Back in the living room I took a shot of bourbon, chased it with another. I climbed the stairs, humming "Love for Sale," the Shearing arrangement.

The bedroom was dark. I groped toward the bed, letting the smell of her perfume haunt the inner beast. The inner beast, still stunned by the long day of hard reversals, was not fully aware of the possibilities. I offered it an image of those spectacular legs, the black rope of her thong dividing those elemental cheeks, reminded it of the energy in those thighs.

A knob of cool flesh nudged my face. I brushed it aside. It wouldn't stay aside. It was a determined knee. A knee. A knee. It moved with a terrible, penduluming insistence. I turned on the light.

I turned off the light. But the Kodak effect of my retina held the image before me. It changed from white positive to red to violet to bruise purple negative. Then it began to recede into the long curvature of the eye's artificial space. It floated, miles away, rose lightly, tilted on an invisible axis,

110 • •

moved high and to the right until it was almost gone, then, with monstrous agility, came back, center stage front. It shimmered and tried to be something else. It became a fish, a frog, a monoplane, a map of Idaho. It was surrounded by a green corona that pulsed and beckoned obscenely. Maybe I yelled, maybe I groaned, or maybe all sound in me seeped into a crevice sixty fathoms below my soul and disappeared forever.

I ran. Out of that room. Falling and straining against woolly nightmare obstacles that wanted me to stay. But I reached the bathroom in time, anyway. All the liquor of the past few days, the meal I'd just eaten—her last supper—came geysering out of me. Between spasms the image of her body floated horribly against the bathroom's white tile. I floated with it, spatially unhinged, like a companion star. Dead star and living star, locked in reciprocal orbit. The puffed face and the swollen lightless eyes took in my troubles with philosophic neutrality. Closing my eyes only changed the hue of the death I could not escape.

I stood when I was able, hours or minutes later. I threw cold water on my face, teeth chattering. And what I did next I cannot account for: I brushed my teeth with her toothbrush. I shaved with the little electric razor she used for her legs, but it was meant only for that fine blond down, and my blue stubble stayed blue. I combed my hair with her comb. I inspected my tongue, decided the moss there was symptomatic of a B-complex deficiency, and swallowed ten multivitamin pills directly out of the jar she kept in her medicine cabinet. Doing these things did not seem peculiar. And the improvised ritual actually gave me strength against vertigo.

Then I went back into the bedroom.

Her face was gray and the narrowed eyes reflected mute pinpoints of light. Her body heat was not totally gone, which meant she had hanged herself from the light fixture recently, possibly while I was eating the supper she'd decided to skip. Her scrawled note on the dresser:

Dear Friends:
I am just too fucked up to live.

She'd done it with pantyhose. I cut through it with a breadknife. I stood on the bed and as the knife broke through the final strands, I guided her fall so that she landed on the mattress. As if that mattered. I pulled her up so that her head rested on the pillow. As if that mattered. I took the remaining piece of pantyhose from her neck, closed her eyes, smoothed her hair, folded the bedspread over her, as if any of these things mattered, and left the room.

Downstairs, I poured myself another drink. Then remembered what it was you were supposed to do in these circumstances. Call the police.

"I want to report a suicide," I said to the first voice that answered. I was put on hold, then, after a full minute, the dial tone came on again. Official interest in suicide was flagging, apparently. I dialed again.

"I want to report a suicide," I said.

A female voice said, "Is this the previous caller?"

"This is."

"One moment."

Again I waited. Finally a voice, weary with experience in such matters, said: "You have a suicide?"

"Yes," I said.

"All right. Just a second." It was the voice of an old desk sergeant, ten months short of retirement. I waited. "All right," he said. "Name please?"

"Lisa Dennison."

"No, no. *Your* name, sir."

"It doesn't matter, does it?"

"It matters."

"I just want to report a tragedy."

"Wouldn't it be nice if everything was that simple?"

"I don't see why you need my name."

"You are refusing to identify yourself then."

112　•　•

I thought about that. "Yes," I said. "That's what I'm doing all right."

"You could get in trouble."

I thought about that. "Not if I don't give you my name."

"You just don't want to get involved, is that it?"

I thought about that. My thoughts were crystal clear but molasses slow in forming. Aftershock. "I guess that's it, officer."

"You guess that's it."

"Yes, I'm sure of it. That's it, all right. I mean, I'm already involved enough. In a personal way, you know?"

"You've been drinking. I can tell."

"Wouldn't you, if you found a girl you'd been intimate with hanging from a light fixture?"

"No I wouldn't. I'm a Mormon."

"I mean *intimate* intimate, officer. Get the picture?"

But I was talking into a dead line. He'd hung up, convinced he was entertaining a degenerate alcohol fantasy of no consequence. I dialed again. To the first voice that answered I said: "Listen carefully. A girl has hanged herself in her apartment in Arabian Heights." I gave the address twice and hung up.

Fear came then. Sobering waves of it. Not specific and containable, but abstract and total. It dried my mouth.

Basho was right: Guts was never my long suit. Easier to walk away from a sticky situation than stay in it. I have no cool, though I've often longed for it. Under fire, I tend to be inflammable. As was Jack Singleton, until the day he was killed. Suddenly, and for no observable reason, he was pure asbestos. We were together in Korea, at the beginning of the commotion. We were part of something grandly known as "Task Force Godbolt," a meager effort to throw an American roadblock across the NKPA's advance. We were told by generals who knew better that the commie robots were no match for Yankee individualism and pride. *We* didn't know better.

● ● 113

We were draftees, snagged off the beaches of California, off the pleated leather seats of our hotrods, and out of the air-conditioned bebop rhythms of our drive-ins. "Yankee individualism and pride" sounded like a movie billboard to us. We had barely learned how to shoot our M-1s without killing our friends. Jack and I, on our second day in Korea, were assigned to a patrol. A regiment of commie robots was rumored nearby. It was a foggy morning. We didn't have any luck. No North Koreans. Then we walked in on what we thought was Dog company command. It wasn't. It was the rumored regiment. Worse luck. We stood there squinting through the rising mist, the light dawning slowly. Then we fell down, sick and paralyzed with terror. But not Jack Singleton. Our sergeant, who had some combat experience, began to yell, "Run, you poor fucking idiot bastards!" but we couldn't move. The commie robots laughed at us and aimed their Russian burp guns almost casually. Then Jack, Jack who had cried like a child the day he lost his 2-S deferment because of poor grades, who wept torrents on the day his draft notice came, who moaned and carried on all through our sixteen weeks of basic training at Ford Ord—this Jack, who developed a palsy on the troop ship that took us to Japan, this same Jack, Jack the Shameless Craven, *strode into the North Korean encampment firing his M-1 from the hip*, screaming curses and racial denunciations on our amazed enemy. All the hostile guns were turned on him instantly, and in that momentary hiatus the rest of us got up and sprinted into the mothering fog and down the narrow road south. I never saw Jack fall. I ran, sprinted, dodged, for what must have been miles, falling face down at every distant burst of gunfire, and finally tripped into a ravine, a thirty-foot fall, landing on my head, which opened like an eye, filling itself with buzzing photons, the light of permanent imbalance.

And now, as the coyote siren of the police ambulance came nearer and nearer, the throaty curses of the long-dead ergeant rose from their Korean burial ground and told me what to do: *Run. Run, you poor fucking idiot bastard.*

The narrow road south this time was Interstate 5, and I followed it to the Mexican border. I hesitated for ten minutes, then crossed over, breathing the alien air deeply.

I stopped in Ensenada, found the bar frequented mainly by tourists, got drunk, then drove to a tourist hotel on the beach.

7

I took a room on the third floor. It had a balcony that over
looked the surf.

The overcast was broken and a full moon traveled above
it, igniting the ocean from time to time with a glare that wa
almost painful. I sat out on the balcony for a while thinking
of nothing, letting the bleak wind ventilate the empty closet
of my soul.

A weariness overtook me. Muscles became lead, nerve
became nonconductive cotton. Breathing in and breathing
out became a conscious effort, something to be sustained.
wasn't sleepy. My eyes wouldn't close. Breathing in and
breathing out and seeing. That's what I was *for*. I had
reached my evolutionary destination. My function in the uni
verse. Breathing and seeing. My meaning. All else was the
illusion. If thoughts were able to form, they fell short of a vo
cabulary. Partial images and impressions rose through the
strata of my mind but I felt no impulse to identify them, give
them pigeonholes, argue them into shapes.

Far beyond the breakers in a sudden lake of quicksilver
a black shape rose like an irrepressible idea, then vanished as
a cloud gloved the moon. My lips formed the word *subma-
rine,* and my ears heard the syllables. When the moon broke

ree again, the sea was empty. Illusion. "Empty," I said, bitterly.

I went back inside, aching from the cold salt air. The bed was empty as the sea, and as cold. Harbinger of times to come. The future. I climbed between the sheets fully clothed, even my shoes. My eyes, which had seen enough, finally closed by themselves, and I disappeared.

I see myself walking corridors. The corridors are narrow and I have to stoop to avoid striking my head on the ceiling. The lamps are institutional. Her swollen face appears in doorways, illuminated briefly by moonlight. A cloud obscures the moon and the face becomes an oval shadow that floats before me. It is my shadow, as I sail higher above the beach, camera in hand, the shutter clicking cleanly, but the mechanism is aging in this coastal air, and the crisp clicks become metallic groans, an oilless seesawing sound that grates on my nerves and I throw the camera away from me but it floats, weightless, becomes a sharp-beaked bird. The bird attacks my face, wants to pierce my eyes. I slap at it, scream, but my arms are slow and when I move them they too make the rusted seesaw sound. I fall, fall, fall toward the room with the coroner's seal on the door, where she is still hanging, her death-flexed arms lifting stiffly to catch me or warn me away.

I sat up in bed, sweating, my heart pounding. I didn't know where I was. I thought hard. I began with Arabian Heights, called Lisa's name, felt my face, the familiar contours, said *Ponce, Arjay Ponce,* into my hands, heard the alien surf answer. Mexico. *This is Mexico.* But a part of the nightmare still claimed me. The sound. The rusted seesaw. A long, dry, metallic squeak followed by a mechanical sigh. Over and over, like a laboring metronome.

It was coming from the walls. I knelt on my pillow and put my ear against the cool plaster behind the bed. It was bed noise from the next room. A couple locked and rocking.

Mexico, tourist hotel, that is the ocean you hear, and Lisa Dennison is dead.

I went out to the balcony again. The sky had cleared. The moon was low and the color of old ivory. Two submarines cruised side by side a mile or two beyond the breakers. A beacon far to the north flashed in thirty-second intervals. I counted more than ten flashes, then went back to bed.

The goddamned seesaw was still running. Elephantine rise and fall. One. Two. One. Two. A drugged waltz. I hit the wall with the heel of my hand. "Snap it up!" I yelled.

I covered my ears with pillows. But the worm of bed-noise drilled through the down.

I went back to the balcony. I looked for subs, counted beacon flashes. Cold and miserable, I went back inside.

See. Saw. See. Saw. Turnip-slow in coming.

I put my ear to the wall again. The woman began to stir. She was making a chirping sound. The man got the message, picked up the pace. The chirping got louder, became a word.

Teacher. Teacher.

I got a glass from the bathroom and placed its rim against the wall. I pressed my ear against the bottom of the glass. Grade-school counterspy technique. The lady wasn't saying teacher.

It was *Deiter.* Dieter, Dieter, over and over, rising in urgency, clarity, and pitch.

Dieter heard his name and responded. Touched by the lash of those syllables, he made the seesaw gallop.

"OH!" she said, solidly, a vowel from the marrow.

"Ach! Liebchen!" he said.

I threw the glass into the middle of the bed and went back out onto the balcony. A distinct sob escaped my lungs. It startled me. I spit into the night, suddenly enraged.

I went back to my listening post, adrenaline pouring into my blood. The seesaw had stopped. It was replaced by a crooning of voices.

Ah, Dieter, Dieter, my thunderbolt!

Mein Rose

—always, ever and ever, my darling—

Ja, ja.

—my life, everything, you understand, Dieter? Everything—

Ja, ja.

—your eyes, your smile, the tenderness, he was never, so never, not once, in all the years, not once, like you, so thoughtful, so—

Ja, es freut mich.

—after you, my love, I can't even hate him any longer, I only pity him, you understand? All I have for him now is pity!

Ich verstehe—

I—my love—I—I

Wieder?

Oh, ja, ja, *wieder!*

Ich amüsiere mich glänzend!

And the seesaw began again. I stood back from the wall and threw the glass at it. An unforgiving rage slammed through me. I overturned a lamp table, kicked at the air. I put my forehead against the wall and yelled. "Goddamn you Rose you! Dieter, you Nazi son of a bitch! You're not going to get away with this!" I picked up a chair and hammered the wall with it, covering myself with a mist of plaster. I thought of setting fire to the hotel itself, but I couldn't find any matches.

The rampage turned inward. I rolled on the floor, sobbing, beating my fists into the carpet. I crawled out on the balcony. There was an adequate distance from balcony to ground, at least thirty feet, and I pulled myself up by the iron filigree, stepped over the rail, counted three beacon flashes, noted, irrelevantly, that there were no subs on the ocean, and jumped. Lisa's living face rose before me, emissary from the other world, and then my mouth was filled with sand. I had fallen into a soft dune, insulated by my madness from the impact. I reentered the hotel, sandy and wild, ran past the nodding desk clerk and back upstairs to my room, where I counted beacon flashes until I calmed. I went to bed then and slept, dreamless, until daybreak.

In the pale light of early morning, I wrote a check for fifty dollars and put it on the dresser along with a note explaining, "For the damage. *Lo siento.*" And I *was* sorry, ashamed, even though I felt better for what had happened.

I stopped in the hallway next to their door. I felt sorry and ashamed about them, too. I knocked. A huge, gray haired man in his fifties answered. Dieter. A woman, also gray, but very small and frail, stood behind him. Rose. They were in their bathrobes.

"About last night," I said. "I was drunk. I'm sorry."

The man looked at me with slowly widening eyes. His face was beefy, splotched with red. Rose grew pale. I took a twenty out of my wallet, pressed it into Dieter's meaty palm. "Please," I said. "My apologies."

Oddly cleansed, I drove out of Mexico.

'God God. I've got the heebie-jeebies."

The waitress who had brought me the L.A. *Times* decided to read the headlines before taking my order. It was 7:30 in San Clemente. I had an hour to eat and make it back to L.A. and P & L. Of course, now that I had the purple badge, I didn't have to worry about punching the clock, especially on Saturday. But neither did I want to take advantage of that particular fringe benefit on my second day as a manager. Damon Spear was going to be looking for excuses to make my life as complex as possible. More complexity is not what I needed.

"Two eggs over easy," I said. "And a side of links."

She didn't look up from my paper.

"And I need a refill," I added, pointing to my cup.

"God oh God," she said, ignoring me. "They get more sickies every year. When's it going to end, I'd like to know?" She tapped the paper with a peglike finger. "Why don't the courts *do* something? I'd vote for the man who'd bring back public hangings, you can bet on that. Say, listen, I'll bet you a year of tips they don't find this creepnik either."

I took the paper out of her hands. "Two eggs over easy. A side of links. And a refill." I spoke slowly, carefully. If she was deaf she at least could read my lips. She took out her order pad. I glanced at the front page. A full-color photo of the president filled the upper right quadrant. "Who are you talking about?" I asked. "The president?"

"What? *No*. Don't be silly. The president is the most normal man in the country. And what a handsome body he has for a man of his age. No, I'm talking about *that* guy, down in the left hand column. The creepnik." She tapped her pencil on a small, blurry photograph that was captioned:

Suspected Slayer

"The creepnik," she said. "That's what I was talking about. God God *God*. Last year, remember, it was the Butcher of San Luis Obispo. The year before that it was The Human Torch—the guy that cremated his mom and dad and himself in the family camper. It just doesn't end! I've lived here all my life—I remember them! The Santa Ana Sniper. The Roaring Rapist of Redondo Beach. The San Pedro Pulverizer. You want a list? I could give you a list!"

I shook my head. I wasn't interested in a list. All I wanted was my breakfast.

"Why don't I move to Vermont? Or Maine?"

"I don't know," I said.

"Why is it that every creepnik in the world winds up down here? Answer me that!"

Her eyes shone with the fires of injustice. "It isn't *fair*," she said. "I've got family. You've got family. All we want is the right to live in peace and decency."

"The government should start an allocation program," I said. "Vermont should be forced to accept its rightful load of deviates."

She turned her head to one side and looked at me. A little diamond of spittle sparkled on her lip. Her eyes narrowed: the assumption of common cause between us evaporated. "No links," she said, all business. "Just patties."

"I'll take it," I said.

She left. I went back to my paper. Another front page story caught my eye:

In spite of everything, that piece of good news still had the power to send a chill of pleasure up my spine.

> Dynablast, a company which has had its share of reversals over the past few years, was awarded the highly coveted Scimitar contract by the Department of Defense, a spokesperson for the company said. Scimitar, the costliest defense contract in over a decade, had been opposed by certain congressmen and citizens' lobbies who insisted that the country did not need another strategic weapon system at this time. A joint statement released by the lawmakers and the lobbyists went on to say that the only purpose such a new system would have, would be to serve the forces of international arms competition, bringing on a serious risk of another world war.

I skipped the next few paragraphs which recounted committee hearings, investigations by subcommittees, the arguments pro and con by forces in and out of government. I went to the last paragraph:

> While detailed descriptions of the new weapon system remain cloaked in top-secret mystery, a spokesperson for the Pentagon has admitted that Scimitar poses no threat to other nations since it is strictly defensive in nature. The spokesperson went on to say, that, if anything, Scimitar would serve to decrease international apprehensions rather than stimulate them. Opponents of the enigmatic project have dismissed these reassurances as typical Pentagon rhetoric designed to sell the public another billion dollar bill of goods.

There was a related article on the second page:

DYNABLAST TO ADD 55,000 TO PAYROLL

My eggs and sausage patty arrived. "Remember the Cucamonga Cannibal? The guy who ate people?" She'd decided to set aside our little differences. Her face was a tight, pale mask, serious with disgust. Tense lips compressed, clarions

• • 123

of alarm in her wide, clear eyes. "When was that? Ten, eleven years ago? Boy, there was a creepnik for you. God God God."

I said: "The guy who ate people?"

She saw that she had me. We were buddies again. She pulled up a chair and sat down. The cafe was not crowded. "Chopped them into bite-size pieces," she whispered. "Made these little packages with Reynolds Wrap. Diced them nice as you please. Stored his victims in his mother's freezer. Remember how they caught him?"

I shook my head, sipped the scalding coffee.

"That's just what I'm trying to tell you! They didn't! They never do! Of if they do, they slap their wrists and turn them loose on the public again. This creepnik walks into the police station pushing a shopping cart full of little hard packages, all frosty. Tells the cops how it's a Mrs. Wax from Anaheim. He *complained* that she gave him bad dreams and diarrhea." She chuckled bitterly at this and rolled her eyes finding such an apogee of delusion merely contemptible "Said he did it for the *taste*. Mrs. Wax being no exception Said she tasted like—get this now—vanilla pork! Oh God the *taste*! Better than veal, leaner than sirloin, he said. It makes my skin crawl!" She leaned close to me and articulated the words again, defying me to miss their significance: *"vanilla pork."*

I toyed with my patty. I wanted her to go away, to dissolve, to emerge in another space-time matrix along with all her relatives, once and for all, forever and forever.

"Can you imagine what goes on in this world?" she said, her voice hushed with a kind of reverence. *"Can* you?" She wore a small gold crucifix on her throat that rocked, tiny and nervous, at the vertex of a threadlike chain.

I poked an egg, watched it bleed yellow on the plate.

"Oh yes," she said, gloomy and triumphant, "vanilla pork." She was leaning very close now, intimate as a doting mother, the needle of air from her lips tickling my cheek.

I cleaved the patty in half with my knife and arched my

124 • •

back, inhaling noisily through my nose. I meant to alarm her. But she only picked up the cream dispenser and held it up to the light, squinting at motes.

"Vanilla pork," she repeated loudly, savoring those syllables as if they had texture, flavor, and bulk. "It's enough to make you want to upchuck." She laughed at the notion. A hard, sardonic laugh, the laugh of one who has been in the world and found it wanting. "The good Lord, wherever he is, must toss his groceries every time he looks in on the L.A. area."

"He probably confines himself to Vermont," I said. The narrow look of distrust returned to her face. She slammed the cream jar down on an envelope of sugar and left me to my breakfast.

I went back to my paper to get my mind off vanilla pork. I decided to see what the latest creepnik had done to earn immortality in my waitress's rogues' gallery. The blurry photo under the president looked familiar.

An attractive suburban housewife was killed late yesterday afternoon by an assailant believed to be the victim's next-door neighbor.

A cloud, which had formed minutes ago (I now realized), passed over my spirit. Adrenaline punched my gut and nausea radiated outward from the blow. The sprinting muscles of my thighs and calves hummed with electricity.

I tried to read on, but my eyes had filled with tears. One phrase stood out, however, and repeated itself in the air before me:

THE SUSPECT, ARJAY PONCE

The paper rattled in my hands, like a snake ready to strike, but I couldn't put it down.

THE SUSPECT, ARJAY PONCE

• •   125

My chair started to walk. The soupy smells of the air became foul and heavy, my eggs grew stiff, the wounded yoke locked in a nasty smile. I dropped my paper on my plate. She came back then, holding a steaming Pyrex.

"Something wrong?" said the waitress, cool and suspicious.

I shook my head. The walking chair was forcing my thighs into the legs of the table.

"You sure?"

I nodded.

"You look like you're having an attack."

"No."

"It's your heart, isn't it?" She was gleeful. Now she understood me. Bad hearts she could deal with. Bad attitudes threw her. She sat down again.

"No."

"That's what killed Kenny."

"I'm all right."

"That's just what Kenny said."

I drank some water, smiled. "Hangover," I said. "Big night." I didn't have the strength to hit her.

"Kenny would drink, then walk around like a corpse for days. 'I'm all right.' 'I'm fine.' My foot he was. He was a sick man."

I tried breathing in and breathing out. *The suspect, Arjay Ponce.*

"Don't fuss over me, Winona. That's all you'd hear from him. You'd think that heart trouble was something to be ashamed of, to hear some men talk."

I made a little cavalier motion with my white hand. She warmed my coffee.

"Men," she said, with affectionate contempt.

I patted my lips with a napkin, made as if to leave.

"I found that old fool sitting in front of the TV set. He passed away in the middle of *Police Woman*. Did he say a word? He did not. Didn't want anyone to make a fuss."

Something like compassion and insanity gripped me. I

126 • •

ook her hand and kissed it. For a split second she accepted he gesture, her face relaxed utterly, then she pulled her hand back as if it had been bitten. A look of immeasurable disgust ook hold of her.

"Sorry," I said. "Sorry. So sorry. Sorry, sorry."

She rubbed at the back of her hand and stood up. I could ee that she was swallowing air.

I put five dollars on the table. "Sorry," I said, stumbling out of my chair. "So sorry. Sorry." I headed for the door. Two highway patrolmen were coming in. I was hunched and moving like a crab, fighting a great colonic spasm. The highway patrolmen stopped and looked at me through their Cool-Ray Polaroids. I weaved around them, my face lacquered with sweat, my yellow eggy smile diverting their thoughts.

Outside, I leaned against the building, breathing the chilly air. I walked toward the pounding sea. The dreamlike quality of the little resort town was not charming.

(The sickies, the sickies. We have our share. The walking wounded. Louella saw his face at the window of the ground-level bathroom. He was watching her pee. Very frightened, but in control, she came out of the bathroom as if nothing had happened. "I'll call the police," she said. "You go out there and see if you can make him stay. He's only a boy." I didn't have a weapon, but I picked up my big Beaulieu 5008S eight-millimeter movie camera and slipped outside with it. He mistook it for a weapon. It looks like a short bazooka or perhaps a submachine gun. "Oh, God, don't shoot, mister," he said. He wasn't a boy. He was a slender, well-dressed man of about fifty. "Lie down," I told him. He got on his knees. "On your face!" I said. He hesitated. I squeezed the trigger and the camera began to whir. "No! Please! Don't shoot!" he screamed, thinking the futuristic weapon was activating itself. "On your face!" I yelled again, and this time he obeyed.)

The street ended at a sea wall. I stepped over it and into the cold sand. The surf in front of me was huge and tricky. Conflicting currents, angling landward from both the south-west and northwest, combined in great pyramidal waves, which broke in several directions at once. The beach slope was steep and as the big waves rose, a dizzying slide of water flowed seaward down the beach at high speed.

I walked the beach south. To my left, stubby, grooved cliffs shouldered the gusting westerly wind. Caught in the gnarled surface of the red clay cliffs, wind from China found its voice, an undulant and ghostly *vrooooo*.

I walked past the famous estate of the fallen president. A one-time center of high strategy. Spanish buildings meant for fiestas were somber and introspective under the lightless overcast. Near the edge of the cliff, a man drove golf balls into the surf. He hunched over each ball with a brooding concentration, and after his swing, he'd stare at the arcing ball with a burning gaze, as if, by sheer force of will alone, to guide its flight to the horizon. I stopped walking and raised my hand, a salute of sorts. He raised his hand in answer and made a fist. I gave him the old "thumbs-up." He made a Churchillian V. I offered the thumb-and-forefinger circle, indicating All's well. He jerked his thumb over his shoulder, meaning the East and all its treacheries. I nodded my understanding and gave the finger to all points the sunrise side of Denver. He twirled his club enthusiastically and gave the air a stunning uppercut with his free hand. I jabbed winsomely with my left. He teed up again and drove a ball over my head and into the breakers. I applauded. He tipped his cap.

We were two losers, down for the moment, but not beyond strategy. I pulled down an imaginary voting machine lever twice, indicating that I'd given him my vote in both '68 and '72. He took off his cap and rubbed his eyes with the back of his wrist. I saluted again, and waved farewell.

I walked back to town, feeling better. I had no strategy, no plan, no immediate course, but I knew now that I'd come up with something. It was only a matter of clearing up a misunderstanding. Similar, in a way, to the situation of the man in the white jump suit on the cliff teeing off at the sea

128 • •

Things, for him, had gotten out of control. That's what I had to guard against.

But how to begin? Turning myself in right away was not the thing to do. I needed time. To compose myself. To build an airtight explanation. Time to discover what the police, in their hasty investigation of the death, failed to take into account.

I went into another cafe next to the bus depot. Bought a paper. I sat at the counter and ordered coffee. The blurry photo in the lower left-hand corner of the front page was me. An old picture, a blown-up section of a group photo.

The suspect, Arjay Ponce, a technical writer for Dynablast, was last seen by his wife, Louella, and Mr. Basho Lovely, owner of The Lovely Fist, a school for self-defense. Mrs. Ponce said her husband became violent and incoherent without provocation, striking Mr. Lovely with a whiskey bottle. Mrs. Dennison, it is believed, was murdered shortly after this incident. When asked if her husband had ever exhibited erratic behavior on other occasions, Mrs. Ponce said, "Yes, and then again, no. Jay was never what one would term an antisocial man, nevertheless, he was capable of imagining grievances of such venom that one wonders, finally, if certitude in these matters can ever be obtained, regardless of the usual intimacies of marriage. I would have never dreamed, until perhaps yesterday, that he would be capable of such a hideous thing." Mrs. Ponce, a social psychologist in her own right, went on to reveal that her husband kept a secret dossier of photographs of his victim taped to the underside of his desk.

I folded the paper, very calmly, and sipped coffee. The trial was on. And I was losing.

Why did I cut her down? I couldn't bear to see her hanging like that, like a carcass in an abattoir. Not good enough. The authorities have no ear for crimes committed out of compassion. *Do not try to confuse this court, sir! Have the fool removed, bailiff!* I opened the paper again. There was another story in the second section.

● ● 129

Police crime lab specialist, T. "Tad" Kendrake, said the assailant had overpowered Mrs. Dennison, strangled her, then hanged the body from the light fixture, hoping to make the murder appear to be a suicide. "But the suspect confused himself," Kendrake said. "After he tied her to the light fixture, he took her down to commit certain illicit sexual acts upon the corpse. We have here a case of exceptional derangement coupled with an almost unprecedented stupidity. Even the suicide note is patently false in that it is crude and uncharacteristically masculine in its tone. Usually this type of individual shows himself to be exceptionally cunning." Kendrake went on to describe how the deviate availed himself of Mrs. Dennison's toiletries, fed himself at her table, and even called the police to report the "suicide" before he left the scene of the heinous crime.

"Oh, the goddamned idiots," I said.

The man seated next to me at the counter glanced at my paper. I folded it and handed it to him.

"Pork barrel," he said, winking.

"What?"

He tapped the headline with his fork. "That Scimitar doubletalk. Pork barrel. Politics. Carload of fatback."

I didn't feel like arguing the point. I nodded.

"Used to be the principle of supply and demand meant something. Time was when there was such a thing as free competition in the open market. You can kiss it all good-bye. This is pure welfare. Get it?"

I nodded. Supply and demand. There's the danger. The principle may be moribund, but within our law enforcement agencies it still has life. Jobs are at stake. Reputations. The public mood, fanned and articulated by the newspapers and TV, demands swift apprehension and punishment for those who louse up its peace of mind. At the moment, I was a commodity. I was worth points in the peace-of-mind market. I was someone's bag of groceries. My capture would promote confidence in the system. Its stock would rise with the public.

130　•　•

Q. Does the pig walk into the sausage machine with trust in his heart?

Q. Does the fatted calf whistle for the butcher?

A. Does a snake piss uphill?

(The sickies. "I have a family," said the peeper. "Let me go, please. I assure you it will never happen again." A cultivated man, a professor of classics at a local community college. "This can break my tenure," he said. He hit a nerve there. "Okay," I said. "On your feet." He got up cringing, waiting for the first blow. He was a pasty-faced man with a little pot belly. His pants were unzipped. He'd been making love to Louella by remote control. "I should put a bullet through your brain," I said, raising the camera. He winced, touched his paunch. Ulcers. They were acting up on him. "I promise you, sir, as a gentleman, I will never do such a thing again. Actually, I don't know what came over me." "Beat it," I said, "before the cops get here." He thanked me, nodding and bowing, and climbed over the grapestake fence and went home. He was my neighbor. Hector Salvo. Professor. "He got away," I told Louella. I described the peeper to the police as a juvenile with heavy acne. "We know the type," they said. "There's an epidemic of this sort of thing going around. Keep your blinds down, lady." The sickies, the sickies.)

Strategy: desert the Oldsmobile. They'd be looking for it now. Take the bus back to L.A. Yes, back to L.A. Running away wouldn't help. I needed friends. I needed evidence, an alibi, a good story, a reexamination of the scene, a rethinking of the facts. They had presumed murder. They had presumed necrophilia. Clearly their conclusions were hastily drawn. Suspecting the worst, they found the worst. But they had to have made serious mistakes in their logical hopscotch. My job: discover and expose those mistakes.

The L.A. bus left in ten minutes. I decided to call P & L. Begin clearing myself with the people I needed most.

I asked the switchboard girl for Spear's office. After a five-minute wait, Spear said, "What is it?"

"It's me, Mr. Spear. Arjay Ponce."

● ● 131

"I don't believe it. Where are you?"

"I won't say, Mr. Spear. I just wanted to tell you that I won't be in today."

"We don't give sick leave for homicidal mania, Ponce."

"I just wanted to tell you that I didn't kill that girl. There's been a terrible mistake."

"Ponce. The police are here right now, asking questions. You want to tell them yourself about this so-called mistake?"

"No! Listen, Mr. Spear. Lisa Dennison hanged herself. I found her that way. I cut her down because I—I, oh, hell, I don't know, I just hated to see her hanging there like that. It was stupid, but not criminal."

"I'm sure the police will be happy to hear that, Ponce."

I heard a series of clicks on the line. We had company. Cops.

"She hanged herself," I said, enunciating the words carefully. "She was messed up. Ask anyone who lives in the condominium. She was well-known as a freak. Ask my wife."

"Your wife thinks you did it, Ponce. She's convinced."

"That's only because—"

"You plowed that girl a bunch and then had the gall to have a tantrum when your wife decided two can play that brand of parchisi."

"No," I said. "You're wrong. She hanged herself because she was schizoid. Probably a manic depressive. This can be verified, Mr. Spear."

"I didn't know you had a medical license, Ponce. Listen, the police know for a fact that she was strangled first and then hanged from the light fixture to fake the suicide. There are finger bruises on her neck. Ten of them, Ponce."

"Finger bruises?"

"Crushed esophagus," said another voice, hoarse and bored sounding.

"Oh good Lord," I said.

"That's right, Ponce," said Spear. "Pray. That's about the only chance you've got."

132 • •

"No, no, I didn't—"

"Found your pecker-tracks in her privates, Ponce. Disgusting."

"What is your location, Mr. Ponce?" asked the hoarse policeman.

"I have to admit you surprise me, Ponce," said Spear. "I didn't have you pegged as a nut. They're calling you The Pantyhose Hangman. I find it all a bit bizarre."

"What is your location, Mr. Ponce?" the cop asked.

"Murder, necrophilia! You alarm me. What's the world coming to?"

"Tell us, Mr. Ponce. We'll send a unit to pick you up. We know you're under a strain."

"Lock up the women, hide the kids, arm the citizenry, call up the national guard, declare martial law, heaven help the old and feeble, The Pantyhose Hangman is on the loose!"

"Please, Mr. Ponce. Tell us your location. In the long run you'll save yourself a lot of unnecessary grief."

"Fresno," I said. "I'm in the Fresno Y, room 436, under the name of Hector Salvo."

I hung up.

Before I got on the next bus to L.A., I bought a pair of Italian sunglasses. Chrome frames, blue glass. Wraparounds. Not the kind of glasses I'd normally wear. Definitely out of character. I also had a full day's growth of beard. Salt and pepper, mostly salt. I went into the men's room and re-combed my hair. I erased the part and gave myself bangs.

I leaned back into the comfortable seat of the Greyhound and watched traffic slide past the window. It was still early, and as we moved north the commuter traffic picked up. I watched the already haggard workers fit their machines into the glittering freeway jigsaw, and felt oddly aloof. I wanted to ride that bus forever. All the way to San Francisco, Portland, Seattle, Vancouver, Alaska, across the polar ice, disembarking in Lapland, where I would live with the white

Indians, the last true primitives in the northern hemisphere, and learn to track the wild, gentle reindeer.

"Oh, *say*," said the man who had taken the seat next to me. He was a small, dapper salesman wearing a bright blue blazer with metallic buttons and a coat of arms on the right breast pocket. He'd been eyeing me flirtatiously for some time. I'd given him a few bullying looks, but they didn't come through the wraparounds. He had a newspaper folded neatly in his lap. The blurry photo—I remembered it now, taken several years ago at a company picnic—grinned at me. I was wearing a baseball cap and a jersey that said *P&L Maulers*. The grin was deranged. (*Smile as if those secretaries over there were going to unbutton their shirts,* whispered the shy cameraman.) I frowned and made my mouth turn down at the corners.

"No," I said. "You don't."

"Sure I do," he insisted, beginning to grin. He was blushing. Several nearby heads turned to look at us.

"*No*," I said. "You don't know me. I'm from the east coast."

He snapped his fingers and clapped his hands, a stylish gesture. "Glenn Ford," he said. "I knew it." He blushed a harder shade of red and swallowed noisily. At least ten passengers were looking at me. *Glenn Ford! Glenn Ford!* Choked whispers traveled the length of the bus. They were suddenly yanked out of their humdrum daydreams. *Glenn Ford!* They brightened. The rancid years of disappointment melted away. Their leaden spirits became buoyant in the presence of a blue-chip star of the old school.

What they saw was the same, short, light-switch nose, the tall imposing forehead, the indecisive crinkles spidering down from the eyes, the diffident mouth. (*I feel as if I'm making love to Glenn Ford,* Louella said, so many years ago. *Say something like Rick Dadier in* The Blackboard Jungle. I said, *I'm not looking for trouble, son.* The laughter of happy days long dead.)

I noticed that objects were being passed back to me. My

fans wanted autographs. I couldn't say no. Saying no would only cause a furor. Exactly what I didn't want. The stars are expected to be men of the people, good guys, someone to have a drink with after bowling. That's why they're stars. People don't go to the movies to get shit on by aristocrats. And so I played Glenn Ford. Mild, gentle, shy, cooperative, someone to write to, someone to date your spinster sister, someone to take on the crooks. Notebooks, lunch sacks, magazine covers, handkerchiefs, books of matches, a tennis shoe, a bible, a card that said *I am deaf and dumb,* were passed back to me, and I signed them all: *With My Best Wishes, Your Friend, Glenn Ford.*

The bus was aglow with marveling moviegoers, too flushed with embarrassment and joy to speak to each other or look my way again.

Imbedded in wholesomeness, I began to feel confident and clean, able to afford some righteous anger. Anger at the psychotic who killed Lisa, anger for the hungry, image-conscious law. I also felt, for the first time, the luxury of pity. Pity for Lisa, that absolute realization of everyman's dreamfuck, and even a twinge of it for her husband, the poor sucker who had been deranged, finally, by that faithless incarnation. His muscles weren't enough to hold her. Gil Dennison, lowlife creep that he is, probably loved his wife (yes, *loved,* but there are versions of love that would make a Gestapo chief cry), and despised her freedom.

But her freedom wasn't an adopted stance. It wasn't the result of choice. She was born to it, fated to it. She was not free to be otherwise. (Our paradoxes will one day make the stones bleed.) And what a dangerous woman she was for a man to marry. There is something in the nature of women like Lisa Dennison that will always be in the public domain. And like the owners of rare paintings, their husbands will soon come to know the gnaw of anxiety when they must leave those ladies unwatched. Gil Dennison came to know that pain, and he refused it. And this is my version of the crime, a version the L.A. police must be helped to discover:

• • 135

Gil Dennison, when he realized her faithlessness was no passing fad, that he could never possess her absolutely, that others (like me) were making equal claims, he strangled her. And then his circuits fused. Seeing her subdued and made constant by death, he claimed her once and for all, one last grotesque coupling, exercising his lawful rights in the vile, unresponsive flesh. Then he ran. And I, the king of good timing, walked in.

Now I needed to think all this out again, and to make the beginning of a plan to prove the story true.

I'm a key saver. On my key ring, I have at least six keys that no longer have locks to open. Functionless keys. Keys for the sake of keys. Keys to unlock what no longer exists, like answers to forgotten questions. And one of those keys was the key to a kingdom. The bomb shelter at Santa Peggy.

Those of us who were in on the shelter (not all the people in the development believed in it—the grasshoppers) were given keys to its door. Most of them were probably misplaced now, the shelter a forgotten white elephant of a past dementia, but I still had mine. And I was sure the shelter was still inhabitable. It was, after all, designed to be waterproof, airtight, quake resistant. In fact, it was safe from everything except a direct hit by a Cuban missile.

I got off the bus across the street from Santa Peggy, entered the development and headed for the children's park. Under the swings, slides, seesaws, and jungle gyms, the big bomb shelter was waiting. Loaded with dried food, bottled water, vitamin pills, and surplus carbines. A man could hold out there for months, maybe years. Beyond the memories of the hunters, the public, the media. A man could enter that tomb a wanted psychopath and emerge anonymous. That, of course, was my last resort. A final desperation I did not anticipate. I'm too claustrophobic to be a successful hermit. Too much an appendage of my world to cut the ties. Going into permanent hiding would only consolidate the case against me. The official books would be closed. I'd be known forever as The Pantyhose Hangman, a necrophilic monster, a running sore on the body of mankind. My children and their children would carry that ignominy like a defective gene. My intentions now were to avoid that. I needed to hide, but I also needed to act.

Santa Peggy. Named after the daughter of the developer. Peggy was a teenage skydiver. One day her parachute didn't open and she fell into a field of wild mustard. The grief-stricken father, seized by a vision of pragmatic tribute, bought the field and built a tract on it, an "undying memorial." A marble pylon in the center of the children's park stands on the point of the girl's impact. A plaque on the pylon says, in tasteful script: *Peggy's Place Forever.* A bronze, haloed parachute tops the monument. The harness of the parachute is empty.

The entrance to the bomb shelter is next to the pylon. A heavy, galvanized steel door in the earth was almost covered now with a loose carpet of crabgrass. The park itself was empty and heavy shrubs blocked the view from the street. I took out my key ring, found the one to the shelter, slipped it into the lock. It didn't turn. I worried for a moment about bending it, but then, after jiggling it back and forth a few times, it began to move, a degree at a time, until the old mechanism surrendered.

The door was heavy but the hinges were not rusted. I climbed into the blackness. It was forty feet straight down and caution was needed. I lowered the door above me and began to grope for the wall switch. I found it, but the lights didn't come on. I took a deep breath of the mossy air and started down through layers of darkness.

The sharp echoes of my shoes on the steel rungs were horror-film slow, and an image of the usual easy victim catatonic with fear, waiting for claw or fang of the inevitable monster, developed in my brain. I shook it off. But something in us does not take holes in the damp ground lightly.

Water filled my right shoe. I froze. The shaft had filled with water! What of the shelter itself? *Flooded.* I stepped down gingerly, searching for the next rung. I knew I had to be close to the bottom. Climbing back up, measuring by fingers the distance between each rung, counting the number of rungs to the water's surface, would give me some idea of its depth. The water was up to my shins. I considered the situation, the bleak alternatives. Took another step down, another, another. Water rose past my hips. And still no floor under my searching toe. The image of a bottomless well sent a chill into my neck hair. I imagined a current. A suction pulling me off the ladder and down into the subterranean lake thick with prehistoric algae. Eyeless creatures with mouths like spoons nudging against the solar warmth of my exotic body.

Another step down, shoving the creatures of my mind aside. Water touched my armpits. But my feet were on the bottom. I groped for the door, a massive wedge of concrete and steel weighing several tons, but easy to open thanks to an ingenious arrangement of springs and weights. I found the handle under two feet of water.

I stopped. If the shelter was not already flooded, it would be stupid to open the door and let in all this water. Not much water in relation to the volume of the shelter, but enough to nasty the place up.

But there was no choice. I reached for the handle again, put weight on it. It was willing. It had to be turned through one hundred and eighty degrees before it would trigger the latch mechanism and the life support systems of the shelter. At one hundred and seventy degrees I remembered a phrase out of the long-lost instruction manual. *Activate sump pump in access shaft if necessary.* The sump switch was on the opposite side of the door. I felt for it, found a rubber-sealed toggle, pressed, heard the pleasant *thunk* of solenoids and the rising whir of an electric motor. Followed by the staccato chirps of the circuit breakers disengaging power.

Jammed. I felt the bottom of the shaft with my foot, but the foot wouldn't do. This would take some deep-diving techniques. I took a deep breath and squatted. The grate was covered with slime. I pulled it off, started the sump again. This time the rising sound of the motor was not stopped by the circuit breakers, and in minutes the water was gone.

I turned the handle to the big door the full one eighty. It opened slowly, massively. I remembered Turhan Bey saying *Open Sesame!* (or was that Sabu?) and the seamless granite parting on the hidden opulence, the wonderful roar of stone as it yielded to human magic. But no sound came from these hermetically sealed hinges (our magic is oiled and muffled) and a blinding light, equal to a cloudless noon, stormed in the growing crevice. I saw nothing but the fires of a molecular storm raging in the stunned rods and cones of my retina, but I stepped inside anyway. The door closed as easily as it opened. I pressed a switch next to it marked SECURE and heard the friendly *chunk* of thick bolts sliding home. No one could come in now without knocking.

My eyes adjusted. When I opened the door, all life support systems of the shelter were activated: lights, blowers, dehumidifiers, heaters. The shelter itself was like a section of subway tunnel. It was tubular in construction, about twenty feet in diameter, and half the length of a football field. Not cozy, but a formidable stronghold. Built-in supply cabinets lined the walls. Every thirty or forty feet there were passageways that led to bathrooms, galleys, dormitories. These were also tubular, but smaller than the main section of the shelter. One of the passageways led to a lounge that was equipped with comfortable furniture, a stereo, and, Lord love the visionaries of this hard world, a *bar*.

I pulled off my wet clothes, found a shower, dried myself under a ceiling of heat lamps. I explored the place naked, the temperature inside now a pleasant seventy-five. I had a drink in the bar—black label Jack Daniels—and sat in a velour recliner, pre-surreal Stan Kenton on the stereo. The recliner had a built-in vibrator. I turned it on and became, for the next half hour, a body without a head, brainlessly content as a dozing cat.

I do not know who you are anymore, Lou had once said after an argument over some domestic trifle—paint or wallpaper, Ford or Olds, carpet or tile, diet or exercise, Nixon or Rocky, Book-of-the-Month or Literary Guild, knobs or handles, *Psychology Today* or *Intellectual Digest*—a fight that escalated quickly beyond the inane pro-and-con logic of the issue itself and into the dangerous irrelevancies of private attitudes. And I, bitter counterpuncher that I was, said, *Lou, you don't know me, you don't know yourself, you don't in fact know shit from sherbet about anyone.* How we break out our big guns for the little sparrows of discontent.

"That's the way it is above ground," I told my standing trooper, smugly emboldened in the total privacy of this steel-and-concrete tomb. The buzzing massage had moved down my spine, excited a doggy vasodilation, the tenfold influx of arterial blood ramming through the sluices, and there I was, forty feet under the lawn, a wanted man on the downhill slope of his life, sporting, nonetheless, a youthfully stiff third leg which demanded and got immediate attention.

I do not know who you are anymore, she said, innocent social psychologist with aspirations, standing on the wormy timber of her cherished premises, arguing for utopia in our time. *I know too damned well who you are,* is what she meant. *My eyes are finally clear. And the simple fact is–I deserve better!* She began sensing her own possibilities a few years ago. (Her consciousness had been raised by a magazine article about a woman who ran away from her family and became a metallurgist for a South American mining firm.) It was inevitable that I should be identified with the forces of restraint. Inevitable and probably justified. All arguments are settled with the establishment of the premises. The rest is ritual dance, predictable as solar eclipses. *There are no games,* says

Damon Spear, and all arguments over honor, dignity, just recompense for faithful service, and the means-to-ends are his. There is only one rule: Prevail. Handily for Louella's cause, Lisa Dennison moved in. It made everything so much more streamlined. No need for a manifesto of freedom, no need for taxing heroics. Lisa had moved the inevitable ahead by a year.

"I do not know who you are anymore," she said. It was a bright Sunday morning. Earlier, I'd taken twelve indifferent frames of Lisa with the little Rollei. I was in a bad mood. Saturday night had been a dud: "Ready?" I'd asked, Trojan in place. She rolled over, away from her book (*The True Meaning of Post-Capitalist Monogamy*) and looked at me blankly over her half-moon reading glasses. "It's Saturday night, Louella," I explained. "Saturday?" she said, bewildered. I slipped my hand under her nightie to help her figure it out. "Oh, Jay," she said, trapping my hand in her thighs. "Please, not tonight. I don't have any urge in that direction at all, not even a little." I freed my hand and kissed her knee. "Well, let's work on it," I said. "You never can tell. There might be a little cold spark we can fan up if we breathe hard enough." She withdrew her knee from my lips. "Oh honest to *God!*" she said. "I try to tell you something of my inner sensitivities and you ridicule me with your barnyard poetics!" I rolled away from her. The fine print on our Saturday night agreement: *offer subject to change without notice in accordance to inner sensitivities.* "Okay," I said. "Okay, okay, okay." But she wasn't ready to let it die a natural death. "You're *in* this book I'm reading, you know. Right here, in chapter six, 'The Brute of the Manor is Deaf and Dumb.' Listen to this. 'Lacking technical power, except as it is doled out within the homeostatic, regressive structure, after which it is essentially impotent though not devoid of nominal cosmetic value, the pre-integrated, post-capitalist, anti-arcadian white-collar worker, *independent of his own twin capacities for role-forfeit and the patriarchal right to arbitrary volitional gainsaying,* will, in every nuncupative instance, insist on standards of inter-

personal response that are, in effect, denials of his own senes-
cent capabilities of conditioned reasoning.' " I didn't wait
for the exegesis. I got out of bed and took off my pajamas.
"What are you doing?" she asked, wary. "Going to take a
shower," I said. "Going to rape my anti-arcadian fist." Then,
Sunday morning, the quick explosions over nothing memo-
rable. And afterward, the sullen judgment, "I do not know
who you are anymore," meaning, *You're not the kind of man I
want to share the future with.* I counterpunched, listing the
many things she also didn't know, and after we spent ourselves in this way, I said, glumly, "Christ, Louella, there's
nothing *to* know." She took it as a weak evasion, but it was
straight to the point, an admission, a horrible one, one that
opened crevices in the delicate stuff of personality.

Nothing to know, nothing to know, except this, this
violet-veined prong, the motherless trooper, the lonely heat-
seeker, raging fount of maximum tingle, exploding lofty
languid bullets forged in the soft anvils of geologic time,
earth's gooey pride and joy, accounting for absolutely everything, but coming so often to nothing. Like this.

I slept then, my mind traveling through confused, cross-
hatched panoramas, dreams of Louella, dreams of Lisa,
dreams in which they were a single woman. We did marvelous things, the three of us, in closets and kitchens, and aban-
doned cars. She scolded me primly, imitating the over-
organized housewife, an exciting game, and we laughed
together until the imprints of my fingers began to appear on
her neck and the soft genital light in her eyes became fog.

I woke in a sweat. The shelter was hot. I checked the
thermostat. The temperature was over ninety. I'd set the dial
at seventy-five, but it had malfunctioned. Hot wind from the
heat ducts washed against me. I hammered the thermostat
with the heel of my hand, but the blowers didn't shut off. I
found a tool chest in one of the supply cabinets, removed the
cover plate of the thermostat, tinkered with the wires and
terminals a while, but the mechanism ignored me. I dis-

mantled it, covering the bare leads of several important-looking wires with electrical tape. That stopped the blowers momentarily, but then a back-up system came on, believing that the primary controls had malfunctioned, and heated air poured out of the ducts with a vengeance. In the meantime, the temperature had climbed to one hundred.

I found clean clothes in another cabinet—gray work denims and a shirt, white socks, high-top work shoes. Practical clothes for the basic labor a ravaged suburb would require. Then I left the shelter.

It was twilight. The rain clouds had blown away. The air was dry and warm. A Santa Ana wind had arisen, driving the storm back out to sea. I stood in the center of the children's park, thinking. For no clear reason, I thought of Skylor Blue. The photograph in *Life* or *Look* had not been, it turned out, a deathbed scene. He had escaped the tubes and wires, the pumps and filter, and the strategies of the mechanics. He had left the hospital in a wheelchair (I recalled now the blurry wirephoto in the Sunday supplement, captioned, "The Indomitable Skylor Blue Cheats Death."). Well, it was an image of escape, I suppose, and escape in all its forms and modulations was my only present necessity. *Arjay Ponce Cheats Death*. Not indomitably, perhaps, but a domitable cheat can learn to live with himself I suspect. Staying alive is what counts.

I walked up the main boulevard of furniture stores, gas stations, car lots, taverns, and taco stands. Warm air from the
interior deserts made the colorful pennants of the car lots flap
gaily. Surplus searchlights threw great arms of light into the
evening sky from the empty parking lots of furniture stores.
Thin blond girls sat forlornly behind the counters of taco
stands, dreaming of stardom or marriage. Overhead, the sky
was a luminous sheet, a baffle for the lights of the city.

I went into a furniture store. It was seven o'clock. I
found the appliance section and went straight to the TV sets,
like a buyer. I tuned a little black and white portable to the
local news. A salesman, weary with boredom, approached
me.

"Help you, sir?"

"Just looking," I said. "Thinking about a portable for the
kids."

"You make yourself to home, hear?" he said, faking
southern warmth. "We have the widest selection on the
street." He moved a few steps away and pretended to make
fine adjustments on a twenty-five-inch color console.

A man with fashionable bangs and angel-hair sideburns
reiterated the major news stories briefly—scenes of fire and

flood, the Capitol building, the White House, the gaunt chil
dren of the Third World, a lake of dead birds in Tennessee
and a fitful ecologist—and then the local news came on.
turned the sound a little higher.

"Meanwhile, right here at home, the manhunt for the
Pantyhose Hangman goes on. The suspect, Arjay Ponce, an
employee of Dynablast, had deliberately misled the police
causing them to focus their attention on the San Joaquin
Valley, a spokesperson for Chief Argyle said today. But it is
now believed that the deranged killer is *still* in the greater
Los Angeles area."

The newscaster turned to his fellow anchorman and
added, cryptically, "Of course, Steve, Los Angeles isn't exactly Milton Freewater, Oregon, is it?"

"Milton Freewater, Oregon?" said Steve, bewildered.
Steve was an experienced straight man. I'd seen their act
before.

"I lost eight hours there once, in my vagabond youth,
Steve."

"Is it a little city, then?"

"Is the Holy Ghost invisible?"

"Then, what you're saying, Des, is that the police department would have an *easier* time of it if the hangman, the
Ponce fellow, had decided to hole up in Milton Freewater
rather than in the City of the Angels, right so far?"

"Listen, pardner," said Des. "If you couldn't find a homicidal psychopath in Milton Freewater who went around
strangling ladies with their own socks and then did all sorts
of nasty things afterward, then you couldn't find a prayer in
the Bible. Dig?"

"Didn't the FBI say something to that effect about our
local *gendarmes* once upon a time?"

"Whoa. Watch it there, Steve. I tell the jokes around
here."

"Not to change the subject, Des, but just what kind of
name is *Arjay* anyhow? I mean, for a homicidal maniac?"

"Listen, any mother who names her kid Arjay can only

146 • •

expect the worst. And speaking of the worst, Steven old sock, what's the weather outlook for Sunday? And you'd better go with the percentages, fella, because the Forty-Niners are in town and ninety thousand fans are going to hold you personally responsible if they're caught with their rubbers in the closet."

The news ended with an interview. I didn't have to look twice at the smooth bronze head to recognize the boss, Byron Towne. The interview was being held in the P & L parking lot.

"Are you at liberty to tell us *any* details about the Scimitar contract, Mr. Towne? Isn't it true that much of the controversy related to the program stems from the unorthodox secrecy that surrounds it?"

Towne cleared his throat. "Karl, let me make an obvious comparison. Suppose that the government lifted all secrecy from the Manhattan Project during the war. What do you think the effect would have been?

"Oh, but surely, Mr. Towne, comparing the present world situation to that of the early forties is a gross distortion. Senator Leander on 'Face Up to the People' last week said that secrecy was being used deliberately to prevent the public and its elected representatives from interfering with the whims of an arrogant and quixotic, if not *paranoid*, defense establishment. Those are *his* words, Mr. Towne, not mine."

"Well, Karl. With all due respects for the Senator, let me just point out an obvious oversight on his part. Am *I* a member of the public, or am I not? Is the secretary of defense a member of the public, or is he not? And what about the fifty-odd senators who patriotically support the program, sight unseen mind you, and their many many millions of constituents? Do you exclude them from Senator Leander's rather sentimental notion of the 'public'? No, of course you don't. Now if one *part* of the public wishes to keep a few vital facts from another *fraction* of the public, a fraction, incidentally, which has no demonstrable need to know, then it seems to me that the imperatives of the situation must take precedence."

"I don't think I follow you, Mr. Towne. Just who is it that determines the imperatives of a given situation, as you call it?"

"Why, the people who have had a responsible part—in the Go or No-Go sense—in creating response-and-afterclap determinations, within, of course, a context of always changing operational parameters."

The reporter stuttered, cleared his throat. "That figure of fifty senators, Mr. Towne. I don't think—"

"All right, forty-five. Forty."

"Gee, I don't mean to haggle, Mr. Towne—"

"Then don't, Karl," said Towne, flashing his enormous argument-settling smile. The ideal corporate executive.

The furniture salesman, who had been watching the same news program on the big color set, said, "Response-and-afterclap determination. What a load of plant food." He was a chunky man of forty or so. His white hair was cropped short into a football coach's crew cut. He wore the customary wide-lapel sports jacket and a canary yellow shirt. His tie was kelly green. "Come on over and watch this big tube," he said to me. "Don't waste your eyesight on that toy." I went over to him and sat down in the platform rocker he was patting. "Say, listen," he said. "I'm going out to get a bite at one of those taco stands. How about minding the place for me for ten minutes?"

"Sure," I said. "Be glad to."

He came back thirty minutes later with a sack full of tacos and two cups of beer. "Sorry it took so long," he said. "But all of a sudden there was fifteen people standing in line for a goddamned taco." He handed me a cup of beer. "I haven't seen fifteen people in a group on this street in over a week. A tour bus must have got lost, or something. This street is dying. I'm not kidding."

The beer was flat and warm. He rooted in the greasy

ack, pulled out a taco, offered it to me. "No thanks," I said.
"I just ate."

"Got ten of them, just in case."

"Just in case?"

"Just in case you wanted some. Listen, it gets lonely out
this way at night. I appreciate the company. I don't give a
rat's ass if you buy a TV set or not."

"Business is slow, is it?"

"Slow? No, it isn't *slow*. Slow would be a heart-warming
improvement. I haven't seen a customer in three days. That
isn't slow. That's rigid. Dead. Stiff."

He'd lost his southern ways. His accent, actually, was
eastern. New Jersey. "How do you manage to stay in business?" I asked.

"Not me, pal. I just work here. The Big Boss lives in
Nevada. He owns a casino. This is just a tax write-off for
him, and a warehouse for his motel furniture. He keeps that
big searchlight out there just to run up a monster utility bill.
Looks good to the IRS in the 'operating expenses' column."
He was eating the tacos in the three-second pauses between
sentences.

A suave man on the TV set was encouraging us to fly immediately to Acapulco. "Look at that horse's ass," said the
furniture salesman. "Pulling down twenty thou for looking
like he'd let you blow him if you played your cards right."
The salesman finished the sack of tacos, filled the bag with
air, popped it. "You know what they told us in salesmanship
school? Sound *southern,* act *southern.* 'Hi, ya'all! Hurry back
now, heah?' 'Well, spank my bottom, ma'am!' What a load of
plant food. Their idea was that people like to feel comfortable, at home. 'Make yourself to home, heah?' I got news. It
don't work. You know what people want? They want to feel
like you'd let them suck you off if they played their cards
right. Look at that joker on the tube. Probably makes his wife
lick the floor. Here's to success." He scoffed, tilted his cup,
drained it.

● ● 149

I thanked the discouraged salesman for his hospitality and left the store. Across the street there was a used car lot:

DOCTOR GO

I crossed over to it. Wheels, an acre of them, my most pressing need.

I found a nicely repainted 1966 Olds and strummed the grill. Doctor Go heard the noise, emerged from his little office, a six-by-eight shack in the center of the lot. Gay pennants flapped on cables that radiated out from a pole above the shack to all four corners of the lot, like the spokes of a great and festive wheel.

"I'll put you in the driver's seat of that big devil for ninety-nine down," he said. He was enormous, close to seven feet tall, close to four feet wide. He was wearing a white blazer that seemed to be made of sailcloth. His jowls curled down over a wine-colored turtleneck sweater. I opened the door of the Olds, slid behind the wheel. It felt good, this promise of freedom. I shrugged noncommittally, smirked, let some air whistle between my teeth, cagey as they come. "Actually," he said, "my name is Floyd Pendergast. Perhaps you've heard of me in another context." I played with the heavy chrome shift lever. Custom. "Go *ahead*," said Doctor Go, impatiently. "Spin the mill, cruise the drag, stomp the hammer out on I-5." I turned the key, the engine came to life. I tried the radio, the heater, the wipers. I turned the engine off. The car would do just fine. "You like the growl of those cubes?" he asked. "Over three hundred and eighty, if cubic inches are important to your thinking. Come on inside, let's talk ways-and-means. I see that you are a working man, correct me if I am wrong."

"Meter reader, PG&E," I said.

I followed him to the shack. A small desk divided the room in two. He wedged himself around the desk and sat down in a big padded chair that wheezed mightily as it took

150 • •

is full weight. I sat on a short stool opposite him. "I don't have ninety-nine," I said.

He frowned. He lit a cigarette. "I despise haggling," he said, peevishly. I looked in my wallet. Two twenties, a five, three singles. "I used to be a dentist, believe it or not," said Doctor Go. "Floyd Pendergast, D.D.S. Call me a liar if you like." I put my money on the desk. "It was those cut-rate fellows with the Ozark affectations that drove me out of a rather lucrative business. You've heard them caterwaul on the radio or television, no doubt. 'Doctor Lonnie John Picket, the dentist who *cares*. Dr. Alvin Sale. Dr. Kenny Overcast, six chairs, no waiting. Sodium Pentothal! Aural relaxers! TV! My God. Mass production dentistry. Once it was an art. Well, it's all water under the bridge. I do quite nicely for myself. No, I am not a bitter man. No, no, not at all." He took a stack of papers out of his desk. "Doctor Go never says no," he said. "A motto." He peeled off a single sheet and handed it to me. "You fill out both sides of this little form, I take the forty-eight dollars like this, and you drive that big devil out of my life forever. That is the way it's done. You're a thief? No problem. My insurance agency in concert with the authorities will surely track you down. You've misrepresented yourself? I shall not pine like a deceived maiden. You are the eventual loser, my friend. So, you see, I am a happy man, any way you look at it. Isn't it obvious?" I filled out the form quickly. He watched without interest. "I always marvel at the basic simplicity of things," he said. "Actually, I'm not much of a salesman. I just sit here and watch them sign pieces of their lives away. This is California. Where the automobile is king."

The car was priced several hundred dollars over high book,
the terms were just this side of felonious, but the down pay
ment and red tape were at rock-bottom minimum. The car it
self was excellent: smooth, powerful, quiet. I'd created a nea
fiction on the purchase agreement form, but small crime
from now on would have to be committed in the name of ef
ficiency. I thought sympathetically of the fallen president
how something like the same logic must have occurred to
him. It's hard to be Simon Pure given the million tricky
parameters of this modern maze. This is the future.

I stopped at a nearby branch of my bank, tapped the
auto-teller for a few hundred—a move that wouldn't be de
tected until the end of the month when the statements were
compiled and mailed out—and continued toward the only
place it made sense for me to go: Arabian Heights.

I drove easily, without fear. The search for the Pantyhose
Hangman, I felt sure, was going on in the sleazy hallways of
skid row, the dry riverbeds where winos sleep, the freight
yards, the dim bus stations, the night beaches. Harmless per
verts were being collared and drilled in all the dollar hotels of
California from San Ysidro to Crescent City. No matter that I
was an upstanding member of the white-collar middle class

from the dependable suburbs: Turning creepnik had given me citizenship in another country, the country where pre-human monsters from the unconscious roam.

I needed to expose the wrongheaded logic of the police: first of all, picking up a dead body, holding it in one arm while tying it to the light fixture with the other, was obviously beyond my physical capabilities. Gil Dennison, on the face of it, was made to order. He had the motive, and he had the brawn. The beating he gave her was the prelude. The cops needed another suspect. A plausible one. *Dennison*. Everything pointing to me was purely circumstantial. Dennison's hand was larger than mine: Comparison of his hand with the finger bruises on Lisa's neck would be a nice way to begin.

The street in front of my old apartment was filled with cars. I drove past, made a U, drove past again. The front door of Lisa's apartment was open. People, young and costumed, were coming and going. I parked.

Music, live and wild, spilled into the street. Through the opened door I saw that the apartment was packed with dancers. A party? For an unreal moment the notion occurred to me that everything had been undone. Some unseen benevolent power had decided to step in and manipulate the affairs of men after too many years of a hands-off policy that clearly hadn't worked out very well. *They've had their chance, now I've got to put things into natural order.* Like cleaning up the playroom after the children had demolished it. Lisa undead, Louella home and cooking an elegant soufflé, Basho Lovely unborn, Damon Spear coaching a losing high school football team in West Texas. Jack Singleton running for president.

"What's going on?" I asked a departing couple.

"Wake," they said.

I climbed the front steps and went in. Someone put a drink in my hand. Something hot and volatile topped with fruit salad. I thanked a tangle of bodies out of which the drink had emerged, squinted through the smoky haze and amplified roar. Roar of guitar, flute, drums. And at least one hundred people, all talking.

A morose, slender man took my hand and pressed it weakly. "Welcome, friend," he said. He was wearing a black armband.

I was suddenly on edge. Something was wrong. The jigsaw puzzle I'd been working on suddenly had an extra piece. "You are—"

"Gil Dennison," he said. "Lisa Dennison's—heh—husband. You from the neighborhood? I'm so down, man. Well, what can I say? I didn't spend much time at home. Isn't this a trip? I mean this—heh—*wake*. Meeting you under hard circumstances, and all, when I am so totally wiped, you'll forgive me if I don't rap long, okay, wow, I guess you call this *dues*, no way around it, right, I mean, we *pay*, man, I don't care who your old man is, right? Heh. What the hell, what the hell, oh, she had some far-out addictions, didn't she, and you can't blame me for that. In men, I mean, addictions, geeks, she dug them. Sweet Jay-zoo, the geeks she dug—heh—woof, man, that sweet li'l ole hump could pull them out from wet rocks, man, *geeks*. I am so stone. Stone to wind. Not to say stoned. I feel guilty, you know? Not uptight-guilty, sort of mellow-guilty, like—heh—when you watch a citizen get snuffed by a gang of hypes, and there you sit with your thumb in your buns, I mean, you *could* have put it on the line, man, and rescued the citizen, but the *dues*, you dig, and so you stand cool and tell yourself you are a philosopher of life and death—heh—uninvolved, and no saver of citizens, uninvolved. I am so stone. Still you never know what would have gone down had you said or done 'this' instead of 'that.' Fuck a duck, fuck a duck."

"Jack Singleton," I said, pulling my hand free of his. "From down the street."

"You—heh—*knew* her, right?" His eyes were red from booze and smoke, and from a deep and chronic agony that had not been relieved by the death of its source. He meant

154 • •

knew' in the older sense. He looked haunted. All his pain had migrated from his brain, which was numb, to his face. I shrugged, started to turn away. He grabbed my sleeve. He was skinny, sickly: toothpick arms, pencil neck, about six feet three and about one hundred and thirty pounds. And he was not the ape on the landing. "It's all *right*, man. I *dig*, dig? I mean—heh—she collected dudes like kids collect string. You dig? I mean, she was a victim of arrested development, like the shrinks say. Got derailed in the anal erotic stage. Collected everything, man. Men and trinkets. Saved her *hair*, man. Kept it in little teak boxes. Hey, Jack," he said, leaning close, "you ever bust her in the buns? She ever let you bang her in the chute?"

I shook my head and pulled away from him. I felt a little sick.

"Come on, man. You can tell me. I mean—heh—they're going to torch her tomorrow. All that meat boiled down to a few ounces of gray ash, man. It'll be all over. Those sweet tight little buns *gone*, man. So, tell me. I can take it. I want to hear about it. Tell me about how you nailed her in the keester, man."

I'd been composing a mental letter to the L.A.P.D. I described Gil Dennison, described the beating he gave Lisa, argued that only a man with railroad-tie arms could have committed the murder in the way it was committed, pointed out that Arjay Ponce was not a weight lifter, indeed, had a verifiable case of bursitis in his left shoulder and could not have hefted Lisa Dennison's ample body with one arm while tying her to the chandelier with the other, suggested that all the motive and all the muscle lay with the powerful but probably often cuckolded husband, who had finally had enough of her. I signed it, A concerned neighbor.

I tore it up. The powerful husband was a wreck, physically and mentally. I looked at him. The bleary eyes were fixed on a point midway between my navel and collarbone, focused on infinity, and the mind that shone through those

● ● 155

wasted eyes was about as murderous as the green heart of a daisy. Gil Dennison was not my man. I looked for the bar. Found it. Traded my gasoline salad for bourbon.

A girl with a Polaroid camera took my picture. She gazed at me, smiling, while the film developed. "I'm in charge of the scrapbook," she said.

"That's nice," I said.

"You know. For the wake. Everybody will get his own copy. It'll be titled and everything. 'Lisa's Wake.' Or maybe just, 'Lisa.' That's probably more tasteful. What do you think? Ten dollars a copy. You don't think that's too much to ask, do you? I think that's a tasteful amount, considering what you'll be getting."

"A bargain," I said.

The camera made a noise, stuck out a tongue of film. She peeled it free. "There you are," she said. "Pretty neat, right?"

She showed me the picture of a stranger. No smiling Glenn. Closer to Anthony Quinn. Grizzly. Rough. Scars or worry creasing the once-smooth brow. A striking transformation. An ugly man I was, traces of nihilism about the down-turned mouth.

"How are you going to make a scrapbook out of Polaroids?" I asked, not curious at all.

"Easy. Each book will be different. That's the idea. Different pictures. Each book will be individualized and will feature the purchaser. So, if you'll give me your name and address, and a check for ten dollars, I'll see to it that you get your copy of 'Lisa' featuring yourself. This is how it will work out. Say your name is Larry: Larry drinking at the bar, Larry listening to the band, Larry discussing current events with Professor Sullivan, Larry eating a tortilla chip, Larry meditating tastefully on the memory of Lisa, Larry saying fond farewell. And so on, et cetera, in that vein. Isn't it a marvy idea?"

"Marvy." I handed the snapshot of Anthony Quinn back to her. "You make your living doing this?"

156 • •

"It started as a hobby. Now I'm in the upper brackets." Pride of achievement blossomed in her attractive young face. "You know, this is still the land of opportunity, isn't it?"

"As P. T. Barnum used to say."

"Who?"

"Barnum. Our twenty-fifth president. Said that an opportunity was born every day."

"Oh sure, I remember him now. We studied him in history or civics or social involvement or something like that. What a truly prophetic thing to say. He was so . . . *tasteful*."

"A wizard of good taste," I said, sliding my empty glass toward the bartender, a graying man who clearly felt himself to be above his lot in life. He refilled my tumbler without looking at me. I didn't thank him.

"How about the ten?" the girl said, nudging me playfully in the arm with her camera.

I took the snapshot from her fingers and let it flutter to the floor: Larry being a shit. "No sale," I said, in Anthony Quinn's voice, gravel-throated and fed to the teeth.

I went into the kitchen to escape the crush of people and the noise. A man in a green and yellow caftan was sitting on the kitchen table, guru style, holding a bottle of Bronco Chablis by the neck. He was talking to a small group of serious-looking people who were seated on the floor in front of him.

"Consent is the key," he said. His audience, all young people, leaned forward, painfully intent, their faces rigid with the struggle to comprehend. They listened to the guru as if each word he uttered meant more than the dictionary said it did. "To go ahead and give your consent—listen up, now—is to give your approval on a whole shitpot of logically connected patterns. I'm telling you that Lisa Dennison gave her *approval* to the man that killed her, this Ponce dude, when she let him slip it to her in the first place."

Several people nodded vigorously, sensing the approach of enlightenment. I moved over to the dishwasher and squatted next to a heavy blond girl with a jade stone on her nostril. She moved a bit, then, without looking at me or saying hello, took my hand in hers. She made a small vibration in her throat as she squeezed my hand. But I wasn't interested in her problem. It was her guru who caught my eye: the king cobra flare of the sterno-mastoids, the bright impersonal eyes, the railroad-tie arms. Oh yes, it was him. The ape. It was the ape.

"Take simple fucking," he said. "Given supposedly without strings. The hope is that there are not any unseen strings, right?" A knowing murmur hummed through the kitchen. The girl next to me tightened her grip on me. The vibration in her throat became ragged and degenerated into a clicking buzz. The guru raised his chablis and lightened it a few ounces. He lowered the bottle and released a wheezing belch. He scratched his crotch, boldly at ease with himself. *If you itch, scratch.* Here was the new man. Man of the future.

"What's he talking about?" I asked the buzzing girl, but her eyes were closed. There was a look of exquisite pain on her face. "I go off," she said hoarsely, "on his voice. I got a tape. I play it and bang I go off."

"Strings," said the guru, lifting an imaginary filament between thumb and forefinger, and we all watched the graceful pantomime transfixed, as if the secret of birth and death were about to be revealed. Then he snapped the fingers that held the invisible string with a loud pop and the audience clucked as if liberated from a lifelong trance of insidious origin. The girl next to me put my hand in her crotch and moaned. Several others giggled with relief. "Strings," repeated the guru, softly this time, his hand still held aloft And then I saw it. The silver butterfly ring on his pinkie.

There was a long breathless silence. Then the guru began to speak again, his voice high-pitched and quick: "Lisa Dennison, as we all know, was stringless. Stringless in mind and stringless in soul. Truly a wonderful individual from the standpoint of stringlessness." He brought his hands together and bowed his head, eyes shut tight as if in meditation. "But her assassin," he whispered, "but her assassin was no

158 • •

stringless. He had strings all over him. And this was what she didn't know, or anticipate. For all her knowledge of fuckology, she was a real country innocent when it came to the strings some of us are hampered by."

The son of a bitch was talking about himself. I freed my hand from the warm V that held it captive and went back into the living room. I pushed into the crowd until I found her. I pulled her to an oasis under the stairs. "I changed my mind," I said. "About the album." I took a twenty out of my wallet and waved it in front of her face. Her eyes widened. She took the twenty and raised the camera. I held my hand in front of the lens. "No, just a second. I don't want to be the star of the album."

"You don't?" She lowered the Polaroid, blinked. "But that's the whole *point*. Larry having a drink. Larry toasting the dear departed. Larry being tastefully pensive."

"I'm not very photogenic. Besides, there is someone here who really impresses me. The man in the kitchen, wearing the caftan—I've forgotten his name—"

"You mean the reverend? Reverend Carp?"

"That's it. Reverend Carp, the man giving the eulogy. Truly a wise person. I'd like to remember Lisa in an album centered on this spiritual advisor. I think it's somehow more appropriate, more . . . *tasteful*."

"What a marvy idea!" she said, struck by a new thought: Push the mourners for *two* albums—one of themselves in tasteful cameo appearances; one centered on the reverend. Marvy.

"But listen," I said, pulling her close to me. "The reverend is wearing a ring. A little silver butterfly. If, somehow, you can manage to get a close-up of the ring, I think it would be terrific. You know, from an artistic point of view. I see that ring as sort of, ah, symbolic of the spirit of the album. Get the idea?" She nodded, trying to concentrate on my instructions, but clearly sidetracked by the digits of a possible windfall.

"Butterfly ring?" she asked.

"On his pinkie. Right hand. Lovely little piece of metal-work. A symbol of metamorphosis, suggesting that life is but a series of quick changes. See what I'm getting at?" I pressed the twenty into her sticky palm. "Take a lot of pictures, okay? More than the usual number. I think the reverend and his butterfly ring should be captured, for posterity."

She looked a bit confused. "Life is a series of quick changes?" she asked.

"Think of it as an album of cameo appearances."

She brightened. "Hey, that's great! I get it! Wow, that's really something, Larry. I'm going to remember that for the album. After the title page I'll have it in Gothics, or something: 'Life is an album of cameo appearances.' Thanks, thanks, thanks, Larry. You're really great." She grabbed the twenty and burrowed into the crowd, camera held high. The image of Lisa's butterfly bruises was still sharp in my memory. Surely the cops had taken photographs of the body, and surely the odd bruises had been circled, numbered, and pondered.

I went to the bar. The sour bartender looked at me. "Where's your glass?" he asked, almost an accusation.

"I don't know. In the kitchen, I guess. Probably next to the dishwasher."

He looked at me as if the missing glass belonged to his mother's crystal collection. "You *were* the bourbon?" he asked, snottily.

"Right. The bourbon."

I, the bourbon, sat at the bar and looked at the new jig-saw puzzle. It was a little tougher than the old one, but all the pieces, except maybe one or two, seemed to be present. I had my man. What I didn't have were witnesses and motive. Motive would probably be easy enough. He killed her for fun. He killed her in order to enlighten her. He killed her because he itched, deep down inside, and only a strangling could satisfy it. The impulse to call the cops now seemed right. But I held back. I wanted more than the butterfly ring, he muscles, and his oily creepiness. I wanted something wrapped in steel ribbons, ready for delivery.

I took my drink back into the kitchen. Reverend Carp was smiling expansively for my photographer. "Come," he said. "Come. The word is a kind of miracle in multiple meaning, isn't it?"

The girl remembered my instructions. When Carp raised his right hand in a priestly gesture, she moved in close and snapped a picture. The butterfly ring, just under his chin, fluttered in the light of the electronic flash.

"Come is consent to enter, come is entering, come is the gushing of fuckjuice. Come is birth, come is the beginning, come is the command to start. And the engine of come, the motor that makes it move, is desire."

The girl moved to his left and took several full-profile shots.

"Let me tell you kids of the unspeakable dream," said Carp, apparently to the photographer, but she wasn't listening. She duck-walked in front of him snapping a quick series of right profiles. He posed for each shot, even though he was absorbed in a complex train of thought. When she raised the camera he froze to avoid the blur.

"The man desires himself. He envies the full-contortionist who is able to satisfy that desire at will. He is alone. In his room, say. It doesn't matter. The door is locked. Suddenly his prick is a foot and a half long. Visualize that eighteen-inch dork, kids." I heard the big blond girl make her buzzing sounds, but I couldn't spot her. The crowd had increased in size, and Carp was glowing with the sense of his own messianic magnetism. "Picture that great torpedo, kids, get an image in your heads of that crowbar."

My photographer moved to the back of the audience and stood on a chair. I signaled to her: *Too far, too far!* She put a fresh cartridge of film into the camera, absorbed in her work.

"Oh yes, he grabs that cyclops, kids, and he looks it in the eye, *hombre a hombre*."

The light from the electronic flash played weakly over the muscular reverend. *Too far, dammit!*

"And yes, you guessed it. He does it, to himself. Self-inflicted head. He wakes up, glued to the sheets, with a case of the shakes, pissed off at the perversity of the unconscious imagination. He hops into the bathroom and brushes his teeth for an hour."

I waved her in. *More close-ups!* I flapped another twenty over my head. *That* caught her eye. She sparkled, she nodded, she crawled like a commando through the transfixed listeners.

"But what does it all mean?" said Carp. "There's your sixty-four dollar question. Let's have a look at the symbols, not the simple components of the act itself."

Carp stood, then, on the table. He unbuttoned his caftan. Opened it. He wasn't wearing shorts. My alert photographer flashed the flasher. A girl in the audience gasped. A boy said, "Hey."

"Are you shocked, kids?" said Carp, becoming lazily erect. "Are you thinking of the component or are you thinking of the symbol? Test yourself. Try to ignore the fact that I'm hung like a buffalo." It rose steadily, excited by the startled audience. "Try to be honest. Really. Come on, now, people. Component or symbol?"

The big girl with the jade stone on her nostril stood up like a volunteer. "Component," she said.

Carp smiled. "Every man wants to satisfy himself. To find the bliss center within. To be free of the restless and endless quest. To stand still and yet to fly. This is the meaning of the symbols. The unspeakable dream, you see, is a *holy* dream, symbolic of the search for ecstatic selfhood, and not merely an expression of the primitive urge to suck oneself off." Carp folded his caftan around himself and sat down again. He bowed his head. "Lord, thy rod has spoken," he said softly, apparently serious.

A boy wanted to fight. He wore a letterman's jacket from a local junior college. He was mad at Carp. Carp avoided him, kept a buffer of fans between himself and the angry athlete. I pulled my photographer to one side.

"Give me what you have," I said.

"Hold on. What about the album? You're entitled to a genuine imitation alligator album cover, a written description of the wake party, an embossed title page, a blow-up of yourself—sort of a mood shot, you know, *il penseroso* . . ."

"Sounds very tasteful," I said. "But all I want is the pictures." I slipped her another five. She handed them over, at least two dozen. All very fine for my purposes.

Carp headed for the door, three steps ahead of the upset athlete. The athlete felt he had been compromised. His girl friend was red-faced about the whole incident. I slipped the photos carefully into my shirt pocket and went after them. There was a clump of stoned mourners sitting on the front steps. They were passing a hand-rolled cigarette around. As I pushed through them, someone handed it to me. I took it, flipped the butt into a shrub, kept going. Someone said, "Far out, these oldies." Someone else said, "An oldie, but *not* a goldie."

The athlete and his girl friend caught up with Carp on the sidewalk. "You rotten phony," said the boy, half-choked on his rage.

Carp shrugged and walked away. The boy grabbed Carp by the shoulder. Carp spun around and hit the boy in the face. The boy fell down and his girl friend screamed. She tried to hit Carp herself. Carp grabbed her wrists and forced her to her knees. The boy got up and tackled Carp. Carp didn't let go of the girl or lose his footing. He raised a knee sharply, catching the boy under the chin. The boy flew away from Carp and landed on his back. Carp laughed at him. The girl was crying. Carp tightened his grip on her wrists. She tried to bite his hand. The boy got up again, very slowly, and staggered toward Carp and the girl. Carp spun the girl away from him and kicked the boy in the balls. The boy fell down again and rolled over several times, Carp walking along next to him, aiming precise kicks that struck the boy with soft explosions, bone on meat, until the boy stopped rolling. The girl ran back into the house, screaming for someone to call the police.

Through all this, I stood back, in the shadow of a hedge, a philosopher of life and death, like Gil Dennison, not willing to put my ass on the line. Besides, I had a selfish mission that took precedence. Carp left the scene, humming a tune, very much undisturbed, a peaceful guru.

I followed at a safe distance. He stopped at a new T-Bird and unlocked it. I walked back to my Olds, and waited. Carp made a U and idled the big car out of Arabian Heights.

He entered the freeway and headed west, driving at a lazy forty-five. Traffic was light and I stayed a couple of hundred yards behind him. It was a lovely night, in spite of the people it sheltered. The stars were out—actually visible. Unusual for L.A. I tuned the radio to the all-news station, learned that the search for Arjay Ponce had moved to Mexico, where the fugitive had written a check for fifty dollars to make reparations after creating a disturbance in a hotel. A man named Dieter Hubler had identified the wanted man, vouched enthusiastically for the fugitive's insanity.

My life in the mouth of an indifferent, golden-throated newscaster seemed about as important as everything else he summarized. Plague in Bangladesh, carnage in central Africa, early blizzards in New England, the price of meat, the price of gas, the price of paper, the death of a famous dog, the birth of triplets to teenagers in Kentucky, the loss of municipal revenue, the return of the brown pelican after an absence of three years, the revelation from a highly reliable source in Washington that Scimitar is a great big ray gun that can melt entire cities in minutes, the life-style of Floridians on pensions, an ex–Cal Tech physicist predicts the end of all life in one century, an ex-priest comes out in favor of castration for deviates, Thomas Jefferson was horny, Walt Disney and Beethoven were born under the sign of Sagittarius, turtles favor mankind, the dolphin is murdered daily, life is hard in Cincinnati between January and May.

The T-Bird left the freeway at Santa Monica and turned up the long avenue that paralleled the deserted beaches. Phosphorescent whitecaps made the ocean a black field filled with blowing newspapers. The sea at night, a black barrier where our proud energy stops dead, a vast portcullis against the nation, the California mind senses it, and we go mad. Carp stopped in front of a beachfront apartment building. I watched him lock up his car, then climb the stairs to the second floor landing, which was visible from the street. He knocked on the door of the third apartment to the right of the stairway. The door opened slightly, then wider, and Carp pushed inside. I decided to sit and wait.

He came out an hour and a half later, tugging the sleeves of his caftan and whistling "Taps." He got into the T-Bird, started it, and laid ten yards of rubber leaving. He was five blocks away before I got my motor started and the emergency brake off. I tried to keep his taillights sorted out from the growing number of cars between us, then got hopelessly

● ● 165

stuck behind a phalanx of cruising teenagers, who gave me the finger each time I blasted my horn. By the time I broke through, Carp was long gone.

He was running. From something. Or toward something. I stopped at a phone booth, turned on the interior lights, took out my Polaroids. They were beautiful. The ring's shape was easy to make out. And so was he. The big thick-fingered hand, the massive wrists, the stumpy forearms, the melony biceps, the bronze grapefruits between shoulder and neck, and the wide cobra neck itself. The daylight blue eyes, the remorseless mouth, the thin lips curling at the corners with the mock solicitude of a torturer. Who would not believe this was the killer? Picture a quiz in the *Enquirer:* my face against his. *Who is the Pantyhose Hangman?* Ninety-nine percent would pick Carp. One of the snapshots was a close-up of his "component." Another, from slightly farther away, showed him presiding over the merry tusk, smiling in that vicious way, eyebrows arched with innocent surprise as the shock waves rolled over his audience. Oh yes, a nasty man, a congenital killer, the ten-thousandth incarnation of the Brute, and capable of anything.

But it wasn't evidence. Even so, I decided it was time to act. He was the man and the cops needed to know. I went into the booth, looked up the number, and dialed. "Homicide," I said to the switchboard operator.

In a minute or so a tired voice came on the line. "Garvey, here. Homicide. What do you want?"

"I have some information," I said, "about the Pantyhose Hangman."

"You do?"

"Yes. First of all, Garvey, you're after the wrong man."

"We are?"

"Yes. And here's why—"

"Wait up, sport. Just a sec."

I heard several loud clicks, a buzz, a muffled voice, some laughter, a woman saying, "Tee Jay, Tee Jay, next or no

166 • •

next, what say, Frank, how in the world, or maybe was it Ensenada."

Then Garvey was back. "Sir?"

"Yes?"

"We'd like your name, please, and the number of the phone there, and the address, okay?"

I knew they were taping the conversation and that they would eventually be able to identify my voice anyway, so I said, loud and clear, "Arjay Ponce, I'm Arjay Ponce, Garvey, the man you're looking for."

More clicks, a loud noise like a chair falling, a shout, a fat dry hand squeaking over the bakelite mouthpiece.

"Ponce? Mr. Ponce?" The voice was now respectful. I had status. I was somebody. A celebrity, requiring a delicate protocol.

"Right here, gov."

"Okay. Now listen carefully, Mr. Ponce. Tell us exactly where you are. Municipality, street, nearest intersection. Okay? We'll send a car for you. Stay calm, sir. Stay calm. We understand what you're going through, but I must caution you to stay very very *calm*. Think of your family, your children. Think of your wife."

My children? My wife? Didn't Garvey read the papers? "Garvey," I said. "My wife sleeps with streetfighters."

I heard the fat hand squeaking. The buzzing. The clicks. Someone yelling, "Turn off that fucking teletype!"

"Sir?" said the diplomatic Garvey. "Are you still there, sir?"

"Listen, Hawkshaw," I said. "The killer in case you're mildly interested is a creep named Carp. Reverend Carp. Some kind of fake guru flash artist who gets off by punching people around." (Someone in the background said, "Drop everything, Linda!") "Reverend Carp, Garvey. Write that down. He's got this butterfly ring, made out of an old silver spoon or something. I'm sure you know what I mean. You check that *ring*, Garvey, against the bruises on Lisa Dennison's shoulder and arm. I think you'll find it fits nicely. See, Garvey, I was *there* all right, in her apartment, but I got there *after* Carp killed her, see, and all you've got against me is circumstantial. Get it?''

No comment, except for the squeaking hand. Tracing equipment was being fumbled into action. Telephone company supervisors were being jangled into decision-making postures that suited their rank. (Oh, how we live for emergencies, how crises make the juices flow; the threat of disaster is too valuable to us for your wonderful threat-free utopia to work for long, Louella.) Switchboards everywhere flashing gay semaphores of alarm. Squad car radios snapping with terse messages in the adrenaline night. Dormant skin rashes flaring into life. We itch, we itch, to save each other, and thank God we *have* to. Yes, Garvey, the fated fatted calf was in the *city* playing with a telephone! Tempting the minions! The coy maniac! Alert the butchers, strop the cleavers, converge!

"Anybody there?'' I asked. "Yoo hoo, Garvey.''

"Units alpha, units delta. Okay, okay, *okay,*'' said Garvey, forgetting to cover the phone. "Get Linda over there, Pete, and, wait up a sec, Frank, you—'' and the mouthpiece was covered again by Garvey's meaty palm.

"Garvey, you goon!'' I yelled. "I'm going to hang up!''

He heard. "Wait, Mr. Ponce. Keep talking, okay?'' He suddenly sounded tired, sapped, distracted by a multiple commotion that had gotten out of hand.

"Garvey, are you listening to me? I'm telling you something. Think of your promotion to sergeant.''

"Okay, Mr. Ponce. I'm right here, I'm going to stick with you, pardner, you're all right, buddy, settle down, kid, we're going to make it, pal, and you can take that to the bank.''

"Garvey, you've been watching TV again. Did you hear anything I told you about Carp and his butterfly ring?''

"Linda is *not,* I say again, NOT, Hawthorne's replacement! Jesus Christ!''

"Garvey.''

168 • •

"Right with you, Mr. Ponce. You said you had butterflies. Gee, I can understand that. I mean, nobody's made of iron. Everybody gets them once in a while. I think the iron-man theory has just about had it, don't you Mr. Ponce? Shoot, I remember when I was a rookie, there was this speed freak, boy oh boy, he had this .357 magnum, *fwup fwup fwup*, that's how they sound, and my pardner, Oscar Handyside—"

I hung up. It's stupid to think they want the truth. They have a carefully worked out version of it, and that's not to be fiddled with. Actual truth is of little interest. What *is* of interest is warm bodies in custody. A one-to-one relationship between criminal deeds and bodies on hand. The connecting logic between deeds and bodies is of secondary importance, provided you can make a reasonably tight case. Logic is pretty much a disreputable specter from simpler times anyway, like the iron-man theory. Innocence and guilt. These are difficult abstractions. They have no place in the well-oiled machinery of justice. No individual is "innocent" or "guilty." Society is guilty. Children are innocent. Everyone else falls in between. We share in the general farrago, waiting for the second coming of Simplicity. Justice, in the meantime, is more than blind. She's deaf. She's dumb.

And she's vain. A crippled beauty, standing with her lovely octopus arms outstretched. It's not enough to be a good citizen. She's not interested in your moral fiber, has no way, given the general farrago, of measuring it. It is only necessary to be a wise citizen. The wise citizen stays far away from those coiling arms, and prays daily for invisibility.

And, oh, how I hoped my little mental essay was wrong. Dead wrong. It had to be wrong. If it wasn't wrong—but the possibility of endless days in hiding was unthinkable. A fantasy leading to deep and mortal divisions in the little kernel of sanity we all have recourse to in spite of trying circumstances.

I drove back to Santa Monica. Parked in front of the

• • 169

apartment on the beach. Thought about it for a minute. Decided to take the bull by the horns. I locked the car and climbed the stairs to the landing, my heart rising in the thoracic cavity and fluttering there.

I rang the bell next to the third door from the stairway. I tried to imagine what kind of girl friend Carp would have. No picture came to mind. I forced an invention. A tall Icelandic blond flowered with blue and yellow butterflies. A thick redhead alcoholic who absorbs punishment the way earth absorbs rain. A black girl who takes all the reverend can dish out for one hundred dollars a session.

Wrong. Wrong. Oh Jesus, *wrong.*

"Oh fuck," I said, as the door opened wider and wider. Not a girl at all. A boy. A man. Thin and frail. Cracked and crusty with dried blood, hunched like a crone, wimpled in blood-caked terrycloth, seesawing on his long narrow feet like a clubbed bindle stiff, a terrible imp whose breathing sounded like gravel rattling in a bag.

"Is that you?" he said, thick-lipped, tongue slow and careful on the loosened teeth. "Is that really you, Arjay?"

"It's me, Tobey," I said, revisited suddenly by an overwhelming absence of simple equilibrium. I leaned on the door frame.

"My God, Arjay." He put his hand on my shoulder.

"I know," I said. "I know."

13

He moved as if he were made out of glass. His nose still trickled blood and he dabbed at it with a Kleenex. I felt seasick and confused. The couch bumped my leg. I sat.

"Arjay," he said, sitting very slowly in an armchair opposite me. "What on earth—"

I held up my hands, waved him off. I closed my eyes, thinking back to the time I saw him in his new office, haloed by the blue ambience of success. How long ago? Only days, but it seemed months. Years. "Wait," I said. "Wait, just wait, Tobey, one bleeding minute."

"Arjay."

"Give it a minute, Tobe." He looked at me as if the newspaper and TV stories were true. But it was a fearless look, as if the worst had happened and there were no more threats to worry about, from me or anyone else. It was a look filled with a sad power. Something darkly final. I leaned back into the couch. "First things first, Tobey," I said. "Then I'll try to explain exactly what I've done and what I haven't done. Okay?" He nodded. "Okay. Tobe, I have to know who Carp is."

He rose carefully and walked across the room to his Kleenex box, a stiff walk, his slippered feet scuffing the carpet. "He works in DC. Sheet metal. I met him the other day at La Mujer. He's a foreman." He held his nose gingerly and rocked it back and forth.

"Broke?" I asked.

He nodded. Carp had himself a stellar evening. First the junior college athlete, then Tobey. Guru SM thug, and fellow employee.

"*Why*, Tobey?"

He looked at me, a ragged, tormented look. It was also an accusation. Use your head, it said. I looked away. The poor twit. Tobey had fallen for Carp, the muscles, the promise of sweet misery. And Carp was only too pleased to oblige. My brain began to sift through a new scattering of random shapes, hoping for an easy mesh. "Tobey, did Carp—"

He scoffed at my stupidity. Sympathy and concern, being useless, were irritants. He nodded, though, and his head sank lower with each nod, until he broke. He held his swollen face in his hands. I went over to him, put my hand on his shoulder, felt the tremors of his frail skeleton. My hand, a mean token, but it was all I could offer. His own restraints made his sobbing noiseless. "Oh fucking shit," I said. "What a pair of wimps we are." And I took him into my arms.

Oh yes, Carp had raped him. And much more than rape. An hour and a half's worth. Simple violation of the body was not enough for Carp. It was only prelude. There was something deep he wanted, something fine and central, a sanctuary.

I went into the kitchen to make some coffee. I filled the electric pot to the ten-cup line, plugged it in. Something was trying to crawl up my throat, something wrapped in sour acid. I think it was the ghost of the child I used to be, looking for a way out, once and for all.

Tobey went into the bathroom, stayed for about ten minutes, then came into the kitchen. He looked better. He had washed the dried blood from his face, composed himself. He

172 • •

sat down at the kitchen table. He put a cigarette to his lips but couldn't bring himself to put fire to it. I took his matches, lit the cigarette for him. He looked at me through the blue sulfur haze, an awful dead-end look that told me who and where we were, and I turned away because it was something I didn't want to know.

"I didn't kill that girl, Tobe," I said.

"No, I don't think you did, Arjay." He'd changed. His pale face showed an interior calm I wasn't prepared to believe. Angelic. Jesus, he was offering encouragement to *me*. I poured out the coffee, shaken by the apparitional quickness of his mood.

"Carp did it, Tobe. I don't understand anything. Nothing makes sense. But I know that Carp did it. I saw him at the girl's apartment the day before he killed her. He'd beaten the crap out of her, wrecked her apartment. He did it, Tobey. Carp is the Pantyhose Hangman, and I need to prove it somehow."

"He's a friend of Damon Spear's," Tobey said, dreamy and remote, almost inaudible, a drifting angel.

"What?"

"Lyle Carp. He and Damon work out together in the company gym. I think Damon is responsible for his promotion to foreman."

I scalded my mouth with coffee. "Carp and Spear?"

"Birds of a feather, Arjay."

I jumped up and went to the sink, filled my mouth with cold water. The tip of my tongue felt as if it had been sandpapered. I began to pace. Living room, kitchen, living room, kitchen. "Tobey, for Christ's sake, what is going on?" I asked, but he just closed his eyes, a powerful satisfaction sweeping over him. I suddenly wanted to knock him off his chair. "Carp and Spear!" I shouted, six inches from his face.

"Weird, isn't it?" he said. He was above the temporal facade, conversing with fellow cherubim.

I paced. Living room, kitchen, living room, bedroom. Saw the bloody sheets, saw myself in the cracked mirror, a hairy maniac, a believable fugitive. The floor beneath my pacing was on a spindle, my legs like Newtonian vectors in Einsteinian space, and the air sang with fluorescent bugs. Plummeting, we were, on Einstein's relative elevator. *Welcome,* said the three heads of Cerberus, the triplicate jaws sifting my entrails. *Survive, survive,* hissed a voice in the mouth of a south-flying bird.

"Tobey," I said, loud with misery. "Make a list for me, right now, of everything you know about Carp and Spear. I want to know every little scrap of information you might have picked up, and I don't care how trivial you think it is." I went back into the kitchen. "Anything and everything, Tobe. I want—"

But he wasn't listening. He was face down on the table and white as his cup. I touched his shoulder, shook him gently. "Tobey?" No response. No one home. Out.

He was still out when I picked him up in my arms and put him on his bed. I sprinkled cold water on his face, slapped his arms and wrists. I yelled his name into his ear and he didn't flinch. And when the floor began to spin with inexorable purpose on its tricky spindle, he didn't seem at all interested. Let it spin, spin away, away.

"Some help in here!" I instructed the lost rescue squads. "Help us!" I yelled again, long and hard into the medicine chest of the bathroom. And found it. Help. The empty plastic bottle. Help. All he would ever need. Tuinal. Mother's little helper. It was a prescription for ninety capsules dated yesterday.

I dialed "O," told O where to send the paramedics, and then I ran.

Ran. Down the evening freeways. North, south, east. For hours. Filling up at self-serve stations. Movement for its own sweet sake, loving the monolithic logic of freeway society. Soaring through cloverleaf vortices, powering through the mathematically banked curves, tributes to Da Vinci, Leibniz, Newton, and Nietzsche. These great domineering ribbons of reinforced concrete leading us godlike to our destiny, the promise fulfilled. Burbank, Van Nuys, Anaheim, Pasadena, Studio City, Oxnard, Azusa, Torrance, Pomona, Long Beach, San Pedro, Cucamonga, Venice.

Sweet motion for its own sweet sake, keeping the speedometer nailed to fifty-five. Sweet, law-abiding motion, the lovely slide of boulevard lights below me, streaking the curved lens of my windshield with reds, blues, and whites, those glowing worlds within the city, the fields of ice blue lights from suburban developments, the domestic dramas among them, sliding across my great lens, second by second, curving past my eye, the hundred thousand scenarios renewing themselves momentarily but reversed in the rearview mirror, right becoming wrong, yes saying no, wife beating husband, cat chasing dog, happiness becoming despair, terror blossoming suddenly and without warning into boundless cleansing joy.

Ran. I ran. No destination. Running for running's sake. Ventura north, San Clemente south, Redlands east; side trips to Newport Beach, Redondo Beach, Culver City, Burbank, Pasadena, Monrovia, Azusa. Under the low-hanging stars, when they could be seen. Gasoline, rubber, glass, steel, electricity, petroleum, polyvinyl, mercury vapor arc lamps, the urge to kick and pin the throttle, popping open the big carbs and merging with it all in one doomsday thrust of the foot. But there were reasons beyond simple fear that said no. To die is one thing, to die unilluminated, without grace, is another. There were pressing questions, they pressed harder than the urge to dive through the sky streaming gasoline fire and noise, and I felt like a frustrated novitiate in an obscure religious order that promised, through bafflement, suffering, and humiliation, *enlightenment*. Perseverance, the single necessary quality of mind, would guarantee results. Never mind the irrational dialectic. Just keep the questions up front: Carp and Spear. Scimitar. Lisa. Murder. And Tobey. There were strings on them, as Carp would say, and the strings were all tied in an invisible (to me) knot. Somewhere.

Tobey. No tolerable place for him in this world now. He believed that. Bought a one-way ticket to the world of sleep. Maybe the paramedics could extradite him. But there are many roads back, and reasons for travel.

I drove to the shopping center across from Arabian Heights, bought a shaving kit at the drugstore, checked into a nearby motel, a seedy place with plastic flamingos on the front lawn. It was called *The Rest or Nest*. It advertised hourly rates. It was still a little too early for the clothing stores to be open, so I climbed into bed, realizing dimly that I was a sitting duck.

Let them come, I told my slumbering self who did not care what I said. Let them come, I told the softening walls, who were more sympathetic. Let them come, I told the light that fed the window, light unchanged through the little years, ancient ageless light, never older than a day. Let them come. Let them come. And if they come, maybe they will see themselves as messengers. Maybe they will see a need and fill it. If I die before I wake, maybe the bullets will be preceded by words, words that I can take with me into the black tunnel behind the clock where the tick-tick is never heard. Words that will reveal the knot at the center of things. Not the center of all things, but at least the center of the things that have argued out my personal fate. Explain the gravitational ties. Turn off the vertigo. These things: Lisa, her perfect face drawing me in. Carp, slamming the door. Scimitar, electrifying the air with paranoia. Tobey, stealing away into the night on the wings of Tuinal angels.

No one came. I slept. All day. Dreamless. Even the inner brain was too tapped out to entertain itself.

I woke in darkness. Called room service for a bottle of Turkey and three cheeseburgers. Turned on the TV. On the educational channel someone was giving instructions in how to build homemade atomic bombs. A pleasant young man chalked the incredibly simple diagram of a one-kiloton device. It was the size of a skull. There was a central core of plutonium oxide surrounded by a steel shell, which in turn was surrounded by an outer shell of TNT. The plutonium, said the youthful mentor, could be obtained at any convenient nuclear reactor with little or no trouble in many cases. The device, when set off, was guaranteed to kill anywhere between ten thousand and half a million people in any large city at a cost of a mere few thousand dollars. An incredible bargain in terms of the dollar-to-deaths ratio. This program was followed by another, called "The Ghastly Horror of Addison's Disease."

My supplies arrived. I overtipped the aging boy. The handful of singles made him linger a moment in the doorway. "Say," he said, his brow-wrinkles compressing, "If there's anything, you know, *else*, I can get you—I mean anything—you be sure to call for Stu. Like, for instance, down the street there's a body shop with outcalls."

Stu the pimp. "Okay, Stu," I said, winking. He winked back and clicked his tongue. We closed the door between us discreetly.

I poured myself a fist-high dollop of Turkey and switched the TV to a commercial station. Several members of the clergy and a bearded civilian were arguing pleasantly about anxiety. I realized then that it was Sunday. *Sunday.*

The days of the week had accordioned for me. My sense of interval was gone. Ever since I stumbled into Lisa's knee, diurnal time had become a linear blur. One long feverish day unable to end itself.

"Man *is* a mirror," said one of the clerics, a smug man with plum-pudding cheeks. "And his fascination with the looking glass—in fable and in real life—is merely emblematic of his spiritual longings, you see." The moderator, a fleshy man with tinted glasses, held up a book and wiggled it seductively. The title of the book was *The Mirrors of God*. "The body is empty, you see," said the cleric, evidently the author. "Inside there is no one, just raw stew and sewage, a baffle of pipings and pumpings, machinery, slime. Man, you see, *is his surface*. Q.E.D. God sees himself from the outside, in a chaos of forms, if you'll forgive the paradox, which, indeed, is not a true paradox at all. Being nonsemantic, I mean. You see. He diversifies beautifully and constantly, without regard to *our* particular difficulties with the vermicular logic of the given."

"Wrong again, Freddy," said a pipe-smoking priest. "If I read you correctly through all that chaff."

"All this talk about mirrors seems excessively figurative to me," said a rabbi. "You are aspiring to literature, I'm afraid, not illumination."

"One and the same thing," said Freddy, author of the book.

"Hey, I don't mean to cornhole your metaphor," said the bearded man, identified on the screen as a professor of clinical psychiatry. "But a man's surface consists of twenty square feet of skin, baby, the total weight of which is a mother-buggering six pounds. I mention this in my book, *Nature and Human Nature*."

"So what you're saying," said Freddy, "is that the exterior of a man is simply—"

"The only reasonable extension of his cornhole interior. A biological inevitability. Go back to your basic phylogenetic

178 • •

parallel. Use your head." The psychiatrist folded his arms, having given the last word.

The rabbi chuckled. "Science and literature. Either one or the other. God is impressed neither by your poetry nor your statistics. God is impressed only by your capacity to believe in him."

"Old hat, Sam," said the priest, smiling generously. "Though I admit I too am somewhat nostalgic for your unembarrassed simplicity. Simplicity for simplicity's sake won't do, though. Not in this day and age."

"Hey, right on, padre," said the psychiatrist.

"I'll have to concur on that," said Freddy.

"Time's up," said the moderator.

I switched to an old movie. *Danger Island.* Peter Lorre as Detective Moto. I poured myself another big drink and climbed back into bed with my cheeseburgers. Peter Lorre was looking into an illegal shipment of diamonds in Puerto Rico. Dull story, nondescript acting, but Peter Lorre, the delightful improbability of the man, held my interest for the full ninety minutes.

Then the barbiturates of food and drink took hold. I went deep into the crystal images that lie at the mind's floor. A consequence of extreme fatigue.

I woke in the middle of Monday. The TV was still on. A commercial for dog food. Three starved collies were eating something out of the hands of children. Magenta worms. I went into the bathroom, relieved myself, looked at the face in the too-bright mirror, hating the easy, cheap optimism of the designers of motel bathrooms, knowing too, that I was the abnormal one, not the cheery millions.

I shaved. Washed. Brushed my teeth with a washcloth. Inspected the bones of my nose. Then I heard Louella say, "Given his shaky perspective of society and of things in general, I have only myself to blame for being surprised." I trot-

● ● 179

ted back to the TV. Louella, with a new hairdo, sat next to a newsman. They were behind a desk. Next to Louella, wearing a bandage roguishly on the left half of his forehead, was Basho Lovely.

"Let me say once again, Mrs. Ponce," said the newsman, "how much I appreciate this exclusive interview."

"I want to tell the story," said Louella, somber, austere, beautiful. "If someone else can be forewarned by my example, then perhaps my loss can be their gain."

"By forewarned, you mean—"

"I'm talking about the violence that seethes deep within the sexually insecure male. You see it everywhere today, in a variety of manifestations. There is a pattern, I think, which can be extrapolated, interpolated, and usefully projected."

"I see. Mr. Lovely, since you are an expert in that specific area—*violence*, I mean, not sexual insecurity, ha-ha—can you tell us something about the dynamics of violence in the average insecure man?"

Basho cleared his throat, drew the microphone toward him. "Well hell yes, I can. They're basically yellow. By that I mean the average insecure individual has a neat system of carefully worked out excuses. As he confronts life-type situations he draws on this system. To avoid making a stand. That's his trademark, being careful never to take a position on a problem. He ducks it. This is his way. *You* know what I mean, I guess."

The newsman chuckled thinly. "Mrs. Ponce, do you go along with that? *Was* your husband—a brutal murderer, a rapist perhaps, a man who attacked and severely injured Mr. Lovely here—a *coward*?"

"Oh yes. Most certainly."

"Let me say something about that attack business," said Lovely, pulling the mike against his chin. "He nailed me in the dark, you know."

"I didn't know that," said the newsman without interest.

180　•　•

"Well, it wasn't *quite* dark," said Louella.

Basho looked at her. A familiar bleak creasing of the forehead caught my eye. Then he made a little *bripp* between his puckered lips. The newsman giggled. Louella, having suffered, was invulnerably serene.

I turned off the set. It was almost noon and I had places to go. First stop, the shopping center. Using my credit cards (no reason now to be cagey), I went to a men's clothing store, *Carlo's Super Threads,* and bought a shirt, a tie, a pair of forty-dollar shoes, and a pin-striped, wide-lapelled, Nino Cerruti suit complete with vest. I left my wrinkled denims and my brogans in the dressing room. Then I went to *The Silver Shears for Guys* and bought a seventy-five-dollar wig. It was blond and long, the hair stylishly unkempt over the ears and down the neck.

I looked good. Unrecognizable. A fop. I modified my walk, inserted an arrogant, calf-flexing lilt, coming down hard on the two-inch heels of my buckled pumps for the sharp Nazi *click.* (Every woman within range stopped breathing for one second and stared. Their men, infuriated by their own comparative proletarian shabbiness, gave me looks of contempt, too aware of my superior appeal, my wealth, my easy ways. The poet was right, women adore the fascists, at least in secret melodramas above a steaming sink.) I stopped at an import shop and bought an ebony cane to signify, in contrast to white, my extraordinary vision.

It was a fine disguise, but disguise was not my motive. My motive was *style*. I drove to Santa Monica, the hospital here. I found Tobey in the Intensive Care Unit. It was a room full of very sick people. Most of them were either unconscious or heavily sedated. Tobey was lying naked on a high bed with rails, attached to an electronically controlled machine.

"He looks terrible," I said to a chubby man in a green smock. A nameplate on his chest identified him as an Inhalation Therapist.

"Not at all," he said. "He looks good. You should have seen him yesterday. Oof!"

"You mean he's going to be all right?"

"I didn't say *that*. But he is dying more *slowly*."

"But he's breathing well. Deep and regular."

"Don't kid yourself." He patted the electronic console. "John Respirator is doing the breathing. Watch this."

He pulled the tube from Tobey's mouth. The small white chest sank, then sank again and did not rise. Next to the electronic console, there was an oscilloscope. The pale green trace jumped feebly every third second.

"His heart?" I asked, pointing at it.

The therapist nodded. He put the tube back into Tobey's mouth. The ribs under the parchment skin flexed, like fingers trying to open. So small and fragile he was, a tiny Frankenstein creature trying to merge with life and leave its death dreams behind. Then, under the machine-guided rise and fall of his chest, something began to happen. The muscles of the abdomen were contracting, causing him to rise slightly, as if he were trying to sit up.

"What's that?" I asked.

"Nothing to get excited about. He's trying to breathe on his own, his system is trying to take over, but it isn't going to happen." He pulled the tube out again and the chest sank like a kite in still air. "No go, no go," said the therapist.

"He's dead," I said.

"Oh no he isn't. Not until John Scope says so."

"Stuff your scope, sonny," I said, tapping my cane on bedrail. "I say he's dead."

The therapist picked up a clipboard. "Say, you're not Dr. Van Opelzelfer, are you?"

I smiled enigmatically. The therapist busied himself elsewhere. I leaned on the bed. The delicate geometry of bone under the negligible flesh glowed like a white apparition against the greater whiteness of the bed. I counted butterflies. Twenty-nine blue hourglasses on the torso. Carefully and lovingly placed. A constellation. A swirling flight of migrating monarchs. A great C, forming an arc from hipbone to hipbone. C for Carp.

I touched Tobey's waxen cheek, knocked the respirator's electrical plug out of the wall socket with my cane, and made a vow.

PART 3

A short, round-faced woman in a quilted housecoat with Chinese dragons on it took me aside and showed me the locked gun cabinet. "This is Arn's collection," she said. She took a small key from a ring of keys and opened the home-made box. I saw what I wanted: a High Standard Victor, a very accurate .22 caliber target pistol.

"How much?" I asked.

"Oh, I don't know exactly," she said, looking nervously over her shoulder at an eavesdropping customer, who was looking at a table full of alarm clocks. "What do you want it for? Are you a sportsman?"

"I'm going to kill somebody," I said.

She gave me a sidelong glance and an inverse grin that flattened her apple cheeks. "Oh *you!*" she scolded, bursting into a frenetic laughter meant to ignite a general hubbub of merriment, but no one took her up on it.

It was a garage sale. I knew the neighborhood fairly well, an older section of Pomona, very quiet. The ad in the *Times* classified section said: Bargains Galore! Everything goes, even my husband's prized gun collection!

"How much?" I repeated.

She looked over her shoulder again at the eavesdropper.

"Well, Arn said I should get a minimum of fifty for the target pistol. So, I guess I'll ask sixty."

I took out two twenties and a ten. There were two extra clips and a box of shells. "Fifty for the gun, another ten for the clips and shells," I said.

Her small eyes, nearly swallowed by their surrounding fat, shone greedily. "How come Arn's giving up his gun collection?" I asked. There were about six pistols in it, automatics and revolvers, a carbine, three World War I rifles, a rusty .45 grease gun.

"Guns are obsolete, he says. He's switching over to electrified darts and disabling gas."

"Oh," I said, slipping the pistol into my pocket. "That makes sense."

The Development Center is a large square building about one mile down the street from P & L. No attempt was made to "fit" the DC building to the dominant architectural styles of the surrounding neighborhood. It was far too large for that. Instead, the high walls of the building were covered with murals in the manner of Diego Rivera. Diego Rivera without, however, social impact. No muscular workers looking hopefully up toward a uniform vision of an egalitarian future against a backdrop of dark satanic mills furious with smoke, heat, blood, and tears. Giant suntanned gringo blonds with good teeth stood in groups of twos and threes joshing, hands on shoulders, content, prospering under the benevolent light of industry, radiant with optimism. Solid blue sky, an occasional gull, and a grove of date palms formed the background. One of the workers, wearing the badge of a foreman, was handing a subordinate a stick of Juicy Fruit.

I pinned my purple badge (I'd kept it safe in my wallet all this time) to my lapel and walked past the security guard who gave me a casual salute. Inside the grounds I picked out a pair of doors and walked toward them as if I knew exactly where I was going. There were several sets of doors to choose from in the east wall, but nothing in my knowledge of the place, which was limited, favored any one set, and so I aimed for the middle of the building.

A rush of noise greeted me: deep rumble of dynamos, bursts of rivet guns, the screech of sheet metal being cut and shaped, hisses, gasps, puffs of smoke, the blinding light of welding machines, a current of voices under it all, shouting, laughing, howling, cursing.

"You here for the tour?" shouted a woman sitting on a stool behind a counter next to the entrance. She was reading a magazine and eating a candy bar.

"Right!" I said.

She leaned back on her stool and reached toward a row of shelves. There were several white hardhats on one of the shelves. She looked at me again, judged the circumference of my skull, picked a hat. "You're early," she said, lips tight, prematurely sour. Thirty-five going on fifty, dimly aware of the injustice, and damned mad about it, but helpless. "Sign for this." She shoved a clipboard at me. "Tours start at three, didn't they get it on the P.A. over there? You've got nearly an hour to kill off." She looked at me furtively, disapproval written all over her. Management fops rubbed her the wrong way. The insignia on her badge identified her as a shop steward. I scrawled my name in a bloated, unreadable hand, ignoring the blue-lined borders. An implosion of rage made her eyes bulge. To control herself, she made an attempt to look busy, stacking hardhats, squaring loose sheets of paper, brushing scraps of candy off her desk. I tapped the counter with my ebony cane. Her eyes widened dangerously.

"Cafeteria open?" I asked.

She nodded. I didn't leave. She looked at me. I was a hot boil on the nose of existence. At the roots of political theory is a simple hatred for personality types. That's healthy enough, I guess.

"I don't remember where it is," I said.

She breathed deeply twice and said, "Follow the E to the dock, turn left and go to the G, go up the ramp and turn at the candy machines."

I saluted with my gleaming stick, tapping it lightly against my hardhat, which was cocked on my blond head at an impudent angle, and strolled away, like a member of the leisure class. Not disguise, but style: I'm a mover and shaker. A cool decision maker.

I followed the huge, alphabetically designated H-beam pillars until I came to the E's. There were many E's. They receded into the distance, blending into a white blur hundreds of yards away. I walked past men and machines, scanning faces under the helmets, hoping to spot Carp.

No luck.

At E-29 a wide esplanade opened to the left, and there, one hundred yards away, a vertical cylinder, glossy purple, reflecting men, lights, and machines in a high convex distortion, was Scimitar. Massive at the base, it rose to well over one hundred feet. It was slightly conical, and it was capped by a distinctly phallic parabolic dome.

"We call it the purple shaft," said a laborer, grinning at my amazement.

"Is it a mock-up?"

He nodded. "Yeah, we just finished 'er this morning. Some kind of cuntbuster, ain't it? Sort of makes you feel like a flea on an elephant's ass, don't it?"

"Speak for yourself, my man," I said, pointing at his skinny, cartilaginous throat with my stick.

The cafeteria was empty. I bought a styrofoam cup of coffee, found a well-used but intact newspaper, sat at a table in the middle of the room. The front page was all Scimitar news.

RUMORED RAY GUN RILES SENATOR
Senator Cyrus Leander charged today that the Department of Defense in league with the executive branch have embarked on an insane course that threatens world stability. Senator Leander

190 • •

made it plain that he would do everything in his power to bring before Congress legislation designed to stop further funding of the program until the president offers "compelling and inexorable arguments for its continuation." The White House, however, refused once again to comment on the charges, claiming that the Senator appeared to be ignorant of the international situation, including the special financial arrangements the Department of Defense, Dynablast, and several subsidiary industries have made with certain Middle Eastern sovereignties. "A major percentage of the funding for the Scimitar program is from external sources," said a White House source.

skipped the next few paragraphs, looking for the ray-gun reference.

Meanwhile, a reliable source within the aerospace industry has disclosed that Scimitar is a radical innovation in the area of nonconventional weaponry. An industry spokesperson, who asked to remain anonymous, said that the weapon is an enormous gamma-ray laser system, a "Super Gaser," powered by solar energy, and it would be stationed in earth orbit, where individual targets would be singled out with heretofore unheard of accuracy.

An artist's conception, based on the description given by the anonymous spokesperson, showed the orbiting cylinder spitting a narrow white beam of light earthward and a puff of flame where the beam struck. Another article, in which several industry scientists were interviewed, condemned the notion of an orbiting ray gun as "absurd," "unworkable," "too expensive," "idiotic," and "a science-fiction writer's pipe dream."

Four workmen came in, on coffee break. They took a table close to mine. Unlike the figures on the mural on the outside of the building, these were little, wizened men who hunched over their coffee, sullen, not disposed toward joshing banter.

I read through the paper to the want ads, but didn't find a word about the Pantyhose Hangman. Public interest was already on the wane. No doubt the police felt less pressured

● ● 191

as a consequence, more inclined to play the passive waiting game. As a commodity my value was sliding downhill. And new threats were attracting the public eye.

One of the workmen took a paper sack out of his coveralls. He looked at me, grinned, patted the bag fondly. The neck of a half pint poked out of the brown paper. He unscrewed the cap, poured a shot into his coffee. He passed the bottle around the table. All the men looked at me and grinned as they spiked their coffee. Insolence, insolence. I walked over to their table, touched the bag with my cane.

"Don't you know you could get fired for doing that?" I asked.

They looked at one another sheepishly. The man who brought the booze adopted a self-righteous pose. "Every body does it," he said. "Even the bosses. They all got liquor in their offices, everybody knows they do."

"Rank," I said, "has its privileges." I wasn't impressed with his snivelling excuses.

The man looked at his hands. I heard his teeth grinding. A dry, milling sound. The others sat stiffly in their chairs, the fumes of their spiked coffee rising into their faces like ac cusations. "I'm going to have to confiscate this, men," I said. I took their bottle, left them the bag. Old Cranshark, 80 proof. I put Old Cranshark to my lips, tasted it. Chemically it would probably be identified as whiskey. "You boys put your jobs on the line today for this swill," I said, wiping my mouth. Fire worms inched through tunnels of meat. I put the bottle to my lips again, made it stand on my teeth. "I'm going to have to take some names," I said, wiping the drool on my sleeve, holding the bottle at arm's length, like a gre nade. "We cannot allow this type of peckerwood goldbrick ing horseplay foolishness, men." I took the bottle in my teeth, held my hands out at my sides like a high-wire artist, tilted my head back until the bottle was vertical again. Old Cranshark burbled home. I kept this pose for a while, imagining myself a human turbine requiring a moment'

...riming. Then I spit the bottle out. It hit the middle of the table and spun lazily. They were gnomes, huddled against a witch's withering wind. I leaned down on my cane from my managerial heights and squinted at their badges.

Umberhocker

Stovekiss

Dill

Butterfield

Gnome names. I looked at each face above the badges. Suspicions confirmed. Gnomes. Blooming gnomes. "You boys sure you work here?" I asked. They nodded, a quartet's mechanical unison. "Who hired you? Who signed your papers?" They looked at each other, very disturbed. They looked at me again, faces blank. "I expected as much," I said, circling them, tapping my cane against their chair legs. I asked them to stand. They did, cautiously. Not one of them was more than five feet four inches tall. Elves. "Get out of my sight," I said. They did. They filed out of the cafeteria. I whistled the working song from *Snow White*. Who did they think they were fooling?

The girl working the counter was staring at me. I went over to her, twirling my cane. "You ever see those men before?" She shook her head. She'd been eating a cookie. There were crumbs on her chin. "They're elves," I said, confiding in her over a tray of green Jell-O wedges. "If you ever see them spiking their coffee again, I want you to call security immediately. There's too much at stake, my dear. You understand?" She nodded, wide-eyed. I touched her shoulder with my cane. Her nameplate said "Minnie Forrest." "Minnie, the elves are responsible, you understand what I'm saying? *Responsible.*" She nodded. She didn't understand a word. "How do you think anything gets done? Where do you think those big lethal shapes that surround us come from, Minnie?" She backed away, inch by inch, toward an urn. Steam serpentined through her hair. "Elves, Minnie Forrest!" I cried, but she was gone, disappeared among the big kettles and roasters and veils of steam.

There were two openings left in tour group A. I signed the tour guide's list and got in line. Twenty-eight hardhats were in front of me. Most were white, the color code for managers. A few were orange—foremen. The murmuring procession moved along in half-steps. The line entered Scimitar at the base through a doorway cut into the lacquered plywood. Close up, the huge weapon looked like a mushroom in the landscape of some gargantuan Oz.

Inside, a stairwell rose to the right. A steep spiral, wide enough for only one person at a time, illuminated by naked sixty-watt bulbs strung on a freely hanging cord that ran the length of the cylinder's core. As the tour moved up the stairs, most of us hugged the wall even though there was a stout guardrail that ran along the inside of the staircase. Still, that central airshaft—fifteen stories from top to bottom—became the subject of nervous banter as we, like acolytes of an eccentric and unpredictable magus, moved step by step toward the mysterious summit. A claustrophobe would not be happy here in the crush of pilgrims on the narrow stairs. A sufferer of vertigo would be even more uneasy as the procession moved higher and higher, coiling upward around a deepening hole. He would measure the vertical drop by counting light bulbs, estimating the distance between each at ten feet. At four bulbs, he would begin to sweat. He would try to distract himself by staring at the fat back in front of him, a shifting field of blue pinstripes, but the sweat would continue to roll into his eyes. He would count bulbs in spite of himself, by quantifying the rise and fall of illumination, a perverse statistician. At six bulbs, he would begin to shake. At eight bulbs, he would feel his feet become gaseous.

There is a simple equation every high school student knows and it can be worked out in your head.

$$s = 16t^2$$

s for distance, t for time. At six bulbs the free-fall trip was just under two seconds. At ten bulbs, two and a half seconds. At fifteen bulbs, just a smidge over three seconds. Time enough for a long thought on the nature of eternity. Time enough to suck in a final argument of air and resonate the vocal cords in a parting howl of protest. Bad thoughts, bad thoughts, but I could not stop myself counting those fucking bulbs.

The stairs ended at a plywood ceiling. There was a circular door cut into it. We waited for the tour guide to tell us what to do. The momentum of the spiraling climb lingered in the balancing mechanism of my inner ear and the big hollow tube spun 1/10 rpm on its central axis, the slight centrifugal pressure forcing me against the wall, hands flat, face ghostly white and damp. I couldn't take my eyes off that fifteenth bulb.

"Say, are you all right?" said the man behind me, the thirtieth pilgrim. No vertigo, acrophobia, or claustrophobia in him. He was leaning back on the guardrail, trusting it absolutely, arms thrown over the bannister, oblivious of the deep pit and the three-second ride to nirvana.

I nodded, faked a grin. My teeth were locked, chalky in

my dry mouth. A tear of sweat jiggled on the tip of my nose, gathering the mass it would need to break the grip of cohesion. I tried not to disturb it.

"You don't look so hot, chief," said my fearless companion. He took out a meerschaum and lit up. Somewhere in the factory a wailing machine sent a low vibration through the mock-up.

The tour guide finally managed to open the trap door in the ceiling. He climbed through it, then stuck his face into the opening and called down to us. "Lots of room up here in the dome, fellas. As you come inside, just take a seat anywhere and Mr. Spear, the Project Manager, will take over and brief you on the film we're going to be looking at today. Okay?"

Spear. I hadn't seen him in the line, hadn't recognized anyone in fact, but then my view had been limited by my twenty-ninth spot in the queue. *Spear.* I touched the hard lump of steel at my navel. A vision of Spear begging for his life sent a shiver of pleasure through me. Grovel, dog! Lick the floor, turd! But Spear wasn't important. His come-uppance would have to be left to fate. It was his sidekick, Lyle Carp, who needed my attention. (Yes, I had spotted a wide flat back under an orange foreman's hat near the front of the line, and I had faith, I had faith.) Oh Carp, how will you face up to the muzzle of my Victor? How will you deal with its winking eye and simple song? I was no assassin, but a scientist, sent to test the quality of grace in the burly poser. Certain important answers might die with him, but I had lost the sense of priorities.

"The film you are about to see won't tell you a whole lot from the technical point of view," said Spear. "But it will tell you something about the political situation we're getting involved in, which is a bit ticklish, to say the least."

We were seated in a semicircle on the floor in the dimly

lit dome. A small screen had been tacked on the curving wall. Spear stood next to the projector. The projectionist waited for a signal. Spear said, "Go, Tony."

Someone turned off the light. Abruptly, the face of the president filled the screen. "Good evening, and merry Christmas, my fellow Americans," he said.

"This flick is scheduled to be aired on national TV Christmas Eve," Spear explained.

The president folded his hands in front of him and leaned toward the camera, his thumbs jumping nervously. "Tonight," he said, "I have an announcement of far-reaching importance, not only for the American people, but for every man, woman, and child on this planet of ours. On this anniversary of the birth of the Prince of Peace, modern technology has given us the means to institute a revolutionary concept in law and order. As you know, law and order is the lifeblood of any society, from Bantus to Bostonians. It is the penicillin that protects a community's security from the counterproductive bacteria, *anarchy*.

"My fellow Americans, you know as well as I how the fevers of anarchy have raged and continue to rage across the body of our planet for more years than any of us cares to remember. You know as well as I how the fever blisters of local warfare have made ugly and lasting scars on the human spirit. And you know as well as I the profound sadness and despair in the knowledge that the ultimate cure—total and unlimited warfare—will ultimately destroy the patient.

"It is with great pride and pleasure, therefore, that I announce to you tonight the renaissance of law and order by means of a new technological miracle, the *Scimitar*."

The president dissolved then and an animated film entitled "Victory Over Anarchy" took his place. The president himself narrated the film.

"Here comes the good part," said Spear.

A Disneyland version of the earth eased into the screen, from left to right. It stopped when it reached the center. Then it began to grow in size like a balloon inflating. On the planet's surface, huge craters marred the otherwise lovely greens, browns, and snowy whites of the continents.

"This is what the human race has been headed for ever since time immemorial," said the president. "The insane fury and destructiveness that lies in the most peaceful bosom—and I have been advised by my psychological experts on this, that this is indeed the case—will eventually vent itself in an orgy of wanton slaughter second to none unless something is done about it and done very, very soon. Look at the chancroids on this earth of ours, and take pause. Think about Beirut, Belfast, Lisbon, Boston, East Los Angeles."

The earth receded again and the chancres of nuclear warfare diminished to invisibility. A purple Scimitar came into view. It was followed by another, then another, then many, like a procession. A single Scimitar arced into the center of the screen, eclipsing the others.

"This satellite," said the president, his voice modulated by the somber pride of personal victory, "is called the Scimitar. Let me show you, now, how it will be utilized."

The satellite split apart to the gay, innocuous music used in every documentary film made by the industry.

"Powered by built-in solar furnaces, a laser beam of almost infinite energy is created within the cylinder. Technically speaking, it is not a laser at all, but a *gaser*. That is to say, a *gamma-ray* laser. Now, as you may or may not know, gamma rays are able to penetrate the earth's atmosphere without an appreciable reduction in their strength."

A brilliant pulse of energy generated within the cylinder and brought to narrow focus inside the mushroom dome shot down toward the earth, which had appeared again for the purpose of the demonstration. The gay music emphasized the discharge with a thrill of violins.

"From a height of hundreds, even thousands of miles, the Scimitar is capable of raising the temperature of a given circular area on the surface of the earth to *five thousand* degrees Fahrenheit!"

• • 199

The music, chastened by this sobering revelation, waxed cautiously triumphant.

"The given area can be varied by means of focusing devices from a two-thousand-yard circle to a circle of mere inches. Think of it. Mere inches! Now, I want to show you what this can mean."

A close-up of the earth revealed a fleet of naval vessels cruising with sinister single-mindedness toward some innocent victim.

"Supposing that these ships represent the attempt by one nation to interfere with the sovereignty of another by launching a sneak naval attack. Let us see what this would mean to the aggressor."

As the brutal warships, snarling anthropomorphically, plowed furrows into the sea (shocked dolphins with little sailor hats leapt out of the way, calling shrilly in dolphin squeaks to their little ones), a Scimitar eased itself into position directly above the fleet. The background music became the mischievous accompaniment for a cartoon character about to spring a painful joke on his adversary. The Roadrunner and the Coyote. Then a bluish light winked from the business end of the purple tube. The beam spread out so that its diameter encompassed a large part of the fleet by the time it reached the surface. The ships in the corona of energy shimmered, faded, disappeared. Poof. Clouds of steam rose from the sea where the ships had been. The Scimitar realigned itself then to include another part of the fleet. Fists of blue light hammered through the overcast until the entire convoy had been puffed into the elements.

This was only the first of many demonstrations of the weapon's usefulness. Fleets of missiles were puffed out of existence on their launching pads, or as they left the atmosphere, still on the upward arcs of their parabolic flights. Bomber squadrons were turned into wistful cloud formations, long feathers of cirrus and stratus, despite their tricky evasive maneuvers. Mechanized armies were erased from battlefields as if they had never been born, raised, and recruited. Even underground munitions depots and factories were destroyed by the efforts of several Scimitars working in concert, the searing heat eventually penetrating to the deepest levels of the subterranean strongholds. And when the Scimitars came under attack themselves, they destroyed their attackers as easily as they had destroyed all the others.

"If this were all the Scimitar could accomplish," continued the president, "well, I, for one, would say, 'Fine and dandy, I'll buy her as she stands.' But the implications are even more far-reaching than the miracles you have just witnessed, my fellow Americans."

The music now became a serious march, indicating final triumph over the most pernicious of foes.

"As you know, one of the chief forms of misbehavior in these past few decades has been the illegal insurgency of small, armed groups, motivated by alien and often indecipherable ideals. This, I know, has been one of your vital concerns as law-abiding citizens who wish only to be left in peace and quiet. Well, let me now lay to rest your deepest fears once and for all! I can hear you all saying, 'High time, Mr. President!' Right? Well listen, the Scimitar can and *will* offer you a total security blanket—like the man on TV says—because it hasn't only the capability of destroying large, mechanized weapon systems, but it's one of the greatest antipersonnel weapons to come down the pike since the discovery of the left hook!"

The triumphant music soared and then a cartoon guerrilla, clothed in black pajamas and carrying an automatic weapon, slinked across the screen. He looked from left to right, and, satisfied that he had not been observed, climbed into the branches of a tall tree where he was invisible except for his glowing, catlike eyes. An unwitting and clearly decent citizen sauntered under the tree and the guerrilla wantonly drew a bead on the man's unsuspecting head. But before he fired the weapon, a flash of blue light came penciling out of the heavens and the would-be assassin became a luminescent shadow of himself and disappeared. Poof. Just like the ships,

• • 201

missiles, tanks, and planes. The good citizen went on his heedless way, turning up his collar against what he believed to be the thunderclap of a sudden summer squall. Other examples of the device's usefulness in target selection showed bank robbers being evaporated before they could get to their getaway cars, muggers watching their hands vanish before they could throttle their victims, a rapist nailed in the act of unzipping, even a mad dog snapping at a child faded in mid-bark.

"Isn't that the cat's pajamas?" asked the president, jovially.

The music, as if sensing the president's buoyant mood, played witty games with violins, flutes, and timpani. The film ended then, and the president came back on the screen, hands still folded before him, thumbs flicking engagingly.

"Now, I'd be the last to deny that the Scimitar has been at the center of a great controversy among certain governmental leaders. The controversy, however, has stemmed mainly from the ironclad secrecy which has surrounded the project until now. I hope that tonight's disclosures have put to rest once and for all the needless hue and cry that for so long has been a source of much confusion in the minds of the people. The people, in their infinite wisdom, will see, I am sure, that with this great new concept in *moral weaponry*, we now have within our grasp, for the first time in recorded history, a way to achieve permanent and lasting *freedom* in our time. Yes, *freedom*, for there can be no freedom in a climate of fear. True freedom, my fellow citizens, is total security. Think about it. Man shall not raise his hand against himself again."

The president faded, and a shot of the White House Christmas tree concluded the program. A choral group in front of the tree was singing "O Holy Night," in march time.

"What a crock of shit," said a jeering voice in the audience. I recognized it. Carp. The wide-backed foreman. Carp. The humbling whims of Providence choked me up for a moment, but then I composed myself and patted the butt of my Victor.

"Well, that bit about the muggers and rapists and mad dogs sounds good but it's not realistic," said Spear. "They're going for public support. Generally speaking, though, this big banana can deliver just about what the film says it can."

I saw Carp, squatting like a baseball catcher at Spear's feet. He was grinning. A secret grin, loaded with contempt. Spear winked at him. Carp stuck his finger in his cheek and made a popped-cork sound. Spear chuckled. Carp whinnied. It was a joke, private and sinister, and no one else understood it.

"Question?" said a man, seated against the wall.

"Fire away, Cecil," said Spear.

"What about the arms limitations treaties? I thought it was settled a while back that we, none of us—Russians, French, and so on—would put strategic weapons into orbit."

"You're talking about nukes, Cece. The treaties specified nukes, I believe," said Spear. He jostled Carp's shoulder and Carp snorted again. "Besides, it's a moot point, since this weapon won't be under our control anyway."

Brisk murmurs of concern rose up and made the domed chamber hum. A stout man, dangerously red in the face, jumped to his feet. "What the hell do you mean it won't be under our control? We're building the son of a bitch, aren't we?"

"That's one of the jokers the president dealt face down," said Spear. "The agreements have all been signed for many moons. Since long after Helsinki. It's all wrapped up. The cat's in the bag and the bag's in the river."

"*You* don't buy this sewage, do you Mr. Spear?" said the red-faced man, mopping his forehead and face with his handkerchief. Spear cuffed the chuckling Carp playfully on the shoulder. Carp began doing isometrics for his pectorals. He was sitting cross-legged, hands pressed together in front of him, eyes shut tight, face tense.

● ● 203

It looked like prayer. Good. Good. All the trappings were being provided as the event of the day unfolded.

"What's done is done," said Spear, mysteriously.

"I smell a rat," said the red-faced man.

"Are ve talkink U.N. control of zis . . . *machine?*" asked another man. He stood slowly. A tall, austere man wearing a black eyepatch. A scar ran the length of his right cheek.

"Not at all, Helmut," said Spear. "That fartbag outfit couldn't police Times Square on Christmas morning. No, this is an exclusive club: Us, United Europe—the Russkies and Chinks will be forced to go along once they see that the thing really works—and of course the Arabs.

"Ze Arabs?"

"It's their bread, Helmut. Their idea, too. I know, the papers have been giving the impression that they're funding about half the contract. The truth is, though, the camel jockeys are footing the whole bill. Our technology, their bucks."

"All right," said the red-faced man. "What about control systems?"

"UJV," said Spear. "They've got the contract for Watchdog, a fleet of one thousand intelligence satellites. All of which will be under the direct control of Arbiter, a monster computer to be buried under the South Pole. Arbiter picks out the targets impartially, from subs to zip guns—so the propaganda tells us—then guides the Scimitars into orbital strike position. We're supposed to witness the end of weaponry in our time, gents."

Carp yawned and rose from his isometric praying. He was bored. Yes, he knew something the rest of us didn't, and so did Spear.

I stood up. "What about bows and arrows?" I asked.

Spear stared at me, my foppery, but didn't recognize his former manager of documents. "I guess we could still have a bow-and-arrow war," he said slowly.

"How about sticks and stones?"

"Right. It's back to the Stone Age, I guess, as far as warfare is concerned, Mr. . . ." He squinted at my badge—too far, too dim.

"In short, we'll still have the furies among us."

"No one suggested that human nature itself would be in any way altered, Mr. . . ."

"Ponce," I said, taking out my Victor. "Arjay Ponce, Mr. Spear."

Only Spear and Carp reacted. Carp dropped to all fours like a dog. Spear kicked him in the ass. Carp leaped to his feet, danced on his tiptoes. Spear jumped behind him. Carp spun away. Spear said, "Look out there, now you, hey, hey, someone tell the—oh dear, shit—everyone now get that fucking trap door *up* hotline to security." Carp went back down on all fours and tried to burrow into the anonymity of tour group A. Spear kicked him in the ass. Someone found the trap door. Carp dove for it. Half of tour group A sat back, still relaxed. Everything that had happened had happened in three seconds, during which time my finger was squeezing down on the light trigger. I fired a round.

It took off Carp's hardhat but otherwise left him alone. He rolled away from the trap door, trying to avoid the pistol's blue finger, which did not waver. Spear had flattened himself on the floor. Tour group A, finally sensing danger, stood up and roared, united at last in panic. Before my vision became obscured, I cranked off another round. Carp squealed. His body folded around the gut-burrowing pellet.

The trap door came off at the hinges. A single animal, Mob, tore it loose. Mob pressed itself like a great cheese into the small opening. I fired another round into the ceiling, to disperse them. They had to disperse because they were obscuring my target. A pinpoint of factory light slipped through the hole. Mob raged at itself through its many-tongued voice, kicked viciously at its more futile parts, passionately single-minded but hopelessly divided against itself. I lost Spear. No matter. It was Carp, Carp, singing under the trample, *gweeeee*, who needed my assistance. I fired again and again into the dome, my lust for the easy trigger running ahead of the cold logic of my mission—the gun shouting *clock! clock! clock!* like the voice of a tiny blue-black angel free at last to announce the cancellation of time—and pale light rained down on us all.

Wood splintered long and mortal and Mob fissioned, a mitotic divorce of noise and form. It was the guardrail failing. Through the trap door, cleared now by the sudden yielding of wood, I saw a freefall of heavy men, the wild flapping of hands grabbing at the flimsy light cord, and then, among the popping bulbs, a thumping rumpus of large bodies, managers and foremen, on the unforgiving concrete, and before the final bulb unlit itself, I counted a half-dozen hardhats rocking gently among the moans. Four white, two orange.

The first derivative of $s = 16t^2$ is $32t$ and its solution yields impact velocity. Figuring t from the fifteen-bulb mark, the four-plus-two hit the floor at a brisk sixty-six m.p.h. I worked the equation out three times, making sure the results were correct. But of course, this was true, this sixty-six, under ideal conditions. For one thing, it presumed a vacuum. Wind resistance, the cushion of friction it provided in the airshaft, was a real factor. Let us call it x. It had to be figured in. This is a professional outfit.

$$v = 32t - x$$

I didn't know how to compute for x. The realization rankled. And something else: $s = 16t^2$ implies perfect, parabolic flight. The trajectory of a stone in mote-free space. Hadn't the four-plus-two tried to fly? Hadn't they flapped, clawed, pushed out against the collapsing distance between their shrinking flesh and the dilating floor? Hadn't they spoiled the equation's purity with their miserable gooney-bird pawing of the air? And then there was the light cord. They grabbed it, delaying Newton's holy acceleration! Get the picture? Forget about the snivelling wind-resistance factor!

206 • •

We've got *real* problems here! X the unknown is not nearly enough. *There are many unknowns.* An infinite series of them. When you think you've got it licked, pow, another one pops us in the keester! Unknown after unknown after unknown, like Chinese marching endlessly into Bob Ripley's sea. A guaranteed supply.

$$v = 32t - (x_1 + x_2 + x_3 + \ldots x_n + \ldots)$$

Listen: enough of these fucking x's and the four-plus-two would all hit like feathers!

So why worry?

I broke a sweat. Oh yes, I heard the moans of those who had tampered with Isaac Newton and had lived. I heard them lament, and the weak, bubbling requests for help. Yes. But it was not my concern. Not my concern. None of my business. I go about my calculations amid the ravings, untouched, pure. With my hands on my ears like shells, their cries become the bleak pipings of gulls hunting chum gubbins, roar and piddle of ocean fondled diurnally by Isaac's long unchanging strokes, nowhere to go but up and down, in and out, sine waves rising and falling, the tangent of death reciprocated by the cotangent of birth, Great Isaac urging us to be mindless under God's simple and visible law, mindless, mindless, mindless, under the simple law.

Someone came up the creaking stairs. Someone else was naming the fallen.

"This guy has had it, pardner."

"He's still up there with a gun making that noise."

"Christ but I hate danger."

A middle-aged man was crying like a baby. His tears leaked into the corners of his mouth and the salt reminded him of the ocean at Venice, no, farther south, La Jolla perhaps, in the summer of 1949, when a girl two years older than himself had jerked him off into the sand using a handful of Coppertone, chanting in time to her stroking

Arjay, Arjay
I just like to watch it
when it jumps up
and spits

They were in a sandstone cave and the sea sounded like a recording of the sea turned up full blast.

17

A woman all yellow and white, call her Sunflower, for she is also very tall, is talking to me in short syllables as her bright needle searches for a vein, it is baby talk, it doesn't count, she is ten feet tall or I am an infant, but it doesn't count, I cannot move, the arm is held still by two men who call her ma'am, she smiles, she has three enormous teeth up front on top where others have only two, her eyes are blue and her hair is the yellow of corn, she coos to me, she warbles, darkness leaks into the picture beginning with the unimportant edges, gradually taking out the central areas until only the drip of her coo and her triple-toothed smile illuminate my brain, then that, too, is filled in with black.

I am not unconscious, absent but not unconscious, a blue wave, if you will, in the rigid air (though I feel the cot pressing against my back), falling *upward*, $s + me = 16t^2 + me$ differentiated twice, yielding this reverse acceleration, thirty-two feet per second per second, *waaaaaeeeee*, sliding up a tongue of light that reaches to the inside skin of the universe, and there, waiting for my rushing atoms to recompose themselves (me added to me, equaling me), I wait.

I was surprised to find myself sitting on a stool. Sun flower was only a nurse, five foot six, nostrils huffing like bellows, and her third tooth was gold. They had buckled me into a straitjacket. A man in white was trying to give me a high gluteal injection. Sunflower was pissed. ("If you're going to do that, make him *stand*," she scolded, but the man in white stabbed me anyway. He said, "First cuckoo in the plant since 1966.") He was pleased, too, all those empty years of minor cuts and abrasions. ("El *bendo*," he said, happily "La flip*ola*, man.")

An ambulance was on its way. Two had already come and gone. There was a lot of confusion out in the hall. "Who is that guy, who is that guy?" someone was yelling, meaning me, but no one had a ready answer. My purple badge was missing, torn off in the excitement, and no one thought to ask *me*, because who wants to take the word of a lunatic anyway.

Carp was on a gurney nearby, trying to sit up. Sunflower restrained him gently, impressed with the size twenty-two neck. His eyes were wide, alarmed, and his teeth were chattering. "I see a spot of black," he said to Sunflower. "It's growing wider and wider!" Sunflower patted his shoulder.

"Ah well," said the company doctor, looking up for a moment from a magazine article about Eddie Fisher.

Three men in blue suits had broken their arms in the same way. Other than that, they had survived the fall remarkably. Two split skulls and one internal hemorrhage were on their way to the hospital. One of the men with broken arms called to the doctor in a hushed but desperate voice. "I think I'm experiencing a severe fibrillation of the auricles, or a dictrotic pulse."

The company doctor tapped his pipe against his shoe. "Leave the highfalutin terminology to the pros, okay?" he said.

The third ambulance came and Carp, along with the three men with broken arms, was wheeled out of the dispensary, leaving me alone with Sunflower, the doctor, and a male attendant. Then Damon Spear came in, his face white and his eyes wild. He flashed his credentials and told everyone to get out. "I've got to interrogate this man," he explained. "He may be an agent of our adversary."

When they were gone, he said, "I'm going to get you out of here," and he picked up a three-pound ashtray and slapped me across the left side of the neck with it and I saw myself falling from the stool, but the white tile floor vanished long before I hit it.

Years later a woman's voice rasped in my ear: "I am Wally Hardmarket—no doubt you've heard of me—and I will unstrap you from that detestable harness after we give you a little pinch." She leaned forward in her oak rocker and the young man standing at her side showed me the syringe. It was big and filled to the top with clear liquid. I had been drugged for some time—my fuzzy body clocks told me that—and now I was going to be drugged some more.

"You've been a rather difficult fellow," she said, and the young man with the needle found a vein in my thigh and pumped it full.

I noticed, with only a twinge of shame, that I didn't have any pants or shorts on. Wally Hardmarket herself was naked, as was her assistant, and seemed completely comfortable that way. She was a middle-aged woman with tubular breasts that rested like basking snakes on the white hummock of her belly. She noticed my fuzzy attentions.

"Don't mistake us for nudists," she said, a bit annoyed. "Just because we don't have on any clothes doesn't mean we subscribe to that particular variety of deviation. We are simply learning to cultivate a correct attitude toward the body. The *aged* body. It is a dungsack, sir. An abomination. Society tends to hush this up with trusses and haute couture. Ah, but it remains a millstone. We believe in rock-bottom truth here."

"Here?" I asked. My tongue felt like a gloved hand. The hand of a listless paretic.

"Here. Sahara Challenge. No doubt you've heard of it. The desert condominium. Welcome to the future."

She began to float. Billow. Enlarge. Her navel was a little toothless mouth smiling vaguely. Her nipples were old cork, mercilessly gnawed by the wino gums of Time. Her face was a pale square, cheeks falling into jowls, the recessed eyes watchful and sharp under a melony forehead that was crammed tight with fierce opinion. I remembered who she was then. Wally Hardmarket. The famous author of self-help books for the already powerful. Advisor to presidents, corporation executives, highly placed ecclesiastics, professors, even sports figures. I'd seen her on a number of talk shows. Always dominating, always making her opinions triumph over less well informed, less articulate, less intelligent guests. I sort of liked her, a raw, knobby woman with a voice that could grate cheese.

I started to say that I hadn't heard of the condominium, but time flared out again, Wally Hardmarket and her assistant disappeared, other bodies came and went, day and night played shadow games on the wall, I tried to count the alternations but lost track, my restraints were gone and I had full mobility but no impulse to escape or even to see if the door to my room was locked, it was a damn good drug, and I slumped into a backwash of hours and days, making mental notes which I immediately forgot, watching TV, feeling agreeable, generous, and absolutely delighted with the way things were turning out. And they wonder why people ruin themselves on drugs.

"We have pragmatic reasons as well as purely idealistic ones," said Wally Hardmarket. "For living in this undraped condition, I mean." She strode in and out of the river of time, commenting on the abstract issues that concerned her deeply.

I looked up from my untouched plate of eggs Benedict and creamed spinach. "Hi," I said. They had left me my watch but it was either strapped on my wrist backwards or it was two o'clock. It seemed more like seven-thirty. *Why* it did, I don't know.

"Germs, for one thing," she said, unfolding a copy of the L.A. *Times* in front of me.

MANIACAL MANAGER RUNS AMUCK

"Clothes," Wally Hardmarket continued, "contain whole colonies of microscopic organisms. For our purposes, this is intolerable. You'll notice the ultraviolet lamps in the ceiling. Germ-killing light."

> An unidentified Dynablast executive fired a pistol into a crowd of fellow employees on a tour of the Scimitar mock-up and escaped capture in the confusion that followed his rampage. Several men were injured critically in the panic. Company officials denied reports that the executive was motivated politically, even though several eyewitnesses indicated that the man became excited and irrational after watching a film presentation which described in detail the weapon's specific functions.

Wally Hardmarket tapped my plate with her fingernail. "Aren't you going to eat that?" she asked.

"I don't like spinach," I said.

"What about those eggs?"

"Cholesterol, DDT, hormones."

Wally Hardmarket scoffed, took my plate, and ate hungrily. "We don't have any real use for you," she said, jaws rotating.

"Get in line," I said, but I felt absolutely superb.

"But we're not cruel. We're not going to be mean. Don't expect a display of arrogance. We're civilized. Overcivilized perhaps. You're here for our temporary convenience. Nothing more. There are those who think you might know something that might endanger our plans. Personally, I don't think you know up from down. No matter. We're not going to hurt you. Oh, you might have a drug hangover by the time this is over. You might find yourself stuck with a habit.

● ●   213

But these things are sometimes necessary. There are minimal risks we all must take. We'll tell you all about it. In the mean time . . ."

She snapped her fingers and the young man with the syringe stepped into the room. Wally Hardmarket leaned forward over her grinning navel, watching the progress of the searching needle. Her nipples were stiff with anticipation.

Years went by. They had given me a room, a third-story apartment overlooking a stretch of uninterrupted desert scenery. Saguaro, ocotillo, prickly pears, big sandy rocks, gray hardpan, miles and miles of it, sky like blue flame, the horizon shifting spastically in the dancing air.

Bed-weak and wobbly, I explored my cell. Legs rubber, head like stone, arms without muscle or bone. The room was motel-simple, decorated by a computer programmed by a manikin. On the walls there were pictures of matadors, seascapes, still lifes, the Bay of Naples. Furniture made out of synthetic wood, the grains rich and dark, surfaces hard and cool as glass. Polyester shag rug. Styrofoam pebbles gunned on the ceiling for acoustic insulation. TV set, a twelve-inch import. I turned it on, flipped the channel selector until I found a picture. It was a picture of me, sitting on the arm of a chair, fine-tuning a TV image of me, sitting on the arm of a chair, and so on. I flipped the dial. Fox Movietone News: the landings at Tarawa, Saipan, Iwo. Formations of B-24s, P-47s knocking over trains, B-25s bombing ammo dumps from low level. Ploesti rocking. Hamburg smoking. A squadron of tanks rolling over North African dunes. Celebrations in Times Square. VJ Day in Chinatown. VE Day in London. Miles of flawlessly marching GI's under a rain of confetti and tickertape. I tried another channel. Cartoons. Betty Boop. Another channel: a movie, *The Head That Wouldn't Say Die*. The condominium, evidently, had its own closed-circuit network. Nothing on the set came from an outside city. I propped up my pillows and watched the movie.

"And now I have complete control of the creature behind

the door," said a young actress. It was her head speaking, mounted in an aluminum tray filled with bubbling liquids. The head was speaking to a humped dwarf called Dr. Henry. Early sixties science fiction, spiritual record of a baffling era.

Dr. Henry, his withered hand gesturing arrogantly, leaned down to challenge the head, face to face. The pan that held the head was fed by a confusion of plumbing and wiring. Dials and meters quivered and clicked on a front panel.

"*You? In control?*" said Dr. Henry, lavishly amused. "Of *what?* A cob-eared manikin powered by a malfunctioning atomic motor? Ha-ha-ha, you make me laugh. I do not mean to be cruel, *liebchen*, but you are nothing but a *head* in search of a *body!*"

The creature behind the door began to thrash, furious, apparently, at the doctor's snotty attitude. A close-up of loosening hinges promised trouble for Dr. Henry, though, if he hung around the underground lab much longer. Dr. Henry, who, like all mad geniuses, had some astonishing valleys in his otherwise Alpine intelligence, moved closer to the weakening door.

"Larry only wanted to *save* you," Dr. Henry explained, "because he felt *sorry* for you. He's better off, believe me, lost in the depths of Krakatau!"

The head merely smiled. "Larry wanted to save me," it said evenly, "because he loved me too much to allow me to remain in this ghastly condition!"

The head wasn't really interested in the argument. It was only trying to keep Dr. Henry talking because the hinges were almost off the door. A gray finger fat as a banana poked through the growing crevice.

"*Loved* you!" said Dr. Henry, whose cruelty, it seemed, ran toward the petty. "Ha-ha-ha! Oh my poor little *dear!* You actually believe that Lawrence Buckforce, the only man to uncover the secret of life yet live to tell about it, *loved* you?"

"He *did* love me!" the head exploded, forgetting for the moment its insidious scheme. "He told me, in my *apartment*, before the accident, that he'd do anything for me!"

● ● 215

Dr. Henry scoffed at the head's gullibility: "He loved a *memory* of the girl who once showed him there was more on the bottom of the Strait of Bonifacio than the lost syllabus of Sibyl Arcane!"

The head, glancing past Dr. Henry, smiled. Dr. Henry had stayed a little too long in the underground laboratory. As the hinges creaked out of the wall, even the monomaniacal mind of the deformed surgeon seemed to grasp the perilous situation. A hand the size of a footstool reached past the askew door and grabbed Dr. Henry by his good arm. The creature behind the door, whose atomic motor was enjoying, apparently, an impressive recovery, roared with delight. The head in the tray cackled insanely.

"*No, no, no! You must not do this!*" Dr. Henry implored, his former arrogance largely destroyed by this turn of events. "I am your only hope for survival in a world of narrow-minded barbarians! Please, *liebchen!* Remember that I am the only one now alive who can resupply your nutrient pump! Without me you have only forty-eight hours to live!"

The creature behind the door and the head in the tray turned a deaf ear to the whining surgeon. *They* hadn't asked for any favors. The lovely head in the tray gave the go-ahead and the creature behind the door tore off Dr. Henry's arm.

I went into a dreamless twilight. Days passed. When I surfaced again, the movie was still on. But it was just starting. The girl, still in one piece, was driving her car on Gafton Street, unaware that one block away a truck carrying a load of plate-glass windows was beginning to skid out of control at high speed in the opposite lane. . . . I watched the awful melodrama unfold, the acting only a shade better than the script.

I watched the movie all the way through. As soon as it ended, it started again. I let it replay without changing channels. I felt wonderful, incapable of being bored, and becoming imbedded in the notion that I had been here all my life and that I owned no existence beyond this little room.

Three men and a girl came into my room. "Time to go," said the girl. I recognized her but couldn't think of her name, or the places we'd been together. I took the girl's hand and slid out of bed. One of the men turned the TV set off. The first reel of *The Head That Wouldn't Say Die* was coming to an end. Larry Buckforce, on the bottom on the Strait of Bonifacio in scuba gear, was making the discovery that would change his life forever.

The girl had nice tits. I recognized them, too. Cheerful uplift. Spirited. A wheezing gorilla with gray furze from tubes to jowl said, "Is he supposed to go to this one?"

Another man, younger, body of a congenital lounger—pale, flaccid, thin, easychair curve to the spine, long tendril fingers—said, "Search me, Dr. Larchmont. You've got the roster."

The third man, an athlete gone to seed, laughed at the younger man's mistake. "Don't bet on it, Homer."

"Don't I know you?" I asked the girl.

She squeezed my hand. Her mouth quivered at the corners. She started to say something, stopped herself.

"Wally Hardmarket been playing with the puromycin again, or what?" said Dr. Larchmont.

"Looks that way, Doc," said Homer.

"What's your name, twinkletoes?" said the ex-athlete.

"My name?" I started to say it. Everyone knows their name. Something came out of my mouth. A muddy syllable.

"What's that?" said the doctor. "I didn't quite catch it, old man."

A tapestry of first names unloomed itself. My tongue thickened. I decided to lie. "Jack," I said, thinking of someone named Singleton whose problems were over. "Maybe it's Jack."

Maybe my name was Jack and maybe it wasn't, but the woman on the stage was Wally Hardmarket. That much I remembered. I tried to assemble an image of my life outside the tall white walls of Sahara Challenge. Fragments came and went. A bellicose nun. A boy named Azad who couldn't speak English and was tormented mercilessly by the entire seventh and eighth grades of Horace Mann Junior High until he burst into tears and nearly killed his closest friend, a harmless boy named Clayton Pastorino, who had committed the unforgivable error of sympathizing with him publicly. A fleeting vision of soldiers running away from a deadly attack. A memory of a wife, mine I guess, staring at me in disbelief, but what I had done to deserve that look was closeted away in some dim crevice of my brain. Images of sleek factories, faces I had known but could not put names to, lumps of conversation, trivial images—an ashtray full of paper clips, a dog asking for a doughnut, a pond full of geese, a slab of meat— but nothing sustained, no series of contiguous events long enough to establish an identity. But, in spite of this, I was still embedded in a feeling of impervious well-being. Drugs, I guess, and I knew I should be very worried, but I wasn't. I vas giddy. I was amused. I was playful. But I was not worried.

It was an auditorium. About a hundred people sat listening to Wally Hardmarket. Everyone was naked. The girl next o me, the one that had helped me out of bed, was taking notes. Everyone was listening carefully, as if something was at stake.

"Historians—*liberal* historians," said Wally Hardmarket, tapping a pointer against a slide projection of a longhaired professor identified (by a typewritten caption) as an advisor to presidents and an architect of foreign policy, "are one of the five seminal roots of the problem."

A man in the rear of the room cleared his throat sonorously and said, "Put it to 'em, Wally!" Wally Hardmarket allowed herself a small pause while the murmurs of "hear, hear," died down.

"It's been their job, as they've seen it, to destroy *myth*. They have taken a malicious pleasure in destroying the one true energizing principle of nations." She struck the image of the professor across the forehead with her stick. "But let me tell you this: a vigorous, self-confident, wholesome, single-minded nation is *energized by myth,* and not by *truth*. Without a body of myth to harness the psychic energies of a people, giving them, consequently, something to live for, every man will be his own judge and jury. No absolute concept of community organization can survive in such an environment. The little people cannot handle this miserable state of affairs! The little people are going off their rockers! This is the definition of decadence. Decadence sets in when myth is destroyed. When a man looks only to himself for ideals, he discovers a fetid gutwagon of confusion. And the neo-mugwumps in our leading schools encourage this nonsense! Look at the Soviet Union, how they have tried to indoctrinate their people in the mythology of socialism, replete with a scruffy pantheon. Better yet, look at China: totally energized by myth! And by their astute mythmaker, Mao! We of the decadent Occident scorn (and we're all guilty here, both

• • 219

liberals and conservatives) the simplistic platitudes that energize the Chinese people, but *they* are strong and we are weak—I'm not talking about planes and tanks and bombs, those things are unimportant in the long term, in the long term a unified society is the only thing that counts—they are motivated and we are stagnant, they are single-minded and we are divided against ourselves and growing more so day by day!''

The girl next to me was writing furiously in shorthand. "Why are you doing that?" I asked.

"For my boss. He couldn't be here today. This is the most important lecture of the series, and he doesn't want to miss a word of it."

"Your boss?"

She looked at me. I liked her, I definitely did, and I had liked her before. Somewhere, sometime. Maybe in pre-Columbian Yucatán. "Damon Spear," she said.

I shrugged. "Who's that?"

"You really don't remember, do you?"

I shook my head.

"Or me."

I looked at her. Yes, I remembered. Something. Nothing particular. Her eyes, maybe. Her hands. Mouth. Breasts for sure. Yes, I knew those twins. I did, I certainly did, indeed I did. I looked up. She was blushing. That seemed wrong. It didn't seem likely that she was a blusher. I frowned.

"Alice," she said sharply. "Alice James."

I thought about that. A bell tinkled one thousand miles away. "The movie actress?" I said.

"There's no movie actress by that name," she said, biting her lip. "I'm a secretary at Dynablast. Mr. Spear's personal secretary."

Someone behind us said, "Save it, will you?"

"Sorry," I said, to Alice James. "But nothing you've said means anything to me."

She looked at her hands. "I—I just want you to know

220 • •

hat whatever it is they've done to you, I have had no part in
t. Will you remember that?"

I nodded. But it didn't matter. Nothing mattered. I felt
ust fine. Dandy.

"But the battle is lost," said Wally Hardmarket. "It's
done. Kaput. The liberal reinterpreters of the past have
urned the trick. Of course, these two-bit mugwumps will be
hot. By someone, if not by us. They will be high on the list
of the masters they think they serve, count on that, my
riends. The masters of the east aren't going to have any
mother's boy professor blabbing the truth about their myths!
And good riddance to them, too! They'll get their just
desserts, believe me! If they think they can go on 'illuminat-
ng the past' with impugnity while picking up their government check when some papa Mao is *their* chairman, they are
uffering from a delusion that dwarfs everyone else's. *Their*
myth is *truth* and they believe in it absolutely, as if the real
ruths of the past are not entombed beyond their feeble
each. But let me tell you this: Truth is a snake in the grass.
Especially historical truth. It always was and it always will
be."

The blimp I was piloting bumped into a wall and began
o spend helium in big farting ruptures. I woke up. Damon
Spear was kicking the bed. "Remember me, idiot?"

"Mr. Spear," I said.

"Give him a fish."

Everything was there, at my fingertips. My name, his
name, Alice, oh sweet Alice, Scimitar, Carp, Tobey Bacon,
Lisa. Too much of it, in fact, crowded into the daylight
egions of the brain. I needed aspirin.

"What's going on here?" I asked.

Spear laughed. A sour little sput-sput. Naked, he was
not as formidable as he was in snappy blue serge. A tumid
paunch, pecks hard but undermined by promising ripples of
nginal lard, massive drumstick thighs balanced dangerously

● ● 221

on pale toothpick calves. Not a candidate for the *Playgirl* fold out. "You weren't supposed to be on that roster," he said, as if that explained something. "Some vagina put you on it by mistake. You're supposed to be under lock and key, until we can make sure about something."

"What roster? Sure about what?"

"For the lecture series. This week it's Wally Hardmarket next week T. Robbie Johanssen, the columnist."

I held my head. There were nails in it. Spikes. Old rusty ones. Bent into question marks.

"As a matter of fact, Ponce, I'd just as soon they'd deep six you now. You're an incredible fuck-up. You might have thrown a serious ripple into the program."

"Deep-six me?"

He drew a fatal line across his throat with a stumpy finger. The gesture, or my reaction to it, made him grin happily. "In fact, I'd like to have the job turned over to big Lyle. That bullet you put into his hip didn't make him one of your big fans, Ponce."

I remembered Tobey, what Carp put him through, cursed my marksmanship, shivered.

Spear laughed. "That's right, killer. Big Lyle *lives*. And he is going to ream you, buddy, when he heals up. I guaran tee it."

My well-being was gone. The euphoria had spent itself. felt very nervous and frightened and physically wasted. Spi wouldn't form. My mouth was filled with mildewed cotton blood pressure behind my eyes made the room throb, there wasn't enough air in the room for both of us, my lungs didn't have the strength to pull in my share, I headed for the door it was locked.

"You're a little souped-up right now, Ponce," said Spear, almost conciliatory.

"Souped-up?"

"Speed, strychnine, metrozol, and a smidge of vasopres sin to undo the puromycin damage. Wally's been having some tests run on you. Consider yourself an unwitting vol unteer, for the time being at least. And I wouldn't get too upset about it if I were you. It's keeping you useful."

I sat on the bed, feeling no injustice, just fear, and breathing deeply. I clung to a phrase. It was Wally Hardmarket saying, "We're not going to hurt you." She was internationally known for her integrity. In the hierarchy of this lunatic asylum, I hoped that she outranked Spear.

"You want to ask me some questions, Ponce? Given your limited powers of deduction, you must be swamped with some real corkers. Why don't you begin by asking me about your promotion to manager? Surely the oddity of that move on the part of people who should know better must have struck you, even *you*, Ponce, as very, very remarkable."

"Lay off the fellow, Damon," said the TV set. "What are you running for, District Attorney?"

19

A weary Buddha shimmered in the tube. *"Como está?"* he said, affably. I looked at Spear. He was staring at a matador above the TV set. "Oh, yes, Mr. Ponce, I can see you just fine. The monitor is in the bull's eye. Yes, that's it. Good. Well then, how have my people been treating you? First class, I trust?"

Spear cleared his throat. "This vagina, sir—"

"Please, Dame. I've heard enough picky-picky for one day, I think. A few minutes ago Wally was here with what's his name—that big furry neurosurgeon we just hired, stereotaxis man, the one with the tumbleweed hanging from his armpits—"

"Larchmont. Dr. Lafcadio Larchmont."

"Right. Larchmont. Anyway, they went on and on about some dumbass triviality, the pros and cons of sintered steel, I think it was, for certain swivel bearings, Larchmont arguing like a blowboll—who the hell does he think he is anyway?— and Wally insisting on the virtues of Pittsburgh. Sintered steel, for God's sakes! Lord, Damon, I am not a *metal*lurgist! For the last ten years, as you know, my world has been esthetics. The cinema. The plastic arts. The poetry of the continental prefuturists—damned exciting stuff!—But chiefly the cinema."

"Skylor Blue," I said, half to myself.

224 • •

The Buddha in the tube smiled. "You recognize me, do you?"

"Yes sir," I said. His face was well known. As in Lisa's photograph, his hair was long and his dark eyes were rheumy, but the tall, bulbous forehead, the hollow cheeks, the lipless mouth, and the prominent jut of his bone white aquiline nose, were just as I remembered them from magazine pictures taken in his celebrity days.

"You've got an excellent visual memory, Mr. Ponce."

"He's stoned on metrozol," said Spear. "Among other things."

"Memory enhancers? But *why?*"

Spear shrugged. "Wally Hardmarket. She and Larchmont are still horsing around with that stuff."

"Ongoing tests, right? Aren't they ever satisfied?"

"You know Wally. The original perfectionist."

"Indeed." The magnified eyes went pensive for a moment, then looked at me. "I'll just bet you're starving for a piece of good news, aren't you, Mr. Ponce?"

"Oh, Christ," said Spear. "Don't tell me you've gone and—"

"Hush your ass up, Dame. Honestly, Arjay—may I call you that?—Dame has been such a bloody grinch lately. Well sure, of course, he's been under the gun, so to speak, and I give him credit for doing a whale of a job amid a lot of flak, living in a kind of no-man's-land for some time now, but still, if we can't maintain good humor, if we can't keep in touch with our own sweet nature, then what's it all *for*, I ask you? Why bother with it at all? Why not just pack it in, for heaven's sake?"

I looked at Spear. His own sweet nature had flown the coop a long time ago. He was cracking his knuckles surreptitiously behind his back and staring at the floor.

"After all, we are idealists here. That's what it's all about, *n'est-ce pas?*"

Spear hissed softly to one side. I heard the word he hadn't intended to utter: *flit.*

"Say what, *boy?*" said Blue. "What was that you said under your breath?" The face on the screen lost its Buddhistic serenity. Its eyes glinted suspiciously.

"I meant this asswipe next to me, Mr. Blue. I don't think he deserves your, uh, hospitality, sir. For the life of me, I don't understand why we don't deep-six him right now, now that he's out of harm's way."

"Don't let him upset you, Arjay. His bark is worse than his bite. Isn't it, Dame? Oh, Dame will bark, but he hardly ever *bites*. He's not exactly what you'd call a kamikaze pilot. He's into the security game, too, just like the rest of us." Blue winked at me, grinned puckishly at Spear. Spear got red, heavily, in the neck and ears. "He always rides tantivy to the fire, but manages to stop well short of the heat."

"That's not fair, Mr. Blue," Spear murmured.

"Of course it isn't, Damon."

Spear shuffled his feet, looked up sheepishly. "I get your point, Mr. Blue," he said.

Blue smiled radiantly. "I perceive merit in Mr. Ponce, Damon. A rather special sort of merit that would naturally elude you. Perhaps if you kept an open mind about the man, you might share my appreciation."

Spear looked at me, tried to smile apologetically. He failed. He looked as if there were a handful of tacks in his throat.

"I'm a humanitarian," said Blue. "That's what it's all about. That's the be-all and end-all of my trip. I have a destiny. I knew it as a boy. I searched and I searched. I guess I've led ten lives because of my questing nature. It may surprise you to know that I once studied for the priesthood. Seminarian, at one time. But it was a dead-end road. For some it's fine. But I am not a passive man, never was, and couldn't arrange my head for the meditative life."

I noticed that as he spoke his lips seemed to rise off his teeth and flutter slightly, as if he'd released a huge volume of gas behind each word. Except there were no audible belches.

226 • •

ust the oddly fluttering lips. And yet it wasn't an impediment because the words were clear and articulated well.

"Believe me, Arjay," he said. "I wish you no harm. And I'm very sorry, personally sorry, for the terrible mix-ups, and the trouble you've had in consequence. I'm afraid I have to take responsibility for a good deal of it, you see."

Spear raised his fingers, keyboarding the air anxiously. "Mr. Blue—"

"Never you mind, Dame. What's right is right. I've taken this man off the hook. We've supplied the authorities with another fish, a worthwhile one at that. One far more to my liking. A very deserving character."

"Not *Lyle?*" said Spear, suddenly alarmed.

"Oh dear heaven above *no*. Lyle can be a nasty banana, but he's been valuable in his way and I expect will continue to be. Besides, he takes himself seriously with all that fuck-or-suck hardass guru stuff, and though I personally think it's silly, I respect his obsession. In his way, he thirsts for spiritual truth."

"Listen Mr. Blue, he *shot* Lyle," said Spear, jerking an outraged thumb in my direction.

Blue sighed, his lips rose off his teeth and flapped, the sound of ducks rising from a pond in the placid mountain air. "The pity, the pity," he said softly, a transcendental sadness touching his features. "Try to accommodate the contradictions, Damon. It's the only thing I can tell you, it's the only thing that offers the possibility of endurance though your most delicate aspirations are drowned in blood. I know you love Lyle Carp as a brother—"

"Oh wait now," said Spear hastily. "It's not like that at all—"

"Historically, we've come to the crux of our problem and must now face our contradictions and embrace them, sadly, sadly, I grant you that, but the alternative is cerebral fission, smoking brains, the soul's poppets unhinged forever, all the stanchions unpinned, in short, the death of the race."

"What are you talking about?" I said, emboldened by Blue's kindness and evident patronage of my continuation.

"You, you asshole," said Spear glumly.

"That's right, Arjay," said Blue, smiling again, the sweet-sad-luminous smile of a visionary.

I felt cold all over, the air that streamed over the membranes of my nasal cavity had ice crystals in it. My mind was a wide pane of glass looking out on the hills and valleys of my life. My nerves quivered in their linings. Every detail of my past life was available to me. The woman in an old recurrent dream who leans down to me like a fragrant mountain quilted in daisies, marigolds, baby's breath, gentian, lupine, buttercups, is my mother, Helga. I am in a crib, discovering my fingers. Wind from the perfumed mountain has music in it. It's her, Helga, no dream, all these flubbed years, *her*. The deleted decades came back in vast purlieus. The first grade in a parochial boarding school, the bed-wetting, the anxiety attacks, the refusal to eat, the chained rage. I began to shake, tears came, the lining of my throat thickened.

"It's over," said Blue.

I swallowed. "Over?"

"As of two days ago, you are no longer wanted for murder."

20

You can't beat the low desert in early winter. Temperature in the high sixties, air as pure as day one, a blue no city inmate sees, the talking breezes, the absolute colors. I strolled in it, within the tall white walls of Sahara Challenge, feeling quite sure that I had lost my mind and all of this was the complex product of broken capillaries high in the cerebral cortex.

A dozen distinguished-looking men and women, all gray-heads, were sunning and talking by the large oval pool. Naked skin beyond a certain age is about as interesting as wilted lettuce. They chatted sociably, without self-consciousness. Wally Hardmarket was there. She saw me.

"Yoo hoo," she called. "Remember me?"

"Is that supposed to be a joke?" I said, glowering. But how could I hold a grudge, having just been restored to the world of innocent bystanders?

Wally Hardmarket stood, joined me at the edge of the pool. "I'm sorry," she said. "Of course I didn't mean it that way. We weren't, you know, just amusing ourselves with your temporal lobes. The annihilation of memory is very important to us here. It's part of the social architectonics of the program. I think we're almost there."

• • 229

"I don't know what you're talking about. Almost where?"

She was a fast talker who looked you straight in the eye, daring challenge. She had large, deep brown, unfathomable eyes that didn't have to squint in the wash of sunlight. "The elimination of history, of course. By pill. We're looking ahead to a fresh start. Weren't you at lecture number nine?"

"I'm not on the roster. I was supposed to be under lock and key until they figured out what to do with me."

"That's silly. We're all under lock and key, in a sense. Once committed to the project, there's no way out. Did you notice the wall around the grounds?"

"Committed?" I was right. A posh banana farm. We're all unlaced. Unberibboned dukes and duchesses. Lost children.

"To the *project*. To a course of action that will change the face of the earth almost overnight, if everything works properly."

I had to watch myself. Humor her. Be patient. You never know. "How nice for you," I said, in my asylum voice.

She laughed. "It must sound quite outrageous to an outsider, I'll concede you that point."

"Outrageous? Not at all. I think it's a peachy idea."

"You're a skeptic, I can see that. Well, that's normal. Quite healthy in fact. I have no doubt but that the great social tragedies of our times could have been nipped in the bud by a skeptical citizenry."

I saw them first out of the corner of my eye. I didn't want to turn my head.

"Hello, Jay," she said. Spear was with her, his arm around her naked shoulder. Her pale body seemed frail, girlish, next to his florid brawn.

"Hello, Alice," I said.

"I've heard the wonderful news. I'm very happy for you. You must have been through hell."

I looked at them. Spear was smirking, but he didn't say

230 • •

anything audible. I felt sure that Blue had given me safe passage in his quirky realm.

"The police picked up the real murderer in a drugstore," said Alice. "And guess what? He was shoplifting *pantyhose!*"

I'd seen the newscast hours ago. Spear took my TV off closed circuit and we'd watched the bulletin from L.A., at Blue's request. "The recent startling turn of events in the Pantyhose Hangman case continues to unearth new surprises," said the anchorman. The police now had a new suspect, witnesses, a telephone confession, a broken alibi, fingerprints, incriminating letters, home movies taken by a neighbor of the killer leaving the apartment shoeless, unzipped, wild. The home-moviemaker was a professor named Salvo. "The elusive executive, Arjay Ponce, originally suspected of the crime, is no longer the target of the intense manhunt that had failed utterly to unearth a single clue as to his whereabouts." And oh, my heart danced, my soul came back, singing, the black cloud on my spirit split and dispersed, and my life became transfused with possibility again. Even when the name of the new suspect registered on me, I did not lose my grip on this joy. "A spokesman for the police department went on to say that Gil Dennison, the victim's husband, had been apprehended in a San Bernardino drug store. He surrendered without resistance and is now being held in the county jail."

"The wrong man," I said, but not with any real sense of diminished happiness.

"What do you care, Ponce?" said Spear. "You're home free, asshole. Count your blessings while you can."

Spear had resigned himself, in spite of his tone, to my unearned status. His manner had lost all its threat. I didn't like him, but now I didn't fear him either. The telecast ended with an interview with Hector Salvo. Salvo described in detail how he just happened to be outside with his brand-new camera on the afternoon of the murder.

• • 231

"How did they get him to lie?" I asked.

"Easy, Ponce. He's a creep. A peeper. He was told what to do, or he'd be exposed as a deviate. This outfit is very good at telling people when to squat, Ponce. The film itself was provided by us."

"Blackmail."

Spear snorted. "Give the man a fish," he said.

Then Blue reappeared on the TV set. "Ta da!" he said, festively. "Everybody's got a string tied to his ass, Arjay. It's been my good fortune to be in a position to do the pulling."

I looked at Alice, tried to cull the depth of her involvement. She seemed innocent, pure, completely ignorant. "Of course it's a frame-up, Alice," I said. "You know that, don't you?"

Her eyes widened. She looked at her boss. Her smile lost its cheer. Spear made a face at me. Wally Hardmarket walked away, uninterested in the day-to-day workings of the project she was allied to.

"This man would trade money for dogshit if someone didn't walk behind him and kick his ass every ten minutes," said Spear, squeezing Alice possessively behind the neck.

"What do you mean, 'frame-up'?" she asked me.

"I mean Gil Dennison didn't kill his wife, that's what I mean. I mean weird Lyle Carp did it. You've met weird Lyle, haven't you? He's your boss's sidekick."

"That's enough, Ponce," said Spear, trying to retake lost ground, but he wasn't credible any more.

I took his hand from Alice's neck and then pushed him into the pool before he understood what I was doing.

I walked away. Alice followed. "What's *really* happening here?" she asked.

I shrugged. "I was hoping you'd tell me." I didn't quite believe her. I wanted to, but I didn't.

Beyond the pool were dunes. We walked to them. We walked to the white brick wall beyond the dunes, followed it for a while, not speaking, until we came to a grove of ocotillo. A small wind clicked in the spiky branches.

"Alice," I said. She turned away from me. "Damon *Spear*, for Christ's sakes."

She turned on me then, eyes blazing. "Don't tell *me* how to get on!"

We sat down on the soft turf. "This damned *au naturel* business," she said. "Can't even carry a pack of cigarettes around." The words were a diversion: the agitation behind them, real. I had no business extending my ragged value system to her. I just plain liked her a lot. But we were a mile away from the common ground we almost had once. Only a mile. Abruptly she kissed my face and stood up. "Let's walk some more," she said.

We walked out of the grove, following the white wall. The place was immense. The condominium itself—squat white brick buildings, the latest in desert architecture—was large enough for several hundred people, perhaps a thousand. There were three pools, large enough to be given proper names in some states, tennis courts, a grassy park, a gymnasium, an auditorium, and a theater. The perimeter was roughly circular and probably three miles around. In other circumstances I would have been impressed.

We came to a grassy depression. Someone, picnickers, had left behind a large blanket. Alice pulled me toward it. We sat down. The depression, an inverse hummock, was a perfect bowl made out of dark, shaggy lawn. The blanket was in the center of the bowl, whose high rim concealed us completely from other strollers.

"I'm not sleeping with him, Jay," she said.

Not meaning to, I made a scoffing *harr*. "Sorry," I said. "It's none of my business. I mean, I'm the last one in the world to tell you—"

She put her finger on my lips, sealing them. "I'm flattered that you care."

"But I have no right."

"That's just it. If you had rights in the matter, well, then,

• • 233

your concern would be expected. Without rights, it's down-right noble."

I worked on that. "That's some kind of logic, lady."

She smiled. I smiled. I took her hand and kissed it. She pressed her face against my chest. I pushed her off. "Wait a second," I said. "What are we doing?" She ignored me. Her lips moved up to my neck and chin, her knee levered my thigh, her breasts made me welcome, her eyes were asking for trouble. "Alice, forget it. This is nuts. I'm a prisoner here, I think; maybe you are too. I don't even know how long I've been here, I don't know if I'm going to get out of it in one piece, I don't know what these goddamned people think they're doing, and now, in spite of that, I'm getting ro-mantic!"

She wasn't listening. I stood up, started to walk away. She caught my hand, pulled me down on top of her.

"Alice, listen, Alice—"

She put her mouth on my words and snuffed them out. I wasn't up for the occasion, knew I wouldn't be, too much was on my mind, the distractions were immense, the sense of dislocation, the confusion, the fear, and I did not feel any possibility of heat. I rolled away from her, crossed my forearms over my eyes, tried to visualize my formerly pre-dictable life, but it seemed like a thin fabrication that wouldn't hold up under a steady gaze.

"Don't be ashamed, no one's looking," she said. "I'll bring it up, if you'll let me."

"Alice, I am not ashamed. I think I'd have something to be ashamed about if I *felt* like making love to you, consider-ing the circumstances."

"Come on, you can do it, Jay," she said, ignoring my reasonable excuse.

I took a long look at her. The coyness in her face rankled me. It seemed indifferent, rehearsed. "Forget about it, Alice," I said. "I have a few other things on my mind."

I could have given her a list. Blue, owner of UJV and sev-

234 • •

eral other thriving enterprises, for openers. What did he want with me? What was he up to? And Lisa: why did Carp kill her? What was the connection? No mere random psycho-sexual attack, of that I was sure. No, it was a deliberate, planned killing. The pop-art snapshot of Blue that had been torn apart *meant* something, too. *What?* And Spear. Why was the project director for the Scimitar program acting like a flunky for Blue? And then there was Alice. Alice, Alice.

The list, which was only partial, made the grass bowl tilt and spin. It brought on a perverse reversal of gravitational polarity. The vectors turned themselves inside out and the arrowheads pointed skyward. I was on my back, pinned to the grassy sky, looking down on a landscape of air. The grass sky spun around my navel. Soon the sun, a great ball of warm mud, would rise and bring on everlasting night. I closed my eyes, crossed my face with my forearms again, tried to remember a grade-school jingle, failed, improvised:

> *dog in fog*
> *dread gully bone*

failed, almost burst into tears, failed, sensed the brink, the thin ice, the gully bone dark, the mighty terror, the place of burning ghosts, the lake of no bottom.

"Easy, easy," said Alice, cooing, touching me, careful as an entomologist.

I groaned. I flapped. I felt a disconnection between me and me. Oh they have fucked me up, axons and dendrites awash with foreign substances, me and me at war, flapping against the green sky, bird-self turned loose and trying to talon the meat of snake-self, oh woe, oh awful woe.

Something screamed. The fire rose against my loins. Birdman and snakeman merged, flying cock the product, hard and angry, hawk eyes alert for prey, prehensile wings to hold it still. It looked up at the woman who was smearing it with clear paste, its heart sending arrows into its veins, a terrible sweet rage of need hammering its brain. The woman tossed the tin of paste aside. "Dimethyl sulfoxide," she said. "Love potion number nine. They love it in Europe."

She decided to play. She ran. I flew after her. She was slow. I caught her and pulled her down. She hit the grass hard and cried. She tried to rub her ankle. I yanked her arm away. She was mine. The wind shrieked out of her. She was mine. Her arms fought me. She was mine. I saw her real fear. I heard her call for moderation. But she was mine, she was mine.

I was tired. I needed to stop. But the fire blazed on. She made sounds, I was hurting her, hurting myself, and the hurting was needed, too. It spread to my lungs and to the muscles of my chest. Breathing hurt, not breathing hurt. Moving hurt, not moving hurt.

Someone giggled. Someone else, trying to whisper, said, *"Shut up!"*

Hurting all over, I stood up, squinted at the rim of the bowl. Three men and the fat snout of a camera looked down at us. Exposed now, they grinned sheepishly and waved hello. A man seated in a director's chair said: "Man oh man, we have some fine footage, kids. Many, many thanks."

I looked at Alice. She hadn't bothered to look up at the men. There was no surprise in her face. Just guilt, maybe a twinge of it, maybe some regret. I knelt down to her, took her face in my hands, made her look at me. "All right," I said. "Start."

"I'm a little sick of myself," she said.

"Just start: what's going on?"

"They said they'd give me five thousand dollars to do it. Mr. Blue is an amateur filmmaker. Didn't you know that?"

"I don't know shit from applebutter."

"He goes for kinky cinema verité."

"Does he now." I walked over to the little tin of dimethyl sulfoxide, picked it up. "And this stuff was planted here?"

She nodded. "Under the blanket."

"What's it do?"

"You ought to know by now. If you're asking me for the physiochemistry of it, then I can't help you."

No, I did not enjoy her tone. No, there was a spiritual malignancy present that needed an exorcist's hand. Things needed to be brought back into line, balance restored, all debts repaid. It was a simple question of *order*. "This is going to hurt me more than it hurts you," I said, smearing the remaining dimethyl sulfoxide on my still churlish trooper.

"Oh no, Jay, I don't want to anymore. I'm really sorry about this. It was a foolish thing to agree to. I don't want to give the impression that they forced me, or anything, it wasn't like that at all. It's just that I really *do* need the money, after all. You can understand that, can't you? I mean. You know."

I guess the look on my face gave her pause. She stuttered. The pain had subsided. I took steps in her direction. She backed away. She paled. She pointed her finger at me and said no, sternly. But there would be no swerving from duty.

She fought. Nails at my face. Kicks meant to disable glanced off my quick thighs. I knocked her down. She got up quickly and ran up the grassy slope toward the men with the camera. I tackled her and dragged her back down by the ankles. I brought her to her feet and knocked her down again.

"Fantastic!" screamed the director. "Toss him the whip!"

But I didn't want the whip. "Kneel," I said, and the director aimed a parabolic microphone at us.

She refused. She shook her head emphatically. No passage, no passage. But I was a shaman with foolproof cures. I hit her in the stomach and turned her over on her knees.

"Please, please," she said, blubbering now.

But I knew what was best. The antidote for greed is humiliation of the body. My Spanish blood, the ghost of Torquemada buried there, understood that principle. A simple moral recipe.

"Lord love a duck," said the director. "He's going to pop her in the caboose!"

I said:

> Had we but world enough, and time,
> This coyness, lady, were no crime.

She only whimpered, uninterested in verse.

"He's one of yours, Miss James. You remember. Andrew Marvell."

The small brown rose was coy. It offered coy passage. Difficult. Miser pinch of the flexed halo. But Torquemada is known for patience. There is thrill in delay. The final yielding postponed becomes magnified in the mind. The greater the sinner, the more profound the conversion. She held for minutes against the invader, then, catastrophically, her strength deserted her, and she yielded.

It was exquisite, the deep violation of that tropical tunnel, that secondary road to paradise, previously untraveled, I felt quite sure, but certain as the much-frequented rosy turnpike to bring the pilgrim home.

She grunted and squealed. I got caught up in a fiery sermon of increasing power and was deaf to everything but my own slamming rhythm.

> Love has pitched his tent
> In the place of excrement,

quoth the madman, wrongly, but his great need was for a logic of couplets, the balance of rhymed pairs. Oh, I gave her iambs till she bawled with pain, pain that made her forget the humiliation, pain that drowned the hyena barking of the director and his flunkies, cleansing pain, pain that reduced her to her essential self, pain that drilled the whole world until it begged on its knees for forgiveness, and I, insular

Torquemada, plowed, nevertheless, those sweet little English muffins till they smoked, my rod of white hot iron relentlessly searching, refusing to warp though I was coming my marrow, coming my brains, coming my liquid soul. Only my own pain, sudden, hard as glass, ripping through my chest, made me stop.

"Holy cow," said one of the director's flunkies. "He's supposed to be the *good* guy!"

21

I woke surrounded by white planes. A cubicle, the smell of alcohol and aerosol sprays, and I am plugged into devices, the most immediate one being a five-inch oscilloscope that repeats green line drawings of a leaning mountain. The line moves from left to right, erecting the same mountain over and over, one each second.

"Ah ha, you're awake at last, you old bugger," said a pleasant voice.

I was too weak to sit up. I rolled my head on the pillow.

"Look up, at the TV set on the wall, Mr. Vance."

It was Dr. Larchmont, poolside, sipping a Margarita. He raised his free hand, wiggled the fingers. An unconcealed monitoring camera stared down at me from the ceiling.

"Ponce," I said.

"Oh, right you are. Sorry."

"What happened, Doctor?"

"Beats me, kid. Coronary, I guess. Not my field, really. I think you got a problem. Might be a touch of the Stokes-Adams syndrome. Ever have endocarditis? I'd lay off smoking and animal fats for a while, if I were you, Mr. Vance."

I sank back into my pillow, horrified. The repeating

mountain on the scope bulged volcanically. Panic, now, was my worst enemy. Calm, calm, stay dead calm.

"Not to worry, old son," said Dr. Larchmont. "If it was a coronary, it was strictly minor league. Let's just call it a spasm due to, ah, stress, okay? I wouldn't sweat it. You did drop like a sack of turnips, though. That's what they're saying. *Whopp!* But you'll be up and around in a day or so. Hey, you might give a thought or two to slowing down, pardner. That root is going to be the death of you yet. Believe me, there's more to life than plowing your brains out on the split-tails, champ."

The picture rolled and he was gone, replaced by a panoramic view of a golf course, music by Wayne King.

"What you need," said Damon Spear, standing in the doorway to the small room, "is a bilateral orchidectomy. You went out of your gourd. A BLO would smooth you out." He came in, closed the door behind him. He was smiling happily. He sat down in the chair next to my bed and crossed his legs. "You look lousy, chump. White as a sheet, like a man on the brink of becoming worm food. I hope you've made your peace, Ponce."

I ignored him. Tried to control my breathing. Panic was gone, but now I had to prevent rage from doing the same damage.

"Should I call a priest?" he said.

I stared at the ceiling, counted by twos to fifty and then back to zero by fours. Got stuck at two, went back to fifty by eights. A workable mantra. Mysticism that isn't plain and simple sucks. I am a simple phototropic fungus trying to clear my brainstem from toxins. Ten, eighteen, twenty-six, thirty-four, forty-two, bingo. The toxins block the light. My mantra shakes them out. The light breaks through the bleakness and fills me with its simple tranquility.

"Or would you rather have a nun?"

Mantra broken, the green electronic mountain grew a crown of trees. I felt branches in my pulse, fibrillating in the wind. Three, six, nine, twelve.

● ● 241

"You know what I'm talking about, don't you?"

I looked at him: His smile was reaching back toward his ears. I knew.

"I bet you'd like to have a few answers before you cash in, right Ponce?"

"I'm not going to cash in," I mumbled.

"Ho, don't count on it. You may have more to survive than a mushy ticker."

My mushy ticker sped up, the green mountain, treeless now but towering like a Matterhorn, flashed on the scope, ground-to-ground lightning. Spear looked at the flaring scope and chuckled. "Ah shit, you're an open book, Ponce. Watch the TV monitor and hang on."

He took a remote control out of his pocket and punched out a combination of numbers. The screen rolled. Then a title came on: *Ponce Sequence, 12-5.* Blurred images for the first few seconds, then a man's back came into view. Beyond the back, a nun. She was on a bed. The images went blurry again, then came back sharply. The man held a drink in his hand. He was spilling it. He bent down and slid the drink under the bed. The nun began to cringe, unconvincingly. Her face, when it could be seen behind the jerky movement of the undressing man, was a mask of theatrical fright. Amateur acting, amateur filming. A flurry of motion nettled the cameraman and when he refocused on the action, the intruder had straddled the nun and had begun to rip away her habit. But the nun fought back, dirty, skillfully. The attacker caught a heel on his chest and a knee pummeled his groin. But that was the nun's big mistake. The streetfighting nun merely enraged the rapist and his strength multiplied. He pinned her, wedged himself past her weakening defenses, howled at the ceiling, the drunk fool, and began the ancient undulating dance of victory. The nun quickly forgot her principles and clamped the invader home with her long brown arms and legs and bled his pent-up aching rivers bone dry. Victor became vanquished, vanquished became

242 • •

victor, the old old turnabout, and no one was complaining. When it was over, the spent intruder looked up directly into the lens of the hidden camera as if he knew it was there and grinned like a tickled baboon. The film lasted about two minutes.

"Quick trigger, Ponce," said Spear. "The old lady must have been holding out on you."

I gave up control of the green mountain. It became surf, a dune, a cupcake. I leaned out of bed and yanked a handful of wires out of the scope and the green trace went crazy for a second, then painted a dull suggestion of the horizon.

"One of our star performers went through a pair of fifty-foot reels before he got it off. Had the girl gnawing the sheets, I want to tell you. Wow, that turkey belonged in a zoo."

I stared at him. He didn't mind. "We were alone," I said.

"Oh no you weren't. Gil Dennison was there, too. The mirror on the wall behind the dresser is one-way glass. Dennison worked the camera on the other side of it."

"Her own husband?"

"You surprise me, Ponce. Come on, now. Try to be up with the times. That's how the boy got *off*. Filming his old lady in the sack with degenerate old men. Our big worry was that it was too obvious, that you'd catch on. We didn't count on your being so cooperatively *dumb*."

There was a long shadow crossing the room. Cloud or blimp, or the Big Solar Turn-off. But the sun walked faithfully behind it. Spear lit a cigar. Savored the first lungful. "The film is fucked in places because that vagina holding the camera got excited during the good parts." He chuckled merrily.

"All right," I said. *"Why?"*

But I had a strong inkling. Set up, I'd been set up. That was clear enough. The Dennisons did their part handsomely, sucking the old degenerate in on his own vanity.

They were working for Blue or Spear. Probably both. And there could be only one reason for putting it on film: blackmail. Everybody has a string on his ass, said Blue. And, if necessary, one can always be tied on. But the uncracked kernel remained: What did I have that was worth blackmail?

Anticipating this question, Spear said, "We wanted your cooperation. But you had to step in shit and get yourself wanted for murder. You are a human monkey wrench, Ponce."

"My cooperation? For what?"

"Lordy, but you are thick," he said, blowing a doughnut toward the ceiling.

I slid my legs out of bed, tested them against the cool tile floor. I was weak, too weak to break the oscilloscope over his head. A memory of pain flickered in the left side of my chest and down the bicep. But I felt reckless.

"Of course, that's why I had you promoted to manager. Because of your basic thickness. Towne gave me a free hand in staffing. I insisted on that. Then I ran a profile on all the goldbricks and time-servers eligible for promotion. You fit nicely—gullible, dumb, good potential for sexual deviation— one of our top choices, in fact. Actually, you were scheduled to be canned—before you had twenty years in the company. They didn't want to have to shell out retirement pay. They don't like the idea of paying good money for dead wood."

That explained a lot: "Tobey Bacon?" I said.

"We outdid ourselves on that one. What a pip!"

I stood up. "All right, Spear. *Why?*"

He chuckled, shook his head. "Boy, we would have had one beautiful relationship, Ponce. I'm only sorry the scheme is nixed. It would have worked beautifully."

I leaned on the arms of his chair, put my face in his. "One more time," I said, slowly. "Why?"

"Oh, why, why, why. *Sabotage,* Ponce. Is your head far enough out of your ass to understand that?"

The door popped open and a big nurse came in.

Hull-o," she said, a Germanic chirp. She was over six feet tall and weighed at least two twenty. She was blond, big-featured, and bristled with competence. "Geud morgning! I ahm Greta. I ahm going to gave you someding nice." She spoke in a Wagnerian singsong. She showed me a tray with a syringe on it. It was filled with something pink.

"What's that stuff?" I asked.

"Elixar, to put you strong as wild bull again, sair. Lyo-philized cells. Directly from Switzerland, zoom, by jet plane."

"Wait a minute—"

"Don't be so stupid all your life, Ponce, for Christ's sakes, man," said Spear. "Mr. Blue is doing you a favor. I'd be just as happy if he kept that stuff under lock and key. The goo in that syringe is worth more than you are."

"Make a cheek," said the nurse, patting my hip good-naturedly, pushing me toward the bed. "Cell terapy," she said, "make you feel like Hun."

Nothing to lose, I climbed on the bed, made a cheek. "What's cell therapy?" I asked.

My nurse laughed, big *Gotterdammerung* haw-haws from her mezzo-soprano bellows. "Sheep fetus," she said. "You mince him up. You freeze-dry, like Sanka. You mix in saline solution. You shoot him, boom, into patient." She swabbed the puncture with alcohol. It burned in me, sheep fire, and I winced. "Soon you feel like stallion again, sair," she said, pulling up my sheet.

She left the room, striding like a Valkyrie. "One thou-sand bucks a shot for that stuff, Ponce," said Spear. "Con-sider yourself privileged."

I considered myself. I didn't feel privileged. I had other things weighing on me at the moment. "You said sabotage. You mean Scimitar?"

"Ponce, the way your mind works, I'm surprised you've managed to feed a family all these years. You're not what they call *quick*."

● ● 245

"Wait a minute. I was in no position to sabotage any thing. And even if I had been, I'm only a small part of th picture—"

He waved his hands. "Hold it, hold it. Don't talk for few minutes, all right? You tend to babble. Hold back a littl and try to use your gourd."

My gourd. I touched its pulpy temples, massaged lightly Blackmail. Sabotage. Scimitar. Dynablast. United JetVac Skylor Blue. Sahara Challenge. Rigged promotions. Murder.

Spear laughed. "All right, Ponce. Don't rupture yoursel Watch this."

He punched out a code on his remote control box. An other bedroom scene appeared on the tube. A naked gray haired man lying on the floor with money spread over hi face. A pert little blond, also naked, squatted over him an sat on the cash.

"They play out their secret fantasies, given half chance," said Spear. "We did a psychological profile, cam up with some damn shrewd guesses. The girls we hired wer first-rate. They drew the old boys out. But I guess I don' have to tell *you*."

He keyed the remote control again. A tall, skinny man i bra and panties squirmed on a furry divan while a heavy-se woman wearing a Prussian helmet snarled viciously an threatened him with a loaf-sized dildo. Spear showed me ex cerpts from a whole library: A stern crewcut professor force three women at gunpoint to stand on a chair. When one los her balance and slipped off, he made her kneel before him He aimed the pistol at the other two and unzipped with hi left hand. A couple made love while a third man jerked of into the jackets of *Forever Amber*. A beach scene: wate nymphs carrying a boatload of pastries to a fat fellow wh climbed in and cavorted. Lubricated with goo, he wedge himself into a cluster of giggling girls. A face I recognized the man with the tics. He painted a miniature landscape on vast, heavily dimpled buttock. The tics, bless his heart, wer calm. Then Tobey Bacon, straddled by Carp. Carp had hir

246 • •

y the ears. The camera was interested in Tobey's expres-
ion: ecstasy and self-loathing; frightened anticipation. Spear
unched out new combinations in quick sequence, and frag-
ents of scenes flashed on the tube in boggling succession.
arieties of bodies in all the possibilities of biped embrace,
ll the thwarted eroticism of middle age exploding in a kalei-
oscopic dance.

"The average manager," said Spear, "is pulling down
bout twenty-five thousand a year. He's got mortgage pay-
ents on his mind, a wife whose only solace of late has been
hat husky check each week, kids, career, status in the com-
unity. He is not going to throw it down the tube by refus-
ng to do a relatively trivial job for us now, is he?"

"What's relatively trivial about sabotage?"

"I'm not talking about gelignite time bombs taped to the
nderside of freight cars. I'm talking about white-collar sabo-
age, the easy kind."

"White-collar sabotage? What's that?"

Spear turned off the TV set, unwrapped a fresh cigar,
olled it between his lips pensively. "See, we figured that
cimitar would not be a cost-plus contract. That the money
alve would have a lot of white-knuckled fingers on it."

That wasn't news. That was one of the *givens*. The days
f the unlimited gravy train, the cost-plus contract, were
ver. A cost-plus contract tells the prime contractor that
hould the cost of the project exceed his estimate, then the
ir Force, Navy, or whoever let the contract in the first place,
grees to pay the overages. In short, a blank check. It was the
reature of wartime exigencies. It got the job done but the
buses were intolerable for a peacetime economy. For a
umber of years now, most defense contracts have been writ-
en without this safety feature for the industry. If costs go
ver the original bid, then the company has to dig into its
wn coffers for at least a decent percentage of the overrun. A
isciplining fact of life the industry did not accept without
ome feverish lobbying and breast-beating.

"All we wanted these carefully selected managers to do

was to spend money," said Spear. "We wanted them to spend it as if they were operating under the old cost-plus rules. Beginning to get the idea?"

My experience as a manager was fairly limited. "Okay, but how can they do that. I mean, aren't there people who keep tabs? Accountants?"

"We put them into the movies, too, Ponce. Did you see that lardass guy force-feeding mayonnaise to the old woman? Chief money-counter. Placed the degenerate myself. Brought him down from the northern facility. He used to test rocket motors. Stone deaf and can't make change without using his fingers."

Spear turned the TV on again and fingered the keyboard of the remote control. Me and Lisa again, trading predilections. Gil, the sneaky devil, had followed us around that night. I guess I was too distracted to notice. We were in a cozy nook, under a stairwell, clamped together like unborn twins.

"It's surprising, Ponce, how many fine, upstanding, straitlaced family men are raving wildass pervs down deep. Makes you wonder about the glue that holds society together, doesn't it?" (We were balled up together. If someone had pushed us, we would have rolled.) "And not so deep at that, come to think of it. Throw a little muff their way and they turn into instant whoremasters. Of course, there were a few eunuchs and churchy types who wouldn't take the bait. There's the low-wattage type who wouldn't recognize his own fantasy if it sat on his face. But they're few and far between. Besides, we figured the overspending didn't have to be all that heavy to sink the program. If every manager we had on film played ball with us and spent a few extra thousand a week, the program would have gone belly up long before the first Scimitar came off the line. Senator Leander and his ratpack would have come on like a Guatemalan gunboat. We were using that dumb son of a bitch against his own interests, but he was too busy listening to his own bullshit to catch on to the scam. Typical, I guess."

248　•　•

"But the funding—"

"Right. Turned out to be a cost-plus deal after all. Thanks to the camel jockeys. We weren't on top of that. We knew the Sheik and his cronies wanted a big hunk of Dynablast, but we didn't know how hot he was for Scimitar itself. We thought he was leading the funding for Scimitar just to get into American aerospace. Just the opposite was true. The contracts were rewritten about a month ago, bringing the Arab commitment up to ninety-nine percent. Byron Towne worked his own con on the Sheik. He convinced the old goat that there were unforeseen complications, political and technical, and the Sheik fell for it and agreed to a new arrangement. He gave Towne a blank check. And that, Ponce, blew us out of the ball game."

Skylor Blue's picture came on the TV set suddenly. "Those goddamned Arabians have got peckers big as your arm!" he said, and faded.

Spear punched out some numbers and a view of the surrounding desert came on. He was upset. Suddenly the reason came to me: Blue was monitoring us. Spear was telling me all this because he'd been instructed to. Well, well, well.

"Spear," I said, feeling nasty. "Why did Carp kill Lisa?"

"You mean Dennison, Ponce. Dennison killed her. Try to remember that. Gil Dennison is taking the fall. Count your blessings while you can." He played with the remote control again, and there, under the watchful gaze of Fred MacMurray, writhed the fierce two-backed beast that couldn't get enough of itself. Tongues, lips, tits, arms, balls, semen, spit, hair, sheening sweat, goo, fingers-in-flesh, flesh-on-flesh, the spasms of simultaneous release. Then Blue again, smiling, serene, benevolent cathode-ray deity on electron wings.

"That's one of the most charming *six-à-neuf* engagements I believe I've ever seen," he said. "One has the sense of total commitment to the act per se, beyond the usual hesitations of self. Really, a *transcendent* performance. I congratulate you."

"I think," I said, searching for an object of proper mass, "I think I've had just about enough."

● ● 249

The oscilloscope wasn't as heavy as I'd thought it was. I swung it by its carrying handle, like a hammer thrower, and let it sail into the TV image, which popped very nicely, sending a shower of little swords through the room.

22

"I don't think I'm on the roster," I said.

She looked at me, then at the list of names again. "Oh yes you are. Arjay Ponce, right? You're right here. Number twenty-nine. Shall we go?"

She invited me into a wheelchair. I shrugged.

"Oh, come on, Mr. Ponce. Be a sport." She was a small, birdlike woman; perky, efficient, crisp. She took my hand and pulled me out of bed. "It's all *right*. I'm on the nursing staff. Miss Simms, and I know what I'm doing."

I'd been left alone for days and felt good. My strength was back and my head was clear. Whether it was the sheep fetus or just the course of nature, I didn't know and didn't care. "All right," I said. "I'll go. But I'm not going to be wheeled."

"Suit yourself," she said, suddenly indifferent. Her friendliness was strictly professional technique.

"Where's your on-off switch?" I asked.

She looked me over, coolly, feature by feature. "Let's say you're not my type, sir," she said.

"That's not what I meant," I said, but she had walked briskly away, her crisp butt vibrant above the speed of her little feet.

An old man with a bad case of the shakes walked to center stage and said into the microphone there: "This is lecture fourteen, entitled *Let's Look Again at Serfdom.*" There was scattered applause.

The old man left the stage. Wally Hardmarket entered. She was greeted by enthusiastic shouts. The man seated next to me said, "I adore that old babe. Her mind works like a shredder. You know what I mean?" I smiled, nodded, kept clapping.

The lecture itself was boring. Wally Hardmarket took us through the reigns in Russia of Alexis, Theodore III, Ivan V, Peter the Great, and Catherine. The nature of peasant revolt was her theme. She took the Don Cossacks to task with great vehemence, accusing them of mindless atrocities against the "paradivine personality." She gave a historical outline of the decline of powers rightfully accorded to the paradivine personality not only in Russia but in many other countries. She proved to us inductively that the contemporary chaos was a direct consequence of the malignant notion that rule by the mob was somehow a superior form of government than rule by the paradivine personality. "Society," she said, "has emasculated itself, beheaded itself, and clothed the mutilated remains in egalitarian slogans." She was in top form, and her audience responded to every inflection, every pause, every ironic interrobang. "No primitive," she said, "from Maori to Tlingit, would dream of taking a course of action based on a popular ballot. The very idea would make them sick with terror. They *depended* on the paradivine personality of their leadership to show them the correct way."

I began to understand. Scimitar, by disarming nations and individual citizens, would guarantee the future: No one nation could accrue the power to impose its social, political, and economic arrangements on another. This clearly was offensive to Wally and her audience. But there was another ore obvious, consideration. Scimitar meant the death of the efense industry itself. Once operational, Scimitar would re-re the arms industry. Dynablast, UJV, Boeing, Lockheed, orthrup, Grumman, General Dynamics, North American, nd so on, would have to close their doors for keeps. Con-acts for civilian projects—rapid transit systems, sewage dis-osal, alternate sources of energy production, the manu-cture of synthetic building materials—would not keep ore than one or two of the giant corporations with their undreds of thousands of employees busy. As I saw it, the reat wasn't against high-minded timeless ideals. It was gainst the mundane, immediate economics. By definition, e paradivine personality would do all right for itself, re-ardless of how well it was armed, in the new, fangless, ocial arrangement. Cream rises to the top no matter what ape the bottle. No, the real issue was the survival of the rgest industrial complex the world has ever known.

Therefore, sabotage. A reverse-Luddite sabotage, carried ut by the white-collar set. But that scheme was decommis-oned. What, then, were these people doing here? What lans were cooking offstage? I looked the crowd over. All niling men and women of distinction, confident, happy, rilling to the relentless logic of their favorite paradivine ersonality.

"History is a snake in the grass," said Wally Hard-arket. "Better yet, it's a tricky, multilayered mosaic. It's ery easy to see how so many people have been fooled into elieving it's all relative. Gosh, but I'd like to give that Ein-ein a healthy kick in his moldy old rump! Looking down at e mosaic from the vertex of time—the present—the mosaic eems lovely in its diversity. To the little people-atoms down ere who happen to live in and compose the mosaic, that iversity must often seem more a *per*versity. Be that as it ay, to enter the realm of disengaged relativistic interpreta-on of the past, is to stumble into the yawning gates of hell self!"

The applause for this was wildly enthusiastic. One b
one the audience stood up and cheered. Someone began
chant. Others picked it up, and soon the entire auditoriun
was ringing with it:

> *O Wally mine,*
> *You're paradivine!*

When the uproar began to fade, Wally continued: "The
would program Arbiter to consider the mosaic relativistically
No one single element under the sword's cutting edge woul
be valued more than another. Think about it! Under it
guidelines, the Conquistadors would never have sailed, th
Roman legions would have milled about in Italy, Englan
would not have ruled the waves, the Germans would hav
been held to clockmaking, the Japanese would have been for
ever thought of as 'those cute little doll-people.' Civilization
indeed, would have been effectively constipated. Blocked
locked, and understocked."

"Hell on earth," said the man next to me.

I said, "What?"

"Nine-tenths of the world's population doesn't thin
clearly," he explained.

"Oh. I see."

He put his hand on mine. Squeezed. *"Do* you?" h
asked, earnestly, his eyes misting over.

"One-tenth of the world's population thinks clearly,"
said.

"Exactly! Exactly!" he said, patting my hand.

"By sheer dint of numbers alone," said Wally, her voic
trembling now under the weight of her worst fears, "the ig
noble, the devilish, the stupid, the corrupt, the nihilistic, th
perverse, the bland, the incompetent, the nay-sayers, th
mugwumps—and you know well who I mean—*would suf*
focate the gifted few!"

"We need to protect ourselves," said my companion.

"The gifted few?"

254 • •

"Precisely! Precisely!" He walloped my shoulder with his tiny hand, blinking back tears.

I looked up at the ceiling. A small bird had accidentally entered the auditorium. It was looking desperately for the sky. The sky had betrayed it. It had suddenly turned opaque and limited. The bird called out to sky-as-it-once-had-been. Its voice was shrill with the urgency of its message. Sky-as-it-once-had-been did not hear. It was locked outside the dome, preening itself against the hard gray sand of the desert. It did not notice the absence of the little bird. It did, however, welcome an interesting hawk from a mountainous place far to the north and showed it a nice fat lizard to eat. The lizard saw the shadow of the hawk. But, because the hawk was a stranger to this desert, the lizard did not see in the silhouette the shape of danger.

"My spirit is weary," said Wally Hardmarket. "And my body is sick."

The audience made doting sounds of encouragement. Wally held up her hand. "Weary, sick, yes, but not dead. Weary, sick, yes, but not confused. Weary, sick, yes, but not *defeated*."

The audience roared. The man next to me nudged my ribs. He was smiling, lips tightening in the grip of a terrible sentiment until the dull white gums were exposed. "God bless her!" he said. Part of the audience heard him, picked up the phrase. "God bless her, God bless her!" they chanted, with increasing good cheer, and the auditorium shook.

After Wally's talk, a film was shown. It was very much like the Disneyesque film I'd seen at Dynablast that illustrated the mission of Scimitar. This film was much shorter, had no distinguished narrator, and its main focus of attention was not on the orbiting super gasers, but on two very odd satellites labeled Alpha and Omega. Alpha and Omega were shaped roughly like human skulls. They were very large, the size of bungalows. To illustrate their size, the twin satellites were shown side by side in a parking lot. A Volkswagen bus was parked between them. A man got out of the bus and stood next to one of the satellites. He climbed into and sat on the lower teeth of what appeared to be an enormous mouth.

Alpha and Omega in orbit moved suavely among the tight formations of Scimitars. They seemed to have a proprietary interest in the big cylinders. Alpha's orbit was essentially polar and Omega's equatorial, but they had a far ranging mobility that allowed them to change altitude and to roam laterally at will. When their orbits intersected, they moved together briefly, exchanged what would appear to be words of affection, (the animator achieved this effect by giving complex expression to the otherwise rigid mouths), the great cyclops lenses of the quasi-faces gazing at one another with the sadness of love sacrificed to a greater cause—sort of a robotic Beatrice and Paolo. In fact, the music which accompanied this dance was from Tchaikovsky's *Francesca da Rimini,* and it seemed touchingly appropriate.

There was triumph as well as sadness in all of this, and the sensitized audience was alive to both moods. After the film ended, they were stone silent for a good thirty seconds Then slowly, one by one, they began to applaud. The applause was moderate, respectful, and lasted five minutes.

23

'So, you're on the roster now," said Spear. He was waiting for me in my room.

I shrugged. He was in a plastic bag.

"There's no accounting for taste," he said glumly.

Actually, it was a plastic suit. It had arms and legs and a neck hole. The TV set—a new one—was on. The glittering eye of the bull was attentive. We were not alone.

"Get a wiggle on, Dame," said Skylor Blue. The TV picture was rolling. When it stopped, Blue was on it. He looked bad. Very tired, face somewhat swollen, skin splotched with what could have been urobilin, eyes dull under the slitted lids. His lips were cracked and dry, and the darting tongue that tried to wet them was black and stiff-looking.

"Put this on," said Spear, handing me a package. It was another plastic suit.

"Why should I?" I said.

"Come on, Ponce, don't play the hardass. It's not convincing. Just put on the suit."

"Suppose I told you to shove that suit? Suppose I told you to take a flying jump at that suit?"

"Please, Arjay," said Blue. "Do it for me."

"You owe him," said Spear. "He put you on the roster."

"Why did Carp kill Lisa Dennison?" I said, ignoring Spear.

Blue released a great, angry belch of air. His lips curled out from the teeth and flapped. He lost his composure. He couldn't talk. "Puh, puh, yaroot!" he said.

"Go ahead," said Spear. "Press your luck."

"Put-on-the-suit-Mr.-Ponce," said Blue, struggling for control. "I-will-tell-you-everything-when-you-get-here."

The TV switched to a view of the desert horizon. A dark band of dust lay on it, a sandstorm. "Your last chance, Ponce," said Spear. "Put it on or don't. Frankly, I'd just as soon you refused. I think Mr. Blue would come around to my way of thinking about you. You'd be off that roster before you could work up a mouth full of spit."

I believed him. The threat wasn't from him this time. It was from the air, the light, the eye of the bull, the sandstorm on the horizon. I sensed an impatience, an urgency; a straining in the underpinnings of the condominium itself as if the struggle against inertia was close to success and the whole works would soon tear itself free of the desert and fly off the planet forever. I put on the suit.

I followed Spear to an elevator. He pushed the *down* button. "I thought he'd have the penthouse," I said.

The doors slid open. "Agoraphobe," he said. "All that desert out there scares him spitless."

The floor of the elevator dropped away briskly, and for one weightless moment I believed I had seen daylight for the last time. It was seconds before the soles of my feet caught up with the floor, and we rode straight down at high speed for what seemed like minutes before a hard deceleration tested my determination to stay upright. The doors slid open then and we stepped into a bright tunnel, big enough to hold boxcars. "Follow close behind me, Ponce," said Spear. "Don't straggle. Don't make sudden moves. Breathe easy. And try not to sweat. Mr. Blue can't take the smell of sweat." Then, to nothing visible, he said, "Damon Spear. Roster Number

258 • •

J-188650. And Arjay Ponce. Temporary Roster Number J-X-999999. Permission requested to advance."

A loudspeaker came on. A female voice said, "Are you scrubbed?"

"Condition P for Peter," said Spear.

A rainbow of light fell across our path. "Proceed to position X-ray," said the voice.

Spear walked slowly to a point within the bright spectrum. I followed. "Sterilizer," said Spear, explaining the process.

"Proceed to position Yankee," said our electronic guide.

We walked to a telephone booth. "You first," said Spear. "Count to three and then get out. Four will cook your ass."

I went in, gave it a quick onetwothree, ducked out. Nothing noticeable happened. Then Spear went in.

"Hard microwave frisker," he explained, emerging.

"Frisker? How could we have any weapons on us?"

"Don't, Ponce, be naive. You could have a pound of relignite sewn into your thoracic cavity, for all anyone knows."

"Proceed to position Zulu," said the loudspeaker.

Position Zulu was the threshold to a vault door. It was circular, at least ten feet in diameter. We waited. Wheels and gears within the disk were moving. Motors clicked on and off, paused and whirred, as intricate combinations, probably from a computer, were fed into them. This went on for a few minutes. Then everything was completely still. The stillness was long and worried, as if the mechanical mind that governed the door was having serious second thoughts about letting us in. Then a groaning electric motor came on, and slowly, one inch at a time, the great door, a cylindrical plug, moved away from us.

It took my eyes a while to adjust to the soft lights. The room was plush. A well-furnished apartment, with a thick pile carpet. There were view windows that overlooked the twinkling lights of a large city. The air was sweetened with

incense or perfume. In sharp contrast to this, a bank of mur
muring computer panels filled an entire wall. In the center o
the room, covered by a white screen, was a raised dais. A
long, shallowly inclined ramp descended from the dais
Muzak violins played medleys of well-knowns arias.

We waited. The room seemed empty. I looked at Spear
He was standing at attention, looking toward the screened
dais. He was sweating heavily. He was nervous. I cleared my
throat.

An enormous grunting belch, originating on the dais
made the screen flap. The noise was followed by severa
lesser eruptions. Then a voice I knew said: "Damn, damn
damn. I'm having a fierce time with the pressure control
Damon, check on Fleckman's progress, will you?"

"Right," said Spear, spinning on his heel. He walked
quickly out of the room, his plastic suit crackling. The big
steel door closed silently behind him.

A light came on within the screened dais. The silhouette
of a large, powerful man filled the panel of the screen tha
was directly in front of me. The man was seated in a chair
leaning forward thoughtfully. *"Dica,"* he said. *"L'aguilla es
colta."*

It was Blue, the legendary billionaire, the man whose
likeness had been torn to shreds and left on Lisa Dennison's
carpet. But the silhouette was all wrong. The figure projected
against the screen was big, vital, powerful. Blue was a very
small man, not much over five feet tall, and had to be nearly
eighty years old by now.

"Pardon me?" I said.

"It's Italian. It means, 'Speak, the eagle listens.' A
famous prefuturist poet, a favorite of Mussolini's, used to re
ceive visitors with that marvelous phrase. Very forceful
wouldn't you say?"

He didn't wait for an answer. He began to recite:

> *O ship of steel*
> *straight and stiff*

plunging lovely
as a naked weapon,
alive, pumping
as if the ribbed bulkhead
contained a terrible heart! . . .

A great bellowing interrupted the cadence. Several more
followed; great, rending blasts. "Ouch!" said Blue. "Damn,
damn, *damn*. Some kind of bloody random squib is—*goddammit!*—don't be one bit surprised if the top of my head
flies out at you—these circuits—the wires are gold, the tran-
sistors are handmade—ouch!—you'd think, wouldn't you,
you'd think—WROPP!—Oh dear God—this is *embarrassing*."
He calmed himself. The sounds of deep breathing filled
the apartment. The breathing slowed. The interrupting blasts
simmered down to unobtrusive sputterings and sighs, then
stopped altogether. "Sorry, sorry, sorry," said Blue. "I get a
little excited. I get a little freaky. I had to leave the seminary
because of my temperament. Loved Rome, hated the excitement. Brought on fits. Did you know I once studied for the
priesthood? Well, I *did*. Probably should have stayed with it.
Considering. Well, here I am, and that's that, right? You
know, what I really hate is incompetence. Bunglers make my
guts rumble. Mistakes are one thing, agreed, but repeated
mistakes are something else. When that Fleckman yahoo gets
down here I am going to hand him his head. I know, I know.
He's the man with the reputation. I hired him on that basis.
What other basis is there? Jesus, I am not running a beauty
contest! I ask for results only! It's the only way to run a bus
ine. 'Top man in the field,' they told me. Well, they were
wrong. It's not unusual though for a man to gain a reputation
he flat doesn't deserve. I admit, I don't understand the mechanism of those politics, but I've seen it time and again. Take
that German rocket expert you've got over there at Dynablast.
He isn't fit to wipe Von Braun's ass, and yet—but wait,
forgive me, Arjay. Surely you have other things on your
mind than my silly old troubles, *n'est-ce pas?*"

I nodded.

"The death, for example, of that awful Denniso woman."

"For example."

"But why do you bother with the small questions, Arjay Surely that rather insignificant event is overshadowed i your mind by our larger purposes, purposes you must hav guessed by now, right?"

I didn't nod. A video screen in one of the compute panels came on. It took me a while to understand what I wa watching. The man on the screen was not caressing th woman in his arms. He was strangling her. He was enjoyin himself immensely. It was slow work. He made it slow. H was doing it in front of a mirror. Behind the mirror was camera lens. He looked into the lens and made his larg biceps bulge mightily. He loved their power. He admired th steep, unnatural arc the biceps made between the shoulde and elbow. The woman was half-sitting, half-reclining, he distorted face pleading with the heedless killer, her lon; sunny legs flexed against the coming dark tide, the bare heel drumming the floor lightly. Then her bulging eyes becam cloudy and indifferent to the process that was taking place i her body. It was at this moment the strangler mounted her hoping, evidently, to time his orgasm to her death spasm When he was through he tied one end of a pair of pantyhos around her neck, picked her up in one arm, climbed up o the bed, and hung her from the light fixture. Satisfied with job well done, he tidied up the room, wrote the suicide note and left. The camera lingered for several morbid seconds o the dead girl, whose fingers still twitched.

"Ugly tragic horrid business," said Blue. "But quite un avoidable, given her treachery."

The lights went out on the dais. The screen in front o the ramp parted. A spider the size of a pony crawled dow the carpeted incline. On the dais, in front of a naked 200-wa bulb, a thoughtful, robust manikin sat. "I avoid such neces sary details" said the spider, "whenever possible. Oh, I don"

262 • •

shun responsibility for actions taken in my behalf. But what, after all, does it profit one to befoul himself with the offal and carrion of necessity when, in truth, there can be no progress without it? No, no, don't try to answer. The answer is obvious and remains unchanged down through the centuries."

I knew what I was looking at. There had been premonitions, warnings, hints. The movie, for example, that played over and over, was making a point. *The Head That Wouldn't Say Die*. Life imitates art. Especially *bad* art. Still, a deep refusal to recognize the truth made the thing before me unreal, partially invisible, a clever deception to test my sanity. I stared and stared until it all registered. Yes, I knew what I was looking at: a severed human head smiling winsomely, embedded in a mechanical spider, eyes glittering, brows raised expectantly, waiting for the compliment, the praise, the dumbstruck gurglings of awe.

I knew also that it was possible: The Russians had accomplished it with animals years ago. No one believed them at the time. The announcement of their success with the severed heads of dogs came at a time of blustering chauvinism during which they claimed to have invented the airplane, the telescope, the internal combustion engine, the telephone, the conveyor belt, mass production, the wheel, farming, the fish hook. The photographs looked tampered with. *All* photographs coming out of Russia in those days looked tampered with. It was as if they had become so accustomed to lying that even the few truths they possessed absolutely were doctored up out of habitual blindness to simple, unadorned fact. Pretty young girls superimposed on the seats of tractors superimposed on good rich earth superimposed against tropical skies, trees in blossom superimposed, the blossoms superimposed on the branches, superimposed birds singing false songs . . . the utopian message totally undermined by the inferior techniques of their photo labs. And then came the pictures of the dogs' heads sticking out of panels, the tongues rolling, and several superimposed scientists milling around importantly, each clearly involved in different contexts. But

• • 263

later reports in American and British scientific journals certified the Russians' success, though their motives were cautiously scorned.

"Why the brown study, Arjay?" said the head of Skylor Blue.

Oh yes, life imitates bad art: Another movie came to mind. A tasteless chiller about the restoration of the Third Reich through this method. The angry head of Goebbels barking orders from a little wooden cabinet studded with gadgetry. Goering whistling "Deutschland Uber Alles" in a galvanized tub. Hitler himself, somewhat charred, going over the revisions to the sequel of *Mein Kampf* while bolted in a formica bassinet. Life imitates schmaltz. But the hard edges of reality quickly unschmaltz it. The ships of *Destination Moon* didn't hold a candle to *Apollo 11*. Yes, I knew what I was looking at, knew it was real, believed in it absolutely, right down to the giddy marrow.

And my body knew what it was looking at too: Life without it was possible. It recognized immediately what the head in the mechanical spider meant to it: The body, the mortal coil, the source of despair, the thing that gets sick, manufactures aneurysms, tumors, cataracts, piles, stones in the bladder, limestone in the arteries, the shakes, the drops, the shits, the tears; the thing that hurts you so terribly, the thing that finally betrays the clever, efficient brain by withering like a leaf, is *superfluous*. ("The body's only purpose is to carry the brain," said Edison, and he should have known.) And a hard tremor rolled through my bowels, climbed steadily toward the already terrorized heart. The brain, on the other hand, knew it was in the presence of . . . no other word for it . . . *salvation!* Even as the body threatened to empty itself through all likely orifices, the mind grew flirtatious. Skylor Blue, his dark eyes shining with pleasure at my reactions, watched my ambiguous convulsions. The fact that he was involved in blackmail, sabotage, murder, and possibly treason, seemed remote and irrelevant compared to the

dark miracle that grinned up at me from its chromium apparatus.

"Well," said the cheerful billionaire, "how do you like
me so far?"

24

A small man, middle-aged and balding, stiff with the con-
strained arrogance of the servile, wheeled in refreshments on
a covered food cart. The head called the little servant
"Chuckie." The cart was loaded with ribbon sandwiches,
fruits, nuts, and things to drink. Blue ran his black tongue
over his leathery lips in greedy anticipation. The dark eyes
sparkled with arachnoid innocence. "Yummers," he said.

When he spoke a compressor was activated. The compressor was on a cart and connected to the spider-vehicle by
a two-inch-diameter hose and an electrical cable. When Blue
moved, the compressor followed, chugging faithfully behind.
The hose, apparently, provided a ready stream of air to Blue's
pharynx. The air hose and electrical cable were connected to
a flange just behind the head.

"One of the few sensuous pastimes I have left," he explained, the eight jointed rods under him flexing silently,
allowing him to look down on the display of treats. "Please
sit down and join me, won't you?"

Chuckie brought me a chair. Before he left us, he placed
a large pan under Blue's vehicle.

"You won't mind giving me a hand?" said Blue, to me.

I shook my head no, a horrified no, meaning *No, I don't*

266 • •

want any part of this, but he understood the opposite, murmuring, "Good, good," the compressor turning over gently,
functioning very well now, allowing Blue an impressive
range of tone and emphasis, allowing him to boom good-
naturedly in the manner of a hungry baron of industry,
"Suppose, then, we start with the Galiano, eh?"

"The Galiano?" I said, not questioning his choice, just
reluctant to move.

"I know, I know," he said. "It's generally considered an
after-luncheon liqueur, but I like to have it first. My taste
buds aren't what they used to be, you see. The Galiano has a
stimulating effect on them. Sort of snaps them awake."

I started to pour the bright yellow liqueur into a small
glass.

"No, no, *no*," said Blue, irritated. "Don't use that glass.
Use the stein, the *stein.*"

I poured an inch into the beer mug.

"I did not say *when,* Arjay," he scolded. "Did you hear
me say *when?*"

I kept pouring. Filled the mug to the brim. "How's that,
Mr. Blue?"

"Please," he said. "I hate formality. Call me Sky. We're
both westerners, aren't we? Back east life is different. Back
there only the press calls Rocky Rocky. His people call him
Mr. Rockefeller. That's the way they feel on top of things
back there. Mister, sir, your honor, your lordship, madam,
mizz, your ladyship, your fine feathered filigreed cockhood,
my lady cunning roundheels, cardinal lardass whosizt, ha-
ha-ha, kiss my globetrotting gash, your honor, phonies,
Arjay, phonies, phonies, phonies, to a man, and we don't
hold with it west of the Big Muddy, do we?"

"Sky," I said, raising the stein.

"Give me," he said, childishly. His eyes were closed and
his lips, trembling with need, puckered out toward the approaching rim of the mug. I put the heavy glass to them and
poured.

It was like pouring water into a drain pipe. He had no

● ●   267

need to swallow. There was no danger of his choking. As I poured, I heard the Galiano hit the galvanized pan beneath the vehicle. Suddenly, the compressor came on, full power. A trumpeting belch shot the last few ounces of Galiano across the room with fire-hose strength.

"Sheeeeee-it!" said Blue, trying to modulate the heavy stream of air. "Hooo-fwoooop! Fah-pong! Kraik-ooo-czurgie!"

The compressor slowed, having played its mindless little joke. "That-goddamned-Fleckman-booby-idiot-I-will-have-his-ass-I-will-have-his-ass-MROP-MROP!"

"Are you all right, Mr. Blue?"

"I said call me Sky, goddammit. You thick or something?"

"Sky. Are you—"

"No I'm not all right. That *hurts*, boy. Nearly blows the top of my head off. Rattles the sinuses. Bejasus."

I poured him a little more Galiano. He accepted it, closed his eyes as the thick sweet stuff coated his battered vocal cords.

"Give me a sandwich, Arjay," he said, the compressor behaving civilly again. "The Braunschweiger. Do you see the Braunschweiger there? It's next to the tongue."

I slid a wedge of bread and meat paste into the dark hole. The jaws worked perfectly. They took six or seven strong chews. Then I heard the dull thud of mangled snack hitting the pan. In all, I fed Blue two dozen sandwiches and two fifths of Galiano. It took about five minutes. When he was finished, Chuckie came back into the room and removed the pan from under Blue's vehicle. It was filled with a disgusting stew of Galiano, bread, Braunschweiger, tongue, figs, pears, almonds, cashews, and the oddly unmolested wedges of a Mandarin orange. The little attendant washed Blue's face with a damp napkin, sponged down the bright legs of the spider, and left, carrying the heavy pan.

"Ah, but you haven't touched a thing, Arjay," said the sated head.

I held up my hand, shook my head.

"Come on, now. Where's your appetite? A man has to eat. Dig in, dig in! I insist."

"No thanks, Sky. I'd rather—I mean, I'm just not very hungry."

"I don't disgust you, do I?"

"Oh no. No no. Not at all. Certainly not."

"Fibber."

"No. I mean it."

"*No. I mean it,*" he mocked.

I picked up a tongue sandwich. It smelled like the inside of a shoe.

"Go on, go on," he said, spidering from side to side nervously.

I popped the little sandwich into my mouth. Dry. Tasteless. I ate three quickly, washed them down with what I thought was water but turned out to be straight gin, a welcome shock to the jumpy interior, my first drink in days, maybe weeks. As I ate, Blue watched me closely. His chalky skin seemed stretched over the bones of his face like fine wrapping paper. His eyes burned with the lonely passion of the voyeur. I realized then what it was he wanted. I stopped gulping the little sandwiches and, cheered on by the gin, began to chew slowly, elaborately, as if each bite were a love affair between my teeth. I closed my eyes, proving my lust, my rapture, faked two or three discreet belches. Blue's mouth went slack, the little black tongue ran listlessly over the dry lips, the teeth glowed like amber bulbs in the dark jaw, spit tried to form but the ducts were filled with dust, and little forlorn clucking noises, like the distant tapping of miners trapped in a pocket of air one mile below the waning afternoon, filled the room.

"Oh bravo," he said weakly. "Bravo, bravo, bravo."

The head dozed. Or maybe it died. It was immobile, the immobility of a shut-down machine. The jaw was frozen slightly open. The eyes were slitted, showing a film of blind mucous, and no pulse beat in the thin veins of his temples. This was the Skylor Blue in Lisa's photograph. No joke, no pop artist's invention, but Blue himself. Lisa. Blue had ordered her death. The reason, which was probably obvious, shouldn't have mattered to me. Not now. But it did. It did.

The erratic compressor chugged into life suddenly and an explosive gust of wind wrenched the head against its moorings, the hard lips flapping a sharp raspberry at me, making the eyes pop open momentarily, but he did not wake. I got up, walked over to the big spider, examined it closely. If I wanted it, if I really wanted it, here it was, on a silver platter. *Revenge.* Seeming to sense my thoughts, the spider raised one of its forward legs and pointed at me. The foot of the leg was a hemispheric suction cup. It hovered an inch from my chest. I backed away, toured the room.

The computer was busy, chattering lustily to itself. I went to the panel that held the large TV tube. There was a toggle switch marked "Library." I flipped it on.

Skin, miles of it. Some scenes I recognized, others were new. I saw myself with Lisa. I saw the other managers exercising their unlocked fantasies. I saw a writhing company of strangers. I saw Carp, self-consciously acting to a rudimentary script: *The Crazed Reverend And His Wayward Flock.* I saw twin Nordic blonds giving Byron Towne a sponge bath. Then Alice, with me, oh Lord, and I hurt her, hurt her mercenary little ass, my crazy face above the fierce laboring loins charged with duty, Higher Cause glowing in the whites of my madman's eyes. Then the bolt of sobering pain, the lunatic clutching his chest, rolling away from his task, the quick camera zooming in on his struggle: agony, true agony, is just as titillating as true ecstasy.

"My hobby," said Blue, awake again, joining me at the tube. "Films, I mean. I love them dirty. Why not? What's more interesting than people having a good time? I'm piecing together a fantastic full-length feature, cinema verité, that will stun the industry when it's released. Oh yes, I'm turning

270 • •

pro. It is going to be a corker. Death, sex, violence, scumbags, excrement by the yard, food, blood, the intestines of animals. A feast for the eye."

I switched off the library.

"*Dica*, Arjay," said Blue, his voice hoarse from the random hurricanes of air. "*L'anguilla escolta.*"

I started to say what was on my mind. I'd been making connections. It had to do with Wally Hardmarket, Alpha and Omega, Scimitar, UJV, Dynablast, the Arabs, and the world situation. A volatile combination guaranteed to fillip the cerebellum without mercy. But I was interrupted before I could start.

A loudspeaker on one of the computer's panels came on and a haughty, nasal voice, neither male nor female, began to speak.

"What good is the body?" it said.

"The body is God's little joke," answered another voice, snottier than the first.

Blue smiled. "That's pretty good, isn't it?" he said. He scooted across the room playfully. When he reached the far wall, he extended his first two legs and gripped the rough grain of the paneling. Other legs followed suit, and Blue, trailing hose and cable behind him, climbed up the wall. He stopped halfway to the ceiling, then scampered laterally a few yards, chuckling happily.

"What is the purpose of sex?" said the first voice.

"To amuse the deserving brain," was the answer.

I sat down. The catechism continued.

"What is a heart?"

"A piece of tripe."

"What is a liver?"

"Dog food."

"What's a kidney worth?"

"A thimble full of piss."

This made Blue roar merrily. He began to climb again. When he reached the ceiling he hesitated only a moment.

• • 271

The air hose and cable played out from the service cart, giving Blue all the leeway he needed for his acrobatics. He walked across the ceiling as easily as he had walked on the floor.

"How does the brain regard the body?" asked the first voice.

"With fear, scorn, disgust, and loathing. A ghastly prison, an injustice, a false limitation, a crime against nature—"

"What, then, is the purpose of the evolution of the physical forms?"

"To nurture the brain until, fully developed, it can nurture itself. Period."

"What can a fully developed brain do?"

"Unshackle itself from the cesspool that hampers it, flee the fetid manure factory, escape the beastly abattoir—"

"In short—"

"Preserve the attainments of the individual mind."

"What does the individual mind, freed from the body, aspire to?"

"Naked power, immortality, congress with the stars, fun without end."

The catechism stopped. Blue, hanging directly over me, winked. "I suppose you're only one guess away from understanding everything, now, right Arjay?"

I nodded. "Those satellites, Alpha and Omega, they're meant to house you and someone else—"

"Wally Hardmarket."

"And since UJV has the contract for the Watchdog system, you probably have some scheme in mind to tie yourselves into the Arbiter computer. You aren't planning to wreck Dynablast's contract to produce Scimitars any longer because you want them for yourself."

"Right on!"

"All right, all right," I said, tapping the heel of my hand against my hot forehead, the hemispheres of my brain threatening to fuse. "Why was Lisa Dennison killed?"

272 • •

The head rolled its eyes and laughed. The compressor lost its restraint. Foghorns of mirth shook the walls. "Remarkable!" said Blue. His voice was like thunder. "Why on earth do you *care?*"

"I care."

"You didn't *love* her by any chance?"

"No. I didn't love her. I don't love anyone—" I stopped myself. Something shook me. I choked. The urge to confess was strong and inexplicable. I touched my face. It was wet. My throat felt raw. My mind stopped one inch short of a precipice. I held my breath. I pulled myself together.

"Tsk, tsk," said Blue. "My, but you're hard on yourself. It's all very simple. She was going to turn me in. To *Time.* She'd taken this snapshot during one of my naps with a miniature camera she smuggled in. She put it in a condom, slipped it into her twat. Clever, what? It was all inert plastic and rubber and it didn't register on the frisker. She'd contacted an editor. She had been my guest, you see. The editor said he'd give her a lot of money and all the free publicity she could use to start a movie career for herself. 'The Secret Life of Skylor Blue Exposed At Last.' You know the sort of thing I'm talking about. Trash. Our little Lisa wanted to be a star. She wanted her name in neon. She was a nasty little self-serving cunt. Aren't they all? Why am I telling you this? I suppose you think I *cared* for her. The way I rant. No. No. No. She let me . . . do things. She had remarkable titties. Her cleft. A perfect ax-cut in teak. She, she. You know what I mean, I'm sure. I'll tell you this: She could have been on the roster. But no. She chose betrayal. And for what? For what? The miserable little strumpet."

"So you sent Carp."

"We were also afraid she might have told you something. That's why we didn't want the police to have you. You really shouldn't have cut her down like that. Don't you know you can get in big trouble doing dumb things for no possible reason? After you turned up berserk in the mock-up, we

• • 273

brought you here. Turned out you didn't know anything at all! I guess the joke's on us."

I'm talking to a bodyless head, I told myself. *No you aren't,* I said. *You've been locked away for good. This is merely the vision of a blistered mind.* I tried to see past my hallucination, to the white walls of my cell, the faces of my loved ones pressing against the glass, the soft soothing strains of "Music for Meditation," the tranquilizing nurses fresh as mint, the bells, buzzers, the whispering voices, the smell of newly cut flowers.

"I didn't believe in the plan to begin with, anyway," said Blue. "It was Damon Spear's idea. Oh, it looked fine on paper. We ran it through the computer. The computer gave the go-ahead. We didn't, of course, program it efficiently. We didn't know at the time that those Arabian Diamond Jims were going to underwrite everything, regardless of overspending. I have to give credit to that boss of yours, Byron Towne. He's a good man. I dislike the man intensely, but he runs a tight con game over there. He put the Sheik in his pocket."

There was a lull. Even the computer slowed its chatter. I looked at the papery head of the spider. I felt something like pity. Pity, that wonderful luxury, had no business among my harassed mental processes. But it was there, anyway. Pity. Pity for this once dynamic industrialist. Pity for me. For Lisa. Pity for everyone in the sinking boat. "I'm no one," I said.

"True," said Blue. "Quite true. In terms of what counts. Your wife despises you. She will replace you with a more stable man. Your children will forget you, or remember you only in nightmares. Your career is gone. You have no friends. You are, in short, valueless to the world that nurtured you. You're just a turd, now, on the cemetery lawn."

Still, I told myself, *here I am, having an audience with Skylor Blue.* And, whatever it meant, I was on his roster.

"Valueless," Blue repeated. "To the world you left."

"Left?"

"Well, I mean, it's your *choice.* Far be it from me to twist your arm. I think, however, you'll see certain advantages in my offer.''

A leg rose toward me. The suction-cup foot touched my knee. A little vacuum sucked at the plastic skin affectionately.

25

"Their insidious object," said the narrator, "was multilateral disarmament. Arms, and the manufacture of arms, would have become obsolete. Civilization would have become, in effect, constipated. Blocked. Civilization, as you know, does not move on its own. The force of arms is always the necessary purgative. We must keep the channel to the future lubricated with the blood of the chimerical enemy."

On the screen a squadron of evil-looking Scimitars ganged up on an innocent munitions plant somewhere in New Jersey. Helpless men and women ran for their lives in the burning parking lots. "Listen to this," said the narrator, clearing his throat, as the renegade Scimitars zeroed in on new victims.

> Last night I saw the monster near: the big
> White monster that was like a lazy slug,
> That hovered in the air, not far away,
> As quiet as the black hawk seen by day.
> I saw it turn its body round about,
> And look my way; I saw its big, fat snout
> Turn straight toward my face . . . .

"Frightening, isn't it?" the narrator asked, interrupting himself. A close-up of a Scimitar menaced the viewer with the blunt phallic crown. The narrator continued:

> But soon its venom was discharged, and it,
> Knowing it had no more power to spit
> Death on the most defenseless English folk,
> Let out a large, thick cloud of its own smoke;
> And when the smoke had cleared away from there,
> I saw no sign of any monster near;
> And nothing but the stars to give alarm—
> That never did the earth a moment's harm.

The narrator paused again, took a deep breath, then read on, with great thumping emphasis:

> Oh, it was strange to see a thing like jelly,
> An ugly, boneless thing all back and belly,
> Among the peaceful stars—that should have been
> A mile deep in the sea, and never seen:
> A big, fat, lazy slug that, even then,
> Killed women, children, and defenseless men.

The poem was accompanied by a cello sawing out three notes of despair.

"C'est moi," said Blue. "On cello, believe it or not. I used to be good. Now I only get by."

"That wonderfully prophetic poem," said the narrator, "was written a long time ago. Still, it matches the sort of gloom that would have overcome us should the traitors of western civilization have succeeded."

The film was titled, *Our Hope For A Decent Future*. It was intended as indoctrination, once Blue and Wally Hardmarket were in control of the Scimitars.

"I suppose you're skeptical," said Blue.

"Skeptical?" I said, feeling the tidal gin numb the stanchions of ordinary logic. "About what?"

"My playing the cello. You wonder, *how*."

Chuckie came in, carrying a cello. He strapped it to a

portable post. He handed Blue a bow, and the spider foot grabbed it in a powerful suction. Blue, his face crimped with a terrible concentration, put the bow to the strings. Through the painful grating, I heard the first half-dozen notes of "Home Sweet Home." Then he dropped the bow, exhausted. Chuckie unstrapped the instrument and carried it, along with the portable post, out of the room. "Let's get shitfaced," said Blue, "I'm in the mood."

I offered him a shot of gin. He waved me off. I took the shot myself. "You said something about an offer," I said.

"Later, later. First I'm going to program myself for shit facedness. I can't metabolize alcohol, you realize, without the goddamned plumbing." He crawled over to the computer. He gave it vocal commands and the lights of the machine danced eagerly. "Hey, but don't you try to take advantage of me when I'm three sheets to the wind, you son of a gun, you," he said, scurrying up to me playfully. The spider legs flexed and the head rose up to nearly my height. Blue stared me in the eye. "I have not been drunk in months, Arjay. I feel like celebrating a little, now that everything's just about in place."

I nodded. The film was waxing toward its victorious finale. The narrator was fairly singing his lines. Alpha and Omega were being transported to their orbital positions by large space shuttles. Once in orbit, the skull-shaped satellites opened their jaws in a robotic grin of triumph. They turned their great lenses toward the camera and zoomed in on the viewer. "Alpha and Omega, Shepherds of the World!" boomed the narrator, almost overcome with joy.

"Those big objective lenses," said Blue, "can pick up hanky-panky in a haystack from a height of two hundred miles."

"What are the jaws for?" I asked.

"Drink up, Arjay, you're lagging behind."

I downed another shot.

"I feel like singing," said Blue. "You know 'My Blue Heaven'?"

278 ● ●

"But first—"

"No. But not first." He gave a hoarse imitation of Mel Tormé. Mel Tormé without an ear.

He waved a suction cup at me, inviting me to join in. I poured myself another shot of gin, watched a grinning Omega put a dozen Scimitars through a kind of close-order drill, after which they set fire to Czechoslovakia.

"Oh, come on," said Blue. "Don't go sullen on me." He tugged my sleeve. "All right, all right. You asked about the jaws. You want to know why we are going to have jaws."

I nodded.

"Well, use your head, man! What do people usually have jaws for?"

"Eating?"

"Exactly. Follow me."

He crawled toward the vault door, the compressor rolling behind him. I followed. The door opened. We went out into the cavernous exterior. On a flatbed truck, evidently having been summoned by Blue, it stood, huge, awesome, glistening gunmetal blue. The great eye, a fifty-inch lens, regarded us with godlike objectivity. The opened jaw with its twin rows of chromium-plated teeth, seemed in the act of forming a single syllable of undeniable veracity. The sight struck a primitive chord deep within me, and I had to resist the urge to fall on my knees and babble for mercy.

"The design was promoted by psychological consider-ations rather than merely functional ones," said Blue. "Sort of makes you want to mess your bloomers, doesn't it?"

From the far end of the tunnel, two attendants brought in a calf. The calf was led up a ramp toward the jaws of the satellite. The jaws widened silently, permitting easier access. The calf began to bleat wildly, resisting its dimly perceived fate. The attendants shoved the animal past the teeth and jumped back. The calf tried to scramble out, but the jaws closed, quick and sure, on the soft flesh. Then the satellite chewed at an unhurried mechanical pace, and the chromium teeth became slick with blood.

"Pow!" said Blue. "Something else, right?"

The bulk of the calf disappeared. The attendants hosed out the mouth and rinsed the teeth. They went to the rear of the satellite and opened a panel. The compacted remains of the calf plopped out onto the truck bed. An attendant hosed the offal from the truck. A gutter, ridged into the tunnel's floor, accepted the mess.

"Actually," said Blue, "this is all Wally's doing. Has to do with her theory that the little people out there need mythological certainties to guide their workaday lives. They'll be required to undergo puromycin therapy to scrub the memory of the past clean. Of course, when the present generation dies out, that won't be necessary. It's going to be a hard program to administer, at best. Frankly, I have my doubts. The idea is to build new libraries with new versions of the past. You understand all this?"

"Understand?"

"Now that calf was only for demonstration purposes. In actual practice, we intend to use people. Criminals, murderers, the congenitally useless. We'll put a nightgown on some mugwump and he'll sprinkle the victim with Wildroot or something and then a host of citizens will chuck him into the jaws. This will all take place in Nebraska once a year or so. We'll shuttle down for the occasion. It'll be during a football halftime, complete with bands, pom-poms, card sections, the works. Got the picture?"

"The picture?"

"I gather you are a bit lost. No matter. It's just that once Wally and I are up there in orbit, controlling those big dongs, we just don't want to be treated as, uh, *threats*. We don't want to be looked at as some kind of doomsday-oriented crackpots motivated by a rarified form of common everyday paranoia. No sir. We'd like to have a little respect. We'd like Mr. and Mrs. Smith to look up into the starry night from the security of their patio and say, 'Alpha and Omega have made all this peace and quiet possible.' Say, listen, we're not just doing this to zap the baddies. We're going to comunicate with the *folks*. We're going to keep a sympathetic ar available to John Doe. You got a complaint—well, just ial up your neighborhood communicator and he'll turn it in. lpha—that's me—will handle the menfolk, and Wally—mega—will take on the ladies. We're aiming to be a locally mnipotent benevolent society of two."

I had a list of questions. "Won't the manufacture of arms ecome extinct anyway?" They were dumb questions. I pur-ied this one anyway. "I mean, that film talked about the in-ustry being wiped out by Scimitar. Isn't that why you ranted to wreck it in the first place? Because it meant the nd of the defense industry?"

Blue chuckled noisily, the compressor threatening to iisfire again. "Heck no! I mean, heck yes! That's why we id it, at *first*. But things got more complicated. When Wally ame into the picture, she brought in a lot of new ideas we adn't thought of. She is a gem. Our own ideas were sort of alf-baked and limited. Wally put everything on a more ing-range, philosophical level. She had the big picture in iind right from the start. That lady's nobody's fool, I want to ell you! Then when she discovered she had cancer, that sort f made everything fall into place. Oh, we'll keep the indus-y, don't worry about that. We *need* conventional warfare. It iakes life more tolerable. God, how boring endless peace rould be! Wally and I will just sort of make sure things don't et out of hand. Those who want a little action in their lives an have it. Those who want to stay home and watch the ac-ion on TV can have *that*, too. The perfect arrangement, if ou ask me."

"Wally Hardmarket has cancer?" I asked.

"Shot through with it, from cervix to armpits. We de-ided then that there should be two sets of brains in orbit—a ystem of checks and balances. A male-female biarchy. Irjay, we're going to get married. With her power of abstract easoning, and my practical knowhow, we're the perfect eam. She thinks of consequences, and I think of how to iake those consequences happen or not happen."

● ● 281

"You want to be God," I said, half to myself.

"Farky pram kaaa-jory!"

"That's what the jaws are for."

"Tloklitakah-reeeeeeek!"

"Pagan ritual."

"Rooooo-plurb! Rooooo-plurb!"

"But won't most people just think it's silly?"

Blue, helpless against the brutal stream of air, held h[is] mouth wide open, refusing to modulate, but the rando[m] flapping of his vocal cords and lips made a crude trumpetir[g] sound anyway.

"I admit it's impressive, but it's also revolting, and, [if] you don't mind my saying so, a little stupid."

He was exhausted from the effort of trying to control th[e] runaway compressor. He looked at me above the tireless far[t] stream with saddened eyes. "Puh, puh, puh," he chugge[d] valiantly.

"I just don't see how it can work," I said. "People w[ill] rebel. It's in their nature. You'll be hated. Underground s[o] cieties will be born. They will mock you in secret. Pamphle[ts] will be printed depicting you as bumbling tyrants. Subt[le] sabotage will be performed, regardless of the risks. Peop[le] will remember their freedom, if not their history, and they[´ll] make up stories about how things most likely used to be. [A] whole mythology of freedom and disobedience will b[e] born."

"Oh shut up," said Blue, the compressor working pro[p] erly again. He looked weak, close to unconsciousness. "Yo[u] you—just—talking . . . like . . . a man . . . with a pap[er] asshole. . . . Arjay . . . my friend . . . ole buddy . [. .] aaahhh shiiiiit . . . I have had it. . . . I have had it. . [. .] Let's go get, get another, another shot of booze, of booze."

He crawled, very slowly, back to the vault door. W[e] went inside.

282 • •

26

My trouble began twenty years ago," said Blue, very drunk now, reeling on his eight bright legs. His hair was wild and his eyes were almost closed. "Heart attacks, big nasty ones, bing, bing, bing. Lots and lots of hard pain, boy. Then the kidneys started to go. It cost me to piss, it cost me not to piss. Here I was, a rich man, and yet the most miserable creature you ever saw. I was scared to die and scared to get out of bed each morning. I was a wreck. Then, about ten years ago, I got a bone disease on top of everything else. Started from the big toe and worked its way up one side of my body, turning the bones to paper. I couldn't sit and I couldn't stand up. I couldn't lie down and I couldn't walk. I couldn't even take a deep breath without it putting me through ten kinds of pure hell. Then one day, I said to myself, Enough is enough, Sky. Let us go down to the river and make our peace. I loaded up my twelve gauge and sucked on the choke for half a day. Just as I was about to toe the trigger, Chuckie, my man, walked in with a Russian. Mikhail Menovich. Normally, I can't stand Russians. They're a bunch of maudlin drunks always breathing into your face and bragging themselves up. But this one pulled the shotgun out of my hands nice as you please and knelt next to my wheel-

chair. I can remove your pain,' he says, and by the look i
his eye alone, I knew he was telling the truth. We flew th
night to Moscow, drove over to the university there, whe
Menkovich was a top-flight neurosurgeon, and before th
sun rose I was riding this contraption, this very san
spider—notice the Cyrillic lettering on the flange?—feelir
wonderful, all the pain was gone, *gone,* not only gone, b
replaced by something else, antipain is the closest I can con
to describing it properly. A kind of unfocused pleasure, lik
when you get a massage and the masseuse is so good yo
don't even know or care where she's working, and you be
come sort of disembodied, a free capsule of ecstasy in a sea
general discomfort."

He was waltzing. Chuckie had brought in some fres
gin. Sweet Dutch gin, and I drank it down straight. The T
screen was showing some stormy footage. The muzak syste
played Strauss. "Blue Danube" Strauss. My mind was wic
open and unafraid. Some symptoms of madness are agree
able. On the TV screen, Lisa was playing with the spide
She tried to straddle it. She ran her fingers through Blue
hair. She clambered up the spider's legs. Reaching the fl
area that held the head, she bottom-walked closer and clos
to Blue's darting little tongue. The screen rolled. A rock ban
wearing dildos raped a life-sized Shirley Temple doll. A m
chanical Santa Claus ate a real foot. A woman spread herse
with salt before a milling herd of Herefords. Nude par
troopers, in a movie called *King Dong,* dropped into a villag
of women terrorized by a talking gorilla with bizarre habit
A large dog mounted a hefty patroness of the arts. A line
children moved their bowels in unison while a prim teach
made a tally. To Liszt, three white horses kicked each oth
to death. A wan hydrocephalic crushed the skulls of kitter
to the music of a beer commercial.

"I'm not saying it was free," said Blue. "The Universi
of Moscow medical school is not what you would call
philanthropic organization. One hundred million, my frien
Cash. This little gadget—of course we've made some big in

284 • •

provements on it, including the computer tie-in—cost one hundred legitimate fortunes."

"That's a lot of money," I said, not caring what I said.

Blue stopped waltzing and scurried over to me. "Say," he said, "you want to get laid?"

I sipped the gin. "Nope. I'm swearing off. Gets you nothing but heartaches. Little pleasure for a lot of pain. Bum deal. Postcoitus *triste,* as they say."

"Really? Well, we'll have to see about that, now, won't we?" He was scheming openly, the way a drunk does.

Chuckie came in with a girl. She was stunning. The materialization of Everyman's dream companion. A tall, doe-yed, husky-chested, suntanned blond with availability stamped all over her.

"Ruff, ruff," said Blue. "Ah, is she not very, very *orbidezza?* So unlike the type of brazen vixen you see so often these days. What do you say now, Arjay? Still sworn off? Going to throw that postcoitus *triste* jive at me again?"

The blond came over to me and sat on my lap. "Beat it," I said. She stood up, still smiling like a centerfold toy, only slightly bewildered.

"Dammit, Arjay!" said Blue. "She's going to think you're queer. Don't let her go off thinking a thing like that, boy! Show her what you're made of!" He was moving in quick circles around us. "Jesus, you're not worried about that little ticker spasm you had, are you? Don't let yourself be buffaloed by a piece of gut, Arjay! Open up the front of that plastic bag and get to work!"

The girl sat on my lap again. I dumped her on the floor. "Take a walk," I said.

"Jesus, maybe you are queer!" said Blue, very excited now. He circled the girl as if he were winding her in a web. "Chuckie!" he yelled. "Bring in my tool!"

Chuckie trotted in and fitted a dildo to one of Blue's legs. The dildo replaced the suction cup. Holding the dildo high, Blue limped on seven legs to the computer and said, "Timed orgasm mode six. Full cortical deployment. Seventy millisecond pulses. Two microvolt occipital lobe feedback squib. Cyclical blockage in Broca's area of the left hemisphere. No scratch that. Theta rhythm extension. Double starburst excitation of the amygdala, triple—oh, shit, that's enough."

Blue hurried back to the girl, who had climbed on a gurney that Chuckie had wheeled in. Chuckie set the brake and left. Blue crawled around the girl slowly, drinking in her beauty. Then he parked the machine in front of her and extended the leg equipped with the dildo. The girl, still smiling blankly, opened her thighs to accept her lover's implement.

"I want to put this fine hydraulic hog deep into your pudgy breadbasket, my dear," said Blue.

"You're the boss," said the girl.

Blue grunted as the connection between flesh and machine was secured. Concentrating hard on the piston rhythm of the hydraulically powered device (though, like the overseer of an industrial machine, completely detached from its labor), Blue said, "Sorry, Arjay, about that crack I made earlier. I know you're not queer. Just not up to your game today. Right?"

"Oh, Mr. Blue," said the girl, tonelessly. "You are really getting it on. You are a terrific stud. This is too super. It really is."

Blue winked at me. "I can accelerate, I can turn up the rpm's, I can turn on the juice, I can secrete elemental gas, can extend, modify curvature, amplify girth, multiply by two, raise the crown, harden and soften, vary the tangent of the angle of entry, differentiate on the egress, slam bam boy if I want, FARP, finesse, tease, TLOK, whip it, snake it, stop and hold, MREEEJ, swivel and wobble, lay it on the YOOOK, spin it—"

"You're too much, Mr. Blue. I mean that sincerely," said the girl.

"Fleckman—AARPH—that son of a bitch, I ROOOOOO YLAAAK!"

I poured myself another gin and walked away from the clamorous union to the fake window where the lights of

286 • •

city glimmered. It was L.A., a view from the Hollywood hills. I picked out my freeway, my suburb, Dynablast, the way home, the area of space responsible for me, frozen now in this photograph, as it was in my brain, the way the face of a dead friend remains stopped in memory, a space that would ghost my mind as long as I continued to have at least a fragment of one.

Chuckie detached Blue's tool and wheeled the exhausted girl out of the room. Sober again, Blue said, "My favorite poet is Shelley. That's where human possibility began, with the Romantics."

I was watching a pattern of lights that repeated itself in a speedy, two-dimensional choreography on the computer. It was hypnotic.

" 'I faint, I fail, I fall upon the grass . . .' " said Blue, quoting his favorite. "Listen, he wrote that not because he's some kind of a pansy, mind you, but because he is in a state of transport due to his vision. Vision! God save the visionaries!"

It was like dominoes arranged in pleasing lines, falling, erecting themselves, falling again. Over and over.

"You begin with the Romantics and you end with the refuturists. Then the world begins to fail. Coincidence? Not in my book. The failure of vision is the failure of spirit is the failure of *policy.* The effete cold-blooded ironical modern poetry is no mere random accident. It is a direct measure of decay. Listen, in the end there is only one guiding force. Either you have it or you don't have it. So, please, do not speak to me of random occurrences!"

I felt a solid correspondence. Between the quick and lovely lights and my neurons. Dendrite fingers flaring with the dance, the excited neurons restructuring the energy and passing it on to the thirsty axon. Synapses clicking like relays, my brain aglow with this simple ballet of lights, off and on, off and on, their basic message, oh how simple and plain, how simple and plain, the mind is a joker, tricking itself, passing the same places over and over again, asking the same questions, as if there were answers a little farther on or a little way back, blink blink blink, or inside, behind, or under.

"I used to write poems myself, believe it or not," said Blue, his voice spreading itself like angel hair among the Christmas lights in my head. "Give a listen:

> Once upon a MROP ek yary
> Gabreet I urdrek meken snarpy
> Elbow the thunders of upper deep,
> Seek falloon in the jeweled skies
> Or dead the Naiads sboible fock
> O, I splong, be-bob-o-let, splong!
> Who alterest all things with thine eyes,
> Mark marp the marn kee-rait the lock
> Time-eaten tower, time-eaten tower!
> Vulture, whose wings are dull
> Falp against rug-wemp piggy hurn,
> Cutting blane skurns bailiff greet
> O terrible aspect of thy feet!"

The rhythm of the poem mixed with the rhythm of the lights nicely. I liked it. "That goddamned Fleckman," I said. "If only that compressor—"

"What are you *talking* about?" said Blue. "The compressor is all right. What makes you think there's something wrong with the compressor? It's working fine now. I'm getting a good strong signal. Five square. I can make that little mother recite Emily Dickinson in a dying whisper that would make a stone beg for mercy."

Blue crawled over to me. He tapped my knee with one of his steel feet. "Think I've got it?" he asked.

"Got it?"

"You know. Talent."

I started to shrug. The lights said no. I nodded. "Sure," I said.

Blue frowned, scurried away. "Miracles are never enough, are they?" he said, face toward the wall.

The lights regarded my thoughts as inferior construc-
ions. Patterns precede that garbage you call thinking, they
id. Diversity, flow, rhythm, and variation. That's what
unts. Why don't you just watch us. Quit looking for a
de. There is no code! Watch!

"I am a miracle!" said Blue, suddenly hot under the col-
r. The eight steel legs clattered wildly as he spun around to
ce me. "But goddammit, Arjay, that is not enough! Don't
nd me that cock-and-bull about how talented I am. You
n't fool me for a second. Oh, sure, I'm *good.* I've got a nice
uch. But I'm no Swinburne! I'm not fit to touch the hem of
ossetti! And if D'Annunzio is Everest, then I'm Boot Hill.
emember Lillian Verna McKenny?

> *My beloved—*
> *The very atmosphere*
> *Trembles with thy coming!'*

hit man! I ask you, what am I next to that?"

I feigned a moment's thought. My brain was a tuned in-
rument. Wordless, its billion strings hummed with light.

"A miracle, that's what I am. Who could doubt it? But
iracles are never enough, are they? You understand me?
ot *enough.* Sunrise is a miracle, if you want to take the
omantic view—which I do—but the following twelve hours
f daylight can be a bloody bore. See what I mean? It de-
ends on what happens to you during the daylight! Take
azarus."

Say something, said the lights. "Lazarus?" I said.

"Sure. No doubt it was a great thrill for him to get back
n his feet after a few days in the moldering grave. But the
ig joke in getting yourself raised up from the dead is that in
ite of the magnitude of the miracle, you're still the same
eadbeat no-talent yahoo you were in the first place. See
hat I'm trying to say?"

I nodded vigorously. The lights were skating big Zees in
y neocortex.

"That old Lazarus began to think, 'Shit, oh dear, I ca⟨⟩ just go back to my old job at the shoe store. I can't just ⟨⟩ back to the wife and kids as if nothing's happened! *Som⟨⟩ thing important has happened to me.* I am special. I ought to ⟨⟩ into politics or religion or science. I ought to be a great m⟨⟩ now. Otherwise, what's the point of this getting raised ⟨⟩ from the bone yard by that friendly wizard? But how am⟨⟩ going to be a great man without a little help from anoth⟨⟩ miracle worker? Hell's bells, all I know how to do is s⟨⟩ undersized wedgies to hefty matrons. Shit, oh dear.' "

Get up and get out now, said the lights. I stood. Chuck⟨⟩ came in, carrying a towel. I sat.

"But I'm in a lot worse shape than that Lazarus. I mean⟨⟩ can't even go back to a daily routine, even if I wanted to. P⟨⟩ ture Lazarus if only his *head* came back to life."

I tried to picture the aborted miracle. It was hard.

"I'm not carping at fate. I'm not diminishing the impo⟨⟩ tance of what Wally Hardmarket has planned for us. I ju⟨⟩ have this . . . feeling . . . that I'm going to spend eternity ⟨⟩ a kind of super bureaucrat. A kind of omnipotent civil se⟨⟩ vant. Notwithstanding the occasional eating of reprobates ⟨⟩ keep the rabble impressed."

I thought: I have no mental resources left. The ligh⟨⟩ agreed. I used to have vertigo. I used to get dizzy. I had ⟨⟩ fancy metaphor for it. A dream. I made a philosophy out of⟨⟩ physiological quirk to account for my own ridiculous fa⟨⟩ ures. I splonged and be-bob-o-letted, as the poet say⟨⟩ Gulled by my own blane skurns in the shadow of the tim⟨⟩ eaten tower. Now I know better: I just haven't got any ment⟨⟩ resources. No brick-and-mortar foundation from which ⟨⟩ secure the mind against the thunders of the upper dee⟨⟩ Right-right-right, flashed the lights.

Gentle Chuckie toweled the head. Bath time. It was ⟨⟩ warm Turkish towel. Blue's neck, where it joined the m⟨⟩ chine—a stainless steel collar studded with rivets—w⟨⟩ chafed and sore-looking. Chuckie squirted a lotion on th⟨⟩ area, rubbed it in with his little caretaker's fingers, wiped ⟨⟩

with the towel. As Chuckie serviced his master, I noticed that two rear legs of the spider rose off the ground slightly and trembled, ecstatically.

"But the worst thing is," said Blue, "I dream incessantly." He was talking to either Chuckie or to me, or to himself.

Chuckie dropped the towel and began to massage Blue's temples. Blue closed his eyes. "There's this hand," said Blue. "Mine, I guess, pushing up out of the earth, where it was inadequately buried. The fingers open to the sunlight like the petals of a flower. Then a filthy dog comes by and sniffs it. He raises his leg. Then I am rolling downhill, just my head, toward a pyramid of bleeding arms and legs and torsos, all human. Then there's the one where I fancy myself a deaf-mute with the organs of a camel."

Chuckie finished his ministrations and left. Blue said, "Come here, would you, Arjay?"

I stood. Discovered that I felt terribly weak. The lights on the computer stopped. They were frozen in a big HO HA. I approached the spider.

"Arjay, would you . . . I mean, would you . . . ever so lightly, the way Chuckie was doing it . . . my temples? . . ."

Dutch gin rose, became fire, became dust, hoped to become ethereal essence, and then to fly, molecularly, back to Holland. I swallowed it back down. I stood behind the head, straddling the air hose and electrical cable. The back of the head was shielded by a bakelite panel. The electrical cable was connected to the panel. On the other side of the connector, thousands of fine, gold wires were strung between the bakelite panel and a shaved, circular area, three inches in diameter, at the back of the head. The skin in this shaved circle was gray. Or rather, it was almost transparent, and the gray was the gray of bone. I touched his cold temples with two cold fingers.

"Oh, m-my," he said, and the compressor stuttered with indeterminate cues. "Oh, sh-shit, oh d-dear."

27

"I blame chiefly the lizard," said Blue.

"The lizard?" His temples felt like dried onion skin.

"Midbrain, the four hills, colliculi, in front of the pons, the vile nucleus, rotten core, region of monstrous dreams, ugly images from the unrecorded and better-forgotten past, inescapable, inescapable. I include its cortical system too, the limbic system. Vile, vile. Is this what it means to be human? The acceptance of this vileness, this ghastly heritage from prehistory? I think not, I think not."

The compressor coughed. It was agitated. It huffed. It didn't want to discuss such things.

"Dreams and headaches," said Blue. "Did I mention the headaches? Atrocious migraine. And nothing helps. Oh, a program to bypass. But it is fleet and tricky. I block the frontal lobes and it shifts to the parietal. Block the parietal and up it pops with a vengeance in the temporal, or occipital. No escape. No escape. Chemicals sometimes help. But not for long. And the side effects are often intolerable. Usually I just throw the switch. *Schwong!*"

"Throw the switch?"

"Program X. Total complete ripple-free blankout. Full stop. It's like perfect sleep or death. No, strike that, no death. Never death. It *is* sleep. Absolute sleep."

"But then you have dreams," I said.

"Exactly!" I felt an impulse of air tighten the fragile skin as the compressor gathered speed. "Dreams from the lizard brain! Visions from the gut brain! The horror! And there's no waking until the timer cuts in. Ordinarily you escape a killer dream by waking. Not me. I stay locked into that country like an exile, an exile among the monsters!"

A sudden gust of air ballooned his cheeks and an angry fart fluttered his lips. *"Where is that idiot Fleckman?"* he screamed.

Chuckie trotted in. "He's on his way, sir," said the little attendant. "He had to go to L.A. for parts. The chopper is over Pasadena now."

Blue made a little, menacing run at Chuckie, stopped short. Chuckie flinched. Blue reached out with one of his front legs and pressed the foot against Chuckie's cheek. Chuckie winced as Blue applied vacuum pressure. "You-tell-him-this," said Blue. "You-tell-him-I'll-have-his-ass-dismantled-if-he-isn't-here-in-twenty-minutes!"

"Yes, sir. Dismantled, sir." Chuckie squirmed but the sucking foot would not release him.

"You got that, Chuckie?"

"Yes, sir! I got it, sir!"

"All right, then." Blue released his servant. There was a circular welt on Chuckie's cheek.

Blue came back to me, a thin smile on his troubled face. "Discipline," he said. "I didn't get where I am today without it. You let up just once in this business and the turkey behind you has got his cock halfway up your ass." His sucking foot whizzed past my cheek. I flinched. He chuckled. "Now where were we?" he asked.

"Dreams," I said. "Headaches."

He looked at me hard, squinting. My tone was wrong. I cleared my throat.

"Yes, dreams and headaches." Then, suddenly sarcastic, he said, "Please let me know if I'm *boring* you, Arjay."

I swallowed, started to say something. His foot inched toward my eyes.

"Never mind," he said, relaxing again. "I'm sorry Forgive me. I'm on edge. You understand." He withdrew his foot, attempted a winsome smile. His painfully cracked lips widened to reveal the purple gums, the long yellow teeth, the black fig that was his tongue. "You know, don't you, what it is I expect from you, Arjay?"

I faint, I fail, I fall upon the grass. I shook my head.

He looked disappointed. "I thought you might have guessed by now. You're not quite as intelligent as one might have hoped." He watched me closely, eyebrows raised "Well, no matter. The important thing is that you have a choice. You are perfectly free to say no. Though, when you consider the advantages, you'll see how foolish that would be."

"Free to—"

"Well, it's a stupid word, isn't it? What does it mean after all is said and done? Free. You know what freedom is Freedom is the ability to choose between French toast and flapjacks in the dining car of a train that is plummeting from a high trestle into a rocky ravine hundreds of feet below That's what freedom is. Big fat deal. Nevertheless, you *are* free to accept or deny my version of French toast, Arjay. Hear me out."

He crawled back up the ramp to the dais. The curtain closed behind him and the bright light came on throwing up the silhouette of the brooding, muscle-bound manikin.

"The lizard brain, the lizard brain," said Blue, nearly sobbing. "It must go. I must excise the monster. Arjay, th dreams are more than dreams. They *occupy* me. They wi themselves alive. I hear their footfalls outside the vault door I hear the scraping of claws and fingernails against the insid surfaces of my skull. They have billeted themselves like un wanted houseguests. They, they . . . Arjay, *there are ghost in here, inside, hideous, hideous* . . . but wait, wait."

The compressor was breathing heavily, gathering contro of itself, seeking calm through discipline.

294 • •

"An amputee," said Blue, carefully, "experiences for quite some time the missing limb. He feels it flex. He feels it relax. He feels the pulse beat in the absent arteries. It itches him, it hurts him. It is a ghost. A real ghost. I think that when a person disappears there remains an itch in the air. Call it his ghost. Arjay, I have been visited by the ghost of my body. Nightly it comes, headless, bumping about, looking for . . . *me*. Oh yes, it is a dream, I know it is a dream, a hallucination perhaps, a collaboration between the limbic brain and the perversities of the imagination, yet, yet, it is no less real for that. Arjay Ponce, *I have seen it!*"

The giddy familiars of panic arrived. I found the gin, drank from the crockery bottle.

"It wants revenge on me. 'It's not my fault,' I tell it. 'It was *you* who came down with those terrible diseases. You're the guilty party!' But it is blind to logic. Arjay, it wants to . . Oh, Christ . . . listen, its sex is hideous and huge, it gropes about, it fumbles toward me following the electrical cables . . . I have to scamper out of its way. I ask the computer for help, I program for Blissout, I hit the Nirvana button, no help, no help, the monster staggers but he does not give up his search, he comes at me Arjay, cock up like a club, he, he . . ."

I began to swill the gin. Program for numb-out. Chuckie was peeking in from behind the door to his quarters. He looked worried. The lights on the computer were blazing. An enormous fart shook the dais. Blue began to sob. ". . . *fuck* me, monster fuck me he would, terribly, he would, I can tell what he wants, he, he, monster my mouth, no defense, I signal for help, radio SOS, Mayday, but he wants to rip me off his bug and monster my neck hole, stuff his big dead wiener into my brains, bang and pump, until they are putty, coming his monsterhood hugely, endlessly, until monster gism pours out my eyes . . . Oh God . . . my ears, my nose . . ."

He stopped. The compressor stopped. It started again, slowly. The sound of calm breathing filled the room. "Wow," said Blue. "I must sound like a basket case to you, Arjay.'

"Oh no," I said, quickly, between swallows. "Heck, everyone has bad dreams now and then."

"Now and then? Did I say *now* and *then?*" Small bleatings from the compressor undermined his emphasis. Check valves were failing, gaskets were yielding, lock washers were loosening, poppets were jamming. Fleckman had a job ahead of him. "*Daily,* Arjay. Each time I nap. And lately, I've been needing more and more naps. I tire easily. I'm not a young buck any longer, you know. Oh. I use amphetamines laced with strychnine, but they only aggravate the situation, ultimately. I may stay awake longer, but then I sleep more deeply and the monster becomes more potent as a consequence. His potency is inversely related to mine. I am the reciprocal of his strength. God damn it, what a lousy deal. You'd think . . . you'd think . . . oh, forget it. Hear me out Arjay, my proposition."

I waited. He said nothing. The dais was filled with silence. The silence of a stopped machine. He had dozed. I took my bottle and toured the room. No doors, except the one to Chuckie's quarters, and of course the big unbudgeable vault. I knocked on Chuckie's door, turned the knob. Chuckie was wearing a plastic bathrobe over his plastic bag. He was sipping Scotch in an easy chair and watching a game show on TV. It was a small, motel-furnished apartment, with a large window. A color photograph of an empty beach filled the window. Chuckie turned away from the TV and looked at me. He didn't welcome me in. He had the face of a leprechaun. A leprechaun in bondage, biding his time. I pushed the door all the way open and entered.

"What's he want with me, Chuckie?" I asked, taking a chair across from the little man.

Chuckie looked at me and scoffed. "What's he want with anybody?"

"Don't fart around with me, shorty. I just might tear your ears off."

296 • •

I saw his disbelief change slightly. He sat up in his chair.

"I'm crazy, Chuck. Plum gone. Lunatics have license. You'd best humor me."

I set my gin-crock down and got on all fours. I crawled toward him, growling and letting spittle drop on my chin. I've always identified with dogs, my secret totem animal, my spiritual equivalent in the four-legged world. It was an act and it was not an act. Or, to put it another way, it was a parallel truth. A previously untapped mode of behavior. Man-dog became dogman. I snapped at his hands.

"All right, all *right*," he said. "I'll tell you."

"Ha!" I said, pleased with myself, but it was a bark. I needed to change roles. Role over pooch. Dog-thoughts preoccupied me. I four-legged it back to my gin. The familiarity of hand-on-bottle drew me up to a neolithic crouch and I became somewhat biped again. Straighter and straighter, until I was me. Whoever that was.

"First of all," said Chuckie, "you're not the only one he's got lined up. There are several hundred people so far. Unfortunately, most of them are professionals. Skinflick actors."

"He wants me to make movies?"

Chuckie giggled. "Something like that. Actually, it's better than movies. He wants to wire you. For sensorial splicing. For feeling. Has he given you that *dove sta amore* line yet?"

"*Dove* what?"

"*Sta amore.* 'Where is love?' It's poetry. He's a connoisseur, you know. *Dove sta amore.* He figures you, and a few others like you, can help him out. He's got the idea in his head that you are some kind of stud."

"That's ridiculous."

"I know. I've seen the movies."

I stopped a growl. "Never mind. What do you mean, 'sensorial splicing'?"

"Larchmont would do it in an afternoon. Larchmont's a

stereotaxis expert, 3-D skull butcher. He'd implant the elec trodes and stimoceivers all through your noodle. Every sen sation and feeling you owned would get piped into the boss. The boss would pick and choose, though. I mean, if you go a toothache, or a case of the clap, he'd tune you out."

Dogsoul yelped. "Oh no. Nothing doing. No brain surgery for me—"

"You haven't heard it all. Don't be so jumpy. There's no real danger. No aches or pains. It's a pretty routine operation for that Larchmont guy. No aftereffects guaranteed. And when it's over, you're on easy street."

Dog needed to pee. I scratched my ear. Tongued the gin. Bristled. Flexed my jaws.

"He'll set you up, anywhere you want to live, with all the money you'll ever need. Big cars, women, money, houses, your own Lear jet, a yacht. All you got to do is live *high*. For the rest of your life. Hugh Hefner without a work load. Getting the picture now? You'll be shitting in high cot ton, Mr. Ponce."

I was getting the picture all right. A picture by Bosch. Bouquets growing out of the assholes of otherwise norma citizens, a depraved gardner fucking a giant strawberry, three men and a sorrowful tuna in a phone booth, a scowling crow pinching the foot of a moron, men crucified routinely to their musical instruments. Bosch was showing us our logica extremes, and here we are, the future.

I said: "But why *me?* I'm over forty. Why doesn't he stick to twenty-year-olds?"

"Good question. But it's not just simple amplitude of sensation he wants. He can program himself for *that*. You've seen him instruct the computer for multiple extended orgasm, haven't you? Easy as pie. He can alter his theta rhythm and make the thrill last for hours, days even. But that's not the whole picture. He can Blissout, he can go Nir vana, he can tune up for Satori, but even so—"

"*Dove sta amore*," I said.

"I guess so. Sensation without feeling bores him, lately.

298 • •

Feeling, according to the boss, gives ecstasy a point of view. Whatever that means. Frankly, I think the old boy is off his rocker. But, far be it for me to look a gift horse in the mouth.''

"What makes him think I can give him anything he can't get from one of his actors?''

"That's the sixty-four-dollar question. But if I were you, I sure as hell wouldn't miss my chance. He's offering you the world. A good chunk of it, at least. Ask him for Catalina Island or something like that and there's a good chance he'll come through. The kind of power he's going to have is something to think about. Then when you get old and useless, he's got a retirement plan that includes free Menkovich surgery and your own spider. That's what it means to be on his roster. Only a few honchos make it. I'm wired for sensorial splicing myself.''

"*You? . . .*"

"Don't laugh. I'm hung like a pony, buster. Don't let my five feet two, eyes of blue throw you. He uses me when he feels brutal. I'm a hard case when it comes to the broads. I ream them, pal.''

In the other room, I heard the compressor turn over. A long loud fart trumpeted the air, like a signal for doomsday.

"See," said Chuckie, "he's going to be a lonely man up there in space all alone. Sure, there's Mrs. Hardmarket, but she's just intellectual company. The boss has always been a man of action. Don't let the poetry fool you. He needs his fun. That's where you and me come in, and about a hundred others. That James woman, for instance—''

"*Alice?* He wants her wired for feeling, too?''

"Sure! Why not? He's got a dozen broads tied in now. He likes to feel what they feel. Don't try to tell me you've never wondered how it is to be on the receiving end. Everybody's a little fruity at times.''

"Has she agreed?''

"What do you think, pal?''

I stood up. "I've got to take a leak," I said.

"No can do. You can't get out of that plastic suit while you're down here. Regulations. The boss is supersensitive to human smells. Sweat, mainly. When he has a woman, she's got to be clean as a whistle, and deodorized, cap-a-pie. If she sweats, out she goes. No exceptions."

"Listen Chuckie," I said, but I was drowned out by the wildest scream of terror I'd ever heard.

Blue almost ran over me as I went through the door. I stopped short and Chuckie bumped into me. Blue was yodeling in terror, the mechanical spider's legs blurring together in their attempt to sprint, followed by the chugging compressor. Blue was running away from something. Probably the headless cocksman.

"O'Grady says 'Freeze!' " screamed Blue. "O'Grady says, 'Stop-dead-in-your-tracks!' "

Chuckie and I stayed in the doorway, out of harm's way. "If I can get to the control panel without getting my ass run over," said Chuckie, "I'll punch the Nirvana button. That should quiet him down some."

Blue made two more circuits of the room, then scooted up the ramp to the screened dais where he bawled like a freighter in a rocky inlet. Chuckie ran to the computer, hit a large red button with the heel of his hand. Blue's ear-splitting lament softened, became a tolerable moan. A perfect, uninterrupted *Om*.

After a minute of this, he came down the ramp, staggering slightly. He looked bad. The skin around his eyes had noticeably darkened, the lightless eyes had the unfocused look of a terminal cancer patient in his last hour, his bloodless skin was paler than before, more transparent, so that a network of veins was easily visible in his cheeks and forehead, and the dark, urobilinlike stains seemed darker. The skin itself seemed looser, as if the connective tissues that held it to his skull had collapsed and one hard pinch and yank would pull it completely away, like a mask.

"He wouldn't play 'O'Grady Says,' " said Blue. "Usually he does. To taunt me, I suppose. Yes, to taunt me."

I said, to Chuckie, "He means the ghost of his body. It's a dream."

"I *know*," said Chuckie, irritated with me.

"No, no. It's no dream," said Blue. "I didn't doze off that time. Oh God." Blue sobbed. The compressor accelerated. A stream of unrippled air poured from the black O under Blue's nose. It stank of hot rubber insulation. Blue exerted himself. The airstream dwindled. "It had me by the ears," he said. "I couldn't get away. He, it, he, it . . . was going to . . . oh dear God in heaven above help me . . . it was like a tent stake . . . enormous . . . brutal . . . I said, 'O'Grady says, shrivel up! Shrivel up!' but it didn't want to play the game, it, he, got rough and started to yank me loose . . . *Chuckie!* Call Dr. Larchmont now, we're going to end this once and for all. I can't stand it another day. Tell him I want that lizard brain scraped out, scraped *out*. We'll leave only me, pure *me*, just the clean clear no-nonsense neocortex! And I do not want a lecture about *risk*, understand? You tell him that!"

Chuckie left the room. Blue darted after him, goosing him hard with his gripping foot. Then he came back to me. "Listen," he said. "Quickly now. Let me give you my terms."

"I've heard them," I said.

Blue squinted at me. "Chuckie?"

I nodded.

"All right, then. All right. What do you say?" He was distracted, nervous, not really concentrating on what he was saying. His eyes darted around uneasily, as if expecting the imminent reappearance of the grim hallucination.

"No," I said.

Blue scurried up close to me. "*What?* No? Surely you heard the benefits? You'll be part of an elite. A select retinue. Less than a thousand people. I call them 'The Feelers.' You'd

• • 301

be Feeler 909. I call them that because they are the ones who emote freely. The affected ones. Listen, I've felt the little wriggle of glee that the typical supercool stud experiences when going off into the tonsils of some would-be-starlet, and it *bores* me. Give me a mix of antagonistic emotions any day—guilt, pleasure, sorrow, joy, jealousy, hate, idyllic love fantasies, childish perversion. The emotion of fools, in short. The emotions of workaday citizens. Devotion and betrayal, ardor and indifference, kindness and cruelty, tenderness and stupid crudity, skill and buffoonery . . . human, *human,* Arjay!''

I heard it coming. It started with an electrical arc, the sound of a grievous short-circuiting. The compressor went berserk. The air hose stiffened around a huge surge of high pressure. Blue started to say it again, *human,* but only the first syllable came out. The jaws flew apart, the lips rose straight out from the teeth, and a blast of sound to rival the Titanic's final roar, *Hooooooooooooooooooo,* poured from the head. I had to put my hands over my ears.

Blue was completely helpless. He tried to move, but the spider seemed stunned, too. The eight legs merely quivered, as if the giant mechanical bug had been doused with a lethal cloud of insecticide. Blue's cheeks began to flap. The stream of air searched out crevices between flesh and bone and his eyelids began to flutter. The skin of his face was working itself loose. Whether it was to stop the noise or to hold Blue's face together, I can't say, but it was clearly a moment calling for desperate action, and I put my hand over his mouth and clamped it shut.

It was a mistake.

28

It was a terrible mistake. A clearer head would have gone to the compressor and jerked out wires, kicked it, overturned it, anything to dampen its brutal determination. It was Skylor Blue's misfortune that a clearer head wasn't on hand. I saw my error immediately, saw also that once made it couldn't be unmade. Pressing my hand against Blue's mouth didn't of course stop the compressor or the wicked flow of air. The air found new channels: Blue's eyes snapped out of his face like champagne corks, the neck bulged mightily, and an enormous fart lifted the head out of its moorings and rocketed it into the air, a weak streamer of wires and plastic tubes, dribbling green liquid behind it. The truncated air hose ripped free of the flange and snaked angrily on the floor, hissing. The spider itself, receiving a chaos of electrical impulses, sprinted into a wall and collapsed.

I ran after the head. It struck the floor a few yards away spinning in a catty-wampus wobble like a crudely designed top. I picked it up. The eyeholes were empty. But the expression on the face was oddly serene, just the same.

29

I was a little stunned. Not in any critical sense. I cradled the sad little head, which had probably been dead for months, in my lap. Stunned, yes, but I felt no wound, no psychic log-jams, no visceral failures. Stunned the way a child is stunned by sunlight after six hours of matinee marvels. Yes, dead for months. The machine kept chattering, in Blue's voice. The loudspeaker in the computer panel said, *Where are my eyes?* Muttered, *I don't like this dark!* miming perfectly, each nuance of inflection imprinted on its clever little engrams. *Oh sweet Jesus* (said the computer), *he's coming at me again!* I held the eyeless head up to the eyeless computer and said, "You are crazy, computer. You've been saturation-programmed by Blue. But Blue is dead. You've been working his jaws and tongue and eyes through the stimoceivers in his brain, fool-ing yourself into thinking you were servant when in fact you were master, servant, and fool, all rolled into one big rug-wemp piggy hurn, cutting up the blane skurns above the ter-rible aspect of your feet. I suppose you actually believed it all made sense. But listen, you big stoop, if you had a brain in your console instead of all that zero and not-zero logical wir-ing, you'd be able to realize a few things, but I guess you're out of luck, you're going to have to spend the rest of your days thinking you're Blue without eyes. But listen, you're just essence of Blue. Blue desire, Blue hate, Blue fear, Blue arrogance, Blue nightmares."

Oh no, don't leave me in here like this, they monster me, they monster my mind, I am tied down, I am locked in, cannot move, cannot see, cannot feel, yet they come to me in the guise of surgeons. Oh Arjay this is hell, hell, hell. Arjay, listen: this is Skylor Blue talking! Hear me! Hear me! It is dark, and stinks of sweat!

But the leathery little head in my hands was serene. Skylor Blue was dead, long dead. The Menkovich technique is merely a sophistication in computer programming technology.

Oh listen Arjay! I'll give you Connecticut! I'll give you the Virgin Islands! I'll give you . . .

"Oh shut up," I said.

30

Fleckman came in carrying a tool kit. Spear was with him. Chuckie and Dr. Larchmont followed. At first they didn't understand what they were looking at. I held up the head. "You're in a lot of trouble, Fleckman," I said. "The compressor blew your boss right off his flange." The head, drained of its fluid nutrients, was drying up rapidly. It no longer looked like a head. It looked like a desiccated eggplant with absurdly human features. I handed it to Fleckman.

"Larchmont!" barked the computer. "Get me out of this! Excise the midbrain immediately! It's filled with sweating monsters! Varieties no one has ever dreamed of! Oh dear God, Larchmont, get on with it! Scrub up, man!"

Larchmont looked at me. He looked confused.

"Pure feedback," I said. "It's an electronic tautology. A is A. B isn't necessary any longer. B for Blue. Get it? The machine is simply acting homeostatically, no doubt as it is directed to by its heuristic circuits. Blue is dead, long live his circuits. Chuckie, get us some gin."

"What in the hell are you talking about, Ponce?" said Spear, gone white.

"I'm a tech writer, remember? I know what I'm talking

about. I saw a machine like this described in the literature. I believe M.I.T. has a similar one. I may be a little thin on theory, but I can see an overall pattern. For instance—"

"Shut up, Ponce!" Spear went to the headless spider and inspected it. "Fleckman, your ass has had it," he said.

Fleckman, a large young man with a high, straight forehead suggesting, deceptively, intelligence, began to blubber.

"Wait," I said. "Fleckman may have been a little negligent, but it doesn't really matter. Blue has been dead for weeks, possibly months."

Spear grabbed the head from me. "Mr. Blue, Mr. Blue," he crooned. Then, to me, he said bitterly, "You're talking doubletalk. You're a stupid man. Everyone knows that. I talk to Mr. Blue every day and you want me to believe he's been dead all this time!"

"Yes," I said. "He's been alive in the same way a frog leg connected to a three-volt dry cell is alive. A little more sophisticated than that, but the same general idea."

"Quit fucking around!" screamed the computer. "I'm in a lot of pain! Larchmont, got your furry ass in gear!"

"Ignore it," I said. "It's only a projection of what Blue would say under similar circumstances. It's purely a statistical response. The machine fed on Blue's brain for years. When Blue died—that is, when his brain functions ceased—the computer just bypassed the dead organ while continuing to activate the head's musculature. A reversal of the input-output relationship. The myoelectric function became an electromyological one. You see? Meanwhile, the nutrient fluid kept the cell structure of the head reasonably intact—"

"KILL HIM, DAMON! KILL HIM RIGHT NOW!" roared the machine. "You know he is talking gibberish! He wants to monster me, too! He wants to MROP my neckhole, he wants to falloon my sboible fock!"

"See what's happening?" I continued. "The computer absorbed everything, even the vocal patterns of casual chatter. Those nonsense syllables are inputs from the faulty compressor. The computer, being fundamentally moronic, just doesn't know any better."

"I think he's right," said Larchmont. "These machines are very capable. The heuristic logic would certainly tend to make it behave homeostatically. It simply intends to survive in the manner it was originally designed for." He approached the computer and it clattered hysterically at him. "The memory banks are immense. Yes, there's a reasonably good chance that Mr. Blue has been dead for some time."

"TREASON, LARCHMONT!" roared the computer. It overloaded its audio amplifiers and they began to oscillate, sending an ear-splitting squeal into the room.

"Kill him, too, Damon! But make him do the operation first! The headache! The headache!"

"Oh shit," said Spear, his loyalty crumbling before the glacial facts. "What am I going to do now?"

"Well, hell," said Larchmont. "You can continue at Dynablast. You're pulling down top dollar there, aren't you? As for me, I still have a very hot practice in Oxnard. It was an interesting idea, but it just didn't work out. Maybe Wally Hardmarket will come up with an alternative some day. Heck, every cloud has a silver lining—"

"You stinking sons of bitches!" said the computer. "I'll get you for this!"

Chuckie brought in the gin. We passed the bottle around. Spear refused it. He held onto the head, gingerly now, as if it were a talisman that had failed its most crucial test.

The computer released a raucous fart. The resentment and despair of a failed life was contained in the sound. The fart was followed by another, and then another. Great sobbing farts of spite, scorn, and bitterness.

"The goddamned *hell*," said Chuckie. "I'm going to vomit!" We looked at him. He was pointing at the head. Spear looked confused. "The ear, the *ear!*" said Chuckie, gagging.

We saw it then. Oh, we did. A white worm, thick as a

nger, inched out of Blue's left ear, its pointed head turning
inquisitively in the baffling world of light.

We stood, frozen, stunned by the worm's hideous vigor,
while the computer continued to give us the raspberry.

31

A great deflation of spirit and purpose was visible every
where in Sahara Challenge. Groups of oldsters who had bee
counting on Menkovich surgery to guarantee their futures s
forlorn, poolside, indifferent to the cheery sun. Wally Hard
market, sitting at a table by herself, was sipping a beer an
staring out into the vast reaches of an intellectual desert stud
ded with the bleached bones of her best ideas. There wer
other famous people here, some I hadn't seen before, all ol
representing a variety of professions. There were artists a
well as business executives—playwrights, novelists, sculp
tors, composers, television personalities—all on the roster
no doubt, because the new world would need old diversions
entertainments, to keep it safe from disruptive thought.

I found my clothes and dressed. No one interfered witl
me. There was no need to. All records—films, videotapes
recordings, written documents—were being burned. If I ha
any intentions of going to the police—and I didn't—my stor
would have to be discounted as the ravings of a disturbe
personality, and my recent history would easily support sucl
a conclusion. All this was implicit. Spear didn't say it. Larch
mont didn't say it. Wally Hardmarket didn't say it. No on
said it. The wide-open gate in the great white wall surround

ng Sahara Challenge said it. *Bye-bye.* As I approached the gate, two flatbed trucks drove through it. Each had a huge wooden crate strapped to it. Alpha and Omega, probably, headed for obscurity, where they would wait for the state-of-the-art of Menkovich surgery to catch up to them. But by then, all the variables will have changed, the reasons for pursuing power will have suffered mutations, technology will have taken its exponential jump ahead, and all the hardware of Sahara Challenge, if it ever comes to light, will seem as quaint as a page out of Leonardo's notebooks. The future is always superceded by the future. It's predictable as leapfrog. Only the frogs, who keep changing to keep things interesting and deceptively original, are unpredictable. Let's hear it for the frogs. As I walked, the high white walls of Sahara Challenge became insubstantial in the shimmering air, a dry land *ata morgana* of passing interest, not to be taken seriously by the traveler. And Scimitar? Should the traveler take that orbiting *fata morgana* seriously? Probably. But most travelers have been living with doomsday at their heels for too long now to get testy with its latest toy. Besides, it was supposed to shoot the bad guys. The only hitch is . . . Forget it. Anyway, it was probably beyond the state-of-the-art. In all likelihood the Arabs had been sold the philosophers' stone by an overconfident industry. Next month's issue of *Heady Revelations* will tell all.

It was a long pleasant walk to the main east-west highway. The day was brilliant, almost hot, and the desert sang its massive silence. I walked for an hour. Cars passed on occasion, but I didn't stick out my thumb and they didn't slow down. It didn't matter. Nothing mattered.

Or everything mattered. But if it did, it all mattered equally (applying a subjective gradient to things-that-matter will only bring us back to where we are now), and taking responsibility for one part of it might require taking responsibility for all of it. And what sane person would do that? Therefore, nothing mattered. To me. As of now.

As of now. *I find myself in the desert as of now,* I told

myself. *Next week, it might be a jail cell or a hospital for me.*
dicants or on the beach at Santa Monica. Look where you we
yesterday. Who in his right mind would have predicted that,
taken responsibility for it? Not you, not you. French toast
flapjacks, the cynical computer instructed, but listen—t
cook may just be out of batter. French toast or nothing, n
friend. So eat, eat, and try to enjoy.

I heard the car approaching from a mile away. When
saw me it began to slow. I didn't turn. It idled a few pace
behind me, and when it realized I wasn't going to stop an
turn, it accelerated sharply ahead of me and slammed on i
brakes. It was peeved. It was a black Cadillac with bett
things to do. Its rear right-turn signal banged at my eye
The rear window was locked in a hard grimace against a
the receding trivia that lined our highways everywhere. Th
door opened and she got out.

"Hello," she said.

"What is this?" I asked. "A low-budget sequel?"

"Don't be that way," she said. She was dressed nicely i
white. "You were rather awful to me, you know. I have rea
sons for holding a grudge, if it were in my nature."

I suppose she did. I never believed in 'temporary in
sanity.' It was either chronic, with degrees of influence, or
was nothing at all, not even a head cold. A convenient appa
rition trotted out by legal hacks to impress the rubes. Dis
counting the dimethyl sulfoxide, I was sane as a potato whe
I punished her, and therefore guilty of an offense against na
ture and humanity. But that didn't matter either.

Her smile kept its spunky determination, but its spiri
faded. "All we want to do is offer you a ride," she said.

"I'm walking, thank you." I felt no spite or humility. Jus
an impulse to walk.

"Leave him," said the Cadillac. The voice was crisp and
tight with renewed strategies. It was the voice of a winner—
Spear's of course—orienting himself toward new battalion
of losers.

312 • •

"You can't *walk*," said Alice. "It's over a hundred miles back to L.A."

I saw that she meant it. It was a ride she was offering me, out of concern only, a *ride*.

"You're very generous to me, Alice," I said, stripping every mote of irony out of my voice. "I'd like to go back to L.A. with you. But not with him. And I really do want to walk."

"But this is the *desert*."

"It's winter. The desert is hospitable. I may settle down here, forever."

"Get in the car," said Spear. "He's off his rocker, can't you see that?"

"Well, I can't walk to Los Angeles with you," she said, taking my hand, perhaps for the last time. Perhaps not. "Frankly, I don't believe you can make it, either."

"It doesn't matter," I said.

"But it *does* matter!" I saw in her eyes that it did. I felt sorry for her. I was touched. If ever a world were possible again, a world where everything mattered, then it would be Alice, sweet cunning survivor among the devouring giants. I blamed her for nothing. She was a victim of herself, as we all were. I felt the grand generosity of the Napoleonic lunatic.

The Cadillac shot forward a dozen yards before the wheels locked again. "Get in this goddamned car or stay!" said Spear. "You're on the payroll for ten more seconds, Alice!"

She squeezed my hand, then let it drop. If there were a possible world, its time hadn't come.

"Call me, won't you?" she said, retreating to the wide black door.

I shrugged. It was the best I could do. But it wasn't enough. What *was* enough really didn't matter. But in spite of that, I said, "Alice, what do you think happened back there, in Sahara Challenge?"

She was climbing into the air-conditioned velour. "Hap-

• • 313

pened?" she said, over her shoulder. "Nothing happened.
was a big party, sort of a working vacation for top executive
You crashed it. They said you were ill. You went crazy wh
you saw them taking pictures of us. That's all." The do
slammed.

"Party? What do you mean *party*?"

The car began to glide away in cushioned grandnes
She rolled her window down. "A kinky bash and semina
for the big aerospace people and other VIPs, given by a ve
big maker of films. Didn't you catch on?"

I shrugged again, but this time I smiled. "What abo
brain surgery?" I yelled, trotting alongside. "Anybody off
to stick a radio in your head?"

She looked at me strangely, a worried look, believing, a
at once, that Spear was entirely right about my mental cond
tion. *"What?"* she said. *"Brain* surgery?"

"Joke!" I yelled. "Joke!" I tapped my finger against m
head indicating the thickness of the bone there. I saw h
diminishing face smile. As the big car collected momentum

I sat down on a rock. *It doesn't matter,* I told a powerf
saguaro that held the sun proudly in its arms.

Yes, replied the king of thorny plants, *but you feel bett
anyway.*